Praise for Sophie Hannah

The Cradle in the Grave

"The title really sells it. It's creepy stuff, which Sophie's things often are, quite necessarily."

—Tana French, author of *In the Woods* and *Faithful Place*

"A perplexing thriller with intrigue and infanticide . . . It's a given that nothing will be as it seems in the latest psychological thriller from Sophie Hannah, who marries complex plots with crisp, conversational prose."

—*Marie Claire* (UK)

"As Hannah sees it things are rarely clear-cut and it is this moral ambivalence that makes her fiction so provocative." —*Daily Express* (UK)

"She writes beautifully, the narrative races along with the reader breathlessly trying to catch up and the subject matter is fascinating. This is her fifth psychological suspense thriller and, like the others, it's destined for bestsellerdom." —Carla McKay, *Daily Mail* (UK)

"Hannah takes domestic scenarios, adds disquieting touches, and turns up the suspense until you're checking under the bed for murders. . . . It's this real-life research that helps make it so convincing—and so unsettling."

—*The Independent*

"Hannah is a master of intense psychological thrillers . . . Full of twists and turns, and terrifying, too."

—*Heat*

"Sophie Hannah has quickly established herself as a doyenne of the 'home horror' school of psychological tension, taking domestic situations and wringing from them dark, gothic thrills. . . . Combining probability theory, poetry, and murder, this is a densely plotted suspenser with a coded puzzle that would grace a Golden Age mystery." —*Financial Times* (UK)

"Sophie Hannah has been rightly praised for intricate and accomplished psychological thrillers which dissect the dark side of human relationships, and her fifth novel . . . covers obsession, manipulation, meltdown, and all points in between." —*The Guardian* (London)

"Enthrallingly complex . . . A multistranded narrative that grips."

—*The Sunday Times* (London)

"Intriguing, unnerving, and engrossing . . . Hannah has timing down to an art. What she has created in *Cradle in the Grave* is more than a murder mystery. It is the most adept of psychological thrillers, in which—as with

Hannah's other novels—the psychosis lying just below the surface of the human personality is exposed. . . . A remarkable novel, and an adventure to read . . . Undoubtedly a first-class whodunit that will keep you reading long into the night."
—*The Scotsman*

The Truth-Teller's Lie

"Meticulously plotted . . . so dark and shocking." —The Associated Press

"Hannah takes pains to throw her readers off balance—and succeeds brilliantly."
—*The Seattle Times*

"Sophie Hannah will leave you bleary eyed after nights of suspenseful page turning."
—Murder, Mystery & Mayhem.com

"Hannah, who understands psychological mayhem as well as Ruth Rendell and maybe even Sigmund Freud, is best read with a crisis counselor on speed-dial. The tight plotting and excruciatingly precise clues make for a superlatively uneasy read."
—*Kirkus Reviews*

The Dead Lie Down

"A master of intricate plotting, Hannah seamlessly melds the police procedural with a gothic-inspired whodunit."
—*Publishers Weekly* (starred review)

"Hannah deals brilliantly with the issues of artistic accomplishment and success, unrequited emotion, revenge, and retribution. This stunning psychological thriller from the author of the equally outstanding *The Wrong Mother* has the complexities of love at its core."
—*Booklist* (starred review)

"A complex, unnerving study of relationships, with none more stressful than that of Sgt. Zailer and DC Waterhouse. Her exemplary skills put Hannah right up there with Ruth Rendell."
—*Kirkus Reviews*

"This utterly gripping thriller should establish Hannah as one of the great unmissables of this genre—intelligent, classy, and with a wonderfully gothic imagination."
—*The Times* (London)

"Beautifully written and precision-engineered to unsettle."
—*The Guardian* (London)

"A master class in plotting that adds twist after twist in a hectic finale."
—*The Sunday Times* (London)

The Wrong Mother

"Shockingly (and refreshingly) blunt riffs about the violent emotions of motherhood and the familial yearnings of men, along with chilling and darkly funny revelations about lust and loyalty, make this novel one of the season's most absorbing reads." —O, *The Oprah Magazine*

"Paced like a ticking time bomb with flawlessly distinct characterization, this is a fiercely fresh and un-put-downable read."
—*Publishers Weekly* (starred review)

"Sophie Hannah just gets better and better. Her plots are brilliantly cunning and entirely unpredictable. The writing is brilliant and brings us uncomfortably close to the dark, ambivalent impulses experienced by the parents of difficult, demanding children." —*The Guardian* (London)

"Sophie Hannah's ingenious, almost surreal mysteries are so intricately constructed that it's impossible to guess how they will end."
—*The Daily Telegraph* (London)

"*The Wrong Mother* is Hannah's most accomplished novel yet. As the revelations tumble forth, the tension is screwed ever tighter until the final shocking outcome. Exemplary." —*Daily Express* (London)

Little Face

"Dark psychological suspense . . . The power this novel packs derives from narrators that play fast and loose with what they know. . . . The solution is a stunner."
—*The Boston Globe*

"Sophie Hannah . . . delves successfully into moral quandaries: What does motherhood mean? What should a mother do when she thinks her child is in danger—especially if her own family doesn't agree?. . . . It's Alice's choices and their consequences that make *Little Face* so compelling."
—*The Washington Post*

"Few authors play with reality and perception as skillfully as Hannah does. . . . Riveting reading." —*Mystery Scene*

"Echoes of *Gaslight* and *Rebecca* . . . a tautly claustrophobic spiral of a story delivered with self-belief." —*Kirkus Reviews*

"The author is a poet by trade and she brings a wealth of psychological and literary subtlety to bear in this impressive novel. Smart and disarmingly unnerving." —*Daily Mail* (London)

"A chilling thriller. I was left thinking about the book for days, and that's usually a good thing." —*The Guardian* (London)

ABOUT THE AUTHOR

Sophie Hannah is the author of the international bestsellers *Little Face*, *The Wrong Mother*, and *The Dead Lie Down*. In 2004 she won the Daphne Du Maurier Prize for suspense fiction, and she is also an award-winning poet. She lives in Cambridge, England, with her husband and two children.

The Cradle in the Grave

Sophie Hannah

PENGUIN BOOKS

PENGUIN BOOKS
Published by the Penguin Group
Penguin Group (USA) Inc., 375 Hudson Street, New York, New York 10014, U.S.A.
Penguin Group (Canada), 90 Eglinton Avenue East, Suite 700, Toronto,
Ontario, Canada M4P 2Y3 (a division of Pearson Penguin Canada Inc.)
Penguin Books Ltd, 80 Strand, London WC2R 0RL, England
Penguin Ireland, 25 St Stephen's Green, Dublin 2, Ireland (a division of Penguin Books Ltd)
Penguin Group (Australia), 250 Camberwell Road, Camberwell, Victoria
3124, Australia (a division of Pearson Australia Group Pty Ltd)
Penguin Books India Pvt Ltd, 11 Community Centre, Panchsheel Park, New Delhi – 110 017, India
Penguin Group (NZ), 67 Apollo Drive, Rosedale, Auckland 0632,
New Zealand (a division of Pearson New Zealand Ltd)
Penguin Books (South Africa) (Pty) Ltd, 24 Sturdee Avenue,
Rosebank, Johannesburg 2196, South Africa

Penguin Books Ltd, Registered Offices:
80 Strand, London WC2R 0RL, England

First published in Great Britain as *A Room Swept White* by
Hodder & Stoughton Ltd 2010
First published in Penguin Books 2011

1 3 5 7 9 10 8 6 4 2

PUBLISHER'S NOTE

This is a work of fiction. Names, characters, places, and incidents are either the product of the author's imagination or are used fictitiously, and any resemblance to actual persons, living or dead, business establishments, events, or locales is entirely coincidental.

LIBRARY OF CONGRESS CATALOGING IN PUBLICATION DATA
Hannah, Sophie, 1971–
[Room swept white]
The cradle in the grave / Sophie Hannah.
p. cm.
ISBN 978-0-14-311994-4
1. Women television producers and directors—Fiction. 2. Sudden infant death
syndrome—Fiction. 3. Mothers—Crimes against—Fiction. I. Title.
PR6058.A5928R66 2011
823'.914—dc22 2011014075

Printed in the United States of America

For Anne Grey, who introduced me to, among many other invaluable pieces of wisdom, the motto 'Take nothing personally, even if it's got your name on it'. This dedication is the exception to that generally sound rule.

Ray Hines

Transcript of Interview 1, 12 February 2009

(*First part of interview – five or so minutes – not taped. RH only allowed me to start recording once I stopped asking about the specifics of her case. I turned the conversation to HY thinking she would talk more freely.*)

RH: I met Helen Yardley once, that's all. What do you want me to say about her? I thought you wanted to talk about me.

LN: I do, very much. You don't seem to, though.

(*Pause*)

LN: I don't want you to say anything in particular about Helen. I'm not trying to—

RH: I met her once. A few days before her appeal. Everyone wanted her to get out. Not only the women. All the staff too. None of them believed she was guilty. That was down to you.

LN: I was only a small part of the effort. There were—

RH: You were the public face and the loudest voice. I was told you'd get me out. By my lawyers, by nearly everyone I met inside. And you did. Thanks to you, and because of the timing, I had it relatively easy, in Durham and in Geddham Hall, give or take a few minor run-ins with idiots.

LN: The timing?

RH: Public opinion was turning by the time I was convicted. Your hard work was having an effect. If my case had come to court a year later than it did, I'd have been acquitted.

LN: Like Sarah, you mean?

(*Pause*)

RH: I wasn't thinking of Sarah Jaggard, no.

LN: She stood trial in 2005. A year after you. She was acquitted.

RH: I wasn't thinking of her. I was thinking of myself, in the hypothetical situation of my trial taking place a year later.

(*Pause*)

LN: What? Why are you smiling?

RH: The group identity is important to you. As it is to Helen Yardley.

LN: Go on.

RH: Us. The women you campaigned for. You say 'Helen' and 'Sarah' as if they're my friends. I know nothing about either of them. And what little I do know tells me we have nothing in common, apart from the obvious. Helen Yardley's husband stood by her throughout, never once doubted her innocence. That's one thing we don't have in common.

LN: Have you had any contact with Angus since getting out?

(*Long pause*)

LN: It must be difficult for you to talk about. Shall we go back to Helen and Sarah? They don't know you any better than you know them, and yet, from speaking to both of them, I can tell you that they feel a strong affinity with you. Because of what you call 'the obvious'. (*Pause*)

LN: Ray, you're unique. Your tragedy is something that only happened to you. I know that. I'm not trying to chip away at your right to be an individual. I hope you understand that. I'm simply saying that—

RH: Sarah Jaggard was acquitted. She was accused of killing one child, not her own. There's even less common ground between me and her than there is between me and Helen Yardley.
(*Pause*)

LN: Ray, you know, I'd understand completely if you said you'd had moments when you hated both Helen and Sarah. *They* would understand it.

RH: Why would I hate two women I don't know?

LN: Sarah was acquitted. All right, she had to endure a trial, but she got a 'not guilty' verdict. That's the verdict you should have got. Meanwhile you were stuck inside, wondering if you'd ever get out. If you resented her – even if you wished in your darkest moments that her verdict had gone the other way – it'd be only natural. And Helen – you said it yourself, everyone knew she wasn't guilty. Her appeal was coming up just as you landed at Geddham Hall. When you heard she was going home, and you knew you weren't, you might well have hated her, wanted her appeal to fail. No one would blame you.

RH: I'm glad you're recording this. I'd like to say very clearly, for the official record, that I felt none of these feelings you're attributing to me.

LN: I'm not—

RH: I didn't resent Sarah Jaggard's acquittal. I didn't want Helen Yardley's appeal to fail. Not for a fraction of a second did I want either of those things. Let's be absolutely clear on that. I would never wish for anybody to be convicted of a crime they hadn't committed. I would never want anyone to lose their appeal if they hadn't done what they'd been convicted of doing.

(*Pause*)

RH: I knew the appeal had gone her way when I heard cheers coming from everywhere at once. All the girls had been glued to the TVs, waiting. The screws too.

LN: Not you?

RH: I didn't need to watch it. I knew Helen Yardley would be going home. Was it her that put the idea in your head that I was jealous of her?

LN: No. Helen's only ever spoken of you in the most positive—

RH: I didn't meet her by accident, the one time I met her. She came to find me. She wanted to speak to me before her appeal, in case she didn't come back to Geddham. She said what you've just said, that it would be natural for me to envy and resent her if she walked free, and she wouldn't blame me for doing so, but she wanted me to know that my time would come: I'd appeal too, and I'd win. I'd get out. She mentioned your name. Said you'd helped her and you were equally determined to help me. I didn't doubt her on that. No one could doubt your commitment, no one who's heard of you – and who hasn't, by now?

(*Pause*)

LN: So perhaps Helen is your friend, after all.

RH: If a friend is someone who wishes you well, then I suppose she is. She's part of JIPAC, she campaigned for my release. I don't understand it, really. She was out, free. Why didn't she just get on with the rest of her life?

LN: Is that what you would have done?

RH: It's what I'm trying to do. There's nothing left of my old life, but I'd like to try and start a new one.

LN: Of course Helen wants to get on with her life. But, having been the victim of a terrible injustice, and knowing you were in the same boat, you and many others . . . Dorne Llewellyn is still in prison.

RH: Look, I don't want to talk about anyone else, all right? I don't want to be part of your gang of miscarriage-of-justice victims. I'm alone, which isn't that bad once you get used to it, and if I ever choose not to be alone, I want it to be my choice. I don't want to think about other women. It's better for me if I don't. You've got your cause – don't try to make it mine.

(*Pause*)

RH: I don't want to rain on your parade, but justice and injustice? They don't exist.

(*Pause*)

RH: Well, they don't, do they? They patently don't.

LN: I believe very strongly that both do exist. I try to prevent one and bring about the other. I've made it my life's work.

RH: Justice is a nice idea and nothing more. We invented it – human beings – because we'd like it to exist, but the fact is that it doesn't. Look . . . For the benefit of the Dictaphone, I'm holding a coaster in mid-air. What will happen if I let go of it?

LN: It'll fall to the floor.
(*Sound of coaster dropping on rug*)

RH: Because of gravity. We believe gravity exists; we're right about that. I could pick up that coaster, and that one, and that one, and let go of them, and they'd all fall to the ground. But what if only one fell and the rest floated at eye-level, or scooted up to the ceiling? What if you saw that happen now? Would you still believe in gravity, if it only *sometimes* made things fall down?

LN: I see what you're trying to say, but—

RH: Occasionally, good things happen to good people. And bad things happen to bad people. But it's chance – pure random coincidence. As it is when it happens the other way round – bad things to good people.

LN: But that's what I call injustice – when the system treats good people as if they were bad.

RH: Justice doesn't exist any more than Santa Claus does.

LN: Ray, we have a whole legal system devoted to . . .

RH: . . . seeing that justice is done. I know. And when I was a child, I sat on the knee of a man in a red and white suit with a long white beard, and he gave me a present. But it was a fantasy. A fantasy that makes people feel better. Except it doesn't – it makes them feel worse when the illusion is shattered. That's why I try to think of myself as someone who's had appallingly bad luck, not as the victim of a miscarriage of justice. Why should I torment myself by believing there's this amazing force for good at work in the world, but that it failed me, or ignored me? No thanks. And people? They don't commit unjust acts in the service of an opposing evil force. They blunder along to the best of their abilities, doing their best – which, mostly, is not good enough – or in some cases not even doing their best, and their behaviour has repercussions for other people, and . . . The point I'm trying to make is, life is chaotic and indiscriminate. Things just happen, and not for any reason.

(*Pause*)

RH: You'd be better off ditching justice and concentrating on truth instead.

LN: You believe in truth?

RH: Absolutely. The truth always exists, even while people are believing the lie. The truth is that I didn't murder my babies. I loved them, more than you can possibly imagine, and never harmed either of them in any way.

LN: I know that, Ray. And now everyone else does too.

RH: The truth is that Helen and Paul Yardley are people who will pour all their time and energy into helping strangers, and maybe Sarah Jaggard and her husband – I can't remember his name . . .

LN: Glen.

RH: Maybe they're that sort too. But I'm not. And it doesn't matter, because you've got them to help you make your programme. You don't need me around to mess it up by saying what I inconveniently think.

LN: You won't mess anything up. The opposite. Your story's—

RH: My story will muddy your waters. I'm a drug addict who either lied in court or lied before I got to court – take your pick. Your average middle-England viewer's going to feel all buoyed up with self-righteous indignation after hearing about Helen Yardley – the respectable, happily married childminder, adored by her charges and their parents, by everyone who knew her – and then you'll move on to me and lose your advantage. A lot of people still think I did it.

LN: Which is why it's all the more important for you to be part of the programme and tell the truth: that you didn't lie, in court or out of it. That you were traumatised and your memory let you down, as people's memories tend to when they're under a massive emotional strain. Tell the truth in this context, Ray – in the context of my film – and people will believe you. I promise you, they will.

RH: I can't do this. I can't get sucked in. Turn that thing off.

LN: But Ray . . .

RH: Turn it off.

www.telegraph.co.uk, Wednesday 7 October 2009, 0922 GMT
report by Rahila Yunis

Wrongly Convicted Mother Found Dead at Home

Helen Yardley, the Culver Valley childminder wrongly convicted of murdering her two baby sons, was found dead on Monday at her home in Spilling. Mrs Yardley, 38, was found by her husband Paul, a roofer aged 40, when he returned from work early in the evening. The death is being treated as 'suspicious'. Superintendent Roger Barrow of Culver Valley Police said: 'Our inquiries are ongoing, and the investigation is still at an early stage, but Mrs Yardley's family and the public can be assured that we are putting every possible resource into this. Helen and Paul Yardley have already endured intolerable anguish. It is vital that we handle this tragedy discreetly and efficiently.'

Mrs Yardley was convicted in November 1996 of the murders of her sons Morgan, in 1992, and Rowan, in 1995. The boys died aged 14 weeks and 16 weeks. Mrs Yardley was found guilty by a majority verdict of 11 to one and given two life sentences. In June 1996, while at home on bail awaiting trial, Mrs Yardley gave birth to a daughter, Paige, who was placed with a foster family and subsequently adopted. Interviewed in October 1997 on the day that he heard the family court's decision, Paul Yardley said: 'To say that Helen and I are devastated is an understatement. Having lost two babies to crib death, we have now lost our precious daughter to a system that persecutes grieving families by stealing their children. Who are these monsters that decide to tear up the lives of innocent, law-abiding people? They don't care about us, or about the truth.'

In 2004, the Criminal Cases Review Commission, which reviews possible miscarriages of justice, referred Mrs Yardley's case to the appeal court after campaigners raised doubts about the integrity of Dr Judith Duffy, one of the expert witnesses at the trial. In February 2005, Mrs Yardley was released after three judges in the court of appeal quashed her convictions. She had always maintained her innocence. Her husband had stood by her throughout her ordeal, working '20 hours a day, every day', according to a source close to the family, to clear his wife's name. He was helped by relatives, friends, and many parents whose children Mrs Yardley had looked after.

Journalist and writer Gaynor Mundy, 43, who collaborated with Mrs Yardley on her 2007 memoir *Nothing But Love*, said: 'Everyone who knew Helen knew she was innocent. She was a kind, gentle, sweet person who could never harm anyone.'

TV producer and journalist Laurie Nattrass played a major role in the campaign to free Mrs Yardley. Last night he said: 'I can't put into words the sadness and anger I feel. Helen might have died yesterday, but her life was taken from her 13 years ago, when she was found guilty of crimes she didn't commit, the murders of her two beloved sons. Dissatisfied with the torture it had already inflicted, the state then robbed Helen of her future by kidnapping – and there's no other word for it – her only surviving child.'

Nattrass, 45, Creative Director of Binary Star, a Soho-based media company, has won many awards for his documentaries about miscarriages of justice. He said, 'For the past seven years, 90 per cent of my time has been spent campaigning for women like Helen, trying to find out what went so dreadfully wrong in so many cases.'

Mr Nattrass first met Mrs Yardley when he visited her in Geddham Hall women's prison in Cambridgeshire in 2002. Together they set up the pressure group JIPAC (Justice for Innocent Parents and Carers), formerly JIM. Mr Nattrass said: 'Originally we called it "Justice for Innocent Mothers", but it soon became clear that fathers and babysitters were being wrongly charged and convicted too. Helen and I wanted to help anyone whose life had been ruined in this way. Something needed to be done. It was unacceptable that innocent people were being blamed whenever there was an unexplained child death. Helen was as passionate about this as I am. She worked relentlessly to help other victims of injustice, both from prison and once she got out. Sarah Jaggard and Ray Hines, among others, have Helen to thank for their freedom. Her good work will live on.'

In July 2005, Wolverhampton hairdresser Sarah Jaggard, 30, was found not guilty of the manslaughter of Beatrice Furniss, the daughter of a friend, who died aged six months while in Mrs Jaggard's care. Mr Nattrass said: 'Sarah's acquittal was the indicator I'd been waiting for that the public were starting to see reason. No longer were they willing to let vindictive police and lawyers and corrupt doctors lead them on a witch-hunt.'

Yesterday, Mrs Jaggard said: 'I can't believe Helen's dead. I will never forget what she did for me, how she fought for me and stuck by me. Even in prison, not knowing if and when she'd get out, she took the time to write letters supporting me to anyone who would listen. My heart aches for Paul and the family.'

Rachel Hines, a 42-year-old physiotherapist from Notting Hill, London, had her convictions overturned in the court of appeal after serving four years for the murders of her baby son and daughter. Julian Lance, Mrs Hines' solicitor, said: 'If it wasn't for Helen Yardley and JIPAC, we wouldn't have been granted leave to appeal. We were lacking key information. JIPAC found it for us. Helen's death is a devastating blow to everyone who knew her, and a huge loss.' Mrs Hines was unavailable for comment.

Dr Judith Duffy, 54, a paediatric forensic pathologist from Ealing, London, gave evidence for the prosecution at the trials of Mrs Yardley, Mrs Jaggard and Mrs Hines. She is currently under investigation by the GMC, pending a hearing next month for misconduct. Laurie Nattrass said: 'Judith Duffy has caused unimaginable suffering to dozens if not hundreds of families, and she must be stopped. I hope she'll be removed from the list of home office pathologists and struck off the medical register.' Mr Nattrass is currently making a documentary about the miscarriages of justice for which he believes Dr Duffy to be responsible.

Part I

I

Wednesday 7 October 2009

I am looking at numbers when Laurie phones, numbers that mean nothing to me. My first thought, when I pulled the card out of the envelope and saw four rows of single figures, was of Sudoku, a game I've never played and am not likely to, since I hate all things mathematical. Why would someone send me a Sudoku puzzle? Easy: they wouldn't. Then what is this?

'Fliss?' Laurie says, his mouth too close to the phone. When I don't answer immediately, he hisses my name again. He sounds like a deranged heavy-breather – that's how I know it's urgent. When it isn't, he holds the phone too far away and sounds like a robot at the far end of a tunnel.

'Hi, Laurie.' Using the strange card to push my hair back from my face, I turn and look out of the window to my left. Through the condensation that no amount of towel-wiping seems to cure, across the tiny courtyard and through the window on the other side, I can see him clearly, hunched over his desk, eyes hidden behind a curtain of messy blond hair.

His glasses have slipped down his nose, and his tie, which he's taken off, is laid out in front of him like a newspaper. I stick out my tongue at him and make an even ruder gesture with my fingers, knowing I'm completely safe. In the two years I've worked with Laurie, I've never seen him glance out of his window, not even when I stood in his office, pointed across the courtyard and said, 'That's my desk there, with the hand cream on it, and the photo frames, and the plant.' Human beings like to have such accessories, I restrained myself from adding.

Laurie never has anything on his desk apart from his computer, his BlackBerry and his work – scattered papers and files, tiny Dictaphone tapes – and the discarded ties that drape themselves over every surface in his room like flat, multi-coloured snakes. He has a thick neck that's seriously tie-intolerant. I don't know why he bothers putting them on at all; they're always off within seconds of his arriving at the office. By the side of his desk there's a large globe with a metal dome base. He spins it when he's thinking hard about something, or when he's angry, or excited. On his office walls, up among the evidence of how successful and clever and humane he is – certificates, photographs of him receiving awards, looking as if he's just graduated from a finishing school for heavy-featured hulks, his grade-A gracious smile fixed to his face – there are posters of planets, individual and group portraits: Jupiter on its own, Jupiter from a different angle with Saturn next to it. There's also a three-dimensional model of the solar system on one of his shelves, and four or five large books with tatty covers about outer space. I asked Tamsin once if she had any idea why he was so interested in astronomy. She chuckled and said, 'Maybe he feels lonely in our galaxy.'

I know every detail of Laurie's office by heart; he is for ever summoning me, asking me questions to which I couldn't possibly know the answers. Sometimes, by the time I arrive, he's forgotten what he wanted me for. He has been into my office twice, once by accident when he was looking for Tamsin.

'I need you in here now,' he says. 'What are you doing? Are you busy?'

Move your head ninety degrees to the right and you'll see what I'm doing, you weirdo. I'm sitting here staring at you, in all your weirdness.

I have an inspired idea. The numbers on the card I'm holding make no sense to me. Laurie makes no sense to me. 'Did you send me these numbers?' I ask him.

'What numbers?'

'Sixteen numbers on a card. Four rows of four.'

'What numbers?' he asks more abruptly than last time.

Does he want me to recite them? 'Two, one, four, nine . . .'

'I didn't send you any numbers.'

As so often when I'm talking to Laurie, I'm stumped. He has a habit of saying one thing while leaving you with exactly the opposite impression. This is why, even though he's said he didn't send me any numbers, I have the sense that if I'd said, 'Three, six, eight, seven' instead of 'Two, one, four, nine', he might have said, 'Oh, yeah, that was me.'

'Bin it, whatever it is, and get in here, soon as you can.' He cuts me off before I have a chance to reply.

I swing my chair from side to side and watch him. At this point, surely, anyone halfway normal would glance across the courtyard to see if I was obeying orders, which I'm not: I'm not binning the card, I'm not leaping to my feet. All of which Laurie would see if he turned his head in my direction, but he doesn't. Instead, he pulls at the open collar of his shirt as if he can't breathe, and stares at his closed office door, waiting for me to walk through it. That's what he wants to happen, and so he expects it to happen.

I can't take my eyes off him, though on the physical evidence alone, I really should be able to. As Tamsin once said, it's all too easy to imagine him with a bolt through his neck. Laurie's attractiveness has little to do with his looks and everything to do with his being a legend in human form. Imagine touching a legend. Imagine . . .

I sigh, stand up, and bump into Tamsin on my way out of my office. She's wearing a black polo-neck, a tiny white corduroy skirt, black tights and knee-high white boots. If something isn't either white or black, Tamsin won't wear it. She once wore a blue patterned dress to work, and felt insecure all day. The experiment was never repeated. 'Laurie wants you,' she tells me, looking nervous. 'Now, he says. And Raffi wants me. I don't like the atmosphere today. There's something not right.'

I hadn't noticed. There are a lot of things I don't notice when I'm in the office these days, and only one thing that I do.

'I reckon it's something to do with Helen Yardley's death,' says Tamsin. 'I think she was murdered. No one's told me anything, but two detectives came to see Laurie this morning. CID, not your regular bobbies.'

'Murdered?' Automatically, I feel guilty, then angry with myself. I didn't kill her. She's nothing to do with me; her death's nothing to do with me.

I met her once, a few months ago. I spoke to her briefly, made her a coffee. She'd come in to see Laurie and he'd done his usual trick of vanishing without trace, having confused Monday with Wednesday, or May with June – I can't remember why he wasn't there when he ought to have been. It's an uncomfortable thought, that a woman I met and spoke to might have been murdered. At the time I thought it was strange to meet somebody who'd been in prison for murder, especially someone who looked and seemed so friendly and normal. 'She's just a woman called Helen,' I thought, and for some reason it made me feel so awful that I had to leave the office immediately. I cried all the way home.

Please let her death have nothing to do with why Laurie's summoned me.

'Do you know anything about Sudoku?' I call after Tamsin.

She turns. 'As much as I want to. Why?'

'Does it involve numbers laid out in a square?'

'Yeah, it's like a crossword puzzle grid, except with numbers instead of letters. I think, anyway. Or maybe it's an empty grid and you fill in the numbers. Ask someone who's got swirly patterned carpets and a house that smells of air-freshener.' She waves and heads for Raffi's office, shouting over her shoulder, 'And a doll with a skirt to cover up the spare loo roll.'

Maya leans out of her office, holding the door frame with both hands as if hoping to block the strong smell of smoke with her body. 'You know those knitted-doll bog-roll holders are highly collectable?' she says. For the first time since I've known her, she doesn't smile, try to hug or pat me or call me 'honey'. I wonder if I've done something to offend her. Maya is Binary Star's MD, though she prefers 'head honcho' – that's her nickname for herself, always delivered with a giggle. In fact, she's only third in the pecking order. Laurie, as Creative Director, is the supreme power in the organisation, closely followed by Raffi, the Financial Director. The two of them control Maya by stealth, allowing her to believe she's in charge.

'What's that?' She nods at the card in my hand.

I look at it again, read it digit by digit for about the twentieth time.

2 1 4 9
7 8 0 3
4 0 9 8
0 6 2 0

A grid, Tamsin said. There's no grid here, so it can't be a Sudoku puzzle, though the layout is grid-like. It's as if the lines have been removed once the numbers were filled in.

'Your guess is as good as mine,' I tell Maya. I don't bother to show her the card. She's always gushingly friendly, particularly to lower-ranking Binary Star employees like me, but she has no interest in anyone but herself. She asks all the right questions – loudly, so that everyone hears how much she cares – but if you take the trouble to reply, she blinks at you blank-eyed, as if you've bored her into an upright coma. And I can tell from her frequent glances over her shoulder that she's eager to get back to her burning cigarette, probably the tenth of the thirty she'll get through today.

Sometimes when Laurie walks past her office, he shouts, 'Lung cancer!' The rest of us pretend to believe Maya's story about having given up years ago. Legend has it that she once burst into tears and tried to pretend it wasn't smoke billowing from her office but steam from a particularly hot cup of tea. None of us has ever actually seen her with a cigarette in her hand.

'I've worked out how she does it,' Tamsin said the other day. 'She keeps the cig and the ashtray in the bottom drawer of her desk. When she wants a drag, she sticks her *whole head* in the drawer . . .' Seeing that I wasn't taking her theory seriously, she said, 'What? The lowest drawer's twice the size of the other two – you could easily fit a human head in there. I dare you to sneak into her office and—'

'Yeah, right,' I cut her off. 'I'm really going to commit career suicide by ransacking the MD's desk.'

'You'd totally get away with it,' said Tamsin. 'You're her baby, remember? Maya's got an underling fetish. She's going to love you whatever you do.'

Once, without irony and in my presence, Maya referred to me as 'the baby of the Binary Star family'. That was when I started to worry that she didn't take me seriously as a producer. Now I know she doesn't. 'Who *cares*?' Tamsin groans whenever I mention it. 'Being taken seriously is seriously overrated.'

Maya quickly loses interest in me and withdraws into her smoky lair without so much as a 'Bye, sugar!' Suits me fine; I never asked to be the object of her frustrated maternal urges. I hurry down the corridor to Laurie's office. I knock and walk in simultaneously, and catch him whizzing his model globe round on its axis with his right foot. He stops and blinks at me, as if he's struggling to remember who I am. In his head, he's probably already had whatever conversation he wanted to have with me, I've agreed to whatever he wanted me to agree to, and done it, and maybe I've even retired or died – maybe Laurie's mind has transported him so far into the future that he no longer knows me. His brain works faster than most people's.

'Tamsin says Helen Yardley was murdered.' *Nice one, Fliss. Bring up the thing you least want to talk about, why don't you?*

'Someone shot her,' Laurie says expressionlessly. He starts to manipulate the globe with his foot again, kicking it so that it goes faster.

'I'm really sorry,' I say. 'It must make it even harder . . . Than if she'd died naturally, I mean. To cope with.' As I'm speaking, I realise I have no idea how to pitch my condolences, towards what sort of loss. Laurie spoke to Helen Yardley every day, often more than once a day. I know how much JIPAC means to him but I've no idea whether he cared about Helen personally, whether he's mourning her as a fellow campaigner or as something more than that.

'She didn't die naturally. She was thirty-eight.' The anger in his eyes still hasn't reached his voice. He sounds as if he's reciting lines he's memorised. 'Whoever murdered her – he's only partly responsible. A whole string of people killed her, Judith Duffy for one.'

I don't know what to say, so I put the card down on his desk. 'Someone sent me this. It came this morning in a matching envelope. No explanatory letter or note, no indication of who it's from.'

'The envelope also had numbers on it?' Miraculously, Laurie seems interested.

'No . . .'

'You said "matching".'

'It looked expensive – cream-coloured and sort of ribbed, like the card. It was addressed to "Fliss Benson", so it must be from someone who knows me.'

'Why must it?' Laurie demands.

'They'd have written "Felicity" otherwise.'

He squints at me. 'Is your name Felicity?'

It's the name that goes on the credit sequence of every

programme I produce, the name Laurie will have seen on my CV and covering letter when I applied to Binary Star for a job. Seen and then forgotten. On a good day, Laurie makes me feel invisible; on a bad day, nonexistent.

I do what I always do when I'm in his office and there's a possibility that I might get upset: I stare at the miniature solar system on his shelf and list the planets. *Mercury, Earth, Venus, Mars* . . .

Laurie picks up the card and mutters something inaudible as he aims it across his office at the bin in the far corner. It whizzes past my ear, narrowly missing me. 'It's junk,' he says. 'Some kind of marketing teaser, waste of a tree.'

'But it's handwritten,' I say.

'Forget it,' Laurie barks. 'I need to talk to you about something important.' Then, as if noticing me for the first time, he grins and says, 'You're going to love me in a minute.'

I nearly drop to my knees in shock. Never before has he used the word 'love' in my presence. I can say that with absolute certainty. Tamsin and I have speculated about whether he's heard of it, felt it – whether he recognises its existence.

You're going to love me in a minute. I assume he's not using the word 'love' in the physical sense. I imagine us having sex on his desk, Laurie utterly oblivious to the large window through which everyone whose office is on the other side of the courtyard can see us, me anxious about the lack of privacy but too scared of upsetting him to protest . . . *No. Stop this nonsense*. I shut down the thought before it takes hold, afraid I might laugh or scream, and be called upon to explain myself.

'How do you fancy being rich?' Laurie asks me.

* * *

Part of the reason I find talking to Laurie so exhausting is that I never know the right answer. There's always a right one and a wrong one – he's very black and white – but he gives you no clues and he's disturbingly unpredictable about everything apart from what he calls 'the crib death mothers witch-hunt'. On that, his views are fixed, but on nothing else. It must be something to do with his brilliant, original mind, and it makes life hellishly hard for anyone who's secretly trying to please him by second-guessing what he'd like them to say while at the same time wanting to look as if they're just being themselves, acting with a hundred per cent integrity and to hell with what anyone else might think. Actually, that's unlikely to be a significant constituency of people, come to think of it. It's probably just me.

'I'd like to be well-off,' I say eventually. 'I don't know about rich. There's only so much money I'd need – a lot more than I've got now, but less than . . . you know . . .' I'm talking rubbish because I'm unprepared. I've never given it a second's thought. I live in a dark, low-ceilinged one-bedroom basement flat in Kilburn, underneath people who have sound-amplifying wooden floors in every room because to lay a carpet anywhere would threaten their upper-middle-class identity, and who seem to spend most evenings jumping around their living room on pogo-sticks, if the noise they make is anything to go by. I have no outside space whatsoever, though I have an excellent view of the pogo-jumpers' immaculate lawn and assortment of rose-bushes, and I can't afford the damp-proofing my flat has urgently needed since I bought it four years ago. Funnily enough, wealth isn't something I dwell on.

'I suppose I'd like to be rich-*ish*,' I say. 'As long as I wasn't getting my money from anything dodgy, like people-smuggling.' I play back my answer in my head, hoping it made me sound ambitious but principled.

'What if you could do my job and earn what I earn?' Laurie asks.

'I couldn't do what you—'

'You can. You will. I'm leaving the company. From Monday, you're me: Creative Director and Executive Producer. I'm on a hundred and forty a year here. From Monday, that's what you'll be on.'

'*What?* Laurie, I—'

'Maybe not officially from Monday, so you might have to wait for the pay-rise, but effectively from Monday . . .'

'Laurie, slow down!' I've never shouted an order at him before. 'Sorry,' I mumble. In my shock, I forgot for a second who he is and who I am. Laurie Nattrass doesn't get yelled at by the likes of me. *From Monday, you're me*. It must be a joke. Or he's confused. Someone as confusing as he is could easily be confused. 'This makes no sense,' I say. Me, Creative Director of Binary Star? I'm the lowest paid producer in the company. Tamsin, as Laurie's research assistant, earns significantly more than I do. I make programmes that no one but me has any respect for, about warring neighbours and malfunctioning gastric bands – subjects that interest not only me but also millions of viewers, which is why I don't care that I'm regarded by my colleagues as the light relief amid all the purveyors of earnest political documentaries. Raffi refers to my work as 'fluff stuff'.

This has got to be a joke. A trap. Am I supposed to say, 'Ooh, yes, please,' then look like an idiot when Laurie falls about laughing? 'What's going on?' I snap.

He sighs heavily. 'I'm going to Hammerhead. They've made

me an offer I can't refuse, a bit like the offer I'm making you. Not that it's about the money. It's time I moved on.'

'But . . . you can't leave,' I say, feeling hollow at the thought. 'What about the film?' He wouldn't go without finishing it; there's no way on earth. Even someone as hard to fathom as Laurie leaves the odd clue here and there as to what makes him tick. Unless the clues I've picked up have been planted by someone determined to mislead me – and it's hard to see how that could happen, since most of them came from Laurie's own mouth – then what makes him tick at a rate of a hundred and twenty seconds to the minute rather than the usual sixty is the film he's making about three crib death murder cases: Helen Yardley, Sarah Jaggard and Rachel Hines.

Everyone at Binary Star calls it 'the film', as if it's the only one the company need concern itself with, the only one we're making or are ever likely to make. Laurie's been working on it since the dawn of time. He insists that it has to be perfect, and keeps changing his mind about the best way to structure it. It's going to be two hours long, and the BBC has told Laurie he can take his pick of the slots, which is unheard of. Or rather, it's unheard of for everyone but Laurie Nattrass, who is a deity in the world of television. If he wanted to make a five-hour film that knocked out both the *News at Six* and the *News at Ten*, the BBC higher-ups would probably lick his boots and say, 'Yes, Master.'

'You're going to make the film,' he tells me with the confidence of someone who has visited the future and knows what happens in it. 'I've emailed everyone involved to say you're taking over from me.'

No. He can't do this.

'I've given them your contact details, work and home . . .'

I want nothing to do with it. I *can't* have anything to do with it. I open my mouth to protest, then remember that Laurie doesn't know my . . . well, it's something no one here knows. I refuse to think of it as a secret and I won't allow myself to feel guilty. I've done nothing wrong. This cannot be a punishment.

'You'll have Maya and Raffi's full support.' Laurie stands up, walks over to the tower of box files by the wall. 'All the information you need's in these. Don't bother moving them to your office. From Monday, this'll be your office.'

'Laurie . . .'

'You'll work on the film and nothing else. Don't let anything get in your way, least of all the filth. I'll be at Hammerhead, but I'll make myself available to you whenever . . .'

'Laurie, stop! The filth? You mean the police? Tamsin said you spoke to them this morning . . .'

'They wanted to know when I'd last seen Helen. If she had any enemies. "How about the entire fucking judicial system, not to mention you lot," I said.' Before I have a chance to remind him that Helen's murder convictions were overturned in the court of appeal by that same judicial system, he says, 'They asked about the film. I told them you'd be exec-ing it as of Monday.'

'You told them before you asked me?' My voice comes out as a high-pitched squeak. My stomach twists, sending prickles of nausea up to my throat. For a few seconds, I daren't open my mouth. 'You emailed everyone and told them I'm . . . When? When did you do that? Who's everyone?' I dig my fingernails into the palms of my hands, feeling horribly out of control. This wasn't supposed to happen; it's all wrong.

Laurie taps the top box file. 'All the names and contacts

you need are in here. I haven't got time to go through it all with you, but most of it's self-explanatory. Any more detectives come sniffing around, you're making a documentary about a doctor determined to pervert the course of justice, and three women whose lives she did her best to destroy. Nothing to do with the investigation into Helen's death. They can't stop you.'

'The police don't want the film to be made?' Everything Laurie says makes me feel worse. Even more than usual.

'They haven't said that yet, but they will. They'll trot out some guff about you compromising their—'

'But I haven't . . . Laurie, I don't want your job! I don't want to make your film.' To clarify, I add, 'I'm saying no.' There, that's better. Perfectly in control.

'No?' He stands back and examines me: a rebellious specimen. Previously compliant, though, he'll be thinking, so what can have gone wrong? He laughs. 'You're turning down a salary that's more than three times what you're on now, and a career-launching promotion? Are you stupid?'

He can't force me – it's impossible. There are some things one can physically force a person to do. Making a documentary is not one of them. Focusing on this helps me to stay calm. 'I've never exec-ed anything before,' I say. 'I'd be completely out of my depth. Don't you want to cooperate with the police, help them find out what happened to Helen?'

'Culver Valley CID couldn't find tennis balls at fucking Wimbledon.'

'I don't understand,' I say. 'If you're going to Hammerhead, why isn't the film going with you?'

'The BBC commissioned Binary Star, not me personally.' Laurie shrugs. 'That's the price I pay for leaving. I lose it.' He leans forward. 'The only way I don't lose it is if I give it to you, and work with you when I can behind the scenes. I need your help here, Fliss. You'd get all the credit, you'd get the salary . . .'

'Why me? Tamsin's the one who's been working on it with you. The woman's a walking miscarriage-of-justice encyclopaedia – there's not a detail she doesn't know. Why aren't you trying to force this promotion on her?'

It occurs to me that Laurie's been patronising me. *How do you fancy being rich?* He's always moaning that he can barely afford the mortgage on his four-storey townhouse in Kensington. Laurie comes from a seriously wealthy family. I'd bet everything I've got – which is considerably less than he's got – that he regards his salary at Binary Star as acceptable, nothing more. The offer Hammerhead made him, the one he couldn't refuse, obviously knocked a hundred and forty grand a year into a cocked hat. But of course a hundred and forty a year would be wealth beyond the wildest dreams of a peasant like me . . . I stop in my tracks and realise that, if that is what Laurie's thinking, he's entirely correct, so perhaps it's unfair of me to quibble.

'Tamsin's a research assistant, not a producer,' he says. 'Look, you didn't hear this from me, okay?'

At first I think he's referring to what he's already told me, about the promotion I don't want. Then I realise he's waiting for me to agree before telling me something else. I nod.

'Tamsin's being made redundant. Raffi's talking to her now.'

'*What?* You're joking. Tell me you're joking.'

Laurie shakes his head.

'They can't get rid of her! They can't just . . .'

'It's industry-wide. Everyone's tightening their belts, making cuts where they can.'

'Who made the decision? Was there a vote?' I can't believe Binary Star would keep me and lose Tamsin. She's got loads more experience than I have, and unlike me, she isn't constantly pestering Raffi for a dehumidifier for her office.

'Sit down,' says Laurie impatiently. 'You're making me nervous. Tamsin's the obvious choice for redundancy. She's earning too much to be value for money in the current economic climate. Raffi says we can get a new graduate researcher for half the price, and he's right.'

'This is so out of order,' I blurt out.

'How about you stop worrying about Tamsin and show me some gratitude?'

'What?' Was that the great crusader for justice who said that to me?

'You think Maya wants to pay you what she's paying me?' Laurie chuckles. 'I talked her through her options. I said, "If there's a line in the budget for me, then there's a line in the budget for Fliss." She knows there's no film without my cooperation, not for Binary Star. Ray Hines, Sarah and Glen Jaggard, Paul Yardley, all the solicitors and barristers, the MPs and doctors I've got eating out of the palm of my hand – one word from me and they walk. Whole project falls apart. All I need to do is bide my time, then sign a new contract with the BBC as MD of Hammerhead.'

'You *blackmailed* Maya into agreeing to promote me?' So that's why she was less gushy than usual when I passed her in the corridor. 'Well, I'm sorry, but there's no way I'm—'

'I want this documentary made!' Laurie raises his voice to a level some might describe as shouting. 'I'm trying to do the right thing here, for everyone! Binary Star gets to keep the film, you get a package that's appealing enough to make you get off your arse and do the work . . .'

'And what do you get?' I feel unsteady on my feet. I'd like to sit down, but I won't, not after Laurie ordered me to. *Not when he's just made a snide remark about my arse.*

'I get your full cooperation,' he says, so quietly that I wonder if I imagined his outburst a few seconds earlier. 'Unofficially I'll still run the show, but my involvement will be strictly between you and me.'

'I see,' I say in a tight voice. 'You're not only blackmailing Maya, you're blackmailing me, too.'

Laurie falls into his chair with a groan. 'I'm bribing you. At least be accurate.' He laughs. 'Fuck, did I read you wrong! I thought you were rational.'

I bite my lip, struggling to take in this latest revelation: that Laurie has an idea of what sort of person I am. It means he's spent time thinking about me, even if only a few seconds. It has to mean that.

'You deserve a chance,' he says in a bored voice, as if it's tiresome having to convince me. 'I decided to give you that chance.'

'You want control of the film even after you leave. You chose me because you thought I'd be easier than anyone else to manipulate.' I hope he's impressed by how calm I am. On the surface, at least. Not in a million years did I ever imagine that I would stand in Laurie Nattrass's office and accuse him of bad things. What the hell am I doing? How many innocent citizens has he sprung from their jail cells while I've been whiling away my spare time leafing through *heat* magazine on the sofa, or shouting abuse at *Strictly Come Dancing*?

What if I've completely misread the situation and I'm the one in the wrong?

Laurie leans back in his chair. Slowly, he shakes his head. 'Fine. You don't want to exec the documentary that's going to win every prize going? You don't want to be Creative Director? Then why don't you make Maya's day: tell her you want out of the deal, and watch her lose any respect for you that she ever had.'

'The *deal*?' I am bloody well not in the wrong here. 'You mean the deal I wasn't party to, the one that involves my life and career?'

'You'll never be offered anything again,' Laurie sneers. 'Not at Binary Star, not anywhere. How long do you think it'll be before you're standing behind Tamsin in the dole queue?'

Mercury, Earth, Venus, Mars, Jupiter, Saturn, Neptune, Uranus, Pluto.

'I don't feel comfortable getting a pay-rise of a hundred grand a year when my friend's losing her job,' I say as unemotionally as possible. 'Of course I'd like more money, but I also like being able to sleep at night.'

'You, lose sleep? Don't make me laugh!'

I take a deep breath and say, 'I don't know what you imagine you know about me, but you're wrong.' Then I feel like a scumbag for implying that I might have an active social conscience, when in fact all the sleep I've lost has either been love-related, or . . .

Or nothing. I can't let myself think about that now, or I'll start crying and blurt out the whole story to Laurie. How hideously embarrassing would that be?

How much would he hate me if he knew?

'Jesus,' he mutters. 'Look, I apologise, okay? I thought I was doing you a favour.'

What happens if I say yes? I could say yes. No, I couldn't. What the hell's wrong with me? I'm panicking, and upset about Tamsin, and it's affected my brain. The state I'm in, it's probably sensible to say as little as possible.

Laurie swings his chair round so that I can't see him. 'I told the board you were worth what I think you're worth,' he says flatly. 'They nearly shat themselves, but I made a good case and I talked them round. Do you know what that means?'

A good case? *Do what I say or I'll put the kibosh on the film* – that's his idea of a good case? He can't even be bothered to put a convincing gloss on it; that's how little he values me.

Without waiting for my response, he says, 'It means a hundred and forty a year is now officially what you're worth. Think of yourself as a share on the stock market. Your value's just gone up. If you tell Maya you don't want it, if you say, "Yes, please, I'd like a pay-rise but not *that* much, because I'm not *that* good, so can we please negotiate downwards?" – do that and you plummet to rock-bottom.' He spins round to face me. 'You're worthless,' he says emphatically, as if I might have missed the point.

That's it: my limit. I turn and walk out. Laurie doesn't call after me or follow me. What does he think I'm going to do? Take the promotion and the money? Resign? Lock myself in a toilet cubicle for a good cry? Does he feel at all guilty about what he's just done to me?

Why the hell do I care how he feels?

I march back to my office, slam the door, grab the damp towel from the top of the radiator and wipe away condensation until my arm aches. A few minutes later, the window is still sopping wet and now so is my jumper. All I've succeeded in doing is flicking the water all over myself.

Why doesn't someone think to put an end to world drought by collecting condensation? My window alone could irrigate most of Africa. Why doesn't Bob Geldof sort it out? It must be Bob Geldof I'm angry with, since it can't be Laurie. I've got a typed document buried somewhere in my desk, instructing me, among other things, never to allow myself to get angry with Laurie.

I used to look at it all the time when Tamsin first gave it to me. I thought it was hilarious, more hilarious still when she told me she gave a copy to every woman who came to work at Binary Star. About a year ago, it started to lose its appeal for me, and I stuffed it in my desk, underneath the flower-patterned lining paper that someone who worked here before me put in all the drawers.

No point trying to kid myself that I can't remember which drawer it's in; I know exactly where it is, even if I've spent much of the last twelve months pretending it isn't there. I pull out the files and the drawer-liner, and there it is, face down. Steeling myself, I pick it up and turn it over.

It's headed, in capitals, 'TAMSIN'S SEVEN COMMANDMENTS', with a subheading in italics, '*To be borne in mind at all times in relation to Laurie Nattrass*'.

The list reads as follows:

1) It's not you. It's him.
2) Have no expectations, or, alternatively, expect absolutely anything.
3) Accept what you can't change. Don't waste time getting angry or upset.
4) Bear in mind that it's only because he's a man that he's got a reputation for being 'brilliant but difficult'. If

he were an equally talented woman who behaved in exactly the same way, he'd be ridiculed as a mental old bat instead of head-hunted for all the best jobs.

5) Beware of imagining that he has hidden depths. Assume his true self is the bit that you can see.
6) Don't be attracted by his power. Some people are powerful in a good way, enhancing the confidence of others and making them believe anything is possible. Not him. Get close to him and you'll find that, as his power seems to grow, yours rapidly diminishes. Look out for a feeling of helplessness and the growing conviction that you must be fairly rubbish.
7) Whatever you do, DO NOT FALL IN LOVE WITH HIM.

According to at least one of Tamsin's criteria, I have failed spectacularly.

2

7/10/09

'Unusual, yes,' said DS Sam Kombothekra. 'Suspicious, no. How could it be?' If trying to be fair to everyone ever felt like too much effort, Sam hid it well.

He and DC Simon Waterhouse were on their way to today's second briefing. It had probably started by now. Sam was walking a little too fast, trying to look as if being a few minutes late didn't make him nervous.

Simon knew it did. Lateness belonged to that vast superset of things that displeased Detective Inspector Giles Proust, known unofficially as the Snowman because his regular avalanches of disapproval descended as tangibly as boulders of ice, and were as hard to shake off. After long years of trying, Simon had finally succeeded in insulating himself against Proust's condemnation: the inspector's opinions no longer mattered to him. Sam was a newer addition to Culver Valley CID and still had a long way to go.

The incident room was packed by the time they got there, with nowhere left to sit and hardly any space to stand. Simon and Sam had to make do with the doorway. Between the bodies and over the heads of dozens of detectives, most of whom had been drafted in from Silsden and Rawndesley, Simon could see Proust's trim, immobile form at the front. He wasn't looking in their direction, but Simon could see the Snowman noticing his and Sam's lateness. A tilt of an eyebrow, a twitch of the jaw – that was all it took. Wasn't it supposed to be women who were passive aggressive? Proust was both: passive aggressive and aggressive aggressive. He boasted a full repertoire of noxious behaviours.

It was clear from the noise in the room that they'd missed nothing; the meeting hadn't got going yet. 'Why now?' Simon addressed his question to Sam's ear, raising his voice to be heard over the mix of murmured conversations and the irregular drumming of feet against table legs. He was still suspicious. More so, if anything, for being told there was no cause. 'Two briefings a day? It's not like this is the first murder we've ever worked. Even with the multiples we've had in the past, he's barely stuck his nose out of his box apart from to carp at you or Charlie, whoever's been skipper. Now he's leading every—'

'Helen Yardley's the first . . . celebrity's the wrong word, but you know what I mean,' said Sam.

Simon laughed. 'You think the Snowman's keen to get his carrot nose and coal eyes in the papers? He hates—'

'No choice,' Sam interrupted him again. 'A case like this, he's going to get publicity one way or another, so he might as well get it for taking a strong lead. As SIO, case this visible nationally, he's got to step up.'

Simon decided to let it lie. He'd noticed that Sam, who normally was courtesy itself, cut him off mid-sentence whenever he talked about Proust. Charlie, Simon's fiancée and former sergeant, put it down to Sam's concern for proper professional conduct: you didn't badmouth the boss. Simon suspected it had more to do with the preservation of self-respect. Even someone as patient and hierarchy-conscious as

Sam could barely put up with what he had to put up with from the Snowman. Denial was his coping mechanism, one that must have been made all but impossible by Simon's constant dissection of Proust's despotism.

Ultimately, it came down to personal preference. Sam preferred to pretend he and his team weren't abused daily by a narcissistic megalomaniac and helpless to do anything about it, whereas Simon had long ago decided the only way to stay sane was to focus, all the time, on exactly what was going on and how bad it was, so that there was no danger it would ever start to seem normal. He'd become the unofficial archivist of Proust's abhorrent personality. These days he almost looked forward to the inspector's offensive outbursts; each one was further proof that Simon was right to have cut off the goodwill supply and all benefits of the doubt.

'You'd think Proust had an evil ulterior motive whatever he did, even if he dragged sacks of grain across the desert to famine victims,' Charlie had teased him last night. 'You're so used to hating everything about him, it's become a Pavlovian response – he must be doing something wrong, even if you don't yet know what it is.'

She's probably right, thought Simon. Sam was probably right: there was no way out of the limelight for Proust on this one. He had to be seen to care, so he was doing it with gusto, while secretly counting the days until he could revert to his usual mode of doing as little as possible.

'He's bound to feel responsible, like we all do,' Sam said. 'Professional considerations aside, you'd have to have a heart of stone not to want to pull out all the stops in a case like this. I know it's early days and there's no proof this murder's connected to the reason we all know Helen Yardley's name, but . . . you have to ask yourself, would she be dead now if it weren't for us?'

Us. By the time Simon had worked out what Sam meant, Proust was banging his 'World's Greatest Grandad' mug on the wall to get the room's attention. *Sound to silence in less than three seconds*. The Silsford and Rawndesley lot were quick learners. Simon had done his best to warn everyone yesterday. It turned out none of them needed the tip-off; spine-chilling tales of the Snowman's mercilessness had done the rounds at both nicks, apparently.

'Detectives, officers, we have a murder weapon,' Proust said. 'Or, rather, we don't have it yet, but we know what it is, which means we're closer to finding it.'

That was debatable, Simon thought. He allowed no statement the inspector made to pass without rigorous scrutiny; everything had to be challenged, albeit in silence much of the time. Was this or that fact a genuine fact, or merely a dogmatically expressed opinion masquerading as the one and only truth? Simon saw the irony; he had the Snowman's perennially closed mind to thank for his determination to keep his own open.

'Helen Yardley was shot with an M9 Beretta 9 millimetre,' Proust went on. 'Not a converted Baikal IZH, as Firearms told us on Monday, nor a 9 millimetre Makarov police gun, as they told us on Tuesday. Since it's now Wednesday, we have no alternative but to believe them a third time.'

An angry-looking Rick Leckenby stood up. 'Sir, you forced me to speculate before I'd—'

'Sergeant Leckenby, while you're on your feet, do you want to tell us a bit about today's gun of choice?'

Leckenby turned to face the room. 'The M9 Beretta 9 mil is US army standard issue, and it's been in circulation since the 1980s, which means it could have come back from Iraq, from the first Gulf War or more recently, or from any other war zone, any time in the last twenty, twenty-five years. Obviously, depending on how long it's been in the UK, that potentially reduces traceability.'

'So we're looking for anyone with links to the American armed forces?'

'Or the British,' said DC Chris Gibbs. 'A Brit could have got it off a Yank and brought it back.'

'No, sir, that's the point I'm trying to make,' Leckenby answered Proust. 'I'd say there's no grounds for assuming the killer's got links with the military. If the gun entered the UK in, say, 1990, there's a good chance it's been through several owners since then. What I would say is—'

'Don't tell us what you *would* say, Sergeant – just say it.'

'The gun on the streets at the moment, used in more than half of urban shootings, is the Baikal IZH gas pistol. You buy them in Eastern Europe, convert them, and you've got an effective short-distance murder weapon. My first thought, at the scene, was that since Mrs Yardley was killed at close range, and since Baikals account for the majority of guns we're seeing lately, and based on the amount of residue on the wall as well as on the body and the carpet around it, the likelihood was that a Baikal killed her. It was only after the bullet was retrieved from her brain and we had a chance to examine it that we were able to link it to the M9 Beretta 9 mil.'

'Which means what?' Proust asked.

'It could mean nothing,' said Leckenby. 'Either gun, Baikal or Beretta, could theoretically be in the possession of anybody.

But my gut feeling is, street shooters don't have M9 Beretta 9 mils. They just don't. So . . . this killer's as likely to be anybody as he is to be gang-connected or a known offender.'

'He or she,' a female DC from Rawndesley called out.

'If the murder weapon is standard US military issue, Sergeant, then we're going to look for anyone with links to the American army, and, as DC Gibbs sensibly suggests, to our own,' said Proust. When he spoke with this sort of slow deliberation, you were intended to understand that he was taking care not to allow the dam of his disgust to burst. 'You've no way of knowing how many hands it's passed through. Guns are like cars, presumably – some sold on every three years, others loyally tended by one careful owner over a lifetime. Yes?'

'I suppose so, sir,' said Leckenby.

'Good. Make sure you have a full resumé of the M9 Beretta, complete with colour pictures, by tomorrow morning, to distribute to everybody,' the Snowman ordered. 'Assuming you haven't changed your mind by then and decided the murder weapon was a turbo-charged pea-shooter from the shores of Lake Windermere. Interview teams – you'll need to start from scratch. Everyone you've already spoken to, Helen Yardley's friends, family, neighbours, etc – you'll need to speak to them again and find the military connection if it's there to be found. CCTV teams – you're looking for any cars with number plates that are either American or armed forces or both. Or – and I hope this goes without saying – anyone known personally to the Yardleys. CCTV could have been a sizeable headache for us, given that the two cameras nearest to Bengeo Street are on the busiest stretch of the Rawndesley Road, but thankfully we've done well with witnesses – more of which in a moment – so for the time being we're prioritising Monday morning between 7.45 and 8.15 a.m. and Monday afternoon between 5 and 6.10 p.m. for the camera outside the Picture House. For the one by the entrance to Market Place, the times we're looking at are slightly different: 7.30 to 8 a.m. and 5.15 to 6.25 p.m. Of particular interest is any car going in the direction of Bengeo Street during one of the earlier time slots and away from it in the later ones.'

The DS with overall charge of the CCTV team, David Prescott from Rawndesley, raised his hand and said, 'A lot of people driving down the Rawndesley Road at rush hour are going to be people Helen Yardley knew. She was a childminder. How many children did she mind whose parents lived in Spilling or Silsford and worked in Rawndesley?'

'I'm not asking your team to red-flag anybody on the basis of CCTV footage alone, Sergeant. I'm simply suggesting that it's an avenue of enquiry.'

'Yes, sir.'

'We don't even know if the killer drove to Bengeo Street or walked, not for certain,' said Proust. 'If he walked, he might have come from Turton Street or Hopelea Street.'

'He could have cycled,' said DC Colin Sellers.

'Or perhaps he fell out of the sky and landed in the Yardleys' front garden,' the Snowman snapped. 'DS Prescott, instruct your officers not to bother with the CCTV footage until we've contacted all the hot-air-balloon suppliers in the Culver Valley.'

The silence in the room was as thick as glue.

Another one for the archive, thought Simon. The killer might have driven or walked, but the idea that he could have cycled to the murder scene was laughable and far-fetched, because cycling wasn't something Giles Proust ever did. Therefore it was contemptible and not worth mentioning.

'Moving on to witnesses, then,' said the inspector glacially. 'Mrs Stella White of 16 Bengeo Street – that's the house directly opposite number 9, the Yardley house – saw a man walking up the Yardleys' path to the front door at 8.20 on Monday morning. She didn't see if he got out of a car – her first sighting of him was on the Yardleys' property. Mrs White was strapping her son Dillon into the car to drive him to school, not paying much attention to what was happening on the other side of the road, but she was able to give us a general description: a man between the ages of thirty-five and fifty with dark hair, wearing darkish clothes including a coat, smartly dressed, though not in a suit. He wasn't carrying anything, she said, though an M9 Beretta 9 millimetre gun would easily fit in a large coat pocket.'

A description like that was about as useful as no description at all, thought Simon. By tomorrow Mrs White, if she was anything like most witnesses, would be saying that maybe the dark hair wasn't so dark, and maybe the coat was a dressing-gown.

'By the time Mrs White drove out on to the road, there was no sign of the man. She says there wasn't long enough for him to have gone anywhere but inside number 9. We know there was no break-in, so did Helen Yardley let him in? If so, did she know him, or did he say something plausible enough to get himself inside when she opened the door? Was he a lover, a relative, a double-glazing salesman? We need to find out.'

'Did Mrs White see or hear Helen Yardley open her front door?' someone asked.

'She thinks she might have, but she's not sure,' said Proust. 'Now, at number 11 Bengeo Street we've got eighty-three-year-old Beryl Murie, who, in spite of her partial deafness, heard a loud noise at 5 p.m. that might well have been a gunshot. She said it sounded like a firework, which is an easy mistake to make if you're unfamiliar with the sound of an M9 Beretta 9 millimetre being discharged, as I think we can safely assume most retired piano teachers are. Miss Murie was able to be precise about the time because she was listening to the radio and the five o'clock news had just started when she heard the loud noise. She said it startled her. She also said it sounded as if it had come from Helen Yardley's house. So, assuming we've got a man entering the house at 8.20 a.m. and the fatal shot fired at 5 p.m., what's happening in between? We can't assume the man Mrs White saw is the killer, but until we track him down and find out for certain, we have to consider the possibility that he might be. Sergeant Kombothekra?'

'Still no joy, sir,' Sam called out from the back of the room.

Proust nodded grimly. 'If another day passes and we haven't found and eliminated Mr Morning Visitor, I'll put my money on him being our man. If he is, and he was in Helen Yardley's house with her for more than eight hours before he shot her, what was happening during those hours? Why not shoot her straight away? She wasn't raped or tortured. Apart from being shot in the back of the head, she wasn't injured. So, did he go there to talk to her, thinking he might or might not shoot her, depending on the outcome of the conversation?'

Simon raised his hand. After a few seconds of pretending not to see it, Proust nodded at him.

'Don't we also have to consider the possibility that the gun belonged to the Yardleys? We can't assume the man brought it with him. It might already have been in the house. Given the Yardleys' history—'

'The Yardleys have no history of illegally possessing firearms,' the Snowman cut him off. 'There's a thin line between exploring all reasonable avenues of possibility and squandering our resources on tosh that, in our desire to be egalitarian, we've elevated to the status of hypothesis. Everyone in this room needs to bear that in mind. We're forty-eight hours into this investigation and we're without a suspect – you all know what that means. We've already alibied and eliminated Helen Yardley's friends, family and close acquaintances. This is shaping up to be a stranger murder, which, for us, is about as bad as it gets, and all the more reason to channel our efforts in the right direction.'

'You were right to raise it,' Sam muttered to Simon. 'Better for us to focus on it and dismiss it than not to think of it at all.'

'Paul Yardley returned from work at 6.10 p.m., found his wife's body and phoned the police,' said Proust. 'He found no one else in the house and neither did the first officers to the scene. Some time between 5 and 6.10 p.m., the killer left 9 Bengeo Street. Someone must have seen him. You know what that means: house-to-house is top priority, and let's extend it. Someone come up with a new mile-radius.'

The Snowman walked over to the board where the enlarged crime scene photographs were displayed. 'Here's the input wound,' he said, pointing at a picture of the back of Helen Yardley's head. 'Look at the scorch marks. The gun was so close it might even have been touching her. From the position of the body, it's a strong possibility that she was in the corner of the room facing the wall when she was shot. A 9-mm bullet in the brain at close range doesn't spin a person round. But there's nothing on the wall next to where she fell, so what was she doing standing there? What was she looking at? Had he marched her over there to kill her because it's the only part of the room that can't be seen from the window? Or was she standing there for some other reason, and he came up behind her, knowing she wouldn't see the gun?'

Simon had missed some of that. He was still thinking about what Sam had said to him. 'Better to focus on it and *dismiss* it?' he said behind his clenched fist so that Proust wouldn't notice. 'Why are the Yardleys less likely to have a shooter than this dark-haired man we can't find?'

Sam didn't sigh, but he looked as if he wanted to. He shook his head to indicate that he wasn't going to risk answering. It occurred to Simon that Sam might find it a damn sight easier to work with the Snowman than he did at present if he didn't also have to work with Simon.

Stand in the corner. Face the wall. Simon considered drawing attention to the symbolism – a teacher punishing a child – then decided against it. Today was one of those days when everyone would disagree with him whatever he said. And he would disagree with the world, as he so often did. A stranger murder? No. Proust was wrong. Collective police responsibility for Helen Yardley's death because eleven out of twelve civilian jurors voted to send her to prison for murder? *Fuck off.*

'Where are we with fingerprints and swabbing?' Proust asked.

DS Klair Williamson stood up. 'Fingerprints – no matches with any on our database. Lots belonging to friends and family, quite a few sets unidentified, but that's only to be expected. We've swabbed everybody for forensic evidence of weapon discharge and got nothing so far.'

'Predictable,' said Proust. 'Gunpowder residue perishes easily. If our killer knows that, he'll have had a thorough wash. All the same, I'm sure I don't need to tell any of you that it would be a grave mistake to drop this angle prematurely. Do your utmost to preserve every possible forensic opportunity. Keep up the swabbing until I say otherwise, and make a note of the names of anyone who gives you an argument about it.'

'Yes, sir,' said Williamson.

'We also want the names of any unsavouries who have raised their heads above the parapet, so keep going through emails, letters, anything you can find – to JIPAC or to Helen Yardley personally. Our killer could have been unknown to her but obsessed with her.'

Simon heard grunts of agreement; people seemed to like this idea. He didn't. Why was no one pointing out the obvious? It wasn't the simple either-or of someone close to the victim versus total stranger, not in this case. There was a third possibility. Surely he wasn't the only one it had occurred to.

'Moving on, then, to the most inexplicable aspect of this killing,' said the Snowman. 'The card protruding from Helen Yardley's skirt pocket.' He jerked his head in the direction of the picture on the board. 'Her fingerprints are on it, as well as another set we can't identify. It's likely the killer put it in the pocket after he shot her and left the top half visible to draw our attention. Also likely is that the sixteen numbers on the card, arranged as they are in four rows of four, have some meaning for the killer. Any new ideas on this – from anyone?'

All over the room, heads were shaking.

'Right, well, we'll wait to hear back from Bramshill and GCHQ.'

There was a general groan and mutters of 'waste of time'.

'What about seeing if there's anybody in the Maths department of a university who knows anything about codes?' Proust suggested. 'And I mean a proper university, not a former polytechnic or an accredited branch of Pizza Hut.'

The reaction to his suggestion was disproportionately enthusiastic. Simon wondered how many tyrants questioned the rapture with which their every utterance was received. The sixteen numbers had been going round in his head all day: 2, 1, 4, 9 . . . Or maybe it was 21, 49, or perhaps you were supposed to start at the bottom and read backwards: 0, 2, 6 . . .

'As a last resort, there's always the press,' said Proust. 'We let them print the sixteen numbers and see what happens.'

'We'd have every loony in the Culver Valley ringing in, saying they'd got the numbers off an extra-terrestrial's lottery ticket,' said Colin Sellers.

Proust smiled. A few people risked laughing. Simon pushed down a rising swell of anger. Any sign that the inspector might be enjoying even the briefest moment of happiness made him want to do damage to somebody. Luckily, such signs were rare.

'What about a profiler?' someone called out. *Someone else who doesn't think the Snowman deserves a lighthearted moment and knows how to put a stop to it.*

Simon waited for Proust to breathe frost, but, surprisingly, he said, 'If we make no progress on the card in the next twenty-four hours, I'll be asking for a profiler to be brought in. In the meantime, while we wait for the code teams at Bramshill and GCHQ to get back to us, we do the dull legwork: which retailers supply this kind of card? What sort of pen does the ink come from? *Well?*' he roared suddenly. A collective shudder rippled through the room.

'Sir, we're still pursuing that,' said the unfortunate DC from Silsford who'd been tasked to find out. 'I'll chase it up.'

'You do that, detective. I want two hundred and fifty per cent effort from all of you. And don't forget your ABC. Let's hear it, DC Gibbs.'

'Assume nothing, believe nobody, check everything,' Chris Gibbs muttered, his face colouring. Simon was the one the Snowman usually nominated to make a tit of himself in front of a crowd. Why had he been spared this time?

'Our mystery caller at 9 Bengeo Street might turn out to be a false lead, so let's make sure he's not our only lead,' said Proust. 'As someone's already pointed out, we could be looking for a female. I want brains switched on and fully serviced round the clock. I don't need to tell you all why this case matters more than any you've worked before.'

'Don't you?' Simon murmured. Beside him, Sam was nodding. And yet the thing that marked out Helen Yardley as different from other murder victims had barely been mentioned, not this morning and not now.

'It's been forty-eight hours,' said the Snowman. 'If we don't get a result soon, they'll cut this squad in half, and that'll just be for starters. You'll all be going back to your own nicks – something I'm sure at least those of you from Rawndesley are keen to avoid. All right, that's it for today. DS Kombothekra, DC Waterhouse – my office.'

Simon was in no mood to wait and see what Proust wanted. 'How come you're happy to ditch the "assume nothing" part when it comes to the gun?' he asked, as soon as he'd slammed the door behind him. This time Sam did sigh. 'Why's Helen or Paul Yardley less likely to own an M9 Beretta than this dark-haired man we can't find?'

'Sergeant Kombothekra, explain to DC Waterhouse why a killer is more likely than his victim to bring a gun to the party.'

'The Yardleys fought to keep their only surviving child, and they lost. Think about what that must have meant to them. You've got a daughter . . .'

'Mention her name, Waterhouse, and I'll yank your tongue out by the root. My daughter has nothing to do with this.'

You ought to hear what Colin Sellers has said about her over the years, what he'd like to do to which bits of her. Simon tried again. 'Paige Yardley lives less than two miles from Bengeo Street, with new parents who've changed her name and won't let her birth family anywhere near her. If I was Helen or Paul Yardley in that situation – someone stole my kid and, to add insult to injury, the law was on their side – I might get myself a shooter. If I'd had to stand in court and watch helplessly as my wife got two life sentences for crimes I was sure she hadn't committed—'

'You've made your point,' said Proust.

'I've made part of my point, and I'll make the rest of it now: Helen Yardley spent nine years behind bars. If she wasn't guilty, revenge might have been on her mind once she got out. And even if—'

'Enough!'

Simon ducked as something flew past his head. Proust's 'World's Greatest Grandad' mug hit the corner of the filing cabinet and smashed. Sam bent to pick up the pieces. 'Leave that!' the Snowman bellowed. 'Open the top drawer of the cabinet. There are two copies of Helen Yardley's book in there. Take one for yourself and give one to Waterhouse.'

The only way Simon could keep his mouth shut was by vowing to do what he should have done years ago and put in an official complaint. He'd do it first thing tomorrow morning. Proust would come back at him with counter-accusations of disrespect, sarcasm, disobedience. *True, true, true.* No one would speak up for Simon apart from Charlie, and she'd only do it because of her personal feelings for him, not because she would disagree with Proust's portrayal of him as every line manager's nightmare.

Sam handed him a copy of *Nothing But Love* by Helen Yardley and Gaynor Mundy. Simon had interviewed Mundy earlier today. She'd told him Helen had written most of the book herself and been a dream to work with. The cover was white, with a picture of a pair of knitted baby bootees at its centre. Curls of yellow paper protruded from the sides of several pages: Post-it strips. Simon glanced at Sam's copy and saw that it was the same.

'Let's start again,' said the Snowman, loading each word with a hefty dollop of patience in the face of provocation. *Not asking for another chance; bestowing one with self-conscious generosity.* 'I called the two of you in here because you're my best detectives – personality disorders notwithstanding, Waterhouse. I need to know that I can count on you.'

'You can, sir,' said Sam.

'Count on us to do what?' Simon asked. He could only occasionally manage a 'sir'. Less and less often these days.

'I want you both to read that book,' said Proust. 'I've read it, and I don't think there's anything in it that adds to what we know already, but you might spot something I missed. The sections I've marked are the parts where I'm mentioned by name. I arrested Helen Yardley three days after the death of her second child, and charged her with the murders of both her children. I gave evidence at her trial. I was a DS at the time. Superintendent Barrow was my DI.'

Not looking at Sam, not reacting at all, took all Simon's willpower.

'As far as I'm concerned, nobody working this murder needs to read the book apart from the two of you. At the briefing tomorrow morning, I intend to tell everyone about my . . . involvement. However irrelevant it is to the business at hand, I'd like it to be out in the open.'

Irrelevant? Was he joking? Testing them?

'I won't be mentioning the role played by Superintendent Barrow, whose name does not feature in the book.'

Had Barrow told Proust to leave his name out of it? Had the two of them been arguing behind the scenes about what to reveal and what to withhold? The Snowman had never bothered to conceal his hatred for Barrow, but it had blended so seamlessly, over the years, with his antipathy for everyone else he knew that Simon had never questioned it or wondered about its origins.

'Ordinarily, as I'm sure you're aware, any officer who charged someone with murder as a DS would not then lead the investigation into the murder of that same person as a DI. The Chief Constable, the Assistant Chief Constable and Superintendent Barrow didn't want me as SIO on Helen Yardley's murder. And yet here I am – SIO on Helen Yardley's murder. Go ahead, Waterhouse. You look as if you have a question.'

'Am I getting the wrong end of the stick, or are you implying that Barrow, the Chief and the Assistant Chief don't want it known that they were instrumental in sending Helen Yardley to prison?' Simon stopped short of asking Proust if he'd threatened to go public about their role in an extremely visible miscarriage of justice if they assigned the investigation into Helen Yardley's murder to any DI but him.

'The Chief and the Assistant Chief weren't involved,' said Proust. 'Though as Superintendent Barrow's superior officers, they have his best interests at heart, as well as the best interests of Culver Valley Police Service.'

Sam Kombothekra cleared his throat, but said nothing.

'So . . .' Simon began.

'In so far as your hypothesis applied to Superintendent Barrow, Waterhouse, I *would say*, to borrow a phrase from Sergeant Leckenby, that your purchase on the stick needs no lateral adjustment.'

'What . . .? Oh.' Simon got it, just in time to avoid making an idiot of himself.

'Will you both read the book?' Proust asked. 'It's not an order. I'm asking you as a favour to me personally.'

'Yes, sir,' said Sam.

Simon had ordered *Nothing But Love* from Amazon this morning, after talking to Gaynor Mundy. He would read his own copy when it arrived, because he wanted to – nothing to do with being asked. *A favour*. He'd have preferred it to be an order. Friends asked favours; the Snowman was no friend.

'Tomorrow morning I want the two of you standing on either side of me for the briefing and tasking, so get in early,' said Proust, more relaxed now that the meeting seemed to be going his way. 'I want everybody to see that I have your full support when I announce that from now on, anyone who makes a remark along the lines of "No smoke without fire" or "Just because they let her out doesn't mean she was innocent" will be formally disciplined, no matter where and in what circumstances that remark is made – as somebody's idea of a joke, under the influence of alcohol. Any bobby who so much as whispers the words in his bedroom in the middle of the night, with his head buried in his duvet – he'll rue the day. From now on, you two are my eyes and ears. You hear any comments like that, you report them to me, whether the commentator is your closest friend or someone you hardly know. You pick up on any bad attitudes, I want to hear about them.'

Simon couldn't believe Sam was nodding.

'I know I can count on your support, and I'm grateful for it,' said Proust curtly. 'Waterhouse, any other points you want to raise, now I've said my piece?'

There was plenty more Simon could have said – had been planning to say – about where he thought the investigation was going wrong, but until he'd had a chance to think about what he'd just heard, he didn't want to say another word in the Snowman's presence. *Count on nothing, shithead.*

'Let's call it a night, then,' said Proust, who would have called it whatever he wanted to call it, whether it was morning, night or the middle of the afternoon.

3

Wednesday 7 October 2009

'It's exactly the kick up the arse I need – that's the way I'm looking at it,' says Tamsin, taking a gulp from her sixth gin and tonic of the evening. 'Control freak like me, any sort of disruption to my routine has to be good for me.' She's started to slur her words. Her top lip keeps slipping on her bottom one, like a smooth-soled shoe over snow.

I could sneak off to the loo, phone Joe and tell him to come and pick her up, but if I leave her unattended she's bound to accost a stranger, and there are at least two men at the bar who look likely to have chloroform-soaked hankies in their pockets. The Grand Old Duke of York is the only pub within walking distance of work that can be guaranteed to have nobody from Binary Star in it, which is why we've braved the bad beer and creepy loners. Tonight, anything's better than bumping into Maya, Raffi or Laurie at the French House.

'My life's been too safe for too long,' says Tamsin decisively. 'I should take more risks.' That's it: no way am I letting her get the tube home. I'll have to wait until she passes out to phone Joe. Another fifteen minutes, half an hour maximum. 'There are no surprises – you know what I mean? Up at seven, in the shower, two Weetabix and a fruit smoothie for breakfast, walk to the tube station, in work by half past eight, running round all day after Laurie, wearing myself out trying to . . .

decipher him, home by eight, eat dinner with Joe, snuggled up on the sofa by half nine to watch an episode of whatever DVD box set we're on, bed at eleven. Where's the spark? Where's the dyna . . . dianne. . . .?'

'Dynamism?' I suggest.

'Whereas now I've got a real challenge: no job!' She tries to sound upbeat about it. 'No income! I'll have to find a way of keeping a roof over our heads.'

'Can Joe cover the mortgage?' I ask, feeling terrible for her. 'Temporarily, until you find something else?'

'No, but we could rent out Joe's study to someone chilled-out who wouldn't mind having to walk through our bedroom every time he needed a wee in the middle of the night,' says Tamsin brightly. 'He might become our friend. When was the last time I made a new friend?'

'When you met me.' I try to prise the gin and tonic from her grasp. 'Give me that. I'll go and get you an orange juice.'

Her hands tighten around her glass. 'You're a control freak too,' she says accusingly. 'We both are. We need to learn to go with the flow.'

'I'm worried the flow might be of vomit. Why don't I ring Joe and he can—'

'*Nooo.*' Tamsin pats my hand. 'I'm *fine*. I whole-heartedly embrace this opportunity for change. Maybe I'll start wearing blue or red instead of black and white all the time. Hey – know what I'm gonna do tomorrow?'

'Die of alcohol poisoning?'

'Go to an exhibition. There must be something good on at the National Portrait Gallery, or the Hayward. And while I'm doing that, you know what you're gonna do?' She burps loudly. 'You're going to be in Maya's office saying, "Yes, please, I'll take that extremely well-paid job." If you feel guilty about earning too much money, you can give some to me. Just a little bit. Or maybe half.'

'Hey – did you just suggest something that makes sense?'

'I believe I did.' Tamsin giggles. 'Socialism in miniature. There'd only be two of us involved, but the principle's the same: everything you have is mine, and everything I have is yours, except I haven't got anything.'

'You need an income. I've just been offered more than three times what I'm on now . . . No, that'd be mad. Wouldn't it?' I haven't drunk as much as she has, but I've had a fair bit.

'What's the prollem?' she slurs, wide-eyed. 'No one needs to find out apart from you and me. Laurie's right: if you blow this chance, everyone'll think you're a dick. And if you hoard your wealth like a Scroogey miser . . .'

'So this is the great challenge that was missing from your life? Forcing me to take a job I don't want so that you can nick half my salary?' I'm not even sure she means what she's saying. I wait for her to tell me she's only kidding.

'You wouldn't have to fund me for ever,' she says instead. 'Just until I sort myself out with a new career. I'd quite like to work for the UN, as an interpreter.'

I sigh. 'Do you speak anything, apart from English and Pissed?'

'I could learn. Russian and French is a good combination, apparently. I did some Googling before I left the office. For the last time *ever*,' she adds pointedly, reminding me of her hard-done-by status. 'If you've got those two languages . . .'

'Which you haven't.'

'. . . then all you need's a translation qualification, which you can get at Westminster Uni, and the UN'll snap you up.'

'When? In four years' time?'

'More like six.'

'How about I support you while you look for a job *in your field*?' I stress the last three words. 'With your track record, you could get one tomorrow.'

'No, thanks,' says Tamsin. 'No more TV for me. TV's the rut I was stuck in until today. I'm serious, Fliss. Ever since I left university, I've been a wage-slave. I don't want to rush out and find new shackles, now that I'm free. I want to do some living – walk in the park, go ice-skating . . .'

'What happened to learning French and Russian?' I ask.

She waves away my concern. 'There's plenty of time for that. Maybe I'll see if there's a local evening class or something, but mainly I want to . . . take stock, walk around, soak up the atmosphere . . .'

'You live in Wood Green.'

'Could you stretch to a flat in Knightsbridge if I'm willing to settle for one bedroom?'

'Stop,' I tell her, deciding the joke has gone on long enough. 'This is exactly why I don't want to be rich. I don't want to turn into the sort of person who thinks it's my God-given right to have more cash than I know what to do with and keep it all for myself. Here I am listening to you witter on, thinking, "Why should I give half my hard-earned fortune to an idle waster?" I'm already turning into that Scroogey miser you mentioned earlier and I haven't even said I'll take the job!'

Tamsin blinks at me, her powers of comprehension impaired by alcohol. Eventually she says, 'You'd resent me.'

'Probably, yes. The ice-skating might just tip me over the edge.'

She nods. 'That's okay. I wouldn't hold it against you. You can call me a feckless scrounger to my face, if you like, as long as I get my share of the money. I'd rather be insulted by you than have to tout myself round prospective employers feeling the way I do now – unwanted and worthless. What am I talking about?' She slaps herself on the wrist, then hits my leg, hard. 'Look what you've done – your negativity's totally dragged me down!'

'I'm turning down the job, Tam.'

She groans.

'Which means I'll probably get my marching orders too by the end of the week. We can go to the National Portrait Gallery together.' *Tell her the truth. Tell her why you can't make Laurie's film. You have nothing to be ashamed of.*

'Bollocks to that!' Tamsin bangs her fist on the table. 'If you're going there, I'm going to the Science Museum instead as a protest at your . . . dickery. Fliss, people dream of things happening to them like what's happened to you today. You've *got* to take it. Even if you decide to leave me to rot in the gutter while you stock up on diamonds.'

'I'm being serious.'

'So am I! Think of all the time you'll get to spend with Laurie, him helping you unofficially – hah!' She gurgles with laughter. 'It's so obvious you're in love with him.'

'It can't be, because I'm not,' I say firmly. Maybe it's not such a huge lie. If I'm aware of all the reasons why I shouldn't love Laurie, which I am, then that has to mean I don't, not wholly. At the very least, I'm halfway in and halfway out. If I'm in love with him, how come I can so perfectly inhabit the mindset of thinking he's a git and the bane of my life?

'You spend *hours* staring out of your window at his office, even when he's not in it.' Tamsin chuckles. 'I'm not going to waste my breath saying no good can come of it. Some good's already come of it – a hundred and forty grand a year for us to split between us.' She gives me a narrow-eyed grin to let me know she's been winding me up about the money. 'You've been rewarded for your good taste. Laurie might be a freak, but he's a shrewd freak. He's seen the way you babble like an idiot in front of him, crazed with lust. You're his perfect pawn: he gets to distance himself from the film in public while retaining control in private.'

'Why would he want to distance himself?' I say, determinedly ignoring everything else Tamsin's just said because if I allowed myself to take it in and believe it, I would have to devote the rest of my life to muffled sobbing. 'He's obsessed with it.'

'In case it goes tits up, which it might very well, now that Sarah's pulled out.'

'Sarah?'

'Jaggard. Oh, my God! Laurie hasn't told you, has he?'

My phone starts to ring. I snap it open. 'Hello?'

'Is that Fliss Benson?' a woman asks.

I tell her it is.

'This is Ray Hines.'

My heart leaps, like a horse over a fence. *Rachel Hines*. I have the oddest sensation: as if this moment was always going to come, and there was nothing I could have done to avert it.

She can't know how significant she is to me, how it makes me feel to hear her voice.

'Why is Laurie Nattrass leaving Binary Star?' She doesn't sound angry, or even put out. 'Does it have anything to do with Helen Yardley dying? I'm assuming she was murdered. I heard on the news that her death was "suspicious".'

'I don't know,' I say brusquely. 'You'll have to ask the police about that, and you'll have to ask Laurie why he's leaving. I'm nothing to do with anything.'

'Really? I got an email from Laurie saying you've taken over the documentary.'

'No. That's . . . a misunderstanding.'

Tamsin has found a pen in my bag and written 'Who?' on a beer mat. She shoves it towards me. I write 'Rachel Hines' beneath her question. She opens her mouth as wide as it'll go, flashing her tonsils at me, then scribbles furiously on the beer mat: 'Keep her talking!!!'

Even if I don't want to?

I heard two women on the tube discussing Rachel Hines, the day after she won her appeal. One said, 'I don't know about the others, but the Hines woman murdered her children, sure as I'm born. She's a drug addict and a liar. You know she abandoned her daughter when the poor mite was only days old? Stayed away for the best part of two weeks. What kind of mother does that? I can believe Helen Yardley was innocent all along, but not her.' I waited for her companion to disagree, but she said, 'It would have been better for the baby if she'd stayed away for good.' I remember thinking it was an odd way to put it: *Helen Yardley was innocent all along*. As if one could start out guilty and then become innocent of a crime.

'I rang to tell you what I'm sure Laurie neglected to mention: that I want nothing to do with the documentary. Evidently you feel the same way.' She sounds nothing like my idea of what a drug addict ought to sound like.

'You want nothing to do with it,' I repeat blankly.

'I've made it clear to Laurie from the start that he'll have to do without me, so I don't know why he keeps copying me in on information I don't need. Maybe he hopes I'll change my mind, but I won't.' She sounds calm, as if none of what she's saying matters to her; she's merely informing me of the facts.

'I'm in a similar situation,' I tell her, too angry about the way I've been treated to be tactful. How dare Laurie inflict her on me without giving me any choice in the matter? Tamsin's jiggling in her seat, desperate to know what's going on. 'Laurie can't take no for an answer,' I say. 'That's when he bothers to ask the question. This time he didn't. I had no idea he was sending out my details to everyone. I don't know why he assumed I'd take on the film without asking me if I wanted to.'

Tamsin rolls her eyes and shakes her head. 'What?' I mouth at her. I refuse to feel bad about any of this; it's Laurie's fault, not mine.

'Why don't you want to?' Rachel Hines asks, as if it's the most natural question in the world.

I imagine myself giving her an honest answer. How would I feel afterwards? Relieved to have it out in the open? It's irrelevant, since I'll never have the guts to put it to the test. 'I don't mean to be rude, but I don't have to explain myself to you.'

'No. No, you don't,' she says slowly. 'This is going to sound pushy, but . . . could we meet?'

Meet. Me and Rachel Hines.

She can't possibly know. Unless . . . No, there's no way.

'Pardon?' I say, playing for time. I grab the pen from Tamsin's hand and write, 'She wants to meet me'. Tamsin nods furiously.

'Where are you? I could come to you.'

I look at my watch. 'It's ten o'clock.'

'So? Neither of us is asleep. I'm in Twickenham. How about you?'

'Kilburn,' I say automatically, then mentally kick myself. There's no way I'm having Rachel Hines in my home. 'Actually, I'm . . . I'm out at the moment, in the Grand Old Duke of York pub in . . .'

'I don't go to pubs. Give me your address and I'll be there in an hour to an hour and a half, depending on traffic.'

Pros and cons race through my brain. I don't want her in my flat. I don't want anything to do with her apart from to know what she wants from me.

'You're worried about having someone who was once a convicted child murderer in your house,' she says. 'I understand. All right, I'm sorry I bothered you.'

'Why do you want to meet me?'

'I'll answer that question, and any others you might have, face to face. Does that sound fair?'

I hear myself say, 'Okay.' Unable to believe what's happening, I recite my address.

'It'll be just the two of us, won't it? No Laurie?'

'No Laurie,' I agree.

'I'll see you in an hour,' says Rachel Hines. That's when it hits me: this is real, and I'm scared.

Three quarters of an hour later I'm at home, trying to cram a drying rack draped with wet washing into my wardrobe. Normally it lives in the bathroom, but that's a part of the flat that a guest might conceivably see, so I can't leave my damp underwear on display there. I succeed eventually in stuffing the rack into the cupboard, but then I can't close the doors.

Does it matter? I'm so jittery, I can't think straight. Rachel Hines is unlikely to force her way into my bedroom.

A panicked voice in my head whispers *How do you know what she's likely to do?*

I pull the drying rack out of the cupboard. Half the clothes fall to the floor. Even if she wouldn't see it, knowing it was there would bother me. It's crazy to put wet laundry in a wardrobe, and I'm not going to start acting like a crazy person before anything's even happened.

I shudder. *Nothing is going to happen*, I tell myself. *Get a grip*.

I put the clothes back on the rack, stand it in the middle of my bedroom and close the door on it. Then I run to the kitchen, which I left in a state this morning: plates and magazines strewn everywhere, toast crusts, milk-bottle tops, orange peel. The fat black bin bag that I should have taken out days ago has leaked oily orange sauce onto the lino.

I look at my watch. Nearly eleven. She said an hour to an hour and a half. That means she could arrive in five minutes. I need at least fifteen to sort out the kitchen. I yank open the dishwasher. It's packed with shiny clean cutlery and crockery. I swear loudly. Who said dishwashers make life easier? They're the devious bastards of the household appliance world. When you want a clean cup or plate, you get a stinking cavern full of curry stalactites dripping baked-bean juice. When you want the damn thing empty and ready to receive, that's the moment it picks to be full to bursting with an entire dinner service, gleaming and ponging of lemon.

I pile the clean stuff randomly into cupboards and drawers, chipping a couple of plates that were already chipped, as most of my stuff is. Then I load the dirty things without bothering to rinse them as I normally would, and wipe the surfaces with a cloth that's probably dirtier than the mess I'm using it to wipe up. I'm quite shallow when it comes to cleaning – tidy and bacteria-infested suits me fine, as long as it looks presentable to the untrained eye.

I take out the rubbish, mop up the oil on the floor and stand back to survey the kitchen. It looks better than it has for some time. The thought pops into my head before I can stop it: *maybe I ought to have murderers round more often.* In the lounge, to a soundtrack of loud bangs from my pogo-jumping upstairs neighbours – their getting-ready-for-bed noises – I pick up about twenty DVDs from the floor and shove them in a cloth shopping bag, which I stuff behind the door.

I don't want Rachel Hines to know what DVDs I own, or anything else about me. I cast my eyes over the bookshelf that fills one whole alcove of my lounge, the one nearest the window. I don't want her to know what books I read, but I haven't got a bag big enough to house them all temporarily, or time to take them off the shelves. I toy with the idea of rigging up some kind of curtain to hide them, then decide I'm being paranoid. It doesn't matter if she sees my books. It only matters if I make it matter.

I plump up the sofa cushions and the one on the chair, then look again at my watch. Five past eleven. I pull open the curtains I closed when I got in, and, looking up to street level, see a man and woman walking past. They're laughing. Her heels clip the pavement as she hurries along, and I have to restrain myself from pushing up my rattly sash window and shouting, 'Come back!'

I don't want to be alone with Rachel Hines.

In the hall, I scoop up all the letters, bills and bank statements that have piled up on the table and put them in the one drawer in my kitchen that opens properly, underneath the cutlery divider. I'm about to slam it shut when the corner of a thick cream-coloured envelope catches my eye, and I remember that I ran out of the flat this morning without opening the post.

That card someone sent me at work, the one with the numbers on it – that arrived in a thick cream-coloured envelope with the same ribbed effect.

So? It needn't mean anything. A coincidence, that's all.

This one's also addressed to Fliss Benson. And the writing . . .

I rip it open. Inside, there's a card with only three numbers on it this time, in tiny handwriting at the bottom: 2 1 4. Or is it supposed to be two hundred and fourteen? The first three numbers on the other card, the one Laurie threw in the bin, were 2, 1 and 4.

There's no signature, no indication of who sent it. I turn the envelope upside down and shake it. Nothing. What do the numbers mean? Is it some kind of threat? Am I supposed to be scared? Whoever the sender is, he or she knows where I work, where I live . . .

I tell myself I'm being ridiculous, and force the tension out of my body, letting my shoulders drop. I concentrate on breathing slowly and steadily for a few seconds. Of course it's not a threat. If someone wants to threaten you, they use words you understand: *do x or I'll kill you*. Threats are threats and numbers are numbers – there's no overlap.

I tear both the card and the envelope into small pieces and take them outside to the bin, resolving to waste no more time on what must be some idiot's idea of a joke. Back inside, I pour myself a large glass of white wine and walk up and down, looking at my watch every three seconds until I can't bear it any longer. I pick up the phone and ring Tamsin's home number. Joe answers on the second ring. 'She's puking her guts up,' he tells me.

'Can I speak to her?'

'Well . . .' He sounds doubtful. 'You can listen to her spraying the toilet bowl with gin if you want.'

'I'm *fine*!' Tamsin shouts in the background. I hear a scuffle; more specifically, I hear Joe losing. 'Ignore Joseph. He likes to make heavy weather of things,' says Tamsin, with the crisp enunciation of someone determined to sound sober. 'Well? How did it go? What did she say?'

'She's not here yet.'

'Oh. Sorry, I've slightly lost time . . . *track* of time,' she corrects herself. 'I thought it was really late.'

'It is – too late to turn up on the doorstep of a complete stranger. Maybe she's seen sense and decided not to come.'

'Have you – gonna say this carefully, right? – *checked* your phone for *texts*?' It sounds like 'shrek-ed your phone for sex', but I know what she means.

'Yeah. Nothing.'

'Then she's coming.'

My watch says twenty past eleven. 'Even from Twickenham, she should be here by now.'

'Twickenham? That's virtually in Dorset. She could be hours. What's she doing in Twickenham?'

'Doesn't she live there?'

'No. Last I heard she was in a rented flat in Notting Hill, five minutes from her ex-husband and the former family home.'

All I know about Rachel Hines is that she was convicted, and later unconvicted, of killing her two children. *Good one, Fliss. Nothing like going into a situation well prepared.*

'Why did I agree to this?' I wail. 'It's your fault – you were nodding at me like a maniac as if yes was the only possible answer.' Even as I'm saying it, I know it's not true. I said yes because I'd just heard that the film might be about to fall apart. Once that's happened and Laurie's at Hammerhead, he'll have no leverage with Maya or Raffi. They'll be able to make me redundant: punish me for daring to think I was Creative Director material, even though I never did, and save themselves a hundred and forty grand a year. I agreed to see Rachel Hines in the absurd hope that somehow it might lead to my becoming indispensable at Binary Star, which is pretty embarrassing, even when I'm the only person I'm admitting it to.

Does that mean I want to make Laurie's film? No. No, no, no.

'I won't let her in,' I say, certain this is the best idea I've ever had.

'There's nothing to be scared of,' says Tamsin unhelpfully.

'Easy for you to say. When was the last time you were visited by a murderer in the middle of the night?' I'm not sure Rachel Hines killed her babies – how can I be? – but it makes me feel better to pretend that I am.

'She isn't a murderer any more,' says Tamsin. Automatically, I think of the woman I overheard on the tube: *I can believe Helen Yardley was innocent all along*. 'Even before she appealed and won, Justice Geilow made a point of saying she didn't think Ray Hines would ever pose a threat to anyone in the future. She as good as said in her sentencing remarks that, though murder carries a mandatory life sentence, she didn't feel it was appropriate, and implied that cases of this sort shouldn't be a matter for the criminal courts at all. It caused an uproar in legal circles. God, I feel sober. It's your fault.'

'Justice who?'

Tamsin sighs. 'Don't you ever read anything apart from *heat*? If you're making the film, you're going to need to familiarise yourself with—'

'I'm not making the film. I'm bolting my door and going to bed. First thing tomorrow morning I'm handing in my resignation.'

'Fine, do that. You'll never know what Ray Hines wanted to talk to you about.'

Good.

'One of her objections to the film was sharing it with the other two women,' says Tamsin. 'Now that Helen's dead and Sarah's pulled out, Ray could be the main focus. Her case. It's the most interesting of the three by far, though I once said that to Laurie and he almost had me hung, drawn and quartered for treason. Helen was always his favourite.'

Helen's case, or Helen the woman? I manage to stop myself from asking. I can't be jealous of a murder victim who lost all three of her children and spent nearly a decade in jail. Even if it turns out Laurie's spent years crying into his pillow on her account, jealousy is not an acceptable option, not if I want to be able to live with myself.

I hear a car pulling up outside. My hand tightens around the phone. 'I think she's here. I've got to go.' I hover uselessly by my front door, trying to contain myself until I hear the bell. When I can't stand it any longer, I open the door.

There's a black car outside my house, with its lights on and its engine running. I climb the five steps that lead from my basement flat up to the pavement, and see that it's a Jaguar. From her telephone voice, Rachel Hines sounded like the sort of person who might own one. I wonder how this fits in with her being a drug addict. Maybe she isn't one any more, or maybe she's a heaps-of-cocaine-off-platinum-edged-mirrors junkie, not your bog-standard shooting-up-in-a-dirty-squat smackhead. *God, if I was any more prejudiced . . .*

I plaster a non-threatening smile on my face and walk towards the car. It can't be her; she'd have got out by now. Suddenly, the engine and lights cut out and I see her clearly in the street-lamp's glow. Even knowing as little as I do about her case, she's totally familiar to me. Hers is a household face, like Helen Yardley's – one that's been on the news and in the papers so often that most people in Britain would recognise her. No wonder she didn't want to meet me in the pub.

I can't believe she wants to meet me at all.

Her face is slightly too long and her features too blunt, otherwise she'd be stunning. As it is, she's the sort of plain that has missed attractive by a hair's breadth. Her thick wavy hair makes me look again at her face, thinking she must be attractive; it's the sort of hair you'd expect to frame the face of a beauty: well cut, lustrous, golden blonde. She looks like somebody important; it's in her eyes and the way she holds herself. Nothing like Helen Yardley, whose absolute ordinariness and accessible friendly-neighbour smile made it easy for most people to believe in her innocence, once her convictions were quashed.

Rachel Hines opens her car door, but still doesn't get out. Tentatively, I approach the Jaguar. She slams the door shut. The engine starts up, and the headlights come back on, blinding me. 'What . . .?' I start to say, but she's pulling away. As she draws level with me, she slows down, turns to face me. I see her look past me at the house and turn, in case there's someone behind me, though I know there isn't. *It'll be just the two of us, won't it?*

By the time I've turned back, she's halfway down the road, speeding up as she drives away.

What did I do wrong? My mobile phone starts to ring in my pocket. 'You're not going to believe this,' I say, assuming it's Tamsin calling for an update. 'She was here about ten seconds ago, and she's just driven off without saying anything, without even getting out of the car.'

'It's me. Ray. I'm sorry about . . . what just happened.'

'Forget it,' I say, grudgingly. Why is it so unacceptable, if you're a decent human being, to say, 'Actually, it's not okay, even though you've apologised. I don't forgive you'? Why do I care what's socially acceptable, given who I'm dealing with? 'Can I go to bed now?'

'You'll have to come to me,' she says.

'*What?*'

'Not now. I've inconvenienced you enough for one day. Tell me a time and date that suit you.'

'No time, no date,' I say. 'Look, you caught me off-guard in the pub tonight. If you want to talk to someone at Binary Star, ring Maya Jacques and—'

'I didn't kill my daughter. Or my son.'

'Pardon?'

'I can tell you the name of the person who did, if you want: Wendy Whitehead. Though it wasn't—'

'I don't want you to tell me anything,' I say, my heart pounding. 'I want you to leave me alone.' I press the 'end call' button hard. It's several seconds before I dare to breathe again.

Back in my flat, I lock and bolt the door, turn off my mobile phone and unplug the landline. Five minutes later I'm rigid and wide awake in bed, the name Wendy Whitehead going round and round in my brain.

From *Nothing But Love* by Helen Yardley with Gaynor Mundy

21 July 1995

On the twenty-first of July, when the police came, I knew straight away that this time was different from all the other times. It was three weeks to the day since Rowan had died, and I'd become an expert at reading the detectives' moods. I was usually able to tell from their faces whether the questioning on that particular day would be relentless or sympathetic. One detective who had always been kind to me was DS Giles Proust. He always looked uncomfortable when I was being interviewed and left most of the questions to his junior colleagues. On and on they would go: did I have a happy childhood? What was it like being the middle sibling? Did I ever feel jealous of my sisters? Am I close to my parents? Did I ever have babysitting jobs as a teenager? Did I love Morgan? Did I love Rowan? Did I welcome both pregnancies? I wanted to scream at them, 'Of course I bloody well did, and if you can't see that with your own eyes and ears then you don't deserve the title of detective!'

I always had the impression that Giles Proust alone among the police didn't merely believe that I was innocent of the murder of my babies, but *knew* it, in the way that I knew it and Paul knew it. He could see I was no baby-killer, and understood how much I'd loved my two precious boys. Now here he was at my door again, with a woman I didn't recognise, and I could see at once from his facial expression that this was going to be very bad. 'Just tell me,' I said, wanting to get it over with.

'This is DC Ursula Shearer from Child Protection,' said DS Proust. 'I'm sorry, Helen. I'm here to arrest you for the murders of Morgan and Rowan Yardley. I don't have any choice. I'm so sorry.'

His regret was absolutely genuine. I could see from his face that it was breaking him up to have to do this to me. At that moment, I think I hated his superior officers more for his sake than for my own. Hadn't they listened to him, all those times he must have told them they were hounding a grief-stricken mother who'd done nothing wrong? I was as much a victim of my boys' deaths as they were.

However terrible the moment of my arrest was for me, I can never think of it without also thinking of Giles Proust and how terrible it must have been for him. He must have felt as helpless as I did, powerless to make the people in charge see and hear the truth. Paul had urged me many times not to assume anybody official was on my side. He was scared I might be naïvely deluding myself, storing up more pain for the future. 'However decent Proust seems, he's a policeman, don't forget,' he would tell me. 'The sympathy could be a tactic. We've got to assume they're all against us.'

Although I didn't agree with Paul, I could understand his attitude. For him it was a way of staying strong. At first he didn't even trust our close families, our parents, brothers and sisters, to be fully on our side. 'They say they're sure you didn't do it,' he would say, 'but how do we know they're not just saying that because it's what's expected of them? What if some of them have doubts?' To this day I am convinced that none of my relatives or Paul's ever thought I could be guilty. They had all seen me with Morgan and Rowan and seen my passionate love for them.

Paul would face no criminal charges, we were told, but he was allowed to come with me in the police car, which was a great comfort to me. He sat on one side of me, DS Proust sat on the other, and DC Shearer drove us to Spilling police station. I sobbed as I was forcibly taken away from my beloved house where I'd been so happy – first with Paul, then with Paul and Morgan, then again when Rowan came along. So many beautiful memories! How could they do this to me after what I'd suffered already? For a moment, I was consumed with hatred for everything and everyone. I had no use for a world that could inflict such terrible suffering. Then I felt an arm round my shoulder and DS Proust said, 'Helen, listen to me. I know you didn't kill Morgan or Rowan. Things are looking bleak for you now, but the truth will come out. If I can see the truth, others will too. Any fool can see you were a good, loving mother.'

DC Shearer muttered something sarcastic under her breath, from which I gathered that she disapproved of what DS Proust had said. Maybe she thought I was guilty, or that DS Proust had breached some sort of protocol by saying what he said to me, but I didn't care. Paul was smiling. He finally recognised Giles Proust for the ally that he was. 'Thank you,' he said. 'It means everything to us to have your support. Doesn't it, Helen?'

I nodded. DC Shearer made another snide remark under her breath. DS Proust could have left it at that, having made his point, but instead he said, 'If this goes as far as a trial, which I very much doubt it will, then I'll be called as a witness. By the time I step down from the box, the jury will be as convinced as I am that you're innocent.'

'What the hell are you doing?' DC Shearer snapped. Paul and I shrank down in our seats, taken aback by her harsh tone, but Giles Proust remained unfazed.

'I'm doing the right thing,' he said. 'Somebody has to.'

I became aware that I had stopped crying. A wave of what can only be described as utmost peace washed over me, and I stopped worrying obsessively about what would happen to me. It was like magic: I was no longer afraid. Whether Giles Proust was right or wrong about my chances of standing trial or what a hypothetical jury would think, it didn't matter. All that mattered was that as I looked out of the window of the police car and watched the post-boxes and trees and shops whizzing by, I loved the world I had hated only a few moments earlier. I felt part of something good and whole and light, something that Paul and Giles Proust and Morgan and Rowan were also part of. It's very hard to explain the feeling in words because it was so much stronger than words.

I didn't know, as we drove to the police station that day, how bad things were going to get for me and Paul, how much more agonising suffering lay in store for us. But as fate went on to rain down blow after blow upon us, even when my spirits were at their very lowest and there seemed no hope of any respite, that peaceful sensation that came over me in the police car on the day of my arrest never left me, even though there were times when I had to struggle to find it inside myself. It's the same positive energy that has spurred me on in the work I have done on behalf of other women in similar situations to mine, and that has been the driving force behind my contribution to JIPAC. DS Proust taught me a valuable lesson that day: that you can always, and easily, give somebody the gift of hope and faith, even in the midst of despair.

12 September 1996

The contact centre was a horrible, soulless place, an ugly grey one-storey prefab that looked lost and forlorn in a vast, mostly empty car park. I hated it on sight. There weren't enough windows, and those there were seemed too small. I said to Paul, 'It looks like a building that's keeping lots of unpleasant secrets.' He knew exactly what I meant. I shuddered and said, 'I can't do it. I just can't. I can't go in there.' He told me I had to, because Paige was inside.

I wanted to see her more than anything but I was scared of the joy I would feel as soon as we were together, because I knew it was something that the social workers could and would take away from me. If I came here for two hours every weekday, which was the deal Ned and Gillian had negotiated for me, that meant I would have to endure some Social Services flunky taking Paige away from me five times each week until my trial, and who knew what would happen after that? Even if I was acquitted, as Giles Proust kept reassuring me I would be, Paul and I still might not be allowed to keep Paige. Ned had explained to me about the difference between the burden of proof in a criminal case, where guilt must be proven beyond reasonable doubt, and the courts that steal children from their parents behind closed doors and under a veil of secrecy. In the family courts, all that needs to happen is for the judge to decide that the child is better off without his or her parents *on the balance of probabilities*, which means nobody needs to prove anything. All it will take is for someone who doesn't know me from Adam or Eve to decide I'm *probably* a murderer, and I'll lose my daughter. 'I've never heard of anything so cruel and unfair in my life,' I told Ned. 'To lose Paige would be unbearable, and what if I go to prison, and Paul loses both me *and* her?' Ned looked me in the eye and said, 'I can't lie to you, Helen. That might happen.'

'Take me home,' I told Paul as we sat in the car park outside the contact centre. 'I've already suffered three terrible losses and I can't cope with any more.' That was how I truly felt. Paige was alive and well, but I lost her when she was wrenched from my arms an hour after her birth to be taken into care. 'I can't lose my daughter all over again every day this week, and next week, and for God knows how long. I won't let them do that to me, or to her.' Up until this point I had been timid and cooperative, and it had got me nowhere. Let them see exactly what they're doing, I thought: depriving a baby of her mother. Why should I turn up and make Social Services feel good about themselves for 'letting' me have contact with my own daughter? They were tearing apart what was left of my family and I wanted them to realise it.

The drive back to Bengeo Street was the most miserable journey of my life. Paul and I didn't speak a single word to one another. At home we made a pot of hot, strong tea. 'You should go back there,' I told him. 'You need to make sure that you get to keep Paige, no matter what happens to me. You'll have to lie, but it's a price worth paying.' Paul asked me what I meant and I spelled it out for him. 'You must pretend to doubt me. Act like you're as worried as the social workers are about me being alone with Paige. Convince them that if they let you keep her, you'll make sure she's never alone with me.'

No words can express how much I hated saying this to Paul. He was my absolute rock and had stood by me unswervingly throughout my ordeal. His loyalty was the main thing sustaining me, yet here I was asking him to pretend to be a worse man than he truly was – a disloyal husband instead of a wonderful brave one. But I knew it was the right thing to do. The only thing that mattered now was stopping those child-snatcher social workers from giving our beloved Paige to another family.

When I lost first Morgan and then Rowan, I didn't think anything worse could ever happen to me, but to lose Paige in this way would be worse, because it would be somebody's fault. The injustice would destroy me, and I feared it might actually kill Paul, however melodramatic that sounds.

'Please,' I begged him. 'Drive back there and see Paige. Ring them now and tell them you're coming.'

'No,' he said flatly. 'I'm not lying to anyone and nor are you. That would make us as bad as them. We'll fight evil with good and lies with truth and we'll win. DS Proust says we'll win and I believe him.'

'Ned and Gillian say we might not,' I reminded him, my eyes full of tears. 'And even if I'm found not guilty in the criminal court, the family court's a different matter.'

'Shut up!' Paul yelled. 'I don't want to hear it.' It was the first time since tragedy had struck our lives that he'd raised his voice to me, and I'm ashamed to say that I took the opportunity to give back as good as I got and vent some of the misery and despair that had built up inside me. The two of us were still screaming at each other ten minutes later when the doorbell rang.

I threw myself into Giles Proust's arms, and must have absolutely terrified the poor man as I shrieked at him that he had to help me make Paul see sense. 'You're the one who needs to see sense, Helen, and quickly,' he said sternly. 'Why aren't you at the contact centre? You're supposed to be there now, but I've just had a call saying you didn't turn up.' I did my best to explain my reasons to him. 'Listen carefully, Helen,' he said. 'However hard it is, you've got to spend as much time as you can with Paige. Don't miss a single visit, or they'll use it against you. I understand what you're scared of, but do you really want to turn your worst fears into reality by giving them ammunition? How do you think it looks if you don't even bother to turn up for the few hours a week you're allowed to spend with Paige?'

'Please listen to him, Hel,' said Paul quietly. 'We've no way of knowing what's going to happen, but at least this way we'll know we did everything we could – we didn't lie or give up the fight. In ten or twenty years' time, whatever our circumstances at that point, we'll be able to look back and be proud of ourselves.'

How could I resist the two of them once they'd joined forces? They were so wise and loyal and strong, and I felt unworthy, like a total coward and a failure.

Giles Proust drove Paul and me back to the contact centre. We'd missed most of our allotted time with Paige, but there was still half an hour left. The contact supervisor looked about twelve. I'll never forget her name: Leah Gould. 'Leah Ghoul, more like,' I said to Paul later. She refused to wait in the corridor and watch us through the window, despite DS Proust almost going down on his knees and begging her to allow us that small degree of privacy. She insisted on staying with us in the horrid, small, too brightly painted room that reeked of the misery of countless families forcibly separated by smiling, officially sanctioned torturers – at least that's how it seemed to me at that moment.

When Leah Gould placed Paige gently in my arms, my misery was sent packing, if only temporarily. A tiny baby is such a joyful, hopeful bundle that it's hard not to respond, and I was suffused with a rush of love for my beautiful daughter. Paul and I showered Paige with cuddles and kisses. The poor child's face was sopping wet within a few minutes, we'd slobbered over her so much! 'No one will take her away from us,' I thought. 'That would be too crazy, given how much we love her and how obvious that must be, even to someone as unemotional and blank-eyed as Leah Gould.' At that moment, I firmly believed the powers-that-be would see sense and Paul, Paige and I would be allowed to have a future together.

I don't really know what happened next but I know that it was one of the oddest moments of my life. Suddenly Leah Gould was standing in front of me, saying, 'Helen, hand the baby to me. Please hand Paige to me. Now, please.' I did as I was told, confused. Time couldn't be up yet; we'd only been in the room a few minutes. I could see from the expressions on Paul and DS Proust's faces that they were also mystified.

Leah Gould virtually ran from the room with Paige in her arms. 'What did I do?' I asked, bursting into tears. Neither Paul nor Giles Proust could answer the question any more than I could. I looked at my watch. I'd spent a total of eight minutes with my daughter.

The episode only made sense when I learned from Ned some time later that Leah Gould was going to give evidence at my trial and say that I had tried to smother Paige right in front of her, in the guise of giving her a cuddle. I remember

I actually laughed when I heard this news. 'Let her say that if she wants to,' I said to Ned and Gillian. 'Paul and Giles Proust were in that room too. No jury will believe they'd fail to notice an attempted murder taking place right in front of their eyes! One of them's a detective sergeant, for heaven's sake!'

Maybe I was naïve. Maybe if Leah Gould's testimony was the only so-called 'proof' the prosecution had had at its disposal, I'd have walked free, and Paul and I would have been allowed to keep our daughter. But though I didn't know it yet, Leah Gould's utterly baseless lie would sound frighteningly convincing alongside the expert opinion of somebody far more mature, articulate and highly esteemed, someone the jury would take very seriously indeed. It's hard to believe, looking back now, that there was once a time when I'd never heard of Dr Judith Duffy, the woman who would play the leading role in the destruction of the rest of my life.

4
8/10/09

The first irritation was Charlie walking into the kitchen. *Her kitchen.* Simon had been living with her at her place for the past six months. Most of the time he preferred it, though the exceptions to this rule were frequent enough to make him certain he wasn't yet ready to put his own house on the market. The second irritation was Charlie yawning. No one who'd had several hours of sleep had any business yawning.

'Why didn't you give me a nudge when you got up?' she said. 'You're my alarm clock.'

'I didn't get up. Haven't been to bed.'

He was aware of her staring at him, then at the book that lay on the table in front of him. 'Ah, your reading homework: Helen Yardley's tear-jerker. Where are Proust's yellow markers?'

Simon said nothing. He'd told her last night, he'd rather saw off his own head than read the copy the Snowman had given him. Did all women make you answer the same question twenty times over? Simon's mum did it to his dad; both his grans did it to both his grandads. It was a depressing thought.

'That can't be the copy you ordered yesterday from Amazon . . .'

'Word,' he said abruptly: a one-word answer, both in form and in content. Word on the Street was an independent bookshop in the town centre, far less trendy than its name suggested. Local history, gardening and cookery books competed for space in the window. Simon liked it because it had no café; he disapproved of bookshops selling coffee and cakes.

'They had an evening event on last night. I popped in on the off-chance on my way home from work, they had the book, so I thought I might as well buy it, read it overnight, speed things up a bit.' Simon was aware of his right heel drumming on the kitchen floor. He forced himself to keep still.

'Uh-huh,' said Charlie lightly. 'So when the Amazon one arrives, you'll have three copies. Or did you put the one the Snowman gave you through the shredder at work?'

He would have done if he could have guaranteed Proust wouldn't catch him in the act.

'If you've still got it, I wouldn't mind having a look at it.'

Simon nodded at the table. 'There's the book, if you want to read it.'

'I want to see which bits Proust marked out for your special attention. I can't believe he did that! The man's ego knows no bounds.'

'The bits about him,' said Simon quietly. 'As if those are the only parts of her story that matter. She thought he was Martin Luther King, the Dalai Lama and Jesus Christ our saviour all rolled into one.'

'*What?*' Charlie picked up *Nothing But Love*. 'The opposite, right?'

'No. She rated him.'

'Then she's guilty of bad judgement at the very least. Do you think she killed her children?'

'Why, because she's full of praise for Proust?'

'No, because she was sent to prison for murdering them,' said Charlie with exaggerated patience.

'I've been told to look out for people like you. The Snowman wants names. Traitors' names.'

Charlie filled the kettle. 'Can I say something without you taking it the wrong way? And if I make you a cup of tea at the same time?'

'Say what you want. I'll take it how I take it.'

'How reassuring. I feel so much better now. All right, then: I think you've got a dangerous obsession brewing. Fully brewed, actually.'

Simon looked up, surprised. 'Why, because I stayed up all night? I couldn't sleep. Helen Yardley's no more important to me than any other—'

'I'm talking about Proust,' said Charlie gently. 'You're obsessed with hating him. The only reason you stayed up all night to read that book is because you knew there were references to him in it.'

Simon looked away. The idea that he'd be obsessed with another man was laughable. 'I've never had a murder victim who's written a book before,' he said. 'The sooner I read it, the sooner I find out if there's anything in it that can help me.'

'So why not read the copy Proust gave you? Instead, you go to Word – which isn't on your way home from work, so you weren't just passing. You went out of your way to go to a bookshop that might not even have been open last night, might not have had the book . . .'

'It was and it did.' Simon pushed past her and into the hall. 'Forget the tea. I've got to get washed and go to work. I'm not wasting time talking about things that never happened.'

'What if Word had been closed?' Charlie called up the

stairs after him. More pointless hypotheticals. 'Would you have gone back to work and picked up the copy Proust gave you?'

He ignored her. In his world, if you shouted a question at someone from far away and they ignored it, you left it at that, maybe waited till later to try again. Not in Charlie's world. He heard her feet on the stairs.

'If you can't bring yourself to read a book you need to read just because he gave it to you, then you've got a problem.'

'She rated him,' Simon said again, staring at his exhausted face in the shaving mirror Charlie had bought for him and attached lopsidedly to the bathroom wall.

'So what?'

She was right. If he found the disagreement of a dead woman unacceptable, he was as bad as Proust and well on the way to tyranny. 'I suppose everyone's entitled to an opinion,' he said eventually. Maybe some of the Dalai Lama's colleagues thought he was an arrogant twat. Did people in flowing orange robes have colleagues? If they did, was that what they called them?

'How much of your time is taken up with hating him?' Charlie asked. 'Eighty per cent? Ninety? Isn't it bad enough that you have to work with him? Are you going to let him take over your mind as well?'

'No, I'll let you do that instead. Happy?'

'I would be if you meant it. I'd get straight on the phone to that five-star hotel in Malaysia.'

'Don't start that honeymoon shit again. We agreed.' Simon knew he wasn't being fair; unwilling to negotiate, he'd given Charlie no say in the matter, then tried to spin it so that it looked like a joint decision.

What was it the Snowman had said? *I know I can count on your support.*

Simon was dreading his and Charlie's honeymoon. Next July was only nine months away, getting closer all the time. He was afraid he'd be unable to perform, that she'd be disgusted by him. The only way to stop dreading it was to reveal the full extent of his inadequacy even sooner.

He brushed his teeth, threw some cold water on his face and headed downstairs.

'Simon?'

'What?'

'Helen Yardley's murder is about Helen Yardley, not Proust,' said Charlie. 'You won't find the right answer if you're asking the wrong question.'

Proust got out of his chair to open the door for Simon – something he'd never done before. 'Yes, Waterhouse?'

'I've read the book.' *Which is why I'm here, giving you another chance to be reasonable, instead of at Human Resources complaining about you.* Except it wasn't a real chance; Simon couldn't pretend there was anything generous-spirited about it. He wanted to prove Helen Yardley wrong. It was ridiculous; embarrassing. Didn't he know Proust well enough after years of working with him?

'It's a pity you never met Helen Yardley, Waterhouse. You might have learned a lot from her. She brought out the best in people.'

'What did she do with it once she'd brought it out?' Simon asked. 'Bury it somewhere and leave clues?' He couldn't believe he'd said it, couldn't believe he wasn't being ejected from the room.

'What's that?' Proust nodded at the sheet of paper in Simon's hand. Was he stifling his anger in order to deny Simon a sense of achievement?

'I think there's an angle we're neglecting, sir. I've made a list of names I think we ought to talk to. All those who had a vested interest in Helen Yardley being guilty, and others who—'

'She wasn't guilty.'

'There are people who need to cling to the belief that she was innocent,' said Simon neutrally, 'and people who need to cling to the belief that she did it because they can't live with themselves otherwise: the eleven jurors who voted guilty, the prosecuting lawyers, the social workers who—'

'Dr Judith Duffy,' the Snowman read aloud, having snatched the paper from Simon's hand. 'Even in my line of work, I haven't met many human beings I'd describe as out-and-out evil, but that woman . . .' He frowned. 'Who are all these others? I recognise a few: the Brownlees, Justice Wilson . . . Waterhouse, you're surely not suggesting Helen Yardley was murdered by a high court judge?'

'No, sir, of course not. I put him on the list for the sake of completeness.'

'Any more complete, it'd be a perishing telephone directory!'

'Justice Wilson played a part in sending Helen Yardley to prison. So did eleven jurors whose names are also on the list. Any of them might have reacted badly when her convictions were quashed. I'm thinking . . . well, maybe someone reacted very badly.' Simon didn't want to use the word 'vigilante'. 'That's why Sarah Jaggard and Rachel Hines are on the list too. Chances are anyone who thinks Helen Yardley escaped justice will think Jaggard and Hines did too. We need to talk to them both, find out if anyone's been bothering them, if they've been threatened or noticed anything out of the ordinary.'

'Make up your mind, Waterhouse. Is this a list of people who have a vested interest in Helen Yardley being guilty, or is it something else entirely?' Proust held the piece of paper between his thumb and forefinger, as if it hurt him to touch it. 'Because it seems to me that Sarah Jaggard and Rachel Hines might have a vested interest in her being *not* guilty, since they were the victims of similar miscarriages of justice, and Helen campaigned on their behalf.'

Helen. Helen and her friend Giles.

'Sarah Jaggard was acquitted,' Simon said.

Proust glared at him. 'You don't think being charged with murder when all you've done is look after your friend's child to the best of your ability constitutes a miscarriage of justice? Then I feel sorry for you.'

As far as Simon knew, the Snowman had never met Sarah Jaggard. Did his outrage on behalf of Helen Yardley automatically extend to all women accused of the same crime? Or was it Helen Yardley's certainty that Jaggard was innocent that had convinced him? If Proust had been an approachable sort of person, Simon might have asked these questions. 'You're right: not all the names on the list have a vested interest in Helen Yardley's guilt. They're all people we ought to talk to, though.'

'Justice Geilow gave Rachel Hines two life sentences for murder,' said Proust. 'She's nothing to do with Helen Yardley. Why's she on the list?'

'You said it yourself: the similarities between the Yardley and

Hines cases are startling. Obsessions can spread. Obviously it's unlikely that Justice Geilow shot Helen Yardley, but . . .'

'She's an even less plausible murderer than Mr Justice Wilson, if such a thing is possible,' said Proust impatiently.

'I've also included the names of the twelve jurors who found Rachel Hines guilty,' said Simon. 'Unlike high court judges, jurors can be anyone. Isn't it possible one of the eleven who sent Helen Yardley to prison spent the nine years she was there thinking of himself as a good guy who helped put away a child murderer, and then couldn't take it when he heard she wasn't guilty after all? Nine years, sir.' Simon allowed himself the luxury of talking as he would to someone who was really listening. 'Think how hard it'd be to change the story after that long, the one you've been going round telling everyone you know, about who you are and what you did. After nine years it's a central part of your self-image. Maybe, that's all I'm saying,' he added for the sake of caution.

Proust sighed. 'I know I'm going to regret asking, but why are Rachel Hines' jurors on the list? You think one of them might have shot Helen Yardley? Wouldn't they be more likely to shoot Rachel Hines, according to your logic?'

Simon said nothing.

'I can read your mind, Waterhouse – always have been able to. Shall I tell you what you're thinking? This obsessed killer, if he's to be found on the Hines jury, might have shot Helen Yardley because she was instrumental in freeing Rachel Hines. Or he might have extended his retributive obsession to all three women and be planning to punish them all, as well as the appeal judges who overturned the murder convictions. Perhaps our killer's a Hines juror who doesn't want to start with Rachel Hines in case that looks too obvious. How am I doing?'

Simon felt his face heat up. 'I think we should show the card with the sixteen numbers found on Helen Yardley's body to all the people on the list and ask if it means anything to them,' he said. 'This case isn't the simple either-or that we're usually faced with: a stranger killer versus someone close to the victim. Most of the people on this list didn't know Helen Yardley personally, but they're not random strangers either. They were as significant in her life as she was in theirs.'

'Laurie Nattrass.' Proust jabbed the list with his finger. 'He's already been interviewed and swabbed. You're not usually sloppy, Waterhouse. Fixated, deluded, yes, but not sloppy.'

'I'd like to talk to Nattrass again myself. I'd like to ask him about the sixteen numbers, ask if anyone he's come into contact with through JIPAC has threatened him or acted out of character, if anything's made him feel uncomfortable recently.'

'Like perishing what?' Proust pushed his chair back from his desk. 'A lumpy chaise longue? A boil on his backside?'

Simon stood his ground, didn't even blink at the volume. 'Those numbers mean something,' he said. 'I'm no psychological profiler, but I'm pretty sure one thing they mean is that this killer's going to kill again.'

'I warn you, Waterhouse . . .'

'He'll leave a similar card next time – either the same numbers or different ones. Either way, it'll mean something. Helen Yardley and Laurie Nattrass represented a lot of the same things to a lot of people. It's possible that whoever killed her might target him next. How about I interview Nattrass, Sarah Jaggard and Rachel Hines, and if none of them can move us forward, if they haven't been harassed recently, if the sixteen numbers mean nothing to any of them, we'll forget the rest of the names on the list and go back to the stranger killer theory.'

'And if Sarah Jaggard was shouted at in the street last week by some alcopop-swilling lowlife, what then?' Proust bellowed. 'We start swabbing Justices Geilow and Wilson for gunpowder residue? Where's the connection? Where's the logic?'

'Sir, I'm trying to be reasonable.'

'Then try, try and try again, Waterhouse!' The inspector's hand shot out as if to grab something. He clenched it into a fist and held it still for a moment, staring at it. *It's gone, knobhead*. Even the Snowman couldn't smash a mug twice.

'There's one person on this list to whom your obsession theory might apply,' Proust said with exaggerated weariness. 'Judith Duffy. She's made it her life's work to ruin innocent women's lives. That smacks of a level of obsession and ... detachment from reality that ought to give us pause for thought, however professionally eminent she is, or has been. We should make it a priority to eliminate her, at least.' Proust rubbed his forehead. 'The truth is, I can hardly bear to utter the woman's name. You think I'm unaffected by all this? I'm not. I'm a person just like you, Waterhouse. You've read Helen Yardley's book. Put yourself in my place, if you can.'

Simon stared at the floor. He wasn't foolish enough to confuse an accusation of insensitivity with a confidence.

'There's a lot the book leaves out,' Proust went on. 'I could write a book of my own. I was at the hospital when Helen and Paul gave their consent for Rowan's life support to be switched off. Didn't know that, did you? Little Rowan was brain-dead. There was nothing that could be done for him, nothing at all. Do you know what I was doing there?'

I don't care. Tell someone else, someone who doesn't hate your guts.

'I was sent to collect the Yardleys, bring them in for questioning. Barrow's orders. A nurse from the baby unit had phoned us within an hour of them bringing Rowan in, accused Helen of attempted murder. Rowan had stopped breathing, not for the first time in his short life. When he was admitted to hospital, he had a Modified Glasgow Coma Score of 5. They put him on a drip and got it up to 14.' Proust glanced at Simon, as if suddenly remembering he was there. '15 is normal. For a while it looked as if he might be all right, but then he deteriorated. Helen and Paul weren't even in the room when his score started to drop again. Helen was too upset – Paul had to take her out. She wasn't even in the room,' he repeated slowly. 'If that's not reasonable doubt, I'd like to know what is.'

'Did the nurse have any proof Helen had tried to kill Rowan?' Simon asked. The only way he could deal with this was practically, by trying to fill in the gaps in the story, focusing on the Yardleys instead of on the Snowman. *He's not baring his soul, he's filling you in on the background. Relax.*

'Paul and Helen were known at the hospital,' said Proust. 'First Morgan and then Rowan had several ALTEs – apparent life-threatening events. Both boys stopped breathing every now and then, for no reason that anyone could identify. Some sort of biological deficiency, I suppose – the most obvious explanation, but it didn't occur to the troublemaker who called the police. She called twice, the second time several hours after the first. Anonymously – no doubt she was ashamed of her despicable behaviour, and worried we'd taken no notice of her first attempt to spread poison.'

Whenever he heard the phrase 'no doubt', Simon doubted. Couldn't a baby's health go rapidly downhill as a result of damage previously inflicted by a parent, even if the parent wasn't present when the deterioration took place? He wanted to ask if there was anything else, apart from Morgan and Rowan Yardley's ALTEs, that had given the hospital staff cause to suspect their mother. Instead he said, 'Everyone working this murder ought to know all this.' A desperate attempt to block intimacy. Simon couldn't stand Proust telling him anything he wouldn't as readily have told Sam Kombothekra, or Sellers, or Gibbs. 'When we're not on shift, we should all be reading up on the background: Helen Yardley's trial, the appeal . . .'

'No.' Proust stood up. 'Not when there's no reason to assume her death is linked to any of it. It could have had as much to do with her physical appearance as with her imprisonment for murder. Judith Duffy, Sarah Jaggard, Rachel Hines, Laurie Nattrass – talk to those four, but no one else on your list, not yet. If we can avoid swabbing Elizabeth Geilow and Dennis Wilson for gunpowder residue, let's do that. Come to think of it, let's make it six: interview Grace and Sebastian Brownlee too. I've yet to come across a juror murderously obsessed with a case he heard thirteen years ago, but adoptive parents, paranoid their daughter might one day want to have a relationship with her biological mother, when the mother is someone as admirable and inspiring as Helen Yardley?' Proust nodded, as if making up his mind.

At what stage did he decide she was innocent? Simon wondered. The first time he met her? Before that, even? Was his staunch support of her a kind of contrariness, two fingers in the face of Superintendent Barrow's assumption that she was guilty? Could Proust have been in love with Helen Yardley? Simon flinched; the idea of the Snowman as an emotional being was repulsive. Simon preferred to think of him as a problem-making machine, human in appearance but in no other respect.

He held out his hand for his list of names. If he left it in here, it would end up in the bin.

'First thing I did when I got to the hospital and saw what was happening, I rang Roger Barrow,' said Proust, settling back in his chair. He hadn't finished with Simon yet. 'He wasn't Superintendent then, and nor should he be now. I rang him, told him I couldn't bring Helen in for questioning. "She's just signed a consent form for her boy's life support to be switched off," I said. "She and her husband are about to watch their son die. They're in pieces." Helen was as innocent of murder as any person I'd ever met, and even if she wasn't . . .' The Snowman stopped, pulled in a deep breath. 'Bringing her in for questioning could wait until Rowan had passed on. Why couldn't it wait? What difference was an hour or two going to make?'

Simon was aware of his own breathing, the stillness in the room.

'"You want her brought in now, get someone else to do it," I said. "No, no," said Barrow. "You're quite right. Go and have something to eat, get yourself a pint, simmer down," he said. As if I'd lost on the horses or something – something trivial. "You're right, bringing the mother in can wait till later." He wanted me out of the way, that was all. When I got back to the hospital, the doctors told me Helen and Paul had been taken in for questioning by two bobbies, minutes after I'd left them – hauled out screaming, like some kind of . . .' Proust shook his head. 'And Rowan . . .'

'He was dead?' Simon blurted out, his discomfort starting to spin into panic. He needed light and air. He needed not to be hearing this, but couldn't find the right words to make it stop. It felt like an assault. Had Proust planned it? Had he watched Simon become hardened to his derision over the years, and decided that enforced intimacy was to be his new weapon?

'Rowan died with neither of his parents there,' said Proust. 'Alone. Doesn't that make you proud to be human, Waterhouse? Assuming you are.' A dismissive hand gesture indicated that he didn't expect an answer.

Simon exited as quickly as he could, giving no thought to where he was going. *The khazi*; his feet knew even if his brain didn't. He went in, headed for a cubicle and just had time to slide the lock across before a wave of nausea bent him double. He spent the next ten minutes spewing up black coffee and bile, thinking, *You make me sick. You make me fucking sick.*

5

Thursday 8 October 2009

I'm in Laurie's office when I hear someone yelling my name. I think of Rachel Hines and freeze, as if by keeping still I can make myself invisible. Then there's more shouting and I recognise the voice: Tamsin.

I get to reception in time to catch the end of what looks like a strange dance. If I didn't know better, I might think Maya and Tamsin choreographed it together: each time Tamsin takes a step forward, Maya blocks her path or puts out an arm to stop her.

'Fliss, will you tell her I'm supposed to be here? I'm getting the imposter treatment.'

'Don't do this, Tam,' says Maya gravely. 'You're embarrassing all of us. We agreed yesterday would be your last day.'

'I asked her to come in,' I say. 'I need someone to get me up to speed on the film, quickly. There was no sign of Laurie when I came in this morning and I can't get hold of him on any of his phones, and anyway, he's . . .' I break off, wondering what I was about to say. He's leaving? He's crackers? 'I needed a reliable expert, so I rang Tamsin.'

'I'm offering my services for free,' Tamsin says cheerily. She's wearing a figure-hugging pink and orange dress that looks new and expensive. I wonder how to check, tactfully, that she's not planning to blow all her remaining money on luxury items as a prelude to driving off a cliff. I know Tamsin: she'll chicken out of the cliff part, but get as far as running up massive debts before latching on to her next faddy idea.

'Look, I've even brought my own refreshments,' she says. 'An old mineral water bottle from the days when I could afford it, full of nice cheap tap water. Yum.' She waves it in front of Maya's face. 'See? No concealed weapons.'

'Thanks *so* much, Fliss, for letting me know.' Maya twitches her nose like an offended rabbit, taking backward steps in the direction of her office. She's been arsey with me all morning. I keep giving her my best, most radiant 'hello's and getting only grunts in response. Binary Star is a different company today. Everybody's keeping themselves to themselves, trying not to meet anyone else's eye. It's like an office in mourning.

For Laurie.

I grab Tamsin's arm and drag her along the corridor to the room I need to start thinking of as my new condensation-free office, muttering, 'Thanks for your contribution.' I slam the door, lock it and put the chain across. If Laurie comes back and wants to get in, tough. He told me I could be him from Monday; all I'm doing is moving the new arrangement forward by two working days. Let him come back and catch me.

Let him come back.

'You're welcome.' Tamsin plonks herself down in Laurie's chair and puts her feet up on his model globe. Her face clouds over. 'You're being sarcastic, aren't you?'

'I could have done without the too-poor-for-mineral-water quip. I have to work here, Tam.'

'I thought you were handing in your notice first thing this morning.'

'I changed my mind.'

'How come?'

There's no reason not to tell her, though I'm not sure it'll make sense to anyone but me. 'I rang my mum this morning. I told her I was worried about being paid more than I'm realistically worth, Maya and Raffi resenting me, stuff like that.'

'She told you not to be an idiot?' Tamsin guesses.

'Not quite. She suggested I say to them that I wouldn't feel comfortable earning so much, and perhaps we could agree a salary that was somewhere between what I'm on now and what Laurie was on, something we could all feel happy with. I listened to her and I swear I could hear myself saying it, sounding ever so reasonable and timid – sounding like *her*, mousey and modest and unassuming and . . .' I shrug. 'Laurie was right. No one asks for less money. I don't care what Maya and Raffi think of me, but . . . I'd lose all respect for myself if I didn't try to make this work.' I feel obliged to add, 'Even though, secretly, I don't think I'm worth anywhere near a hundred and forty a year.'

'You're suffering from Reverse L'Oréal Syndrome,' says Tamsin. '"Because I'm not worth it". So, you're going to make the film?'

'You don't think I can do it, do you?'

'If it can be done, you can do it,' she says matter-of-factly. 'Why wouldn't you be able to?'

I consider telling her what makes me different from her or Laurie or anyone else at Binary Star, why I can't hear the names Yardley, Jaggard and Hines without feeling a cold dragging in the pit of my stomach.

I didn't tell my mother about Laurie's film. I mentioned

the promotion and the pay-rise, but not what I'd be working on. Not that she'd have tried to stop me. Mum would be more likely to dance naked in the street than say anything that might lead to an argument.

Tamsin's the only person at work I've ever been tempted to tell. Trouble is, she's never silent for long enough. This time's no different. 'The question is, do you still have a film to make after Ray Hines left you stranded on the pavement? Have you spoken to Paul Yardley? Talked Sarah Jaggard back on board?'

'I haven't done anything yet.'

'Apart from spreading the contents of five box files randomly across the room,' says Tamsin dubiously, eyeing the papers on the floor and on every available surface.

'I was looking for something and I didn't find it. Does the name Wendy Whitehead ring any bells?'

'No.'

'What are the chances of it being buried somewhere in all this lot? I've skim-read as much as I've had time to, but—'

'Don't bother,' says Tamsin. 'Any name that crops up even once, I'd know it. I know every expert witness, every health visitor, every solicitor . . .'

'What about just Wendy, then? She might have got married and changed her surname. Or divorced.'

Tamsin considers it. 'No,' she says eventually. 'No Wendys. Why?'

'She rang me last night.'

'Wendy Whitehead?'

'Rachel Hines.'

She rolls her eyes. 'I know. I was there, remember?'

'No, I mean later. After she'd driven away without getting out of the car. Almost immediately after. She apologised, said she still wanted to talk to me, but I'd have to come to her.'

'Did she say why she drove off?'

'No. I saw her looking behind me, sort of like . . . I don't know, it looked as if she was staring at somebody over my shoulder, but when I turned round there was no one there. I turned back and she'd driven away.'

'You think she saw something that scared her off?'

'What could she have seen? I'm telling you, there was nothing there. Just me. No one walking past, no neighbours looking out of their windows.'

Tamsin frowns. 'So who's Wendy Whitehead?'

I hesitate. 'This might be something you'd rather not know.'

'Is it bad?'

I don't know how to answer that without telling her.

'Is Joe shagging her behind my back?' Tamsin kicks the globe over. 'That'd be typical of my luck at the moment.'

I can't help smiling. Joe would never be unfaithful to Tamsin. His favourite hobby is making no effort whatsoever. You can almost see him looking at other women and thinking *Don't need to bother, already got one of those*. 'It's got nothing to do with your personal life,' I say. I can't stand the suspense, even though I'm the one with the information, not the one waiting to be told. 'Rachel Hines said Wendy Whitehead killed her daughter and son.'

Tamsin snorts and slumps back in Laurie's chair. *My chair*. 'No one was in the house when Marcella Hines died apart from her and Ray. Same with Nathaniel four years later – he was alone with his mother at home when he died. Wendy Whitehead certainly wasn't there, if she even exists. What's more interesting is why Ray Hines is lying, and why now.' I open my mouth but I'm not quick enough. 'I know why,' Tamsin says. 'To reel you in.'

'So what do I do? Go and see her? Ring the police?' I spent most of last night asking myself these questions, unable to sleep for more than half an hour at a time.

'Go and see her for sure,' says Tamsin. 'I'm curious. I've always been curious about her – she's a strange woman. She's gone to great lengths to keep Laurie at a distance, but she can't seem to get enough of you.'

If there's even the tiniest chance that it's true, then I ought to tell the police. And if Wendy Whitehead turns out to be a real person, one who didn't murder Marcella and Nathaniel Hines? She might be interrogated or even arrested, and I'd have caused trouble for an innocent woman. I can't do that, not without finding out more. *Not without being sure it isn't exactly what Rachel Hines wants me to do.*

Why hasn't Laurie rung me back? I've left messages for him everywhere I can think of, saying I need urgent advice.

Marcella and Nathaniel. Now I know their names. I haven't thought much about having children, but if I did, I wouldn't give them names like that. They're the sort of names you choose if you think you're someone to be reckoned with. I wonder if this is my Reverse L'Oréal Syndrome kicking in again; what would I call my kids, Wayne and Tracey? *Because I'm not worth it.*

Wayne Jupiter Benson Nattrass. *Oh, for God's sake, Felicity, grow up!*

Why has Rachel Hines waited until now to mention Wendy Whitehead? Why would she go to prison rather than tell the truth?

'Tell me about her,' I say to Tamsin. 'Everything you know.'

'Ray? She drew the short straw when it came to husbands, that's for sure. Have you read the transcripts of Laurie's interviews with Angus Hines?'

'Not yet.'

'They're somewhere in all that lot.' Tamsin nods at the mess of papers. 'Dig them out, they're worth a read. You'll think Angus can't possibly have said those things until you come across the press cuttings in which he's quoted as saying the exact same things.' She shakes her head. 'Have you ever had that, where you hear something from a person's own mouth, something they'd have no reason to lie about, and you still can't believe it?'

'What does he do? What's his job?'

'He's some kind of editor at *London on Sunday*. He ditched Ray as soon as the verdict went against her. Paul Yardley and Glen Jaggard couldn't have been more different. They were with their wives all the way, totally supportive. I reckon that's why Ray Hines is such an oddster. If you think about it, she suffered an extra trauma. Helen and Sarah were let down by the system, but not by the people closest to them. Their families never doubted their innocence. When you get a chance to read all the notes, you'll see that Helen and Sarah consistently refer to their husbands as their rocks, both of them. Never mind a rock, Angus Hines isn't even a pebble!'

'What about the drugs?' I ask.

Tamsin looks puzzled. 'Sorry, was I supposed to bring some?'

'Rachel Hines is a drug addict, right?'

She rolls her eyes. 'Who told you that?'

'I heard two women talking about her on the Tube once. She mentions it herself somewhere too . . .' I look around for the relevant bit of paper, but can't remember which corner of the office I dropped it in, or even what it was.

'Her interview with Laurie,' says Tamsin. 'Read it again – assuming you can find it among the debris of my once-immaculate filing system. She was being sarcastic, taking the piss out of the public's ridiculous perception of her. She's no more a . . .'

The door opens and Maya comes in carrying two mugs of something hot on a tray. 'Peace offering,' she says brightly. 'Green tea. Fliss, I need to speak to you as soon as poss, hon, so don't be too long. Tam, please say we're still friends. We can still have jolly nights out together, can't we?'

Tamsin and I take our cups, too stunned to speak.

'Oh, and I picked this up from reception by mistake, hon.' Maya pulls an envelope out of the waistband of her jeans and hands it to me. She flashes a sickly smile at us, waves the tray in the air and leaves.

A cream-coloured envelope. I recognise the handwriting; I've seen it on two other envelopes.

'Green tea?' Tamsin snaps. 'Slime is green. Snot is green. Tea's got no business being—'

'Tell me about Ray Hines not being a drug addict,' I say, tossing the envelope to one side. I know there will be numbers in it, and that I won't be able to work out what they mean, so I might as well forget them. It's someone's idea of a joke, and eventually they'll deliver their punchline. It's probably Raffi. He's the comedian around here. One of his favourite topics of conversation is funny things he said and how much everyone laughed at them. 'If she isn't or wasn't a druggie, why did anyone think she was?' I ask, trying to sound as if my mind's still on Rachel Hines.

Tamsin stands up. 'I've got to get out of here. You've been summoned, and if I stay, I'll end up killing somebody.'

'But . . .'

'Laurie wrote an article called "The Doctor Who Lied" – it's somewhere in all this mess. Everything you need to know about Ray Hines is in it.'

'What paper was it in?'

'It hasn't been published yet. The *British Journalism Review* are taking it, and the *Sunday Times* are publishing an abridged version, but both have to wait until Judith Duffy loses her GMC hearing.'

'What if she wins?'

Tamsin looks at me as if I've made the most idiotic suggestion she's ever heard. 'Read the article and you'll see why that's not going to happen.' She leaves the office with a parody of Maya's wave and a 'Bye, *hon*'.

I manage to restrain myself from begging her not to leave me. Once she's gone, I try and fail to persuade myself to put the cream envelope in the bin without opening it, but I'm too nosey – nosier than I am frightened.

Don't be ridiculous. It's some stupid numbers on a card – only an idiot would be scared of that.

I tear open the envelope and see the top of what looks like a photograph. I pull it out, and feel a knot start to form in my stomach. It's a photo of a card with sixteen numbers on it, laid out in four rows of four. Someone's held the card close to the lens in order for the picture to be taken; there are fingers gripping it on both sides. They could be a man's or a woman's; I can't tell.

2 1 4 9
7 8 0 3
4 0 9 8
0 6 2 0

I look for a name or any writing, but there's nothing.

I stuff the photograph back into the envelope and put it in my bag. I'd like to throw it away, but if I do that I won't be able to compare the fingers holding the card to Raffi's fingers, or anyone else's.

Don't let it wind you up. Whoever's doing it, that's exactly what they want.

I sigh, and stare despondently at the papers on the floor. The envelope has made me feel worse about everything. I haven't got a hope in hell of making Laurie's film. I know it; everyone knows it. All these interviews and articles, the medical records, the legal jargon . . . it's too much. It'll take me months, if not years, to get on top of it. The idea that all this has become my responsibility makes me feel sick. I have to get out of the room, away from the piles of paper.

I close the door behind me and head for Maya's office, half hoping she'll fire me.

'You're a dark horse.' Maya folds her arms and looks me up and down as if searching for further evidence of my shady equestrian qualities.

'I'm really not,' I say. Then I take a deep breath. 'Maya, I'm not sure I'm the best person to—'

'Ray Hines rang me a few minutes ago, as I expect you already know.' Wisps of smoke are rising from her desk. Tamsin's bottom-drawer theory must be right.

'What . . . what did she want?' I ask.

'To sing your praises.'

'Me?'

'She's never rung me before, and never returned my calls. Funny that, isn't it? That she'd call me now. Apparently – though this is news to me – she had reservations about Laurie, ungrateful sloaney toff that she is.' Maya smiles. It's the sort of smile a waxwork might reject as being a little on the stiff side. 'Sorry, Fliss, hon, I don't mean to take my anger out on you, but, boy, does it make me mad. When I think how hard Laurie worked to get her out, and she has the nerve to say she never thought much of him . . . as if it's up to her to dish out judgements, as if Laurie's some jumped-up nobody from nowhere instead of the most garlanded investigative journalist in the country. She said he couldn't see the wood for the trees, except she's so stupid, she got it the wrong way round. Her exact words were "He can't see the trees for the wood". She'd still be in prison if it wasn't for him. Has she forgotten that?'

I give my best all-purpose nod. I want to know exactly what Rachel Hines said about me, but I'm too embarrassed to ask.

'Do you by any chance know where Laurie is?' says Maya.

'No idea. I've been trying all day to get hold of him.'

'He's bloody well left.' She sniffs and looks out of the window. 'You watch – we won't see him again. He was supposed to be in until Friday.' She bends down behind her desk. When she reappears, she's holding a well-stocked glass ashtray in one hand and an unambiguous, entirely visible cigarette in the other. 'Don't say a word,' she tries to joke, but it comes out more like a warning. 'I don't normally smoke in the office, but just this once . . .'

'I don't mind. Passive smoking reminds me of how much I used to enjoy the active version.' And makes me feel superior to the poor, weak fools who haven't given up yet, I don't add.

Maya takes a long drag. She's one of the oddest-looking women I've ever seen. In some ways she's attractive. Her figure's great, and she's got big eyes and full lips, but she's completely missing the chin-neck right-angle that most people have between their faces and their torsos. Maya's open-plan face/neck area looks like a flesh-coloured balloon that's been stuffed into the collar of her shirt. She wears her long dark hair in exactly the same style every day: straight at the top and elaborately curled at the bottom, held back by a red Alice band like a Victorian child's doll.

'Be honest with me, sugar,' she purrs. 'Did you ask Ray Hines to ring and talk you up?'

'No.' *No, I fucking didn't, you cheeky bitch.*

'She said she'd spoken to you several times yesterday.'

'She phoned me and said she wanted to talk. I'm going to ring later, set up a meeting.' I leave out the part about Wendy Whitehead, and, to be on the safe side, the story of last night's abortive rendezvous. Until I know what any of it means, I'm reluctant to hand it over.

'She's one step ahead of you.' Maya picks up a scrap of paper from her desk. 'Shall I read you your orders? Marchington House, Redlands Lane, Twickenham. She wants you there at nine tomorrow morning. Have you got a car yet?'

'No. I—'

'You passed your fourth driving test, though, right?'

'It was my second, and no, I didn't.'

'Oh, bad luck. You'll do it next time. Get a taxi, then. Twickenham by public transport's impossible – quicker to get to the North Pole. And keep me updated. I want to know what Ray's so eager to talk to you about.'

Wendy Whitehead. I hate knowing things that other people don't know. My heartbeat is picking up speed, like something walking faster and faster, unwilling to admit it wants to start running. Tamsin's right: Rachel Hines wants to reel me in, and she's afraid it isn't working. I didn't phone her back first thing this morning. It's mid-afternoon and I still haven't made contact. So she rings the MD, knowing I'll have to meet her if the order comes from Maya.

She's clever. Too clever to say, 'He can't see the trees for the wood' by mistake.

'Fliss?'

'Mm?'

'What I said about nobodies from nowhere . . . I didn't mean you, even if it sounded like I did.' Maya flashes me a poor-little-you smile. 'We all have to start somewhere, don't we?'

6

8/10/09

'How about if I buy the first drink tonight?' said Chris Gibbs, not seeing why he should have to.

'No.'

'How about I buy all the drinks?'

'Still no,' said Colin Sellers. They were in an unmarked police pool car, on their way to Bengeo Street. Sellers was driving. Gibbs had his feet up, the soles of his shoes against the door of the glove compartment, safe in the knowledge that it wasn't his to clean. He'd never have sat like this in his own car; Debbie would go ballistic.

'You'll do a better job than me,' he said. 'You've got the patience, the charm. Or is it smarm?'

'Thanks, but no.'

'You mean I haven't come up with the right incentive yet. Every man has his price.'

'She can't be that bad.'

'She's deaf as a fucking door knob. Last time I was hoarse when I came out, from shouting so she could hear me.'

'You're a familiar face. She's more likely to—'

'You're better with old ladies than I am.'

'Ladies full stop,' Sellers quipped. He thought a lot of himself because he had two women on the go, one of whom he was married to and one he wasn't, though he'd had her so long he might as well be married to her; two women who reluctantly agreed to have sex with him in the vain hope that one day he might be less of a twat than he was now and always had been. Gibbs had only the one: his wife, Debbie.

'Ask her nicely, she might give you a hand-job. Used to be a piano teacher, so she'll be good with her hands.'

'You're sick,' said Sellers. 'She's like, what, eighty?'

'Eighty-three. What's your upper age limit, then? Seventy-five?'

'Pack it in, will you?'

'"All right, love, wipe yourself, your taxi's here. It's four in the morning, love, pay for yourself."' Gibbs' impression of Sellers was as unpopular with its inspiration and target as it was popular with everyone else at the nick. Over the years, the Yorkshire accent had become considerably more pronounced than Sellers' real one, and quite a bit of heavy breathing had been added. Gibbs was considering a few more minor modifications, but he was worried about straying too far from the subtlety of the original. ' "All right, love, you roll over there into the wet spot, cover it up with your big fat arse." If you want me to stop, you know what you have to do.'

A few seconds of silence, then Sellers said, 'Sorry, was that last bit you? I thought you were still being me.'

Gibbs chuckled. '"If you want me to stop, you know what you have to do"? You'd really say that, to an eighty-three-year-old grandmother?' He shook his head in mock disgust.

'Let's both do both,' said Sellers. He always caved in eventually. A couple more minutes and he'd be offering to interview both Beryl Murie and Stella White on his own while Gibbs had the afternoon off. It was like the end of a game of chess: Gibbs could see all the moves that lay ahead, all the way to check-mate.

'So you're willing to do Murie?' he said.

'With you, yeah.'

'Why do I have to be there?' said Gibbs indignantly. 'You take Murie, I'll take Stella White – a straight swap. That way we don't waste time. Unless you can't trust yourself alone with Grandma Murie.'

'If I say yes, will you shut the fuck up?' said Sellers.

'Done.' Gibbs grinned and held out his hand for Sellers to shake.

'I'm driving, dickhead.' Sellers shook his head. 'And we're wasting time however we do it. We've already taken statements from Murie and White.'

'They're all we've got. We need to push them for what they didn't think of the first time.'

'There's only one reason we're back here,' said Sellers. 'We've got nowhere else to go. Everyone close to Helen Yardley's got a solid alibi, none of them tested positive for gunpowder residue. We're looking for a stranger, to us and to her – every detective's worst nightmare. A killer with no link to his victim, some no-mark who saw her face on TV once too often and decided she was the one – someone we've no chance of finding. Proust knows it, he just won't admit it yet.'

Gibbs said nothing. He agreed with Simon Waterhouse: it wasn't as simple as someone close to the victim versus stranger murder, not in the case of a woman like Helen Yardley. Someone could have killed her because of what she stood for, someone who stood for the opposite. The way Gibbs saw it, Helen Yardley's murder convictions had started a war. She'd been killed by the other side, the child protection control freaks who assume parents want to kill their kids unless someone can prove otherwise. Gibbs kept this insight to himself because he didn't think he deserved the credit for it; as with all his best ideas, Simon Waterhouse had planted the seed. Gibbs' admiration for Waterhouse was his most closely guarded secret.

'He's really lost it this time.' Sellers was still talking about the Snowman. 'Telling us we aren't allowed to say or even think Helen Yardley might have been guilty. I wasn't thinking that – were you? If her conviction was unsafe, it was unsafe. But now he's put the idea into all our heads by telling us it's forbidden, and all of a sudden everyone's thinking, "Hang on a minute – what if there *is* no smoke without fire?", exactly what he's saying we mustn't think. All that does is make us think it's what he *thinks* we're going to think, which makes us ask ourselves why. Perhaps there's some reason we *ought* to be thinking it.'

'Everyone's thinking it,' said Gibbs. 'They have been from the start, they just haven't been saying it because they're not sure where anyone else stands. No one wants to be the first to say, "Oh, come on, course she did it – sod the court of appeal." Would you want to stand up and say that, when she's been shot in the head and we're all breaking our bollocks to find her killer?'

Sellers turned to look at him. The car swerved. 'You think she killed her babies?'

Gibbs resented having to explain. If Sellers had been listening . . . 'I can see what you're all thinking because I'm the only one *not* thinking it. What that Duffy woman said – it's crap.'

'Duffy who?'

'That doctor. When the prosecutor asked her if it was possible that Morgan and Rowan Yardley were both SIDS deaths, she said it was so unlikely, it bordered on impossible. SIDS is crib death – Sudden Infant Death Syndrome, where the death's natural but no reason can be found.'

'I know that much,' Sellers muttered.

'That was the quote: "so unlikely, it borders on impossible". She said it was overwhelmingly likely that there was an underlying cause, and that the cause was forensic, not medical. In other words, Helen Yardley murdered her babies. When the defence called her on it and asked if, in spite of what she'd said, it was possible for SIDS to strike two children from the same family, same household, she had to say yes, it was possible. But that wasn't the part that impressed the jury – eleven out of twelve of them, anyway. They only heard the "so unlikely, it borders on impossible" part. Turns out there's no statistical basis for that, it was just her talking shit – that's why she's up before the GMC next month for misconduct.'

'You're well informed.'

Gibbs was about to say, 'So should you be, so should everyone working the Yardley murder,' when he realised he would be quoting Waterhouse word for word. 'I reckon Helen Yardley would have walked if it hadn't been for Duffy,' he said. 'All the papers at the time printed the "so unlikely, it borders on impossible" quote. That's what springs to most people's minds when they hear the name Helen Yardley, never mind the successful appeal or Duffy being done for misconduct. And that's just regular people. Cops are even worse – we're programmed to imagine everyone on our radar's guilty and getting away with it: no smoke without fire, whatever legal technicalities might have got Helen Yardley out. I only know different because of Debbie's experience.'

'Your Debbie?'

Would he bother mentioning someone else's Debbie? What did he know about Debbies that weren't his? Sellers was an idiot. Gibbs wished he hadn't said anything now; at the same time, he was looking forward to flipping his trump card. This was his own original material, nothing to do with Waterhouse. 'She's had eleven miscarriages in the last three years, all at ten weeks. She can't get past that point, no matter what she does. She's tried aspirin, yoga, healthy eating, giving up work and lying on the sofa all day – you name it, she's done it. We've had all the tests, seen every doctor and every specialist, and no one can tell us anything. Can't find any problems, that's what they all say.' Gibbs shrugged. 'Doesn't mean nothing's wrong, though, does it? Obviously something is. Any doctor worth shit'll tell you medicine's always going to throw up mysteries no one can solve. How many miscarriages has Stacey had?'

'None,' said Sellers. 'How come you've never . . .?'

'There you go – all the medical proof you need, and proof that Duffy's a cunt. If one woman can miscarry eleven pregnancies and another miscarry none, it stands to reason that one woman might lose two or even more babies to crib death, and others not lose any. Doesn't make it murder, any more than Debbie murdered all the foetuses she lost. Hardly takes a brain of Britain to work out that some medical issues might be there in one family and not in another, like big noses or a tendency to get varicose veins. Like having a microscopic dick's a problem in your family and not in mine.'

'Apparently there's a rare genetic condition that only affects men with dark curly hair and the initials CG,' Sellers said with a straight face. 'When they look at their own penises, their vision distorts and they see them as five times the size they really are. Sufferers also tend to have a problem with body odour.'

They'd arrived at Bengeo Street. It was a horseshoe-shaped cul-de-sac of 1950s red-brick semis with small front gardens, token patches of green. Many of the houses had extensions built on to their sides. It gave the street an overcrowded look, as if the buildings had over-eaten and were straining to fit into their plots. The Yardleys' house was one of the few on the street that hadn't been extended; no need, with no kids to fill it up, thought Gibbs. It was still cordoned off by police tape. Paul Yardley was staying with his parents, for which Gibbs was grateful. Dealing with Yardley was a nightmare. You'd tell him there was no news and he'd stand there and look at you as if he didn't recognise your answer and was waiting for the real one.

Gibbs looked at his watch: half past four. Stella White's red Renault Clio was parked outside number 16, which meant she was back from picking up her son from school. Sellers had rung Beryl Murie's bell and looked as taken aback as Gibbs had been two days ago to get, by way of a response, a wordless electronic version of *How Much is That Doggy in the Window?* that was audible across the street. 'Forgot to warn you about the deaf doorbell,' Gibbs called out.

Stella White opened her front door as he approached. She was holding a child's muddy football boots, a blue plastic alien toy and a toast crust. Her jeans and V-necked jumper hung off her thin frame, and there were dark circles under her eyes. If this was what life with children did to you, maybe he and Debbie were the lucky ones.

'DC Gibbs, Culver Valley CID.'

'I was expecting a DC Sellers,' Stella White said – upbeat, smiling, as if a DC Gibbs was some kind of bonus, or treat.

Sorry to disappoint you.

'Change of plan.' Gibbs showed her his ID, and allowed himself to be ushered into the front room. Television noise was coming from the next room, the one with the closed door: some sort of horse-racing commentary.

'Your husband watching the racing?' he asked. The room they were in looked as if it had had some money spent on it: thick swagged curtains, real wood floor, a slate and marble fireplace. Subtle colours that you couldn't easily describe, nothing as straightforward as red or blue or green. Debbie would have loved it, though she'd have been unwilling to live on Bengeo Street, however smart the house was inside; it was too close to the Winstanley estate, on the wrong side of town.

'I haven't got a husband,' said Stella. 'My son Dillon's got a thing about horses. At first I tried to stop him watching the racing, but . . .' She shrugged. 'He loves it so much, I decided it was mean to deprive him.'

Gibbs nodded. 'Any sort of interest's got to be good, hasn't it?' he said. 'When I was a kid I wasn't interested in anything. Nothing. I was bored out of my mind until I was old enough to drink and . . .' He stopped himself just in time, but Stella White was grinning.

'Exactly,' she said. 'I'm just so glad he's passionate about something – it almost doesn't matter what. He studies form and everything. Get him on the subject of racing and you can't shut him up.'

'How old is he?'

'Four.' Seeing Gibbs' surprise, Stella said, 'I know. It can be a bit embarrassing. He's not a child prodigy or anything – just a normal kid who's crazy about horse-racing.'

'Next you'll tell me he speaks twelve languages and can cure cancer,' said Gibbs.

'I wish.' Stella's smile dimmed. 'I don't want to embarrass you by springing this on you, but I find it's easier if I do, and then it's out of the way. I've got cancer.'

'Right.' Gibbs cleared his throat. 'Sorry.'

'Don't worry, I'm used to it – the cancer, people's reactions to it. I've had it for years, and I've lived a better life because of it.'

Gibbs didn't know what else he could say apart from sorry. A better life? Who was she trying to kid? He was starting to wish he'd stuck with Beryl Murie.

'Please, have a seat,' said Stella. 'Can I get you anything to drink?'

'No, I'm good. I could do with Dillon joining us, if you can tear him away from the horses. I'd like to go over what you've already told us about the man you saw approaching Helen Yardley's front door, see if you remember anything new.'

Stella frowned. 'I doubt Dillon saw him. I was strapping him into his car seat – he sits in the back, so he'll have had a view of the back of the seat in front and not much else.'

'What about before you put him in the car? Presumably the man approached the house from the road. Might Dillon have seen him further down the street, before you strapped him into his chair?'

'He could have, I suppose, though I didn't notice him, not till he was right outside Helen's house. But to be honest, I don't think Dillon saw him at all. The detective who came last time talked to him, and it wasn't much use. Dillon said he'd seen a man, but that was pretty much it – he couldn't say when or even *where*, and by that point he already knew *I'd* seen a man . . . I think he was just saying it because he'd heard me say it.'

'If only the man had been a horse,' Gibbs attempted a joke.

'Oh, then he'd have remembered every detail.' Stella laughed. 'Dillon's quite good with detail usually, even when horses aren't involved, but he couldn't tell the detective anything: hair colour, height, clothes. Not that I was much better.' She looked apologetic. 'I *think* he had darkish hair and darkish clothes, I think he was tallish, regular build, and at the upper end of young or the lower end of middle-aged. I seem to remember he was wearing a coat, but who wouldn't have been? It's October.'

'Not carrying anything, as far as you remember?' Gibbs asked.

'No, but . . . he could have been, I suppose.'

'And you didn't notice if he had a car, or if there were any cars not usually parked on Bengeo Street that were there that morning?'

'I wouldn't know a Volvo from a Skoda,' said Stella. 'Sorry. I'm completely car-blind. There could have been twenty bright pink Rolls-Royces parked on the street and I wouldn't have noticed.'

'Not a problem,' said Gibbs. 'If I could have a quick chat with Dillon, though . . .' He produced his best smile. 'I'm not expecting him to tell me anything, but it's worth a shot. A lot of the blokes I know who are into the horses are also into cars.'

'Okay, but . . . if by any chance he starts to talk about Helen's death, could you . . .' Stella stopped. She looked embarrassed. 'I know this is going to sound weird, but could you try to be as positive about it as you can?'

Gibbs chewed his lip, stumped. Positive, about a woman who'd been fucked over by the legal system, robbed of her only surviving child and then shot in the head?

'This is going to sound very convenient from a woman with terminal cancer, I know, but I'm trying to bring up Dillon to believe what I believe: that there is no death, or there doesn't have to be. The spirit is what matters and that never dies. Everything else is trivial.'

Gibbs sat as still as a stone. He should have stuck with Beryl Murie, quit while he was ahead. 'What have you told Dillon about Helen Yardley's murder?'

'The truth. He knows she was a special person. Sometimes special people are chosen for soul challenges that most of us couldn't cope with, which is why Helen had a harder time than most, but now she's moved on to the next stage. I told him she'd be happy, if happiness is what her spirit needs, in her next life.'

Gibbs managed a non-commital nod. He looked again at the room he was in: fireplace with four framed photographs on the mantelpiece above it, two chairs, a two-seater sofa, bellows, a brass bucket for coal, a poker for the fire, two wooden coffee tables. No joss-sticks, nothing tasselled, no yin-yang symbols; Gibbs felt as if he'd been conned. 'What did you tell Dillon about the person who killed Helen?' he asked. Whoever he was, he was the one Gibbs wanted to move on to the next stage, the stage of being banged up for life and, ideally, beaten to mincemeat in some shithole of a prison.

'That was hard, obviously,' said Stella. 'I tried to explain to him that some people are afraid of experiencing their pain and try to redirect it to others. If you don't mind my saying so, you strike me as falling into that category.'

'Me?' Gibbs sat up straighter in his chair. *Get me the fuck out of here.*

'Not that I'm saying you'd do anything violent – of *course* you wouldn't.'

Gibbs wasn't so sure.

'It's just ... I sense a lot of clouds close to the surface. Underneath those, there's a light burning brightly, but it's ...' Stella laughed suddenly. 'I'm sorry. I'll shut up – I've got bigmouthitis as well as cancer, I'm afraid.'

'Can I have a word with Dillon?'

'I'll go and grab him.'

Left alone in the room, Gibbs exhaled slowly. What would Waterhouse think about a woman who saw perks where others saw tragedy, and violent death as a great opportunity, facilitating a soul's entry into a happier next life? What if you decided a friend of yours had suffered enough in her present incarnation and it was time for her soul to move up a level? Gibbs wondered if he ought to mention it.

Through the wall, he heard the sound of Dillon's muffled anger as the TV was switched off. He stood up and walked over to the display of photographs above the fireplace. One was of Dillon in his school uniform. He looked as if he was saying the 'ch' part of the word 'cheese'. There was a picture of Stella and Dillon together, and two of Stella alone, in running gear. In one she had a medal on a ribbon round her neck.

When she came into the room with Dillon, Gibbs said, 'Runner, are you?' It was something he'd considered taking up, before deciding he couldn't be bothered.

'Not any more,' said Stella. 'I haven't got the strength for it now. When I first got my diagnosis, I realised there was one thing I'd wanted to do all my life that I still hadn't done, so I trained and I did it: two or three marathons a year for about five years. I couldn't believe how much healthier it made me feel. Not only feel,' Stella corrected herself. 'I *was* healthier. The doctors gave me two years to live – I've managed to wangle an extra eight.'

'That's not bad.' Maybe thinking positive about death had its upside after all.

'I've raised pots of money for charity. Last time I ran the London Marathon, all the money I raised went to JIPAC – you know, Helen's organisation. I did a couple of triathlons, too, also for charity. Now I'm mostly doing public speaking – to cancer patients, doctors, Women's Institute, University of the Third Age – anyone who'll have me.' Stella smiled. 'If you're not careful, I'll show you may cardboard box full of press cuttings.'

'Can I watch telly?' Dillon asked impatiently. He was wearing a blue tracksuit with a school logo on the top. There were traces of chocolate round his mouth.

'Soon, love.' Stella stroked the top of his head. 'Once we've finished chatting to DC Gibbs, you can go back to your horses.'

'But I want to do what *I* want to do,' Dillon protested.

'Can you remember Monday morning?' Gibbs asked him.

'It's Thursday today.'

'That's right. So Monday was . . .'

'Before Thursday it was Wednesday, before Wednesday it was Tuesday, before Tuesday it was Monday. That day?'

'Right,' Gibbs agreed.

'We saw the man with the umbrella, beyond,' said Dillon.

'Umbrella?' Stella laughed. 'That's a new one. He didn't—'

'Beyond?' Gibbs knelt down in front of the boy. 'You mean ahead?'

'No. Beyond.'

'Did you see the man outside Helen Yardley's house on Monday morning?'

'I saw him and Mum saw him.'

'But he didn't have an umbrella, sweet-pea,' said Stella gently.

'He did.'

'What colour was the umbrella?'

'Black and silver,' said Dillon, without missing a beat.

Stella was shaking her head in apparent amusement. She mouthed something at Gibbs that implied she'd explain later, once Dillon had been returned to the TV room.

'Did you see the man getting into or out of a car?'

Dillon shook his head.

'But you saw him outside the Yardleys' house, on the path.'

'And beyond.'

'You mean he went into the house?' Gibbs signalled to Stella not to interrupt.

She ignored him. 'Sorry, but . . . sweet-pea, you *didn't* see him go into Helen's house, did you?'

'Mrs White, please . . .'

'The more times he's asked, the more he'll invent,' said Stella. 'Sorry, I know I shouldn't leap in, but you don't know Dillon like I do. He's very, very sensitive. He can see that people want him to tell them things, and he doesn't want to disappoint them.'

'He was in the lounge,' said Dillon. 'I saw him in the lounge.'

'Dillon, you *didn't*. You're only trying to help, I know, but you didn't see the man in Helen's lounge, did you?' Stella turned to Gibbs. 'Believe me, if he'd had a black and silver umbrella with him, I'd have seen it. It wasn't even raining. It was bright, sunny and cold – what I call perfect Christmas Day weather, except in October. Most people want snow at Christmas, but I—'

'It wasn't bright,' said Dillon. 'There wasn't enough sun to make it bright. Can I watch the horses now?'

Gibbs made a mental note to look up last Sunday's weather forecasts for Monday. Someone cautious might have taken an umbrella with him even on a sunny morning, if rain had been predicted. *And if it hadn't?* Could the gun have been inside the closed umbrella?

'It *was* raining,' said Dillon, looking up at Gibbs with a hard-done-by expression on his face. 'The umbrella was wet. I *did* see the man in the lounge.'

Judith Duffy lived in a three-storey detached villa in Ealing, on a windy tree-lined street that felt neither like what Simon thought of as 'proper London' nor like anywhere else in particular. He decided he wouldn't like to live here. Not that he could have afforded to, so it was probably just as well. He rang the bell for the third time. *Nothing.*

He pushed open the gleaming brass letterbox and looked through it, saw a wooden coat stand, a herringbone parquet floor, Persian rugs, a black piano and red-cushioned stool. He took a step back when his view was blocked by purple material with a button attached to it.

The door opened. Knowing that Judith Duffy was fifty-four, Simon was shocked to see a woman who could easily have been seventy. Her straight iron-grey hair was tied back from her narrow, age-hollowed face. In the photograph of her that Simon had seen, the one the newspapers always used, Duffy had looked much rounder; there had been the hint of a double chin.

'I don't think I invited you to peer through my letterbox,' she said. It was the sort of phrase that begged, Simon thought, to be delivered with barely suppressed outrage, but Dr Duffy sounded as if she was merely stating a fact. 'Who are you?'

Simon identified himself. 'I've left you two messages,' he said.

'I didn't return your calls because I didn't want to waste your time,' said Duffy. 'This will be the shortest interview of your career. I won't talk to you or answer your questions, and I won't allow you to do whatever test it is that establishes whether or not I've fired a gun. Also, you can tell your colleague Fliss Benson to stop bothering me – I won't talk to her either. I'm sorry you've had a wasted journey.'

Colleague Fliss Benson? Simon had never heard of her.

Duffy started to close the door. He put out his hand to stop her. 'Everyone else we've asked has agreed to be swabbed, and cooperated with us in any way they can.'

'I'm not everybody. Please take your hand off my door.' She closed it in his face.

Simon pushed open the letterbox again and saw purple. 'There's someone I can't find,' he addressed Duffy's cardigan, the only part of her he could see. 'Rachel Hines. I've spoken to her ex-husband, Angus. He said she's staying with friends somewhere in London, but he doesn't know where. I don't suppose you've got any idea?'

'You should ask Laurie Nattrass that question,' said Duffy.

'I'm planning to, soon as he rings me back.'

'So it's everyone minus one, then.'

'Pardon?'

'Cooperating. Laurie Nattrass can't be cooperating if he hasn't returned your calls.'

Do we have to have this conversation through a letterbox? 'Mr Nattrass has already been swabbed, alibied and eliminated, as you would be if you—'

'Goodbye, Mr Waterhouse.'

Simon heard the shuffle of her feet on the wood floor as she moved away. 'Help me out here,' he called after her. 'Between you and me, and I shouldn't be telling you this, I'm worried about Mrs Hines.' No matter what the Snowman said, no matter what Sam Kombothekra said, Simon's instincts told him he was looking for a serial killer, or a person with the potential to become one – someone who left cards bearing strange numerical codes in the pockets of his victims. Was Rachel Hines one of those victims? Or was Simon's imagination as out of control as Charlie was always telling him it was?

He let out a heavy sigh. As if in response, Judith Duffy took a few steps towards the front door. Now Simon could see her again, her shoulder and her arm. Not her face. 'I had lunch with Ray Hines on Monday,' she said. 'There, I've given you my alibi – and hers – so you can go away happy, and even if you aren't happy, you can go. Neither of us knew that it was the day someone would murder Helen Yardley. At that point it was just Monday 5 October, same as any other Monday. We met at a restaurant, spent the afternoon together.'

'Which restaurant?' Simon got out his pad and pen.

'Sardo Canale in Primrose Hill. Ray's choice.'

'Do you mind my asking . . .?'

'Goodbye, Mr Waterhouse.'

This time, when Simon pressed the letterbox, he met with resistance. She was holding it shut from the inside.

He went back to his car and switched on his phone. He had two messages, one from a man he assumed was Laurie Nattrass whose message was a strange noise followed by the words 'Laurie Nattrass' and nothing more, and one from Charlie, saying that Lizzie Proust had rung to invite the two of them for dinner on Saturday night. Didn't Simon think it was weird, she wanted to know, given that they'd known the Prousts for years and no such invitation had been forthcoming until now, and what did he want her to say? Simon texted the word 'NO', in capitals, to her mobile phone, dropping his own twice in the process, in his eagerness to get the message sent. The Snowman, inviting him for dinner; the thought made Simon's throat close like a clenched fist. He forced his mind away from it, unwilling to deal with the violence of his reaction and the element of fear it contained.

He rang one of the three mobile numbers he had for Laurie Nattrass, and this time someone answered after the first ring. Simon heard breathing. 'Hello?' he said. 'Mr Nattrass?'

'Laurie Nattrass,' said a gruff voice, the same one that had left the message.

'Is that Mr Nattrass I'm speaking to?'

'Dunno.'

'Pardon?'

'I'm not where you are, so I can't see who you're speaking to. If you're speaking to me, then yes, you're speaking to Mr Nattrass, Mr Laurie Nattrass. And I'm speaking to Detective Constable – and I'm spelling that with a "u" instead of an "o" and an extra "t" between the "n" and the "s" – Simon

Waterhouse.' As he spoke, his words rose and fell in volume, as if someone was sticking pins in him and each new jab made him raise his voice. Was he insane? Pissed?

'When and where can we meet?' Simon asked. 'I'll come to you if you like.'

'Never. Nowhere, no-how.'

It was going to be like that, was it? One of those easy conversations. Could this man really be an Oxford- and Harvard-educated multi-award-winning investigative journalist? He didn't sound like one.

'Do you know where I might find Rachel Hines?'

'Twickenham,' said Nattrass. 'Why? Ray didn't kill Helen. Looking to fit her up again, are you? You can't step into the same river twice, but you can fit up the same innocent woman twice. If you're filth.' It wasn't only the volume that varied from word to word, Simon noticed – it was also the speed at which Nattrass spoke. Some sentences spurted out; others were delivered slowly, with an air of hesitation, as if his attention were elsewhere.

'Do you happen to have an address or contact—?'

'Speak to Judith Duffy instead of wasting my time and Ray Hines'. Ask her what her two sons-in-law were doing on Monday.' It was an order rather than a suggestion.

Two sons-in-law. And, since these days the police looked at things from an equal opportunities perspective, two daughters. Were they worth checking out?

'Mr Nattrass, I need to ask you some questions,' Simon tried again. 'I'd prefer to do it in person, but . . .'

'Pretend your phone's a person. Pretend it's called Laurence Hugo St John Fleet Nattrass, and ask away.'

If this man was sane, Simon was a banana sandwich.

Nattrass was certainly drunk. 'We're considering the possibility that Helen Yardley was murdered as a result of her work for JIPAC. As you're the . . .'

'. . . co-founder, you're wondering if anyone's tried to kill me. No. Next?'

'Has anyone threatened you? Anyone acting out of character, any strange emails or letters?'

'How's Giles Proust? Leader of the band now, isn't he? How can he be objective? It's a joke. He arrested Helen for murder. Have you read her book?'

'Helen's . . .?'

'*Nothing But Love*. Nothing but praise for dear old Giles. What do you think of him? Cunt, right?'

Simon started to say 'Yeah,' then turned it into a cough, his heart racing. He'd nearly said it. That would have been his job down the pan.

'If he thought Helen was innocent, why did he arrest her?' Nattrass demanded. 'Why didn't he resign? Morally colour-blind, is he?'

'In our job, if you're told to arrest someone, you arrest them,' said Simon. *Morally colour-blind*. If there was a better description of the Snowman, he had yet to hear it.

'Know what he did when she got out? Turned up on her doorstep with everything his henchmen had confiscated when they arrested her – Moses basket, crib, bouncy chair, Morgan and Rowan's clothes, the lot. Didn't even ring first to warn her, or ask if she wanted a van-load of reminders of her dead babies. Know how many times he visited her in prison? None.'

'I wanted to ask you about a card that was found in Helen Yardley's pocket after her death,' Simon said. 'It's been kept out of the press.'

'2,1,4,9 . . .'

'How do you know those numbers?' Simon didn't care if he sounded abrupt. Even at his rudest, he was no competition for Nattrass.

'Fliss had them. Felicity Benson, Happiness Benson. Except she's not very happy at the moment, not with me. She didn't know what the numbers meant. I chucked them in the bin. Do you know what they mean? Know who sent them?'

Felicity Benson. *Fliss*. Simon had no idea who she was, but she'd just leaped straight to the top of the list of people he wanted to speak to.

Angus Hines

Transcript of Interview 1, 16 February 2009

AH: Well? I assume you have questions you want to ask me and aren't here for the sole purpose of recording silence.
LN: I'm surprised you agreed to be interviewed, frankly.
AH: You mean that if you were me, you'd hide away in shame?
LN: I'm surprised you agreed to talk to me. You know where I stand. You know I'm making a film about—
AH: You mean I know whose side you're on?
LN: Yes.
(*Pause*)
AH: You think it's appropriate to take sides?
LN: Not appropriate. Essential.
AH: So, for the sake of clarity, whose side are you on?
LN: Ray's. And Helen Yardley's, and all the other innocent women who've been locked up for killing children they didn't kill.
AH: How many altogether? Ever totted up the grand total?
LN: Too many. JIPAC's pressing for five cases to be reviewed at the moment, and there's at least another three that I know of – innocent women in the British prison system thanks to the lies of your friend Dr Judith Duffy.
AH: My friend? Oh, I see. So on one side we have you, my ex-wife and the scores of unjustly maligned mothers or

baby-minders, victims of what I believe you've called a modern-day witch-hunt . . .

LN: Because it is one.

AH: . . . and on the other side there's me, Judith Duffy – anybody else?

LN: Plenty. Anyone who played a part in ruining the lives of Ray, Helen, Sarah Jaggard and other women like them.

AH: And in your righteous war, with its clearly defined armies, who's on the side of my children? Who's on the side of Marcella and Nathaniel?

LN: If you think—

AH: I am. I'm on their side. It's the only side I'm on. It's the only side I've ever been on. That's why I'm willing to be interviewed – by you, by anybody who asks me. You can try as hard as you like to cast me as a villain in your BBC documentary, but provided you represent me accurately, I believe the viewing public will see the truth behind your lies.

LN: Me? What have I lied about?

AH: Deliberately? Probably nothing. But going through life with blinkers on and spouting your prejudices at every opportunity is a form of lying.

LN: So I'm blinkered?

AH: You can't see the trees for the wood.

LN: The wood for the trees. The expression is 'You can't see the wood for the trees'.

AH: (*Laughs*) 'Oh! Let us never, never doubt/What nobody is sure about!'

LN: I see. So I'm blinkered because I've always believed in your wife's innocence? Unlike you, who betrayed her?

AH: I don't think I did betray her. And, for the record, I too now believe she's innocent. And I believe it all the more strongly for having once believed otherwise – something I wouldn't expect someone with your simplistic outlook to understand.

LN: Is that your way of saying sorry? Have you apologised to Ray for doubting her? Have you even tried?

AH: I've nothing to be sorry for. All I've done is refuse, throughout, to insult anybody, my wife . . .

LN: Ex-wife

AH: . . . or my children, by lying. When the police first let it be known that they suspected Ray of murder, I doubted her innocence, yes. I also doubted her guilt. I was in no position to say for sure how Marcella and Nathaniel died, since I wasn't at home when it happened, on either occasion. The police were suspicious – I didn't see why they would be if there were no grounds for suspicion. They'd have had better things to do, surely? Two deaths for no apparent reason in the same family is unusual. Marcella and Nathaniel were perfectly well in the days before they died. There was nothing wrong with them.

LN: Are you a paediatrician? I'll have to amend my notes. It says 'photographer' here.

AH: Then you'd better make an amendment, as you say. I was promoted some time ago. I'm Pictures Desk Editor at *London on Sunday*. Someone else does the donkey work now. I get to sit at a desk eating chocolate biscuits and looking at Big Ben out of my window. See how easily you can mistake an incorrect assumption for a fact? I don't make assumptions, unlike you. I made none about Ray. She loved the children – her love for them was genuine, I had no doubts on that front. At the same time, I was realistic enough to wonder whether certain psychological . . . conditions might exist in which love for one's child is compatible with doing it harm. Because of Ray's history.

LN: Oh, come on! She sits on a window ledge to smoke a cigarette – next thing she knows, the filth are out in full force, cordoning off the area around the house, standing in her bedroom where she can hear every word they're saying, on their mobiles to her GP asking about the percentage likelihood of her jumping.

AH: That's one version of the story, one of the many she's served up over the years: the 'all I wanted was some peace and quiet and a fag' remix. In court she tried to pass the whole thing off as an episode of post-natal madness, claiming she had no clear memory of either the window ledge or the cigarette.

LN: There's nothing wrong with Ray, psychologically or in any other way. She's a normal, healthy woman.

AH: Does it strike you as normal behaviour to climb out of a dangerously high window and sit on a small ledge, smoking? Not to mention that this happened on Ray's first day back after she'd inexplicably walked out on me and Marcella when Marcella was only two weeks old. Then, nine days later, she just as inexplicably walks back in, refusing to say a word about where she's been or why she left, and when pressed on the subject, she rushes upstairs and climbs out of the window. If that was your wife behaving like that and then she was accused of murdering your two children, you're telling me you'd have no doubts?

LN: If Ray was suffering from post-natal depression, whose fault was that? You snored your way through the first fourteen nights of Marcella's life while Ray was up every hour and a half breastfeeding. She'd endured two weeks of looking after a demanding baby with zero help from you, and she decided . . .

AH: . . . that if I didn't experience first-hand how hard it was, I'd never understand, so she took off and left me to my own devices. The 'my husband's a sexist bastard' feminist remix.

LN: You can call it that if you want. I call it the truth.

AH: Nine days after her departure, Ray returned to find I hadn't coped on my own at all, as I'd been supposed to – I'd summoned my mother instantly, being an unreconstructed man. Since Ray's only desire had been to turn our home into a utopia of gender equality and me into Mary Poppins, she was furious with both me and Mum. She climbed out of the window to get away from us. You see? I'm as familiar with the lie as you are.
(*Pause*)
The fact is that from the moment I brought Ray and Marcella home from the hospital, I did my fair share of the childcare, if not more. If Marcella cried in the night, I was the one who got out of bed first. While Ray fed her, I made us both cups of tea, then sometimes we'd talk, or sometimes we'd listen to the radio. When we were bored of both, we'd open our bedroom curtains and try to look into neighbours' windows, see what was going on. Nothing much. Lucky bastards were sleeping.
(*Long pause*)
I was always the one who changed Marcella's nappy and settled her back to sleep. Not once or twice – every

time. By the time I got back into bed, Ray would already be asleep. I did all the supermarket shopping, all the washing and ironing, cooked the evening meals . . .

LN: Then why did Ray walk out on you?

AH: Not only me. Me and Marcella. You don't ever wonder whether a woman who's capable of deserting her newborn baby might also be capable of killing that same baby a few weeks later?

LN: Never.

AH: A woman who has no qualms about lying under oath, implying in court that she was suffering from post-natal depression, then telling you later that it was all part of some feminist stand she'd decided to take?

LN: Not everyone who lies is a murderer.

AH: True. Ray certainly lied, but, as I said before, I no longer believe she harmed Marcella and Nathaniel.

LN: We all lie from time to time, but hardly any of us kill our own children. Most men might give their wives the benefit of the doubt. Paul Yardley did. Glen Jaggard did.

AH: You need first to have a doubt in order to give someone the benefit of it. Everything I've heard about Yardley and Jaggard suggests they never doubted. You were talking about normality before. Do you think that's normal? Natural?

(*Pause*)

I didn't think Ray was a murderer. All I knew was that our two babies were dead, four years apart, and some people thought Ray might have been responsible. I didn't think she was a murderer and I didn't think she wasn't a murderer. I didn't know.

LN: The result of your not knowing was that Ray had to spend the run-up to her trial living with a man who wasn't her loving husband any more but a sinister data-gathering stranger, watching her for signs of guilt or innocence. How do you think that must have been for her? And then when the verdict went against her, you gave an interview outside court saying you were glad your children's killer had been brought to justice and that you'd be starting divorce proceedings as soon as possible. Unless you were misquoted?

AH: No. That's what I said.

LN: You didn't even have the decency to speak to Ray in private first, before announcing your abandonment of her to a scrum of reporters and photographers. In fact, you didn't talk to Ray again until after her release, did you?

AH: I don't see this as being a loyalty issue. Is it disloyal to wonder if your wife might have murdered your children when that's the question everyone else in the country is asking themselves? When you hear her lie in court? She didn't only lie about why she left home . . .

LN: Even without any creative editing on my part, people are going to think you're a cold-hearted monster. What if Ray had been acquitted? How would you have felt about her then?

AH: This isn't about feelings. I love Ray. I always have and I always will, but I wanted justice for Marcella and Nathaniel. I was in a difficult situation. Since I knew I'd never know for sure – and no one can live with uncertainty for ever, especially not me – I made a decision: whatever the court's verdict, I would abide by it. If the verdict had been not guilty, I would have believed Ray was innocent.

LN: Let's have this absolutely clear: you're saying that if it had gone the other way, your doubts would have vanished just like that?

AH: I would have seen to it that they did. I'm not saying it wouldn't have taken some self-discipline, but that was my decision. That's why we have a justice system, isn't it? To make decisions that no man alone can be expected to make.

LN: I suppose you've never heard of the Birmingham Six?

AH: I've heard of them. And of the Guildford Four, and the Broadwater Farm Three, Winston Silcott and his cronies. And of the Chippenham Seven, the Penzance Nine, the Basingstoke Five, the Bath Spa Two . . .

LN: You're talking rubbish.

AH: How many fake examples will I have to invent before you take my point?

(*Pause*)

AH: You know, in a way it's quite comforting talking to you. You haven't got a hope in hell of understanding someone like me. Or Ray.

LN: How did you feel when Ray won her appeal and had her convictions overturned?

AH: I wondered whether it might mean she was innocent.

LN: Did you feel any guilt at that point?

AH: Me? I didn't kill my children, or lie in court, or arrive at an incorrect verdict. What did I have to feel guilty about?

LN: Do you regret divorcing your wife?

AH: No.

LN: But you no longer believe she's a murderer?

AH: No. But I did when I divorced her, which means it was the right thing to do at the time, based on the information available to me then.

The Doctor Who Lied: The Story of a Modern-day Witch-hunt

Laurie Nattrass, March 2009

(Tamsin – this is for British Journalism Review *as soon as Duffy loses her GMC hearing)*

It's one of the staples of fiction: the doctor with the God complex, conceited enough to imagine he can draw a murder to the police's attention, explain how it was committed (injection of potassium between the toes) and still elude detection as the culprit. He never does, for that would deprive the lead sleuth of the opportunity to say, 'You've developed a God complex, doctor. You get a kick out of choosing who lives and who dies.'

In fiction, it makes for another predictable evening in front of the television. In real life, it's considerably more frightening. Harold Shipman, the GP who murdered hundreds of his patients, died without admitting his guilt or offering any explanation for his crimes. He was a contemporary bogeyman, an unassuming monster who moved among ordinary people undetected, passing himself off as one of them.

Following hot on his heels in the monster stakes is Dr Judith Duffy. Last week [adjust if necessary] Dr Duffy was struck off after a GMC hearing found her guilty of misconduct. Despite never having murdered anybody, Dr Duffy was responsible for ruining the lives of dozens of innocent women whose only crime was to be in the wrong place at the wrong time when a child died: Helen Yardley, Lorna Keast, Joanne Bew, Sarah Jaggard, Dorne Llewellyn . . . the list goes on and on.

Here's a horror story to rival the most terrifying tale any author of penny-dreadfuls could dream up. Dr Duffy doesn't make an appearance until later, but bear with me. In August 1998, Ray (Rachel) Hines, a middle-class physiotherapist from Notting Hill, London, gave birth to a baby girl, Marcella. Ray's husband Angus, who works for *London on Sunday*, saw no need to amend his lifestyle. He continued to work long hours and go out drinking with colleagues; meanwhile Ray, having temporarily given up the work she loved in order to stay at home with a baby who never slept for more than an hour at a time, became progressively more exhausted. So far, so familiar. Mothers everywhere will be nodding as they read this, muttering rude comments about men under their breath.

Most women believe themselves to be the equals of their male partners until the advent of the first baby, at which point most – even in this day and age, astonishingly – accept that the days of equality are over. The men continue to go out into the world, and come home insisting they need a good night's sleep in order to perform well the next day. The trouble is, there's a baby to be looked after, so someone has to put their career on hold, if not abandon it altogether. Someone has to summon up the energy, after a punishing day without a break, to cook, clean and iron.

Someone must relinquish their freedom and identity for the greater good of the family unit. Those someones are invariably women.

This is what happened to Ray Hines, but fortunately for Ray, or perhaps unfortunately, she is not most women. Having had the privilege of meeting her more than once, I can tell you that Ray is exceptional. Before tragedy and injustice devastated her life, Ray was one of the UK's most successful businesswomen, co-founder of the market-leading PhysioFit franchise. I once asked her to tell me how this came about. She said, 'I had a bad back as a teenager'. Referred to an incompetent physiotherapist who sat reading a magazine while Ray walked on a machine, Ray decided to do something about the standard of physiotherapy provision in the UK and made a career out of it. That's the sort of woman she is. Most of us would have asked our GPs to refer us to a better physiotherapist, and left it at that.

Ray decided she wasn't willing to be the sacrificial lamb of the family. When Marcella was two weeks old, Ray left home without telling Angus where she was going. For nine days, she stayed away, phoning home regularly but refusing to say where she was or when she'd be back. Her hope was that when she returned, Angus – who would presumably be struggling to cope alone – would have realised the error of his ways, enabling the couple to go forward on a more equal footing.

No such luck. Ray came back to find Angus's mother living in her house, attending to all things domestic with great flair and enthusiasm. Angus would for ever after be able to say, 'My mum coped, so why can't you?' That's why Ray lied to Angus, initially, about the reason for her nine-day absence: she felt humiliated by her failed plan, and told him she had no idea why she'd walked out and couldn't remember where she'd been for the nine days she wasn't at home. Angus rejected that answer as unsatisfactory and wouldn't stop badgering her, so she ran up to their bedroom and locked the door. When Angus and his mother started to berate her through the door, she opened the window and climbed out onto a rather precarious ledge, to escape their harsh voices.

She lit a cigarette and thought about her options. She didn't think Angus would change for the better; if anything she thought he might get worse. She wondered, fleetingly, if she ought to disappear for good. Angus, his mother and Marcella would manage fine without her. She loved Marcella, but she wasn't prepared to live out the rest of her life as the family slave, and she wondered if this made her a bad mother, since most of her good-mother friends seemed to welcome slavery, or at least tolerate it with reasonably good humour. Not for one second did she think about jumping off that ledge.

Fast-forward three weeks. 12 November 1998, 9 p.m. Angus is out with friends from work. Ray has given Marcella her last feed of the day and settled her in her Moses basket. Life is, generally, better. Marcella is sleeping well and therefore so is Ray. Angus has suggested that Ray should go back to work as soon as possible, which is also what she wants, and they've agreed that Marcella will start at a local nursery when she's six months old. Angus regularly jokes that this will be brilliant for Marcella, and names the children of several of their friends who have been 'spoilt to the point of vileness' by having their mothers at their beck and call for the first five years of their lives.

Ray goes upstairs to her bedroom, and lets out a howl when she sees Marcella. Her face is blue and she's not breathing. Ray summons an ambulance, which arrives three minutes later, but it's too late. Ray and Angus are distraught.

Enter one Judith Duffy, a perinatal and paediatric pathologist and Consultant Senior Lecturer in Infant Health and Developmental Physiology at the University of Westminster. Duffy performs the post-mortem on Marcella and finds nothing to suggest she did not die naturally. There is one fractured rib and some bruising, but Duffy says both were probably caused by attempts at resuscitation. The ambulance staff agree. Marcella is a victim of Sudden Infant Death Syndrome (SIDS), which means that no explanation for her death can be found.

Fast-forward four years. Ray and Angus have another baby, Nathaniel. One morning, when Nathaniel is twelve weeks old, Ray wakes to find Angus's side of the bed empty, and light streaming in through the curtains. She is terrified. Nathaniel always wakes her up before it's light, so something must be wrong. She runs to his Moses basket and the nightmare begins all over again: he is blue, not breathing. Ray calls an ambulance. Again, it's too late.

Again, the post-mortem is performed by Dr Judith Duffy, who finds swollen brain tissue and evidence of subdural bleeding. She concludes that Nathaniel must have been shaken, even after consultation with an eminent colleague, Dr Russell Meredew, who disagrees. Crucially, Meredew points out that there is no tearing of the nerves in the brain, as there would have been if Nathaniel had been shaken. Dr Duffy tells Dr Meredew – OBE, incidentally, and winner of the Sir James Spence Medal for his contribution to extending paediatric knowledge – that he doesn't know what he's talking about. She says she has no doubt that Ray Hines shook Nathaniel to death, and smothered Marcella.

There is no alternative now but for the police to become involved, and in due course Ray is charged with the murders of her two children. Her trial begins in March 2004.

But wait a moment, I hear you say. Didn't Dr Duffy perform a post-mortem on Marcella and find nothing suspicious? Yes indeed. Her answer to this, in court, is that she examined the evidence again and revised her opinion. She argues that even if the fractured rib was caused by efforts to resuscitate Marcella, the bruising cannot have been, since Ray admits she was too scared to attempt any sort of resuscitation, and Marcella was already 'cyanosed' by the time the ambulance arrived. This means that there would not have been sufficient blood pressure to cause bruising when medics pressed down on Marcella's chest to try and get her heart beating again.

Again, Russell Meredew disagrees. He explains that it is possible for bruises to appear when blood pressure is almost down to nothing, or even – though this is rare – after death. He has seen many instances of the former and one or two of the latter. He also points out that Myocarditis, a viral inflammation of the heart muscle, is a more likely cause than shaking for Nathaniel's brain swelling and subdural haemorrhage.

It's almost impossible for any fair-minded person to comprehend what happened next, or rather what didn't happen. Without the death of Nathaniel, Dr Duffy would not have become suspicious about Marcella's death. Two things had made her think Nathaniel Hines hadn't died naturally: subdural bleeding and swollen brain tissue. Once Dr Meredew had explained that both could result from a naturally occurring virus, why wasn't that the end of the murder trial? Why didn't the prosecution realise their case had fallen apart? Why didn't Justice Elizabeth Geilow throw it out of court?

Inconceivable though it is, Russell Meredew – a man I'd trust to carry me across an enemy minefield – later confided to me that at the point when Dr Duffy told him she'd changed her mind about the cause of Marcella's death, she hadn't looked again at the file. 'She can't have reviewed the details – she'd come to me straight from Nathaniel's post-mortem. It's hard not to conclude that she suspected foul play in the case of Nathaniel, and decided that meant Marcella couldn't have died naturally.' Meredew added that he didn't doubt that Dr Duffy had at some point dug out Marcella's file and had another look at it, but, as he brilliantly put it, 'If you go searching for flying pigs and there's a pale pink sky, what conclusion are you going to draw: a beautiful sunset or flying pigs as far as the eye can see?'

The jury, of course, would have been familiar with Dr Duffy's name. She was the expert who, at Helen Yardley's trial for the murder of her two sons in 1996, said that for crib death to strike the same family twice was 'so unlikely it borders on impossible' – a memorable sound-bite indeed. I believe Ray Hines' jury remembered it, and thought that it meant Ray couldn't be innocent of murder, just as eleven out of twelve jurors in 1996 had concluded it meant Helen Yardley was guilty.

Russell Meredew did his best to save Ray. He called Dr Duffy's assertion that Marcella Hines was smothered and Nathaniel shaken to death 'a nonsense', explaining that smothering is 'covert homicide', whereas shaking is usually linked to losing one's temper. Smotherers are devious but controlled, so it's unlikely that any mother would smother one baby then shake the next, even assuming she were murderously inclined.

The court heard that there was an extended family history of similar tragedies in Angus Hines' family. Angus's nephew was stillborn, and his grandmother lost a baby to SIDS. His mother suffers from a disease called Lupus, where the body eats itself from within. Asked to explain what all this meant, Dr Meredew was unambiguous: 'It's highly probable that the defendant's husband's family contains a genetic auto-immune disorder. That would explain the stillbirth, the SUDIs (sudden unexpected death in infancy), Lupus – all things you'd expect if there was an auto-immune malfunction.'

Was the jury listening? Or were they all thinking about 'so unlikely it borders on impossible'? Did they take against Ray because she wasn't a good witness? She contradicted herself several times, denied things she'd previously said to the police, and was accused by the prosecution of lying.

What no one knew was that Ray's lawyers had advised her to lie. She was betrayed by the very people whose job it was to protect her. Her defence team decided that the true story of why she left Angus and Marcella alone for nine days, and the smoking on the window ledge episode, would make her appear unsympathetic to the jury; they would think she was a feminist agitator. Instead, Ray was encouraged to pretend that she had been suffering from post-natal depression, didn't know why she'd left or where she'd gone when she was away, didn't know why she'd come back, had no memory of climbing out on to the window ledge. Not only was it illegal and immoral for Ray's lawyers to give her this advice (unsurprisingly, they now deny they did so), it was also a fatal miscalculation.

Ray was found guilty of two counts of murder and sentenced to life in prison. Her lawyers sought leave to appeal, citing Russell Meredew's claim that Dr Duffy couldn't have looked again at Marcella's medical notes at the point at which she'd told him she'd changed her mind and now suspected Marcella was murdered. But this was impossible to prove. It was Dr Meredew's word against Dr Duffy's. Leave to appeal was denied.

Then, in June 2004, two months after Ray was convicted, there was a breakthrough: a volunteer working for the organisation Helen Yardley and I set up together, JIPAC (Justice for Innocent Parents and Carers), spoke to somebody who worked with Dr Duffy – let's call him Dr Anonymous. He produced a copy of an email Dr Duffy had sent him in which she lamented her own idiocy in having allowed her arm to be twisted over Marcella Hines' post-mortem. Desmond Dearden, the coroner on whose desk Marcella's file landed, knew Angus Hines personally, and told Duffy they were a nice family. Astonishingly, he seems to have semi-blackmailed her into ignoring her suspicions and recording instead that Marcella Hines had died of natural causes. Here is an extract from Duffy's email to Dr Anonymous:

> Why did I imagine even for a minute that Desmond knowing the family was any sort of guarantee? Why didn't I take umbrage at his not-so-subtle implication that if I didn't toe the line on this one then he wouldn't send any more coroner cases my way? The truth is, I wasn't sure about Marcella Hines. I was suspicious – aren't I always? – but I wasn't sure, as I have been in other cases – Helen Yardley, for example. I think I wanted to prove to myself that I'm not the terrible monster Laurie Nattrass thinks I am, and that, in a situation where I could think either the best or the worst of somebody, I'm capable of thinking the best. I know it sounds lame, but that's what must have been going on in my mind. And, yes, I'll admit it, I hated the thought of no more coroner cases coming my way. And now look what's happened! Another Hines baby is dead, and I'm under oath being asked why I 'changed my mind' about Marcella Hines' entirely natural death. If I could turn back the clock and give the cause of death as unascertained . . . but there's no point wishing, is there?

What happened next? Well, yours truly forwarded the email to Ray Hines' defence team, who forwarded it to the Criminal Cases Review Commission. Incredibly, leave to appeal was once again denied. The CCRC should have focused on Dr Duffy's lack of professional integrity and what that meant for a case in which she and her coterie, the hawks of child protection, were the only witnesses for the prosecution. Instead, they took in only that Duffy had harboured suspicions about Marcella Hines' death for longer than she had at first disclosed. Perhaps they imagined that this fact imbued those suspicions with greater validity. JIPAC has demanded to know why, as soon as this email came to light, Judith Duffy wasn't sacked and struck off, but so far we have received no satisfactory answer. Likewise, we have made enquiries as to why a coroner as corrupt as Desmond Dearden is still in post. The response is a deafening silence.

Hope finally came for Ray Hines when there was a breakthrough in Helen Yardley's case. A document came to light, courtesy of another Dr Anonymous, in which Dr Duffy consistently referred to Helen Yardley's son Rowan as 'she'. That's right: the expert who was so sure Rowan was murdered didn't even know what sex he was.

Next, the pathologist who had performed the post-mortem on Rowan Yardley came forward. After Rowan's death, she had contacted several people she regarded as expert and asked their opinion about the high level of salt she'd found in Rowan's blood. Judith Duffy, not knowing at that point that Rowan's brother Morgan had died, also with high blood-salt, three years previously, sent a reply in which she said that, 'the instability of blood chemistry after death renders it diagnostically immaterial. Dehydration is the most usual cause of high serum sodium'. Dr Duffy concluded by saying, 'Unless you're looking for a specific poison, blood results cannot and should not be relied upon.' A mere eighteen months later, Duffy had forgotten that this was ever her view, and testified in court that Helen Yardley's sons had died of deliberate salt poisoning. She presented Morgan and Rowan's high blood-salt levels as all the proof of murder that anyone could need.

The CCRC finally saw sense. Helen Yardley was granted leave to appeal. A year later, so was Ray Hines. Some unkind personage must have leaked information to the press, because various accounts of Judith Duffy's disgraceful behaviour appeared in national newspapers, and public opinion started to turn against the woman who was once lauded as a champion of children everywhere. Suddenly, Helen Yardley, JIPAC and I were no longer the only voices calling for Duffy to be stopped.

In February 2005, Helen Yardley's murder convictions were quashed. This evidently gave Dr Duffy no pause for thought, for in July 2005 she was back in the witness box testifying against Sarah Jaggard, the latest innocent woman on trial for killing a child – Bea Furniss, the daughter of a friend of hers. Thankfully, the jury saw sense and unanimously acquitted Sarah. They listened to Bea's grief-stricken parents, who were adamant that Sarah had adored Bea and would never have harmed her.

Did Dr Duffy listen? Had she listened when Paul Yardley and Glen Jaggard – two of the most solid, reliable men I've ever met – said over and over that their wives would never harm or kill a child? Did she listen to the scores of parents who had entrusted their sons and daughters to Helen Yardley's care, who said that Helen was incapable of violence or cruelty, that they would happily use her as a childminder in the future? Did Dr Duffy hear Sarah Jaggard's parents, two mild-mannered retired school teachers, or her sister – a midwife, no less – say that Sarah was loving and caring, that there was no way she would ever lose her temper and shake a defenceless baby?

The sad truth is that Dr Duffy listened to none of the real experts, none of the people who knew Helen or Sarah personally. Hers was the only opinion that mattered, and she would have stopped at nothing in her attempts to ruin the lives of innocent women, using her status as expert in the criminal and family courts to wreak further destruction on already ravaged families. Paige Yardley, the child Helen conceived and gave birth to while at home on bail awaiting trial, was forcibly taken from her birth family on the say-so of guess who? Dr Duffy told the court that Paige was 'at grievous risk of harm' and ought to be removed from her home 'without delay'.

Now Duffy's career and reputation lie in tatters, and not a moment too soon. It beggars belief that she was involved in the care arrangements for Paige Yardley when it was known she would appear for the prosecution at Helen's trial. It defies common sense, not to mention common decency, that she was allowed to give evidence as an expert witness at Sarah Jaggard's trial. Helen Yardley had been free for five months at that point, and the extent of Duffy's misconduct in connection with her case was well known. What better things had the GMC to do than take action against her, and why did it take them so long?

How time must have dragged for Ray Hines, who was not freed until December 2008. Unlike Helen Yardley and Sarah Jaggard, who had plentiful support from family and friends, Ray had been disowned and divorced by her husband Angus when she was found guilty. She had been reviled in the press as a 'drug addict', after Angus told a reporter she was a regular marijuana smoker. In fact, she only used the drug occasionally, when the bad back from which she has suffered all her life caused her so much agony that she'd have tried anything. She is as far from the stereotype of a grubby, sofa-surfing junkie as it's possible to be. She is a proud, spiky woman who holds her head high and refuses to cry for the cameras. She admitted in court that she can't think straight unless her home is tidy and that she believes it's bad for women to give up their careers and stay at home with their children. How Judith Duffy must have hooted with glee when she saw how easy it would be to take this remarkable woman and turn her into a murderous she-devil.

Even now, with Ray Hines free and Judith Duffy deservedly disgraced, JIPAC's work is far from done. 62-year-old Dorne Llewellyn of Port Talbot in South Wales is just one of the many women still behind bars for a crime she didn't commit: the murder, in 2000, of nine-month-old Benjamin Evans. Dr Duffy testified that Mrs Llewellyn must have shaken Benjamin, causing the brain haemorrhage that killed him, but couldn't answer when counsel for the defence asked how sure she was that the shaking episode, assuming there was one, had taken place while Benjamin was in Dorne Llewellyn's care. Interestingly, one of Dr Duffy's staunchest supporters is Benjamin's single mother, Rhiannon Evans, who was 15 when Benjamin was born. Now 23, she is a prostitute and well known to local police.

The case is currently under review by the CCRC. JIPAC is praying for a speedy and successful appeal. The only evidence against Mrs Llewellyn is the opinion of a doctor who's been struck off for misconduct, so how could any appeal judge uphold her conviction? Surely for our country's esteemed judicial system to make another heinous mistake in a child death case, having already made so many, is, to quote Dr Duffy, 'so unlikely it borders on impossible'?

7

Thursday 8 October 2009

I'm sitting at Laurie's desk making a list when the phone rings. Since talking to Maya, I've done more background reading than I'd have thought possible in such a short time, and made so many phone calls that my right ear feels as if it's on fire. I have appointments to see Paul Yardley, Sarah and Glen Jaggard, and most of the lawyers and doctors I've been reading about. I smile at my list of ticked names, ignoring the cross next to Judith Duffy's that spoils the display, and pick up the phone.

'What are you playing at?' Laurie demands.

'Where have you been? I've left hundreds of messages.'

'I'm not going to let you make a mockery of everything I've worked for.' He mumbles something I can't make out. It sounds insulting. How many insults can you pack into three seconds' worth of mumble? Maybe two if you're a nobody, but at least twenty if you're the great Laurie Nattrass. 'I'm not doing this over the phone,' he says. 'You'd better come round.'

'To your house?' A townhouse in Kensington: that's all I know. I'm ashamed to feel my eyes filling with tears. How can he be so angry with me? What have I done? 'I don't know where you live,' I say.

'If that's your idea of an insurmountable obstacle ...' There's a click, then he's gone.

I refuse to cry, so I practise blinking for a while, then ring Tamsin and ask for Laurie's address. She recites it from memory. 'Have you been summoned?' she asks, from which I infer that I might not be the first person this has happened to.

Why do I love Laurie so much, when he treats me like a servant? Why do I think he's gorgeous when he's at least a stone overweight, his eyes are always bloodshot and his skin looks as if it hasn't seen sunlight for years? I put this question to Tamsin.

'Aha!' she says. 'So you admit it: you love him.'

'Isn't admitting it supposed to be the first step towards recovery?'

'Ha! I *knew* it!'

'Is being jeered at by your friends the second step?'

'You love him for the same reason everyone loves him: he's a mystery. You don't know what he is, and can't see any way to find out. That's kind of addictive, until you realise you'll never get the satisfaction you crave.'

If Tamsin knew the truth about me, would she change her mind about why I love Laurie? Would she say I'm deluding myself that by getting close to him, I can shake off the taint I've been carrying around with me? By loving the man who helped to free Helen Yardley and Rachel Hines, I can maybe . . .

Except I can't, not if he doesn't love me back. The more he treats me like his worthless skivvy, the more tainted I feel. What am I doing kidding myself that I can make Laurie's film, that I'll do such a brilliant job that he'll respect me and love me and I'll finally be able to move beyond the shame? I'll end up making something pallid and average because I feel guilty, then hiding its existence from my mum when it's broadcast, so that she won't be devastated.

Whatever I do, whether I make the film or not, I'm going to feel horribly guilty. That doesn't seem fair.

'I read Laurie's "Doctor Who Lied" rant,' I tell Tamsin.

'Fantastic, isn't it?' she says. 'If ever an article's going to make the entire legal system hang its head in shame, it's that one.'

'I thought it veered between pathetic and downright offensive.'

'Yeah.' She sniggers. 'Course you did.'

'I *did*,' I insist. It's true, isn't it? So why do I feel as petty as a jilted girlfriend sewing prawns into the linings of her ex's curtains?

I get rid of my helpful and not at all annoying friend, and leave the office, armed with Laurie's address. I stop the first taxi I see, praying the driver will be shy, unfriendly or a Trappist monk. My wish is not granted. I get a twenty-five minute lecture about the West being in decline because it doesn't produce anything any more, and a prediction that soon we Westerners will all be slaving away for a pittance on Korean assembly lines. I restrain myself from asking if, in exchange, a Korean person will come over here and be made to feel like shit by Laurie Nattrass.

How can he disapprove of what I'm doing? I haven't done anything yet, apart from contact the people whose names are in the files *he* left for me.

Laurie's house is one of a row of immaculate white stucco villas on a quiet, tree-lined street. The front door, glossy black-painted wood with two stained-glass panels, stands open. As with most things about Laurie, I have difficulty interpreting this. Does he want me to go straight in, or is he too busy and important to bother with mundane tasks like shutting doors properly?

I ring the bell and shout hello simultaneously. When nothing happens, I take a tentative step inside. 'Laurie?' I call out. In the hall there's a bike leaning against the wall, a grey and black canvas rucksack, a briefcase, a jacket scrunched up on the floor, a pair of black shoes. Above the radiator, four shelves run the length of one wall, housing a collection of neatly folded newspapers. Opposite these are two large framed photographs, both of what looks like an Oxbridge college. Where did Laurie go to university? Tamsin would know.

Between the two photos is a small square sticker that totally ruins the effect: a circle of gold stars against a navy background with a thick black line running diagonally through it. There's another sticker on a grandfather clock at the far end of the hall, stuck to the wood: 'Say No to the Euro'. It offends me, not because I give a toss about the euro one way or the other, but because the clock looks old and valuable, and shouldn't be used as a fly-posting site. It stands slightly wonky, as if it's too tired to straighten up.

The white-painted wooden steps directly in front of me are heaped with books and papers. Every step has a pile of something on one side, though not the same side in each case: anyone who wanted to go upstairs would have to zig-zag. I see JIPAC-headed paper, and several copies of *Nothing But Love*: one hardback and two paperbacks. I bet Helen Yardley didn't write any of it herself.

If I wrote a book, would Laurie read it?

I am not jealous of Helen Yardley. Helen Yardley lost all three of her children. Helen Yardley was murdered three days ago.

I pick up the hardback of *Nothing But Love* and turn it over. On the back cover, there's a photograph of Helen with her co-author, Gaynor Mundy. They've got their arms round each other to suggest deep friendship as well as a close professional relationship. Bound to have been the photographer's idea, I think cynically – the two women probably loathed each other.

I'm about to put the book down when I notice Helen Yardley's hand, draped over Gaynor Mundy's shoulder, and my mouth turns dry. Those fingers, the nails . . .

I drop the book and root in my handbag for the cream envelope. I try to feel pleased that I didn't bin it, but part of me wishes I had. If I'm right, I don't want to think about what it might mean.

Pulling out the photograph, I compare the fingers gripping the card in the picture to Helen Yardley's fingers on the cover of her book. They're the same: small square nails, neatly cut. Without stopping to think, I tear the photo and the envelope it came in into little pieces and drop them into my open bag like a handful of confetti. I notice that I'm shaking.

For God's sake, this is ridiculous. How many people must there be who have well-trimmed squarish fingernails? Millions. There is absolutely no reason to assume Helen Yardley is the person in the photograph I was sent, holding the card with the sixteen numbers on it – no reason whatsoever. There's no reason to think that because she was murdered . . .

I shiver, and force my attention away from my silly morbid fears. 'Laurie, are you there?' I call up the stairs.

Still no reply. I look in both downstairs rooms: a wet-room twice the size of my kitchen that contains a shower, basin, loo and more small square black tiles than I think I've ever seen before in my life, and a huge L-shaped kitchen-dining-lounging space; from its elegant finish in several different shades of nut and earth – brown and beige for posh people – I guess that it would prefer to be described as a space than a room. It looks as if it recently contained a party of eighteen who panicked mid-way through a slap-up meal and did a runner. Was Laurie one of them? How many of the twelve empty wine bottles did he drink, and who helped him? Did he host some kind of JIPAC shindig here last night?

I swan-neck my way up the stairs to the first floor, treading carefully, aware that one misplaced step could provoke a paper-quake and do irreparable damage to Laurie's filing system. I spot an envelope addressed to Mr L. H. S. F. Nattrass and a cardboard Nike shoebox with the word 'Accounts' scrawled on it in green-marker pen. L.H.S.F.: that's three middle names he's got, as well as all his awards, money and the world's admiration. I've only got one middle name and it's a terrible one: Margot. If I weren't so tired of psychoanalysing my romantic impulses, I'd wonder if my love for Laurie might be misinterpreted jealousy. Do I want to be his girlfriend, or do I wish, deep down, that I was him?

I come to a landing and a choice of four doors, one of which is ajar. As I move towards it, I see shapes in the gloom: the end of a bed and the lower part of a pair of legs. 'Laurie?'

I push open the door and there he is: Mr L. H. S. F. Nattrass, in a crumpled grey suit. The curtains are closed. Laurie's sprawled on a double bed that I assume is his, staring at a small TV on a chair in the corner of the room – an ancient one, by the look of it. There's a metal aerial balanced precariously on top that's almost as big as the TV itself. On the screen, a woman is crying in a man's arms, but there's no volume. Laurie stares at them as they mouth words at one another.

Can he tell what they're saying? Does he care? A purple silk tie lies on the duvet beside him.

I turn on the light, but he still doesn't look at me, so I decide I won't look at him either. Instead, I take the opportunity to have a good nosey at his room, something I never thought I'd get to do. It's disappointingly similar to his office. *My office.* There are framed posters of constellations and planets on the walls, two globes, a telescope lying beside its case, a pair of binoculars, some weights, an exercise bike, three books: *The Nazi Doctors*, *Knowledge in a Social World* and *Into That Silent Sea: Trailblazers of the Space Era, 1961–1965*. Wow, they sound like fun bedtime reading.

Poking out from under the bed is a dustpan and brush with a packet of disposable razors and a canister of shaving gel in the pan, as if they've been swept up off the carpet. Coins – silver, copper and gold – are scattered everywhere: on the bed, on the floor, on top of a chest of drawers. It makes me think of the bottom of a wishing well.

'What do the H, S and F stand for?' *Laurie Horrible Selfish Fucker Nattrass.*

'Hugo St John Fleet,' he says, as if these are perfectly normal names to have. No wonder he's a nutter.

'I love black and white films.' I nod at the screen.

'What about technicolour sentimental crap on a black and white TV – do you love that?'

'Why are you angry with me?'

'You leave a message for me saying you're trying to set up an interview with Judith Duffy and you need to ask why I'm angry?'

'I've set up interviews with lots of people,' I tell him. 'Judith Duffy's the one person so far who's refused to—'

'Judith Duffy ruins lives! Turn off that drivel, for fuck's sake.'

Is he talking about *his* television, that *he* switched on when I wasn't even here?

'I'm not your servant, Laurie.' With feeling, I add, 'And I don't love black and white films – I only said it because it's . . . well, it's so hard to talk to you, and I have to say something. Come to think of it, people who bang on about how they love black and white movies really annoy me. It's blatant film racism. A film can be good or bad whatever its . . . colour scheme.'

Laurie examines me through narrowed eyes. 'Ring your GP. Tell him the anti-psychotics aren't working.'

'Who's Wendy Whitehead?'

'*Who?*'

'Wendy Whitehead.'

'Never heard of her. Who is she?'

'If I knew, I wouldn't need to ask you, would I?' I make a show of looking at my watch. 'I've got things to do. Was there something you wanted to say to me?'

Laurie hauls himself off the bed, looks me up and down, then turns to pick up his tie. He drapes it round his neck and, holding it at both ends, pulls it back and forth so that it scratches against his shirt. 'Judith Duffy'd cut off her own legs sooner than talk to anyone from Binary Star,' he says.

'I thought of that. I didn't tell her where I worked, just my name.'

'Are you waiting for me to pat you on the head and tell you how clever you are?' he sneers. I'm glad he's being so rude and offensive; it's the best thing that could have happened. As of this moment, I officially don't love him any more. That deluded phase of my life is so over. 'You want me to make this film, don't you?' I say icily. 'How am I supposed to do that without—'

Laurie grabs my shoulders, pulls me towards him. His mouth collides with my lips. His teeth bang against mine. *A tooth for a tooth*, I think automatically. I taste blood and try to push him away, but he's stronger than I am, and makes a cage out of his arms to trap me. It takes me a few seconds to realise that what he thinks he's doing is kissing me.

I have just had sex with Laurie Nattrass. Laurie Nattrass just had sex with me. Oh, my God, oh, my God, oh, my God. Proper, complete sex, not the silly Bill Clinton kind. Or rather, not only the silly Bill Clinton kind. Which, of course, isn't at all silly as long as no one suggests it's an end in itself. Bad choice of words. What I mean is, it's no substitute for the real thing, the thing that Laurie and I just . . . oh, my God.

It can't be true. It is true. It only doesn't seem true because he's now acting as if it didn't happen. He's staring at the TV screen and doing that thing with his tie round his neck again, as if his hands are having a tug of war. Would he notice if I discreetly reached for my bag, pulled out my phone and rang Tamsin? I could do with talking to someone impartial. Not about the sex itself – that would be crude, and I'd be too embarrassed to use any anatomical words – but about the weirdness that started when the sex finished. That's the part I'd really like to put under the microscope of gossipy analysis: the way Laurie managed to have all his clothes back on within three seconds, and what he said as he sat back down on the bed beside me, seeming not to notice that I was still naked: 'Stupid mistake. My fault.' At first I thought he was talking about us, but then he said, 'Her phone number was in the files I gave you. I should have taken it out. Thought you'd have more sense than to ring her, though.'

Can it have happened the way I remember it? Surely there was an organic, transitional phase I failed to notice, some word or gesture on his part that bridged the gap between intimacy and discussion of the film. I wish I could check with Laurie that until a few minutes ago he was lying on top of me, but I'm getting the strong sense that he's moved on and wouldn't welcome a recap. Besides, how would I put it: 'Could you be so good as to confirm the following details?' Ridiculous. Obviously.

I don't need to check anything with anyone, for God's sake. I was here, wasn't I? The trouble is, it's too recent – maybe four minutes, maximum – since we . . . er, brought things to a conclusion. I've been mulling it over and I've decided that the temporal proximity of the event doesn't mean my memory's any more likely to be accurate than if it had happened five years ago. In five years' time, I hope to be able to be clinically objective about this afternoon, so that knowing what actually happened between me and Laurie won't be a problem then as it is now.

I wish I could talk to Tamsin.

If I lie still and don't put my clothes back on, will Laurie have sex with me again?

'Duffy won't ring you back,' he says. 'She'll assume you're an enemy. By now she thinks everyone's an enemy.' He seems pleased about this, as if it's what she deserves. I'm not convinced it does the world any good for any person to have only enemies, not to mention the individual involved, no matter what they've done, but I say nothing. 'Every detail of her personal and professional life has been judged by the tabloids and been found wanting,' says Laurie with relish. 'From her neglect of her own children when they were small in favour of her career, to the beefed-up qualifications on her first ever CV, to the two marriages she sabotaged by being a workaholic. By now the whole world knows what a bitch she is, and she knows it.'

'Mm-hmm,' I say brightly, this being the best I can do in the circumstances. As subtly as possible, I shuffle to the edge of the bed and pull on my knickers, bra, shirt and trousers. I can see my bag. It's not fully zipped up; I can see the edge of my phone poking out. Oh, what the hell. If Laurie can stare at the TV, mess about with his tie and talk about work . . .

I reach for my phone and switch it on. The message icon flashes on the screen, but I'm not interested in what anyone might have to say to me, only in the earth-shattering news I have to impart. I send Tamsin a text saying, 'Laurie pounced on me. We had sex. Immediately after, he dressed, acted like nothing had happened and started talking about Judith Duffy. Good sign that he can be himself around me instead of putting on false romantic act?' I sign off with an F and two kisses, and send it. Then I turn my phone off again. Just because I was desperate to tell Tamsin doesn't mean I'm ready to deal with her reaction. I smile to myself. By deliberately including in the text a question that only a self-deceiving lovestruck fool would ask, I have inoculated myself against becoming that self-deceiving lovestruck fool. Tamsin will realise I was sending up the sort of girly women we hate, who never swear or burp in public and are much less canny than we are.

'I read the article you wrote,' I tell Laurie. '"The Doctor Who Lied".'

There, see? Sex, love – they're just bodily functions as far as I'm concerned. I've forgotten all about both, in fact. They're trivialities, to be squeezed into the gaps between making brilliant, award-winning documentaries.

'Best thing I've ever written,' Laurie says.

'What? Oh, right: the article.' It's hard to concentrate when every inch of your skin is fizzing, and you feel as if you're lurching through space, high above the real world and the ordinary mortals who inhabit it. *Concentrate, Fliss. Be a grown-up*. 'I'm not sure you should publish it in its present form,' I say.

Laurie laughs. 'Thank you, Leo Tolstoy.'

'Seriously. At the moment it comes across as . . . well, biased. And nasty. As if you enjoy sticking the knife in. Doesn't that kind of . . . I don't know, weaken you? Undermine your argument? You present Judith Duffy as a hundred per cent evil and everyone who takes a stand against her as flawless: brilliant, trustworthy, heroic. I lost count of the enthusiastic adjectives you used to describe the people who agree with you. You talk about Dr Russell Meredew as if he's the second coming. It makes the whole thing sound too much like a fairy story, with handsome princes and boo-hiss villains. Wouldn't it be better to present the facts and let them speak for themselves?'

'Tell me you're not going to interview Judith Duffy,' Laurie barks at me.

I can't, so I carry on with my lecture. 'You say the friends and family of Helen Yardley and Sarah Jaggard are the "real experts", the people who actually knew them. You imply Judith Duffy ought to have taken notice when they said the women were innocent . . .'

'I more than *imply* it.'

'But that's crazy,' I say. 'No one wants to think that someone they love might be a killer. It reflects badly on them, doesn't it? Their choice of best friend, or partner, or childminder. Surely their opinions are the least objective and reliable? And you can't have it both ways. If the nearest and dearest are the real experts, what about Angus Hines? He thought Ray was guilty, but you didn't let that sway you any more than Judith Duffy let Paul Yardley or Glen Jaggard's views sway her.'

Laurie stands up. 'Anything else, before you leave?'

He's kicking me out for having the wrong opinion. Or maybe he would have kicked me out anyway.

'Yes,' I say, determined to show I'm not intimidated by him. For an insane second, I consider telling him I'm speaking from personal experience, the worst experience of my life. No one can be objective about the culpability of a loved one. It's simply not possible. I have days when I think my dad must have been corrupt through and through – evil, almost – and days when I think he deserves no blame at all, and miss him so much I feel I might as well be dead too.

'I didn't like the bit in the article about Benjamin Evans' mum being a single mother and a prostitute,' I say eventually. 'You seemed to be suggesting that those two things made her more likely than Dorne Llewellyn to have shaken—'

'You read an out of date version,' Laurie cuts me off. 'Editor of the *British Journalism Review* agreed with you, so I took that bit out. I'll email you a copy of the sanitised version, in which I don't mention that Rhiannon Evans is a hooker who sings Judith Duffy's praises at every available opportunity and is keen for Dorne Llewellyn to stay in prison for the rest of her life.'

'Don't be angry with me, Laurie.'

He snorts dismissively. 'Do you know how easily your job could disappear? Carry on pursuing Judith Duffy and that's what'll happen. If you think I'm going to stand by and let you and her use my film as a vehicle for airing her distorted—'

'I'm not going to do anything like that,' I yell at him. 'I want to talk to her, that's all. I'm not saying you're wrong about her. She's the bad guy – fair enough. But I need to know what sort of bad guy she is if I'm making a documentary about the damage she's done. Is she well intentioned but prejudiced? Stupid? Is she an out-and-out liar?'

'Yes! Yes, she's an out-and-out fucking liar who destroys people. Will you stay away from her? This is the last time I'm going to ask you.'

Is he really so intolerant that he wants no point of view heard but his own? Is he worried about me? If so, might that mean he loves me?

Felicity Benson, how can you not despise yourself?

I didn't mean it. I've got a whole self-mockery thing going on here that's way more sophisticated than unrequited love.

I'd give anything to be able to tell Laurie what he wants to hear so that we could both be happy, but I can't bring myself to be a compliant idiot simply because it would please him. If I'm making this film, and it seems I am, I want to do it in the way I think it should be done.

'I've just worked it out,' I say. 'Why I love you. It's because we've got so much in common. We both treat me as if I don't matter, as if I'm nothing.' Not any more, I vow. From now on, I'm not nothing.

'*Love?*' says Laurie, in the way a normal, civilised person might say 'Genocide?' or 'Necrophilia?': shocked and appalled.

I pick up my bag and leave without another word.

Outside, I hail a taxi and take a while to remember my own address. Once I'm moving, and breathing again, I switch on my phone and see that I have two new messages. The first is a text from Tamsin. 'You big, big, big, BIG eejit!' it says. The second is a voicemail message from a Detective Constable Simon Waterhouse.

8

8/10/09

Sam Kombothekra didn't like the way Grace and Sebastian Brownlee were holding hands. It wasn't suggestive of tenderness, but rather of taking a defiant stand against the enemy. They looked like two people about to charge into battle together.

'Gunpowder residue,' said Grace, her voice full of disbelief. Sam would have bet good money on this being the first time the phrase had been uttered beneath these high corniced ceilings. The Brownlees evidently believed that a period house ought to be filled with period furniture, and the sort of tastefully patterned wallpaper a bona fide Georgian might have chosen, as if the present era could be banished if one tried hard enough.

Paige Yardley's adoptive mother was a small slender woman with mid-brown hair cut in a neat bob. Her husband was tall and balding on top, with wild gingery-blond tufts above his ears that suggested he was unwilling to lose any more hair than he absolutely had to. He and his wife worked for the same law firm in Rawndesley, which was how they'd met, they'd told Sam. Sebastian Brownlee had mentioned twice so far that he'd had to finish work three hours earlier than he normally would in order to get home for this meeting. Both he and Grace were still wearing their work suits.

'You're not suspected of anything,' Sam reassured Grace. 'It's routine. We're asking everyone who knew Helen Yardley.'

'We didn't know her,' said Sebastian. 'We never met the woman.'

'I realise that, sir. Nevertheless, you and your wife are in a unique position in relation to her.'

'We consent,' said Grace in a clipped voice. 'Take your swabs, do whatever you need to, and get it over with. I'd rather not see you here again.' An odd way to put it, Sam thought. As if she might come down to breakfast one morning and find him sitting at her kitchen table. Come to think of it, the Brownlees seemed the type who might insist on taking all their meals in a formal dining room.

Sam had no reason to suspect them of anything. They had given him a full account of their movements on Monday. Together with their thirteen-year-old daughter, Hannah – the girl Sam couldn't help thinking of as Paige Yardley – they had left the house at 7 a.m. At 7.10, they had dropped Hannah off at the home of her best friend, whose mother gave the two girls breakfast and drove them to school on weekday mornings. Sebastian and Grace had then driven straight to their firm's office in Rawndesley, arriving there as always at about 7.50. After that, Sebastian had either been in the office or out at meetings with clients for the rest of the day. 'You're in luck,' he'd told Sam. 'Fee-earning solicitors like us have to make a note of how we spend every minute of our time, so that the right people can be billed.' He'd promised Sam copies of his and Grace's time-sheets for Monday, and contact numbers for all the people in whose company they had spent any of those individually itemised minutes.

Grace, who worked part time, had left the office at 2.30 p.m. and gone to pick up Hannah and her best friend from school, as she did every weekday. She and the two girls had then gone swimming at the private health club, Waterfront, to which both the Brownlees and the friend's family belonged. Grace had been able to give Sam the names and numbers of several acquaintances of hers who had seen her either in the swimming area or having a drink and a snack in Chompers café-bar with the girls afterwards. After leaving Waterfront, Grace drove Hannah's friend home, and she and Hannah got back to their house at 6.15 p.m. Sebastian Brownlee arrived home at 10, having eaten dinner with clients in Rawndesley.

Sam was certain everything the couple had told him would hold up. What was bothering him, then, if it wasn't that he thought they were lying? 'What time will Hannah be back?' he asked. There were framed photographs of her all over the living room wall. In Sam's experience, this many pictures of the same person in one room and no pictures of anyone or anything else could mean one of two things: a stalker with a dangerous obsession, or an adoring parent. *Or two adoring parents.*

Hannah Brownlee had glossy centre-parted brown hair, wide grey eyes and a small nose. She had Helen Yardley's face, only a younger version.

'You're not swabbing my daughter for gunpowder residue,' said Grace Brownlee angrily.

'That wasn't what I—' Sam began.

'I took her to my mother's house because I knew you were coming. I didn't want her involved. Tell him, Sebastian,' she snapped. 'Let's not prolong the agony.'

'Hannah knows a local woman was murdered. People have been talking about it at school and it's been on the news, we could hardly keep it from her, but . . .' Sebastian glanced at his wife. She responded with a look that made it clear she wasn't going to help him out, so he turned back to Sam. 'Hannah has no idea Helen Yardley was her birth mother.'

'I've always been in favour of telling her,' Grace blurted out. 'I was overruled.'

'I wanted my daughter to have a regular, carefree childhood,' Sebastian explained. 'Not to grow up knowing she was the child of a murderer, someone who'd smothered two of her babies and would almost certainly have done the same to Hannah if Social Services hadn't stepped in. What father would place a burden like that on his daughter's shoulders, to be carried for *life*?' He aimed this last word at Grace.

'I take it you think Helen Yardley was guilty, then.' Nothing depressed Sam more than bigotry. What made Sebastian Brownlee so sure he knew better than three court of appeal judges?

'We know she was guilty,' said Grace. 'And I agree with everything Seb's just said, except there's something he always fails to take into consideration.'

Sam wondered if it was therapeutic for the Brownlees to conduct this argument in front of him, a stranger. 'What's that?' he asked.

'A significant number of adopted children reach an age when it starts to matter to them to know where and who they come from. If I could guarantee Hannah would never be one of them, of course I wouldn't be in favour of telling her, but there are no such guarantees in this world. I wish her birth mother had been anyone but Helen Yardley – *anyone*. If I could, I'd bury my head, and Hannah's, deep in the sand and forget all about the truth, but I can't, or at least I can't be one hundred per cent certain that I'd get away with it, not for ever. If Hannah finds out when she's older, the shock'll be devastating. Whereas if we'd told her as soon as she was old enough to understand, if we even told her now . . .' Grace shot a pleading look at her husband.

'How old is old enough to understand that your natural mother wanted to kill you?' said Sebastian angrily. 'That she *did* kill your two brothers?'

'What have you told Hannah, then?' Sam asked. 'About her birth parents.'

'Nothing,' said Grace. 'We told her *we* knew nothing, that we asked the social workers not to tell us. She knows she was adopted, but that's all.'

If Simon Waterhouse were here, would he be thinking that, since Hannah was absent, it was impossible to verify what she did or didn't know? What if she knew she was Helen Yardley's daughter, and Grace and Sebastian were lying because . . .

No. Impossible. Thirteen-year-old girls from Spilling didn't tool up with M9 Berettas and murder their mothers. Sam made a mental note to check that Hannah had been at school all day on Monday. 'What makes you so sure Helen Yardley was guilty?' he asked Grace.

Sebastian Brownlee touched his wife's arm: a sign that she shouldn't answer. 'We're busy people, Sergeant – as, I'm sure, are you,' he said. 'We'd like to go and collect our daughter, and you're not here to debate Helen Yardley's guilt. Shall we get on with what needs to be done?'

'I'd like an answer to my question,' said Sam. His throat was dry. The Brownlees hadn't offered him a drink.

Sebastian sighed heavily. 'How do we know she's guilty? All right, let's start with baby Morgan, the first son she murdered.

Leaving aside the massive amounts of haemosiderin found in his lungs, all of different ages – not just one bleed, in other words, but several distinct bleeds, a clear indicator of repeated smotherings – leaving that aside, and the fact that four medical experts who testified for the prosecution said there was no way that much haemosiderin would be present if the death was natural, there was also the small matter of Morgan's serum sodium level, which was about five times what you'd expect for a child his age—'

'The level of salt in his blood,' Grace cut in with the explanation Sam needed. 'She used salt to poison him.'

Salt poisoning *and* smothering? Sam didn't believe Helen Yardley had deliberately harmed either of her sons, but even if she had, why would she simultaneously try to kill them in two different ways? In the interests of fairness, he had to admit you could easily turn that around: if you really want to hurt someone, maybe you attack them in any and every way you can think of.

'Morgan had been rushed to hospital more than once in his short life because he'd stopped breathing. Funny that, isn't it?' Sebastian Brownlee demanded. 'A perfectly healthy baby just stops breathing – how convenient. Each time he decided to perform his stopping-breathing-for-no-reason trick, it was the same time of day – between five and six in the evening, at the end of a long day of his mother being at home alone with him while his father was at work. You tell me why a baby would stop breathing, over and over again, at the same time of day.'

'Don't shout at him,' said Grace. Sam was about to tell her it was okay, but stopped himself.

'The defence's liar-for-hire doctors said maybe he had a respiratory disorder, maybe he was dehydrated, maybe he was suffering from nephrogenic diabetes insipidus – diabetes where your salt levels are up the pole instead of your sugars. They were making it up as they went along, and the jury knew it!' Sebastian let go of his wife's hand, stood up and started to pace. 'Let's move on to Rowan, baby number two. He also had too much salt in his blood. All the doctors agreed this was what killed him – the question was: had his mother poisoned him or did he have this rare form of diabetes? Or a faulty osmostat – that's the mechanism that regulates sodium in the blood. I suppose you could say there was no way of telling for sure, but the medical experts who testified for the prosecution thought it fitting to point out that the post-mortem had turned up a skull fracture and several healing fractures, of different ages, at the ends of Rowan's long bones. Metaphyseal fractures, they're called. Ask any paediatrician, or any social worker for that matter – they're the sort of fractures you get if you take a child by the wrist or the ankle and hurl it at the wall.'

Grace Brownlee flinched.

'The skull fracture was bi-lateral – also extremely rare for a non-inflicted injury,' Sebastian continued loudly, as if he was in court rather than in his own living room, addressing a larger audience than his wife and Sam. He paced up and down, his hands stuffed in his trouser pockets. 'Most skull fractures are simple and linear, confined to only one bone in the skull. Oh, the defence's doctors had a field day! One had the nerve to say that the skull fracture couldn't have caused Rowan's death because there was no brain swelling.'

'Seb, calm down,' said Grace in a resigned voice, as if she didn't expect him to take any notice.

'It might not have killed him, but it's still a fucking skull fracture!' Having made this declaration, Sebastian sat down again, shaking his head. Was he done? Sam hoped so. His own fault for asking.

'One expert witness for the defence said the fractures could have been caused by something called Transient Osteogenesis Imperfecta, but there's no evidence that such a thing exists,' said Grace. 'OI's real enough, though rare, but Transient OI? No proof whatsoever – not so much as one recorded case. As Judith Duffy pointed out at the trial, OI has other symptoms, none of which applied to Rowan Yardley – blue sclera, wormian bones . . .'

'When Duffy said there was no such thing as Transient Osteogenesis Imperfecta, the defence QC tried to make her look arrogant by asking how she could possibly know that for sure,' Sebastian took over. 'Could she point to any research that proved OI could never take a transient form? Of course she couldn't. How do you prove that something doesn't exist?'

'I can't remember who's supposed to have said it, but it's true,' Grace muttered. '"The greatest fool can ask a question that the wisest man cannot answer."'

'The defence tried everything. They even wheeled out the old chestnut of what-if-he-fell-off-the-sofa? I'm a lawyer,' Sebastian announced, as if Sam might not already be aware of his occupation, 'and if there's one thing I know, it's this: when you're running more than one defence, it's because you know you've got no single line of defence that's going to work.'

A loud sigh from Grace made him stop and look at her. 'None of this is how *I* know Helen Yardley was guilty,' she said. 'You can argue endlessly about medical evidence, but you can't argue with an eye-witness account from someone who had no reason to lie.'

'Leah Gould,' said her husband, taking her hand again as if to thank her for reminding him. 'The contact supervisor at the care centre where the Yardleys went to visit Hannah.'

Paige, thought Sam. Not Hannah; not then.

'Leah Gould saved our daughter's life,' said Sebastian.

'Helen tried to smother Hannah in front of her,' said Grace, her eyes filling with tears. 'Pressing her face against her chest so she couldn't breathe. Two other people saw it too – Paul Yardley and a detective sergeant called, of all things, Proust – but they lied in court.'

Sam did his best not to react. The Snowman, lie under oath about having witnessed an attempted murder? No. Whatever other bad things he was capable of, he wouldn't do that. Sam knew Helen Yardley had included her version of the incident in *Nothing But Love* – Simon Waterhouse had told him. Sam needed to read the book, however much he didn't want to.

'You'd expect her husband to lie,' said Sebastian bitterly. 'For better or for worse, even if you're married to a killer, but a police officer?' He shook his head. 'Unfortunately, at the trial, DS Proust's remembrance of things past was flawed to say the least. He testified that in his opinion Leah Gould had overreacted, that all Helen did was hug Hannah tightly, as any loving mother would if she thought she might be about to be separated from her daughter for years, if not for life. Eleven out of twelve jurors ignored him. They trusted Leah Gould not to have plucked an attempted murder out of thin air.'

'Though that's exactly what she herself ended up claiming to have done,' said Grace bitterly. 'That dreadful Nattrass man made so many waves in the media that everyone, even most of the original prosecution witnesses, ended up on the side of the convicted murderer against her victims. Nattrass made sure every tabloid scumbag got his very own Judith Duffy scoop, whether it was her promiscuity as a teenager, her callous childcare arrangements as a young mother, the job she'd been fired from as a student . . .'

'It wasn't about the evidence any more,' said Sebastian, clutching his wife's hand in a way that looked to Sam as if it might be painful for her. If it was, she said nothing. 'It had become political. Helen Yardley had to get out of jail free, and quickly; she was becoming an embarrassment to the system, even though all Nattrass had in his arsenal was a case against Dr Duffy, one prosecution witness among many. All right, her behaviour was questionable, but she was only a small part of the case. Except, suddenly, she wasn't. Some of the other doctors who'd testified against Helen Yardley changed their tune – none of them wanted to become Nattrass's next victim. The prosecution team didn't push for a retrial when they could and should have. Ivor Rudgard QC will have had it spelled out for him by someone from the Lord Chancellor's office as was: drop this or you'll never make red judge. So Rudgard dropped it.'

'Next thing you know, Laurie Nattrass interviews Leah Gould in the *Observer*, and she says she's no longer sure she saw Helen Yardley try to smother her daughter by pressing her face into her jumper. She now thinks it's likely she panicked for no reason, and she deeply regrets the part she played in convicting an innocent woman.' It was clear Grace could hardly bear to utter those words in connection with Helen Yardley.

'Of course she'd say that once Helen Yardley's free and everyone's talking about witch-hunts and the persecution of grieving mothers,' said Sebastian. 'It isn't easy to be the lone voice of dissent. More than ten years after the event, you can convince yourself that things were different from how they actually were, but the fact is that when she was in that room at the contact centre, Leah Gould pulled Hannah away from Helen Yardley and she believed that, in doing so, she saved Hannah's life.'

Sam was starting to feel sorry for the Brownlees. Their obsession was weighing them down, sucking the life out of them. He suspected they went over and over the story, feeling fresh outrage each time they reached the part where Helen Yardley was freed. 'How long have you lived in this house?' he asked.

'Since 1989,' said Grace. 'Why?'

'So before you adopted Hannah.'

'I'll ask again: why?'

'The Yardleys' house is on Bengeo Street, only about five minutes from here.'

'In terms of distance, perhaps,' said Sebastian. 'In all ways that matter, Bengeo Street is worlds away.'

'When you adopted Hannah, did you know where the Yardleys lived?'

'Yes. There were . . .' Grace stopped, closed her eyes. 'There were some letters forwarded to us by social services. From Helen and Paul Yardley to Hannah. Their address was on the letters.'

Needless to say, Hannah had never clapped eyes on them.

'Did you consider moving?' Sam asked. 'Once you decided not to tell Hannah who her birth parents were, didn't you think it might be a good idea to move out of Spilling – to Rawndesley, perhaps?'

'*Rawndesley?*' Sebastian reared in horror, as if Sam had suggested he move to the Congo.

'Of course we didn't,' said Grace. 'If you lived in this house, on this street, would you ever move?' She gestured around the room.

Did she want Sam to answer honestly? Had she really said that? Staring at her, wondering how to respond, he suddenly had it. He knew why he was suspicious of the Brownlees, in spite of their solid alibis and middle-class respectability: it was something Grace had said as she'd let him in. He'd shown her his ID, explained that he was DS Sam Kombothekra from Culver Valley CID, but that there was nothing to worry about, his visit was a formality, nothing more. Grace's response had been almost exactly what you'd expect from a blameless woman. Almost, but not quite. She'd looked Sam in the eye and said, 'We did nothing wrong.'

It was dark by the time Simon got to Wolverhampton. Sarah and Glen Jaggard lived in a rented flat above a town-centre branch of Blockbusters on a busy main road. 'You can't miss it,' Glen had said. 'The sign's been vandalised and someone's scratched out the first "B", so now it's "Lockbusters". Talk about sending the wrong message,' he'd attempted a joke. 'No wonder we've been burgled twice since moving here.'

The Jaggards had been homeowners once, but had sold their house to cover Sarah's legal costs. Simon hadn't been convinced by Glen Jaggard's determined cheeriness on the phone. He detected in it the underlying fatigue of someone who feels he has no alternative, in the face of life's unremitting grimness, but to be upbeat all the time.

The flat looked as if it had an upstairs and a downstairs, judging from the windows. It was a decent size: probably about the same square footage as Simon's two-up two-down cottage, or Charlie's two-bed terrace. We ought to sell the pair of them and buy a bigger place together, thought Simon, though he knew he'd never suggest it and that, if Charlie did, his first reaction would be fear.

He remembered the Snowman jumping down his throat when he'd suggested Sarah Jaggard wasn't the victim of a miscarriage of justice. How could she be, when she'd been unanimously acquitted? Proust evidently thought that to be tried for manslaughter constituted miscarriage of justice enough, and Simon wondered if the woman he was about to meet agreed. Did she see herself as a victim, rather than someone who had triumphed over adversity? The shabby exterior of her home and the deafening traffic noise outside it made Simon think that she might, and he wouldn't blame her if she did.

Rusty wrought-iron steps led up to the flat, speckled with the black paint that must once have covered them. There was no doorbell. Simon knocked, then watched through the panel of cracked opaque glass as a large shape lumbered towards him along the hall. Glen Jaggard threw open the door, grabbed Simon's hand and shook it, simultaneously leaning forward to pat him on the back with his other hand, a manoeuvre that put the two men in awkward physical proximity. Simon took in Jaggard's checked shirt, jeans and walking boots. Was he planning on climbing a mountain later?

'You found Lockbusters, then?' Jaggard laughed. 'I couldn't believe it when our DVD player packed up about a week after we moved in. Talk about sod's law: you move to a flat above a DVD rental place and your DVD player packs in!'

Simon smiled politely.

'Go through to the lounge.' Jaggard pointed down the hall. 'There's tea and biscuits in there already. I'll get Sarah.' He took the stairs two at a time, calling out his wife's name.

Simon had been in many people's homes over the years, but this was a first: tea being made before he arrived. If he'd been late, would he have had to down it cold?

He was expecting the Jaggards' lounge to have nobody in it, since Glen and Sarah were both upstairs, and was surprised to find Paul Yardley there, looking terrible. His eyes were puffy, his skin waxy and greasy. *Like the congealed fat in a frying pan after you've cooked sausages*. The first time Simon had interviewed him after his wife's death, Yardley had said vehemently, 'Most people in my position would be thinking about topping themselves. Not me. I fought for justice for Helen once, and I'll do it again.'

Now, with equal intensity, he said, 'Don't worry, I'm not staying,' as if Simon had protested at his presence. 'I only came here to talk to Glen and Sarah about Laurie.'

'Laurie Nattrass?' On the wall behind Simon there was a framed newspaper photograph of Nattrass, Yardley and a tearfully smiling Helen, holding hands like a row of paper dolls. Taken on the steps of the court building after Helen's successful appeal, Simon guessed. It was the only picture the Jaggards had put up in the living room of their rented flat. Beneath the grainy black and white image was the headline 'JUSTICE AT LAST FOR HELEN'.

From the relative lack of furniture – two red chairs, one with a torn seat, a coffee table, a TV – and the bareness of the walls, Simon guessed that most of the Jaggards' possessions were in storage. *We won't be here long, no point filling the place with our stuff*. That's what Simon would tell himself, in their position. He wouldn't want to unpack anything that mattered to him and bring it to this dump with its damp-stained ceilings and cracked plaster. Did the Jaggards dream about buying a place soon, far away from the video shop with the damaged sign, so that they could put the past behind them once and for all?

Hadn't Sarah Jaggard also been photographed outside court after her acquittal? Simon was sure she had; he remembered seeing it on the news and in the papers. With Laurie Nattrass by her side, unless his memory was playing tricks on him. Why wasn't Sarah the one up on the living room wall?

'Do you know where Laurie is?' Paul Yardley asked. 'He's not returning our calls – not mine, not Glen's or Sarah's. He's never done that before.'

Nattrass had been eliminated; he'd been in meetings at the BBC all day Monday, so there was no reason to keep track of his movements. 'Sorry,' Simon said.

Paul Yardley stared at him for nearly ten seconds, waiting for a better answer. Then he said, 'He wouldn't ignore us. Do you know where he is?'

There was a creak of floorboards from above, followed by the sound of very slow footsteps, as if a ninety-year-old was coming down the stairs. Yardley sprang out of his chair. 'Don't worry, I'm going,' he said, and was down the hall and out of the flat within seconds. Simon made no move to stop him or ask where he was going; he knew he'd feel bad about that later. Talking to a man who'd lost everything was no fun, but you had to make the effort.

He picked up one of the three chipped mugs on the coffee table and took a gulp of tea that was somewhere between hot and cold. He wanted a Bourbon biscuit as well, but didn't take one.

Glen Jaggard steered Sarah into the room with both hands. She was tall and thin with wispy brown hair, dressed in pink striped pyjamas and a white towelling dressing-gown. She looked at Simon briefly before averting her eyes.

'Sit down, love,' said her husband.

Sarah lowered herself into one of the red chairs. Everything she did – walking, sitting – had an air of awkward inexperience about it, as if she was doing it for the first time. She was nervous in her own home. *If that's how she thinks of it; if she doesn't think of her home as the place she had to sell to stay out of jail.*

Simon had familiarised himself with her case as best he could. She'd been charged with the manslaughter of Beatrice Furniss, a six-month-old for whom she had babysat regularly. Beatrice – or Bea, as she was known – was the child of Pinda Avari and Matt Furniss. Before she was arrested, Sarah was a hair stylist, and Pinda, an IT audit manager for a chain of bookmakers, was one of her longstanding clients as well as a friend. On the evening of 15 April 2004, Pinda and Matt went to a party, having dropped Bea off at the Jaggards' house. Sarah put on a Baby Mozart DVD for Bea, which they watched together. Glen Jaggard and three of his friends, who were also his colleagues at Packers Removals, were in the next room playing poker. Bea had never had a set bedtime, as Pinda and Matt were against imposed routines for babies, but at about nine o'clock she fell asleep on Sarah's knee.

Sarah put her down on the sofa and settled in to watch TV. An hour later, she glanced down at Bea beside her and noticed that the baby's skin had a blue-ish tinge and she thought, though couldn't be sure, that there was something funny about her breathing. She tried to rouse Bea, succeeded in waking her, but was frightened by how floppy she was. At one point Bea's eyes rolled back in her head and that was when Sarah feared something was seriously amiss. Carrying Bea gently, trying not to panic, she took her through to the kitchen to Glen and his friends. They took one look at Bea and told Sarah to phone an ambulance. By the time it arrived, Bea had stopped breathing. The crew was unable to resuscitate her.

The post-mortem found the cause of death to be extensive bleeding in the brain and eyes. The paediatrician who had performed it took the stand at Sarah's trial and said she believed Bea had died as a result of being shaken. Dr Judith Duffy, called as an expert witness, backed her up. Nothing, she agreed, would cause the sort of subdural and retinal haemorrhages Bea Furniss had suffered apart from violent shaking. The defence disagreed, and produced a research paper, published in the *British Medical Journal* and referred to in court and subsequently in the press as Pelham Dennison, to prove that the symptoms many doctors believed to be indicative of shaking could occur naturally. Even better, Sarah Jaggard's lawyers produced Pelham and Dennison in person to explain their research. Both doctors told the court that bleeding in the brain and eyes needn't be caused by inflicted trauma, and could as easily be the result of a non-induced hypoxic episode – in other words, a period during which a baby is deprived of oxygen owing to a breakdown of one of its internal systems.

Both Dr Pelham and Dr Dennison pointed to a history of heart arrhythmias in Bea's family; her maternal grandfather and her uncle had both died of a disease called Type 2 Long QT syndrome, which affects the heart. If Bea had also been a Long QT syndrome sufferer – and it was a genetic defect, so likely to be passed down through the generations – this might be sufficient to cause hypoxia, which might in turn cause death. Judith Duffy poured scorn on this hypothesis, pointing out that tests had conclusively proved Bea Furniss hadn't suffered from Type 2 Long QT, or from any of the six other identified variants of the disease. In response to the suggestions made by Pelham and Dennison that there might be other as-yet-unidentified forms of Long QT syndrome and that Bea Furniss might have suffered from one of those, Dr Duffy said that obviously she could not prove this was not the case, but that somebody ought to explain to the jury about the difficulties of proving a negative. Furthermore – and Dr Duffy took this to be the most significant point – there were clear stretching injuries to the nerve roots in Bea's neck, which were found at post-mortem to be swollen and torn. This damage could only have been done by shaking, said Dr Duffy.

The prosecution's theory was that Bea had been crying or screaming, and Sarah had shaken her in a fit of temper. Glen Jaggard and his three friends who had been in the house that night testified that Bea hadn't cried at all. The prosecution tried to claim first that the men might not have heard the crying over the combined noise of their poker game and the TV in the next room, and then that Glen Jaggard and his friends had a vested interest in protecting Sarah. One of the poker players, Tunde Adeyeye, took exception to this line of questioning and told the court in no uncertain terms that he had no interest in protecting people who killed babies, and that he was as certain as he could be that Sarah Jaggard had done nothing of the sort.

Pinda Avari and Matt Furniss, though 'visibly devastated by grief' according to one reporter who'd been in court, gave moving evidence in support of Sarah. Pinda said, 'If I believed somebody had killed my darling baby, I would want that person brought to justice more than anything and wouldn't rest until I made that happen, but I have no doubt whatsoever that Sarah loved Bea and would never have harmed her.' Matt Furniss said more or less the same thing.

The prosecution changed tack, and hypothesised that Sarah Jaggard had shaken Bea to death while she, Glen and the baby were alone in the house, before Glen's friends got there. That, argued counsel for the Crown, would explain why Tunde Adeyeye and the other two poker players had heard no noise from the baby. Did they make a point of assessing Bea's condition before commencing their game? Did they get a good look at her, before Sarah brought her into the kitchen in an apparent panic? All three men had to admit that they had called out hello to Sarah when they arrived but paid no attention to Bea, and couldn't swear that she hadn't died earlier, when they weren't present. Dr Judith Duffy seized on this when she was called back to the witness box, saying that the time window for Bea's death was consistent with this possibility; death could have occurred at any time between 7 and 10 p.m., and Glen Jaggard's friends had only arrived at 8. The defence argued that, since Pinda and Matt had only dropped Bea off at 7.45, it was highly unlikely that Sarah would have so quickly lost her temper with the baby. It was simply not credible, Sarah's barrister maintained, that a woman with Sarah's gentle and patient temperament, a woman with no history of violence whatsoever, would lose control of herself and become a baby-shaking monster within the space of fifteen minutes.

Dr Duffy wasn't a popular witness. More than once, the judge threatened to clear the courtroom if the heckling didn't stop. Laurie Nattrass was among the hecklers, and was quoted in one newspaper as saying he was happy to be held in contempt of any British court when those same courts were in the habit of making a mockery of justice.

After a trial that lasted six weeks, and during which Sarah Jaggard fainted several times, the jury returned a unanimous verdict of not guilty. On hearing this, Sarah fainted again. Simon knew he ought to feel sorry for her. He oughtn't to be thinking about the stretching injuries to Bea Furniss's neck that could only have been brought about by shaking. *According to Judith Duffy, who was about to go up before the GMC for misconduct.*

'I heard Paul Yardley asking you about Laurie,' said Sarah. If she wanted or expected Simon to respond, she showed no outward sign of it. 'I let him down. We all did. That's why he doesn't want anything to do with us.'

Simon found himself wishing Glen Jaggard hadn't left them alone. He could have done with a feeble Lockbusters quip round about now, to dilute the bleak, oppressive atmosphere Sarah had brought into the room with her. She seemed ... Simon struggled to find the right word. *Hopeless*. Entirely without hope, as if her life was over and she didn't particularly care. 'How did you let Laurie down?'

'I told him I'd changed my mind about the documentary. About being in it, and . . . After Helen died, I begged him not to go ahead with it. So did Glen, so did Paul. We were all scared of drawing attention to ourselves, in case . . .' Sarah grabbed her mouth with her hand, as if to stop herself from crying, or from saying more.

'You didn't want a documentary linking you to Helen in case the killer made the same link and went for you next,' Simon guessed.

'I felt like such a traitor. I loved Helen like family, I *worshipped* her, but I was scared. There are people out there, sick people, who'd give anything to get their hands on women like us – me, Helen, Ray Hines. I've always known that. Helen never believed me. She said everyone knew we were innocent, Laurie had proved it – she was like him, she believed in good winning and evil being stamped out, but that's not the way the world works.'

'No,' said Simon. 'It isn't.'

'No,' Sarah echoed bitterly. 'And part of the reason it isn't is because of cowards like me.'

Simon could hear Glen Jaggard whistling in another room: the theme tune from *Match of the Day*. 'So Helen and Laurie are your heroes,' he deduced aloud, looking again at the framed photo on the wall.

'Laurie's not scared of anything or anyone. Neither was Helen. You can see their courage in their faces, can't you?' For the first time, Sarah sounded animated. 'That's why I love that picture, even though—' She grabbed her mouth again.

'Even though?'

'Nothing.'

'Even though what, Sarah?'

She sighed. 'Angus Hines took that photograph.'

'Ray's husband?' That didn't sound right. 'I thought he was a newspaper editor.'

'He is now, at *London on Sunday*. Before that he was a press photographer. He hated Helen for being more loyal to his wife than he was. He visited her in prison once, to taunt her – no other reason. He wanted to torment her.'

Mentally, Simon added an item to his list: find out what Angus Hines was doing on Monday.

'Imagine what a shock it was for Helen to see him there, outside the court, when she'd just won her appeal. I'd have collapsed, but not Helen. She was determined not to let his presence spoil such an important moment. Look, you can see her determination.' Sarah nodded at the picture. 'I can't believe she's dead. Not that I wasn't scared before – I've always been scared – but it's so much worse without Helen, and now Laurie's not ringing . . .'

'You've got Glen,' Simon pointed out.

'I'm even scared of being swabbed, or whatever it is you're going to do to me.' Sarah ignored the mention of her husband. 'Isn't that crazy? I know I didn't kill Helen, but I'm scared the test'll come back positive anyway.'

'That won't happen,' Simon told her.

'Even before Helen was murdered I was frightened of Laurie's film and the effect it would have. The thought of being back in the limelight made me feel sick, but I didn't dare tell Laurie I wanted out. And then when Helen was killed . . .' Sarah let out a loud sob and buried her face in her hands. 'I was shattered, but I had the excuse I'd been waiting and hoping for. I thought I could persuade Laurie to give up on the film, I thought he'd understand my fears. Even if we never found out for sure that Helen was killed by some crazy child protection vigilante, if there was even a chance that was why . . . But Laurie sounded so cold when I tried to explain, so remote and distant. That was the last time I spoke to him. I don't suppose he cares what happens to me now.' Sarah sniffed. She picked up one of the mugs from the table, took a sip, then held it against her face as if it was a comfort blanket. Simon was on the point of steering the conversation away from Laurie Nattrass when she said, 'Now he's leaving Binary Star and someone else is making the film, some woman called Fliss. I don't understand it. Why would Laurie hand it over to someone else?'

Fliss Benson. Simon had left her a message and was still waiting for her to get back to him. So she was making the crib death documentary, was she? And she'd had a card with the same sixteen numbers on it, Helen Yardley's sixteen numbers, if Laurie Nattrass's word could be relied upon. *Four rows of four. 2, 1, 4, 9 . . .*

Simon reached into his pocket for the small Ziploc bag he'd brought with him. He held it up in front of Sarah Jaggard's face so that she'd have no difficulty seeing it through her tears. 'Do these numbers mean anything to you?' he asked.

She dropped her tea in her lap and started to scream.

Part II

9

Friday 9 October 2009

'Cream coloured. Sort of ribbed,' I say, for what must be the tenth time. 'You know, a bit stripey, but not stripes of colour, more like . . . texture stripes.' I shrug. 'That's the best I can do, sorry.'

'And you don't remember the numbers?' DC Waterhouse asks. He's hunched awkwardly over his notebook in the middle of my sofa, dead centre, as if invisible people are squashing him in on either side. Every so often he looks up from his note-making and stares at me hard, as if I'm lying to him, which I am. When he asked me if I'd received any other unusual communications, anything that had worried me, I said no.

I should tell him about the second and third anonymous envelopes, but the prospect fills me with dread. *In case he tells me that three is so much worse than one, three constitutes a real risk.* He might look even more concerned than he does now, and the worry on his face is making me feel quite paranoid enough at its present level. Besides, there's no point saying anything – it's not as if I've still got the second card or the photograph to show him.

Yeah, right. The pieces of the picture are in your bag. How hard would it be for him to put them together and identify those fingers as belonging to Helen Yardley?

I wish I was better at self-deception. It's dispiriting, constantly listening to myself calling myself a liar.

'2, 1, 4, 9 – those were the first four numbers, the top row,' I say. 'I don't remember the others. Sorry.' I glance discreetly at my watch. 7.30 a.m. I need DC Waterhouse to leave, quickly, so that I can get to Rachel Hines on time.

He turns over a page in his notebook and passes it across to me. 'Could those have been the sixteen numbers?' he asks.

The sight of them makes me queasy; I want to push them away. 'Yes. I . . . I'm not sure, but I think . . . Yes, they could be.' Seeing him nod and open his mouth, I panic and blurt out, 'Don't tell me. I don't want to know.'

What the hell did I say that for? Now he'll think I'm scared of something.

He gives me a curious look. 'What don't you want to know?'

I decide I might as well be honest, by way of a change. 'What the numbers are. What they mean. If it's got anything to do with—' I break off. I know better than to invite trouble by voicing my worst fear.

'If it's got anything to do with what?' DC Waterhouse asks.

'If I'm in danger, I'd rather not know.'

'You'd rather not know?'

'Are you going to repeat everything I say? Sorry. I don't mean to be rude, I just . . .'

'I haven't said you're in danger, Miss Benson, but let's suppose you were: you wouldn't want to know about it, so that you could protect yourself?'

This is what I dreaded; he's making it too real, threatening the sustainability of my denial. Now that he's put it like that, I have to ask. '*Am* I in danger?'

'There's no reason to assume that at this stage.'

Fantastic. That makes me feel heaps better.

Waterhouse watches me.

I open my ill-considered gob again, to break the uncomfortable silence. 'The way I see it, if someone's determined to . . . kill me, or whatever, then they're going to do it, aren't they?'

'Kill you?' He sounds surprised. 'Why would anybody want to do that?'

I laugh. I'm glad I'm not the only one playing games here. He's told me he's from Culver Valley CID. He hasn't mentioned Helen Yardley, but he must know I know that she was killed in Spilling in the Culver Valley, and that his interest in the sixteen numbers must have something to do with her murder.

'I'm not saying someone wants to kill me,' I tell him. 'I'm saying that, if they did, they could do it easily. What am I supposed to do, hide in a bullet-proof bunker for the rest of my life?'

'You seem frightened,' says Waterhouse. 'There's no need to panic, and, as I said, no reason to assume—'

'I'm not panicking about being attacked or killed, I'm panicking about panicking,' I try to explain, fighting back the tears that are prickling my eyes. 'I'm scared of how scared I'll have to be if I find out why you're asking about the card and the numbers. I'll be in a whole new realm of fear – too terrified to get on with my life, too frightened to do anything but curl up into a ball and die of dreading what might happen to me. I'd rather not know, and let whatever's going to happen happen. Seriously.'

It might not make sense to anyone else, but it makes perfect sense to me. I've always been phobic about hearing bad news. When I was a student, I had a drunken condomless one-night stand with a man I hardly knew, someone I met in a nightclub and never saw again. I spent the next ten years worrying about dying of AIDS, but there was no way I was getting tested. Who wants to spend the last few years of their life knowing they've got a terminal illness?

Waterhouse stands up, walks over to the window. Like everyone who's ever admired the view from my lounge – a greenish-stained light-well wall leading up to an uneven pavement – he makes no mention of the charming aspect.

'Try not to worry,' he says. 'Having said that, you need to take a few basic precautions. You live here alone?'

I nod.

'I'm going to try and organise for someone to keep an eye on you, but in the meantime, have you got a friend you can stay with? I'd like you to spend as little time as possible on your own until you hear different.'

Keep an eye on me? Would he say that if the threat to me wasn't serious?

This is getting ridiculous. Ask him what's going on. Make him tell you.

I can't bring myself to do it, even though the truth might be an improvement on what I'm not quite allowing myself to imagine. Maybe I'd feel better if I heard it.

Yeah. Course you would.

'I'd also like you to halt all work on the crib death murders documentary for the time being, and broadcast the fact that that's what you're doing,' says Waterhouse. 'Contact everyone involved. Make sure they know it's postponed indefinitely.'

Resistance rears up inside me like a tidal wave. I don't know why I'm nodding mutely like an obedient sap when I have no intention of following his instructions. Either I'm lying again, or I'm agreeing with him because I know he's right in theory, I know that's what I ought to do.

I also know I can't. Can't give up on the film now, can't stop myself from going to Twickenham this morning. Despite the fear and the guilt, the pull inside me is too strong, like a current I have no hope of fighting. I have to talk to Rachel Hines, hear what she has to say about Wendy Whitehead, the woman she claims killed her children. I have to go deeper in.

It's nothing to do with truth or justice. It's me. If I don't see this through, all the way to the other side of whatever it leads to, I might go my whole life without ever fixing on who I am or how I feel – about myself, my family, my past. I'll be nothing – the nobody from nowhere, as Maya so graciously put it, trapped for ever, still tainted. I'll have missed my one chance. That terrifies me more than the idea of someone trying to kill me.

As if he's reading my mind, Waterhouse says, 'We're having trouble getting in touch with Rachel Hines. Do you have her contact details?'

The police must think the film is connected to Helen Yardley's murder.

'They're probably in a file somewhere. I think she rents a flat in Notting Hill, close to where she used to live with her family,' I parrot what Tamsin told me. Part of me would like to be helpful and give Waterhouse the Twickenham address, but if I do that, he'll make it his next stop, and I can't let that happen. I can't have him in my way. I'm the person Rachel Hines is going to speak to this morning; no one else.

'She doesn't seem to be staying there at the moment,' he says. 'You don't have any other address for her?'

'No,' I lie.

10

9/10/09

'Two new faces for you today.' Proust tapped the whiteboard with a pen. 'Or rather, one face and one police artist's best attempt at a likeness. The woman in the photograph is Sarah Jaggard. Some of you might have heard of her.'

About half and half, thought Simon. There were as many people nodding as looking blank.

'She was tried in 2005 for the manslaughter of Beatrice Furniss, the baby of a friend,' said the Snowman. 'She was acquitted. She has several links to Helen Yardley. One: Helen campaigned, under the auspices of JIPAC, on Mrs Jaggard's behalf. Two: Laurie Nattrass – I assume you've all heard of him – was until very recently making a documentary about three crib death murder cases, two of which were Helen and Sarah Jaggard. Three, and this is closely related to two: Dr Judith Duffy, regular star witness for the prosecution in suspected abuse cases, testified against both Helen Yardley and Sarah Jaggard at their trials. Duffy's on the verge of being struck off by the GMC for misconduct.'

A taut silence filled the room as everyone stared at the face beside Sarah Jaggard's: a sketch of a man with a shaved head and uneven front teeth. Apart from Proust, only Simon, Sam Kombothekra, Sellers and Gibbs knew why his as-yet-unidentified ugly mug was up on the board. Was Simon the only one who objected to being among the chosen people? 'The home team', Rick Leckenby and a few others had taken to calling them, seemingly without malice.

There was another meeting of the select few scheduled for immediately after the briefing. In Proust's glass-walled office in the corner of the CID room, where everyone else working Helen Yardley's murder would once again be able to see but not hear the inspector consulting his inner circle. It was no way to run a murder investigation.

'Last Monday, 28 September – so a week before Helen Yardley was shot – Sarah Jaggard was attacked near her home in Wolverhampton by the man whose unprepossessing image we have here.' Proust pointed to the board. 'Mrs Jaggard has understandably suffered from depression since her arrest in 2004 and is on anti-depressants. On 28 September, she went to her GP for a repeat prescription. On leaving the doctor's surgery, she went straight to the nearest chemist, the Moon Street branch of Boots. As she was approaching the door, in full view of the shop window, a man came up and grabbed her from behind. He put one arm round her neck and the other round her waist, and dragged her into a nearby alleyway. Once he had her where he wanted her, our assailant turned Mrs Jaggard round, enabling her to get a good look at his face, produced a knife and held it against her throat.

'Mrs Jaggard can't remember his exact words but he said something to the effect of, "You killed that baby, didn't you? Tell me the truth." Mrs Jaggard told him that no, she didn't kill Beatrice Furniss, to which he replied, "You shook her, didn't you? Why don't you admit it? If you tell me the truth, I'll let you live. All I want's the truth." Mrs Jaggard told him again that she didn't shake the baby, had never harmed a child and never would, but that didn't satisfy him, and he continued to repeat himself, threatening that unless she told the truth, he would kill her. In the end, Mrs Jaggard became so terrified, and so convinced he was going to kill her if she didn't give him what he wanted, that she lied. She said "All right, I did shake her, I did kill her."'

Simon saw confusion on some of the faces around him, though a few people were shrugging as if to say, 'Anyone would say that, if someone had a knife to their throat.'

'Sarah Jaggard *did not* shake Beatrice Furniss, who died of natural causes,' said Proust, his metal-grey eyes raking the room for signs of dissent. 'She was being threatened by a madman. A madman who didn't know his own mind, as it turned out, because the minute she lied and said she'd shaken the baby to death, he started to tell her that she didn't. He said words to the effect of, "Don't lie. I told you, I want the truth. You didn't kill her, did you? You didn't shake her. You're lying." At which point Sarah Jaggard tried again to tell the truth: that she hadn't harmed baby Beatrice in any way, that she'd only said she had in fear of her life. The man got angry at this point – *angrier*, I should say – and said, "You're going to die now. Are you ready?"

'Mrs Jaggard fainted in shock, but not before hearing a woman's raised voice. She was too frightened to make out what the voice was saying. When she came round to find herself flat on her back, her attacker was gone, and there was a woman standing over her, a Mrs Carolyn Finneran, who had come out of Boots and noticed a skirmish in the alleyway. Hers was the voice Mrs Jaggard heard before she fainted.' Proust paced the room as he spoke: his gang-plank walk, one foot slowly and carefully in front of the other. *If only there were an ocean for him to fall into.*

'If Mrs Finneran hadn't appeared when she did and scared our man away, it's reasonable to assume Sarah Jaggard might have died on 28 September,' said Proust. 'In any event, given the link between her and Helen Yardley, that this attack happened a week before Helen's murder is something we couldn't afford to ignore even if we didn't have something more concrete linking the two incidents. I won't keep you in suspense.'

The Snowman stopped in front of an enlarged copy of the card that had been found in Helen Yardley's pocket after her death: the sixteen numbers. 'Once Sarah Jaggard had been helped to her feet by Mrs Finneran, the first thing she did was reach into her jacket pocket for a tissue to wipe her face. She pulled out more than she bargained for: there was a card there, identical to the one you're all familiar with.' Proust held out his hand. Colin Sellers, standing behind him like a performing seal waiting for his cue, handed him two transparent plastic folders. Proust held them up so that everyone could see the cards inside. 'Same numbers, same handwriting – though that hasn't yet been officially confirmed by the people whose overpaid job it is to tell us what we already know. Exactly the same layout – the numbers divided into four rows of four horizontally and four columns of four vertically, and nothing else on the card except the numbers: 2,1,4,9, et cetera.'

An eruption of whispers and murmurs filled the room. Proust waited for it to subside before saying, 'Mrs Jaggard is adamant that this card was not on her person when she left home to go to the doctor's, and that there's no way it could have made its way into her pocket unless her attacker put it there. The numbers mean nothing to her, or so she told DC Waterhouse. She kept the card in the hope of working out what it meant, thinking it had to mean something. She informed neither her husband nor local police about the attack.' The Snowman raised his hand to halt the loud expressions of incredulity. 'Don't be so sure you would have behaved differently in her position. Her only experience of the law is a negative one. The thought of inviting the big boots of plod to re-enter her life when they'd crushed it once before was unappealing to say the least. She was also terrified that, if this man were caught, he would say she'd admitted to killing Beatrice Furniss. She decided a better way to deal with what had happened was never to leave the house again. Her husband Glen noticed a deterioration in her condition, but had no idea of the cause.'

'So we've got a serial, or an aspiring serial?' Klair Williamson asked.

'We don't use that word unless we have to,' said Proust. 'What we have is a strong interest in these sixteen numbers. No help so far from Bramshill or GCHQ, or from the Maths departments of the universities I contacted. I'm considering going to the press with it. If we need to wade through a thousand lunatics to find out what these numbers mean, then that's what we'll do. And, while I'm on the bad news, my request for a psychological profiler did not meet with a favourable response, I'm sorry to say. The usual excuse: lack of money. We're going to have to do our own profiling, at least until bust gives way to boom.'

'I thought boom and bust had been abolished,' someone called out.

'That was a lie told by a man every bit as criminal as the shaven-headed individual who held a knife to Sarah Jaggard's throat,' Proust snapped. 'A man . . .' – he tapped the police artist's image with his pen to make it clear who he was talking about – '. . . that Mrs Stella White, of 16 Bengeo Street, says *might* be the man she saw on Helen Yardley's driveway on Monday morning. He *might* have had a shaven head, even though in her original account, he had darkish hair. Her son Dillon says it's definitely not the same man, but then he also says it was raining on Monday, and that the man outside Helen Yardley's house had a wet umbrella with him. We know this is not true – there was no rain and none was forecast. Even if Helen Yardley's killer concealed his gun inside a fastened umbrella, that umbrella wouldn't have been wet. I think we're going to have to write off the Whites, mother and son, as being among the most unhelpful witnesses that have ever hindered our progress. Nevertheless, the cards in the pockets are a firm link between Baldy and Helen Yardley's murder, so at the moment he's our best bet.'

Baldy? thought Simon. Had the Snowman looked in the mirror lately?

'Why would he use a gun for Helen Yardley and a knife for Sarah Jaggard?' a young DC from Silsford called out. 'And why attack one in her home and the other outside a shop? It doesn't fit in with the sixteen numbers in their pockets. That's typical serial, but the change of method and setting . . .'

'It's not the same man,' said Gibbs. 'Stella White said darkish hair, twice – to DS Kombothekra and then to me.'

'Shave your head tonight, DC Gibbs. We'll see if you've got enough hair by this time next week to be described as darkish.'

'You're not serious, sir?'

'Do I strike you as a frivolous sort of person?'

'No, sir.'

Simon raised his hand. 'If I can respond to the point about serial—'

'I don't know if you can, Waterhouse. Can you?'

'The attack on Sarah Jaggard wasn't a success. He was interrupted before he'd finished with her. With Helen Yardley, he decided to do it differently, better: in her house, husband safely out at work, gets her all to himself for a whole day, no one to disturb them, and shoots her at the end of it. The repetitive part, the signature that's typical of serials: that's the cards with the numbers on. That's the focal point for him, and it would have provided enough continuity to allow him to be flexible about the details.'

'I'll take that as an application for the post of in-house profiler, Waterhouse.'

'We've been wondering why the killer might turn up at 8.20 in the morning, stay all day and only shoot Helen Yardley at 5 in the afternoon.' Simon went on.

'And it's looking highly likely that's when she *was* shot,' Proust chipped in. 'The post-mortem gives us a ninety-minute window: 4.30 to 6. Deaf Beryl Murie did us proud.'

'Extrapolating from what we now know, might the killer have been doing to Helen Yardley what he did to Sarah Jaggard, only for longer?' Simon suggested. '"Tell me the truth. You did kill your babies, didn't you?" She'd have said "No, I'm innocent," for as long as she could hold out, then panic would have taken over. He'd have been telling her she'd only live if she told the truth, and she'd take that to mean he wanted her to confess to guilt. She'd have said anything to stay alive: "Yes, I killed them". He says, "No, you didn't. You're lying. You're telling me what you think I want to hear. You didn't kill them, did you? Tell the truth." "No, I didn't kill them. I told you I didn't kill them but you didn't believe me." "You're lying. I know you killed them. Tell the truth." And so on.'

'For eight and a half hours?' said Sam Kombothekra.

'A chilling performance, Waterhouse. I particularly liked the manic glint in your eye as you delivered the psychopath's lines. Can you account for your whereabouts on Monday?'

'Why would he have kept it up for so long?' asked Gibbs. 'He'd have been able to see within half an hour that she was changing her tune every time he got angry and accused her of lying.'

'Maybe he thought if he kept it up for long enough, she'd see that changing her story back and forth wasn't getting her anywhere, wasn't getting rid of him or putting a stop to the fear,' said Simon. 'He hoped she'd settle on one or the other – guilty or innocent – and wouldn't contradict it no matter what he threatened her with. Whichever she fixed on, he'd know it was the truth.'

'And we enter the realm of fantasy,' Proust intoned.

'In that situation, most people wouldn't be capable of rational thought,' said Klair Williamson. 'You wouldn't be calm enough to think, "Right, telling him what I think he wants to hear isn't working, so from now on I'll stick to the truth."'

Simon disagreed. 'If someone holds a gun to your head and keeps ordering you to tell the truth or else he'll kill you, eventually you're going to tell the truth. You've tried lying to please him – it's got you nowhere. Pretty soon your terror convinces you that he *knows* the truth, so you daren't lie any more.' Simon was pleased to see a few people nodding. 'We don't know much about this man, so we can't afford to ignore what he's told us himself, via Sarah Jaggard: all he wants is the truth. She said he kept saying that. If he's the same man who killed Helen Yardley – and I think he is – he spent the whole of Monday trying, literally, to scare the truth out of her.'

'And killed her at five o'clock because . . .?' asked Rick Leckenby.

'He failed.' Simon shrugged. 'Maybe Helen refused to give him an answer. Maybe she said, "Go ahead, shoot me if you want to, but I'm not telling you anything." Or maybe she told him the truth and he didn't like it, so he killed her anyway.'

'I just can't see it going on like that for eight and a half hours,' said Sam Kombothekra. 'Maybe one, or two . . .'

'Let's get back to work,' Proust said pointedly. 'Before Waterhouse is tempted to build a leisurely lunch and siesta for the killer into his fantasy. Felicity Benson, thirty-one years old, single.' He tapped the name on the whiteboard. 'Known as Fliss. She lives in Kilburn in London and works for the TV production company Binary Star. She's supposed to be taking over Laurie Nattrass's documentary, the one about, among others, Helen Yardley. On Wednesday – two days ago – she opened an envelope addressed to her at work and extracted from it a card that made no sense to her, with our friends the sixteen numbers on it. She showed it to Mr Nattrass, who threw it in his office bin. Sadly, it's well on its way to a landfill by now; the chances of our finding it are zero. Miss Benson is alive and well, and I've asked for some resources to be devoted to keeping her that way. The higher-ups are stalling, as I knew they would. In the meantime, Miss Benson has agreed to stay with a friend and spend no time alone apart from when answering a call of nature, at which times the friend should remain close at hand.'

Proust paused for breath. 'I believe this young woman's in danger.'

No one disagreed.

'However, to play devil's advocate for a moment, there's clearly a variation here as well as a link,' he went on. 'The card is part of a pattern, but Miss Benson simultaneously breaks the pattern by having been neither attacked nor killed, which is why Superintendent Barrow isn't authorising protection. Strange logic on his part, since protection, as I understand it, is preventative and future-focused. Perhaps if Miss Benson were already dead, Superintendent Barrow would see fit to protect her.' The Snowman ran his hand over his shiny head. 'That's about it for now. Without neglecting any previously assigned tasks, we need to pursue the Wolverhampton angle – we might hit the jackpot and get Baldy on CCTV. We still need brands and suppliers for the card, the pen, the ink. Top priority is drafting something for the press. Oh, and we need a telegenic volunteer we can put in front of the cameras. That's you, Sergeant Kombothekra – your own fault for having clean hair and a winning smile.'

'What about the third woman featured in Nattrass's documentary?' Klair Williamson called out.

'Rachel Hines,' said someone.

'Has anyone contacted her to see if she's been sent the same numbers?' Williamson asked.

Proust packed up his files and headed for his office as if she hadn't spoken.

* * *

'One of you had better explain to me and explain fast about Laurie Nattrass and Rachel Hines, in a way that makes sense this time. Where are they?'

Clever, thought Simon. Making it their fault instead of his: the hurried account they'd given the Snowman was so garbled, he could hardly have presented it at the briefing. How could he have answered Klair Williamson's question, when he had so little information? And whose fault was that? The select few doubled as the scapegoats.

'I've told you everything I know,' Simon said. 'Nattrass told me Ray Hines was staying in Twickenham, Angus Hines said she was staying with friends, and Fliss Benson didn't know where she was. Since my first and only conversation with Nattrass, I've been unable to contact him. He's not at his house, at either of his offices . . .'

'He has more than one?' Proust's eyebrows shot up.

'Officially, today's his last day at Binary Star, but he's not there, and he seems to have started at another company already, Hammerhead,' said Colin Sellers. 'He's not there either, and he's not returning calls. Until we find him, we can't ask him about Ray Hines' Twickenham friends. Her ex-husband's given us a list of her friends, but none are in Twickenham.'

'We've eliminated Angus Hines for Helen Yardley's murder, sir,' said Sam Kombothekra.

'In one of his seven offices, was he?'

'He wasn't, sir. He had the day off on Monday. Between 3 p.m. and 7 p.m. he was in a pub called the Retreat in Bethnal Green with a Carl Chappell. I spoke to Chappell myself, sir – he's confirmed it.'

'While Judith Duffy was having lunch with Rachel Hines in Primrose Hill.' Proust sucked in his lips, stretching the flesh tighter on his face. 'Why would you have lunch with the person whose lies turned twelve jurors and one husband against you and deprived you of your freedom for four years? And why would Doctor Despicable wish to dine with a woman she believes is a child murderer? One of you, get her to talk. Maybe she knows something about the Twickenham contingent.'

'What about her two daughters and their husbands?' Simon asked.

'Is that premature? No, I don't think it is,' the Snowman answered his own question. 'I wouldn't put it past them to blame Helen Yardley and Sarah Jaggard for ruining their mother's life, or their mother-in-law's. Apart from anything else, we can't afford to ignore a suggestion made to us by Laurie Nattrass. If he turns out to be right, we'll never hear the end of it. You never know, one of the sons-in-law might be Baldy himself. Get on to it, one of you. With regard to tracking down Nattrass and Rachel Hines, pursue any link, however tenuous – her lawyers, people she met in prison, his friends and media contacts. Presumably they've both got relatives.'

'Yes, sir,' said Sam.

'If this is about revenge on the people responsible for Duffy's downfall, Laurie Nattrass and Rachel Hines would be on that list, along with Helen Yardley, Sarah Jaggard and Fliss Benson.' Proust frowned. 'Yet Nattrass told Waterhouse only that Benson had been sent the sixteen numbers, not that he'd had them himself.'

'Maybe the killer's only interested in women,' Sellers suggested. 'In which case, you'd expect Ray Hines to have been sent a card.'

'If we don't know where she is, maybe the card-sender doesn't either,' said Sam. 'Which makes finding her all the more crucial, before he does.'

'It might be about a different sort of revenge,' said Gibbs, looking at Simon. 'Nothing to do with Duffy's downfall or with Duffy, but on baby-murderers and the people who side with them against their victims.'

'Baby-murderers, detective?' The Snowman stood up and walked round his desk. To Simon's left, Sam and Sellers were as still as the most ambitious participants in a game of musical statues. Simon made a point of shifting from one foot to the other and yawning, boycotting the fear-freeze.

'*Baby-murderers?*' Proust breathed in Gibbs' face.

'I meant from the killer's point of view. I don't think—'

'Are you the killer?'

'No.'

'Then speak from your own point of view. Say what *you* think: women slandered as baby-killers, women wrongly convicted as baby-murderers!'

'You mean say what *you* think,' Simon muttered, loud enough for Proust to hear. *You want trouble, I'll give you trouble. Come on, you tyrannical fuck. Don't waste your hostility on someone who's not going to make the most of it.*

The inspector didn't take his eyes off Gibbs. 'All the right words are yours for the choosing, detective – all the words that make it clear you're on the side of good against evil.' Gibbs stared sullenly at the floor.

'You attack one woman, get interrupted, leave the numbers in her pocket,' said Proust conversationally, as if nothing unusual had happened. 'A week later, you shoot dead a second woman, leave the numbers in *her* pocket. The day after you kill the second woman, you send the numbers by snail mail to a third woman, whom you neither attack nor kill. Why? What's going on in your mind? Waterhouse?'

'My mind, sir? Or do you mean the killer's mind?' *All the right words are yours for the rejecting in favour of all the wrong ones, Baldy.*

'I don't want to give myself nightmares, so I'll plump for the latter.' The Snowman smiled, perching on the edge of his desk.

Why doesn't it matter what I say? How come Gibbs can make you angry and I can't? Simon couldn't work out if it was favouritism or a calculated neglect. He remembered Charlie's caution: *Helen Yardley's murder is about Helen Yardley, not Proust. You can't find the right answer if you're asking the wrong question.*

Knowing Charlie would be disappointed to see him behaving like a child, he forced his thoughts back into line. 'Fliss Benson's convinced Laurie Nattrass has gone into hiding because of her,' he said. 'It's probably too stupid to be worth a mention, but . . . they spent part of yesterday afternoon in bed together at his place.' He wondered if he should have said 'having sex' instead. Would that have sounded more natural? 'It had never happened before, and she thinks he regretted it straight away. Immediately afterwards, she says, he started acting distant and virtually threw her out. She's tried to ring him several times since, with no success, and he hasn't returned her calls.'

'He could return yours, though, couldn't he?' said Proust. 'He must know you don't want to speak to him about his intentions with regard to Miss Benson.'

'He wouldn't . . .' Sellers stopped, shook his head.

'Don't keep us in suspense, Detective. What would you do if you'd recently ejected a clingy woman from your bed and wanted to make sure she didn't find her way back into it?'

'Well, I might . . . I might switch off my mobile, go to the pub or to stay at a mate's house and kind of . . . forget to check my messages for a day or two. Just until things had died down. I mean, normally I wouldn't, normally I'd be happy to have any woman back who wanted more, but . . . she's tried to ring him several times since yesterday afternoon? That type's enough to spark off a spell of hibernation, sir – so much hassle, the sex isn't even worth it.'

'I don't think our inability to get hold of Nattrass has got anything to do with Fliss Benson, and I told her that,' said Simon. 'I thought we ought to consider it, that's all. More for what it says about Benson than anything else. She seems convinced it's all about her. I can imagine her being obsessive. She's kind of odd.'

'Takes one to know one, Waterhouse.'

'I asked her to halt all work on the documentary until further notice and she agreed, but . . . she struck me as one of those who'll agree to your face then do what she wants behind your back.'

'Women, you mean?' said Sellers. He was rewarded with a thin-lipped smile from the Snowman.

'I don't want to be told every time I turn up to interview someone that Benson and her camera crew have just left,' said Simon. 'I've looked into the possibility of getting an injunction, and been told there's no chance. Binary Star's documentary is about old cases, not Helen Yardley's murder, so there's no contempt issue.'

'We're going to have to rely on goodwill,' said Sam Kombothekra.

'Goodwill?' Proust eyed him coldly. 'I'd sooner place my trust in the tooth fairy.'

'What do you want us to do about Paul Yardley, sir?' Sam asked.

'Talk to him again, but go gently. Remember who he is and what he's been through. It's possible he forgot, which I suppose would be understandable in the circumstances, but we need him to tell us that he didn't ring emergency services straight after he found Helen's body. He first tried Laurie Nattrass's direct line at Binary Star, then his home number, then his mobile. Then he rang the police.'

'Would you forget phoning someone three times, however grieving and shocked you were, if the police were asking you to think back over your every movement?' asked Simon. 'Going gently's all well and good, but what Yardley's been through is irrelevant if he's lying to us and getting in the way of us—'

'Paul Yardley is not a suspect,' Proust cut him off. 'He was working when Helen died.'

'His alibi is one colleague, that's it – a mate he's worked with for years,' Simon stood his ground. Not only for the sake of disagreeing with Proust, though that was a fringe benefit. 'Yardley made three attempts to contact Laurie Nattrass before alerting us to his dead wife on the living room floor, and he didn't think to mention it to anyone? You can't tell me that's not a bad sign.'

'Paul Yardley isn't a liar!' Proust smacked the flat of his

hand against the desk. 'Don't make me take you off this case, Waterhouse, because I need you on it!'

That's right: you want to yell at me, not have me round for dinner.

'I want to interview Stella and Dillon White myself,' said Simon. 'I don't think we can discount what Dillon said about the wet umbrella and the rain.'

'You never stop, do you? Sergeant Kombothekra, explain to DC Waterhouse why, in our job, we're sometimes obliged to discount things we know not to be the case, like rain on a sunny day, or the guilt of innocent people.'

'Have you read the transcript of Gibbs' interview with Dillon?' Simon asked Proust. 'What kind of four-year-old says, "I saw him beyond" about a man he saw across a narrow cul-de-sac?'

'He sounded like . . .' Gibbs screwed up his face. 'What's a soothsayer?'

'This meeting is over,' said the Snowman, with the sort of pronounced finality most people would hold in reserve in case they ever needed to announce the end of the world. 'I for one shan't mourn its passing.'

'Sir, if I can—'

'No, Waterhouse. No to all your suggestions and requests, now and for ever more.'

Simon wanted to punch the air in triumph. That had to be it now, surely: the end of Proust's sick special-friend campaign. There would be no more confidences, no more invitations; no flattery or favours asked. Traditional unvarnished hostility had been reinstated, and Simon felt lighter as a result, able to move and breathe more freely.

It didn't last long. 'Got your diary with you, Waterhouse?' the Snowman called after him as he was leaving the room.

'We need to sort out an evening for you and Sergeant Zailer to come to us for a bite to eat, since you can't do tomorrow night. Pity. Why don't the two of you talk it over and get back to me with some dates that'd work for you?'

11

Friday 9 October 2009

Marchington House is a mansion. Its size shocks me to a standstill. I crane my neck and gawp at the pillared entrance, the carved stone arch around the door, the rows and rows of windows, so many that I don't even try to count.

How can someone like me walk into a place like this? The house I grew up in is about half the size of the outbuilding I can see at the far end of the garden, beyond what looks like an enormous black eye-patch on the grass, a rectangular tarpaulin that I assume covers a swimming pool.

I nearly laugh, imagining how the owners of Marchington House would react if they were told they had to spend even one night in my flat in Kilburn. *I'd rather die, darling. Go to the east wing scullery and ask the maid for a vial of arsenic from the poison cabinet.* My hands tighten around the strap of my shoulder bag. I've brought with me everything I thought I would need, but I can see now that it's not enough. *I'm the wrong sort of person for this.* I might have a top-of-the-range digital recorder with me, but that doesn't mean I know what I'm doing here.

Why is Rachel Hines here? Does the house belong to her family? Friends?

Please can we make friends? As a kid I used to say that to my dad when I'd been naughty and he was cross with me.

Pathetic as I know it is, I'd give anything to hear those words from Laurie. It would make a welcome change from hearing him say, 'This is Laurie Nattrass. Leave a message and I'll get back to you.'

I've resolved not to ring him or think about him at all today. I've got more important things to worry about. *Like the person who sent me a card with sixteen numbers on it, who might or might not want to kill me. Like the lies I told the police.*

I force my feet to move in the direction of Marchington House's front door. I'm about to press the bell when I notice the rings of stone around it, like ripples in water that have set. How many stonemasons were involved? One? A dozen? I take a deep breath. It's hard not to feel inferior when faced with a doorbell surround that looks as if it's had more time and care devoted to it than all the places I've ever lived in put together.

This house is too good for a woman who . . . The thought surges up before I can stop it. I force myself to follow it through: a woman who killed her two children. Isn't that what I believe, or has reading Laurie's article changed my mind?

I expect to be waiting a while, but Rachel Hines opens the door within seconds of my ringing the bell. 'Fliss,' she says. 'Thanks for coming.' She holds out her hand and I shake it. She's wearing pale blue flared jeans and a white linen shirt with a strange, plum-coloured woollen thing over it, some kind of shawl, but with arms and a neck. Her feet are bare. *She feels at home here.*

'Would you like me to put some shoes on?' she asks.

I feel the heat rush to my face. How can she know what I was thinking? Was I staring?

'I've learned to read body language over the years.' She smiles. 'Call it a finely tuned survival instinct.'

'You must be less nervous than I am,' I say quickly, because I'd rather tell her than try to keep it to myself and fail. 'Bare feet means relaxed, or it does to me, anyway. But . . . I don't mind. Not that I'd have any right to mind.' *Shut up, you fool.* I realise I've been manipulated; my confession was entirely unnecessary.

'That's your interpretation of my bare feet? Interesting. The first thing I'd think would be "under-floor heating". And I'd be right. Take off your shoes and socks and you'll see – it's like having your feet caressed by warm sand.' Her voice is deep and soft.

'I'm fine,' I say stiffly. If I were paranoid, I might start to think that all her dealings with me so far have been designed to throw me off balance. I don't know why I'm using the conditional tense, come to think of it – that's exactly what I *do* think. 'Paranoid' is such a pejorative word; sensibly cautious is what I am.

Apart from when you lied to the police.

'Do you see how our minds are incapable of thinking freely?' she says. 'It matters to me that this house has under-floor heating, more than it would to most people. Your nervousness matters to you – maybe it makes you feel ineffective. In the space of about ten seconds, we've both used my bare feet to reinforce the patterns our minds are determined to follow.'

Is this conversation going to get easier? She's harder to talk to than Laurie.

You're not supposed to be thinking about him, remember?

She stands back to let me in. 'I'm less nervous than you are because I know for sure that you're not a murderer. You don't know that about me.'

I don't want to have to respond to that, so instead I look around. What I see takes my breath away: a large hall with a glossy pale stone floor and skirting boards made from the same polished stone, about three times the height of any I've seen before. Everywhere I look there's something beautiful: the figure-of-eight newel-post, top and bottom circles hollowed out in the middle like something Henry Moore or Barbara Hepworth might have made; the chandelier, a falling shower of blue and pink glass tears, nearly as wide as the ceiling; two large oil paintings side by side, taking up an entire wall, both of women seemingly falling through the air, with small pinched black mouths and their hair flying out behind them; two chairs that look like thrones, with ornate wooden backs and seats covered in shimmery material the colour of moonlight; the water-feature sculpture in the corner – a human figure, the body made of rough-edged pink stone, the head a perpetually rolling white marble ball with water sliding off it as it moves, like a sheet of clear hair. I'm most impressed by what can only be described as a sunken glass rug, a rectangle of clear glass unevenly flecked with silver and gold, set into the stone in the centre of the hall, with light glowing through from beneath.

For about two seconds, I try to kid myself that this trying-too-hard interior wouldn't suit me at all, that I find it vulgar and over-the-top. Then I give up and face the fact that I'd chop off my right arm to live in a house like this, or to have a friend or relative who did that I could stay with. Tonight, on police advice, I've arranged to stay at Tamsin and Joe's, on a hard futon in their cobwebby, rattly-windowed computer room. I hate myself for making the comparison. I am officially a horrible, shallow person.

'You don't know for sure that I'm not a murderer,' I say, to prove that Rachel Hines isn't the only one capable of unexpected pronouncements.

'I know that I'm not,' she says.

'Wendy Whitehead.' I hadn't been planning to mention her name so soon. I'm not sure I'm ready to know. That's how good a truth-hunter I am: *please don't tell me anything – I'm too scared*. 'Who is she?'

'I thought you might want a drink before—'

'Who is she?'

'A nurse. Well, she was. She's not any more.'

We stare at one another. Eventually I say, 'I'll have a drink, thanks.' If I'm about to become the only person apart from Rachel Hines who knows the truth about her children's deaths, I need to prepare myself.

This can't be happening.

I follow her into a kitchen that's more haphazard than the hall but still beautiful: oak floor, curved white work surfaces that look like a sort of spongy stone, a double Belfast sink, a stripe of pale green glass with water pulsing through it running all the way along the floor on one side, breaking up the wood. Against one wall there's a cream-coloured Aga, except it's three times longer than any I've seen before. It's only slightly shorter than a minibus, come to think of it. In the centre of the room there's a large battered pine table with eight chairs around it, and, behind that, one of those free-standing island things, shaped like a teardrop, its curved sides painted pink and green.

Against the wall nearest to me, there's a purple backless sofa with a matching footstool pushed up against it. Both have been designed to within an inch of their lives. Together, they look like a wiggly exclamation mark. I notice a calendar on the wall: twelve months at a glance, with a tiny rectangle of space assigned to each day of the year. At the top it says 'Dairy Diary'. A Christmas present from the milkman? There's handwriting on it, but I'm not close enough to read it. Above the purple sofa are three paintings of stripes that warp when you look at them. I try to read the pencil signature at the bottom of the nearest one: Bridget something.

Above the minibus-Aga there's a framed photograph of two young men punting down a river. They're both good looking: one serious-faced and dark with a nice smile, the other blond and well aware of his sex appeal. A couple? Did they meet as students at Cambridge, hence the punt? If I was the sort of prejudiced person who leapt to conclusions about gay men and stunning interior design, I'd be concluding round about now that this might be their home.

'No family resemblance whatsoever, is there? You wouldn't believe three siblings could come out so different from one another.' Rachel Hines nods at the photograph and hands me a glass of something dark pink. 'Those two hogged all the good looks. And the charm.'

Not a gay couple, then. Of course. The sons of Marchington House would have studied at Cambridge. No sexed-up polytechnics for them. Rachel Hines probably went to Cambridge too, or Oxford. Any parents who install a strip of whooshy green glass in their kitchen floor would want all their children to get the very best education possible.

I wonder where those parents are. Out at work?

'It wasn't Wendy Whitehead's fault that Marcella and Nathaniel died. I tried to tell you that on the phone, but you cut me off. Please, have a seat.'

Not her fault? I realise how dry my mouth is, and take a sip of what turns out to be cranberry juice. 'You said she killed them.'

'She thought she was protecting them. So did I, which is why I let her do it.'

I wait for her to explain, trying to ignore the chill that's creeping up my back. For a second, as she stares at me, her poise seems to slip and she looks trapped, helpless. 'Can't you work it out? I've told you she's a nurse.'

'I've read Laurie's notes. There was no nurse at your house when . . . You were alone with both babies when they died.'

'Wendy gave Marcella and Nathaniel their first DTP jabs. You don't have children, do you?'

I shake my head. *Vaccination.* She's talking about vaccination. I remember reading something in a newspaper a while ago about crazy hippies who refuse to immunise their children and rely instead on ginseng and patchouli oil to ward off disease.

'They scream when you take them for their jabs. You have to hold them while the needle goes in, but you don't feel as if you're hurting them. You think you're doing your duty as a good mother. You make no comparisons or analogies, you don't think about the other circumstances in which people are injected against their will, all of them horrendous . . .'

I push her out of my way, walk over to the kitchen table and slam down my glass. I'm glad I didn't bother sitting. 'I'm going. I never should have come here in the first place.'

'Why?'

'*Why?* Isn't it obvious?' I can hardly contain my disappointment. 'You're making this up as you go along. Nothing was said at your trial about any DTP jabs.'

'Well spotted. You could ask me why.'

'Now you're making out that what happened to Marcella and Nathaniel was down to routine childhood vaccinations, trying to compare them to lethal injections on death row.'

'You don't know what I'm trying to say, because you didn't let me finish. Marcella was born two weeks early – did you know that?'

'What's that got to do with anything?'

'If you leave now, you'll never find out.'

I bend to pick up my bag. Now that I know I'm not going to be exec-ing a documentary about a murderer called Wendy Whitehead who nearly got away with it, I've no reason to stay. Rachel Hines must know that. What lie will she try next?

'Why are you so angry with me?' she asks.

'I don't like being messed around. Don't pretend you haven't been toying with me from the first phone call – insisting on coming to my house in the middle of the night, then driving away. Ringing me and saying Wendy Whitehead killed your children, conveniently forgetting to mention anything about vaccinations . . .'

'You hung up on me.'

'I lied to the police, thanks to you. They asked me if I had an address for you and I said no. I'm supposed to suspend all work on the film until they give me the all-clear. I shouldn't be here.' My bag slides off my shoulder. I try to catch it and fail. It drops to the floor. 'You sent me those cards and the photograph, didn't you? It was you.'

She looks puzzled, but puzzled looks are easy to fake. 'Cards?' she says.

'Sixteen numbers in a square. The police think whoever

sent them might try to . . . attack me or something. They didn't say so, but I can tell that's what they think.'

'Slow down, Fliss. Let's talk about this calmly. I promise you I didn't send you any—'

'No! I don't want to talk to you! I'm walking out of here now, and you're not going to contact me again – I want your word on that. Whatever game you've been playing with me is over. Say it! Tell me you'll leave me alone.'

'You don't trust me, do you?'

'That's an understatement!' In my whole life, I have never spoken to anyone so viciously.

'My word's worthless, then.'

'Good point,' I say, heading for the front door. My lie to the police won't matter if I correct it as soon as I can. I'll ring DC Simon Waterhouse and tell him Rachel Hines is at Marchington House in Twickenham and that I'm sure she's the person who sent me those numbers. I don't know why it didn't occur to me before. I got the first card in Wednesday morning's post. It was on Wednesday that she phoned me for the first time. Did she sit down on Tuesday and make a list? *Item one: abandon all other projects and devote all time henceforth to messing with Fliss Benson's head?*

'Fliss!' She grabs my arm, pulling me back towards her.

'Let go of me!' I feel dizzy, unsteady on my feet, as if by touching me she's injected pure, undiluted panic into my bloodstream. I think of DC Waterhouse telling me not to go anywhere alone.

'Do you think I killed them?' she asks. 'Do you think I murdered Marcella and Nathaniel? Tell me the truth.'

'Maybe you did. I don't know. I'll *never* know – neither will anyone, apart from you. If I had to guess, based on what little I know of you, I'd say yes, I think you probably did it.' There, I've said it, and fuck you, Laurie, if you're telepathic and heard me say it and you're shaking your head in disgust. You never bothered to ask me what I thought about your protégées, did you? Helen and Sarah and Rachel. My opinion doesn't matter. It matters as little as the sex we had yesterday.

Without warning, I burst into tears. *Oh my God, oh my God, oh my God*. I try to regain control, but it's useless. I feel like someone who can't swim, powerless in the face of a gushing waterfall. It doesn't even feel as if the tears are coming from me and, for a few minutes, I'm too shocked by what my body is doing without permission to notice that someone is holding me tight, or to realise, because no one else is here, that that someone must be Rachel Hines.

'I'm not going to ask you. You probably don't want to talk about it.'

I shake my head. I'm sitting on the wiggly purple sofa in the kitchen, concentrating on drinking my cranberry juice, sip by sip. Perhaps by the time I finish it, I won't feel so horrendously embarrassed. Rachel's sitting at the table at the far end of the room, trying to keep a tactful distance. *As if either of us is likely to forget that she's just spent the last half hour mopping me up*.

'I didn't send you a card with numbers on it,' she says. 'Or any photographs. Did you ask the police why they thought the sender might attack you? If you're in danger, you've a right to know what's going on. Why don't you—?'

'I don't need a life coach,' I mutter ungraciously.

'And if you did, you wouldn't recruit me,' she says, neatly

summarising my views on the matter. 'I can explain why I drove away on Wednesday night, but it might offend you.'

I shrug. I'm already feeling unloveable, humiliated and terrified – offended might as well join the club.

'I didn't like your house.'

I look up, to check I've heard right. '*What?*'

'It looks dirty. The paint's flaking off the window frames . . .'

'I don't own it. I rent the basement flat, that's all.'

'Is it nice?'

I can't believe I'm having this conversation. 'My flat? No, it's not *nice*. It's about – ooh, let's see – five million times less nice than this house. It's small and damp and all I can afford.' I wonder if I ought to qualify this: *all I could afford, until recently*. Why bother? As soon as Maya hears Rachel Hines' revised opinion of me, not to mention Laurie's, I'll be unemployed and probably homeless. Even mouldy flats in Kilburn cost money.

'I looked at the outside of your house and I knew I wouldn't like the inside. I tried to tell myself it didn't matter, that I'd be okay, but I knew I wouldn't. I pictured us sitting and talking in a dingy lounge, with posters stuck to the plasterboard walls with drawing pins, and a throw over the sofa to hide the stains, and . . .' She sighs. 'I know how awful this sounds, but I want to be honest with you.'

'I can't complain, can I? I accused you of being a child-killer.'

'No, you didn't. You said you didn't know. There's a big difference.'

I look away, wishing I hadn't let her provoke me into expressing an opinion.

'Ever since prison, I've . . . I can't stand to be anywhere that isn't . . .'

'A stunning mansion?' I say sarcastically.

'The wrong physical environment, any kind of ugly surroundings – it makes me feel physically sick,' she says. 'It never used to. Prison changed me in lots of ways, but that was the first thing I noticed, the first night I was out. Angus and I had split up. I had no home to go to, so I went to a hotel.' She takes a deep breath, drawing in her chin.

Only three stars, was it? I don't say it. It's too easy to be cruel to her, and I know I'd enjoy it too much. *It's not her fault I started blubbing and made an exhibition of myself.*

'I didn't like the room they put me in, but I told myself it didn't matter – I'd only be there a few nights while I sorted out somewhere more permanent to live. I had this nauseous feeling that wouldn't go away, a bit like car sickness, but I tried to ignore it.'

'What was wrong with the room?' I asked. 'Was it dirty?'

'Probably. I don't know.' I hear impatience in her voice, as if she's been asked the same question countless times and still can't come up with an answer. 'It was mainly the curtains that bothered me.'

'Dirty?' I try again.

'I didn't get close enough to find out. They were too thin and too short. They stopped at the bottom of the window instead of going down to the floor. It was as if someone had pinned two handkerchiefs to the wall. And they were attached to one of those horrible plastic tracks with no pelmet or anything to cover it. You could see bits of string poking out behind the material at the top.' She shudders. 'They were disgusting. I wanted to run from the room screaming. I know it sounds crazy.'

Just a bit.

'There was a picture on the wall of a stone urn, with flowers strewn around its base. I didn't like that either. It was sort of washed-out looking. No proper colours.' She rubs her neck, plucks at the skin with her fingers. 'I wondered at first if it was because it was an urn – you know, the death connection – but I decided it couldn't be. Marcella and Nathaniel weren't cremated, they were buried.' Her matter-of-fact tone makes my skin prickle. *You know, the death connection*. How can someone whose two babies have died say that so casually?

'Anyway, there was nothing I could do,' she goes on, unaware of my reaction. 'I couldn't ask to change rooms without a good reason, and I didn't have one, not until I turned on the taps in the bathroom and nothing came out. No water. I was so pleased, I burst into tears, ran to the phone – I had my legitimate reason, and I knew they'd have to move me. Silly thing was, I didn't really care about having no water – I could have got a bottle from the mini-bar and used it to brush my teeth and wash my face. I just wanted to get away from those damn curtains.' She looks at me with a weak grin. 'The ones in my new room were better. They were still too short, but at least there was a pelmet, and the material was thicker. But . . .' She closes her eyes. I wait for her to tell me that there was something even more appalling in the new room: the previous occupant's toenail clippings in a pile on the bedside table. The thought makes me feel sick; I try to erase it from my mind. *The jury will disregard the image of hard, yellow slivers of toenail*.

'The picture of the urn was there, up on the wall – the same wall as in the previous room, directly opposite the bed.' From her haunted expression and her shaky voice, anyone would think she was recalling a scene of carnage. Perhaps she's about to. I realise I'm holding my breath.

It's a while before she speaks again. When she does, she says, 'Not the exact same picture, obviously. An identical copy. They must have put one in each room – clones masquerading as art. Hideous, mass-produced . . . crap!'

So? Is that it?

'I *was* sick then – properly, physically sick. I packed my things and got the hell out of there, didn't have a clue where I was going. I flagged down a taxi in the street and heard myself reciting my old Notting Hill address to the driver.'

'You went to your ex-husband?' *Why not here, to Marchington House?*

'Angus. Yes.' There's a faraway look in her eyes. 'I told him I couldn't stay in the hotel, but I didn't tell him why. He wouldn't have understood if I'd said there was no difference between a hotel room and a cell at Geddham Hall.'

'But . . . you'd split up. He thought you'd . . .'

'Killed our children. Yes, he did.'

'Then why go to him? And why did he let you in? *Did* he let you in?'

She nods. When I see her coming towards me, I stiffen, but all she does is sit down at the far end of the sofa, leaving a comfortable distance between us. 'I could tell you why,' she says. 'Why I behaved as I did, why Angus behaved as he did. But it wouldn't make sense out of context. I'd like to tell you the whole story, from the start – the story I've never told anybody. The truth.'

I don't want to hear it.

'You can make your documentary,' she says, with a new energy in her voice. I'm not sure if she's begging or issuing an order. 'Not about Helen Yardley, or Sarah Jaggard – about me. Me, Angus, Marcella and Nathaniel. The story of what happened to our family. That's my one condition, Fliss. I don't want to share the hour or two hours or however long it is with anyone else, however worthy their cause. I'm sorry if that sounds selfish . . .'

'Why me?' I ask.

'Because you don't know what to think about me. I could hear it in your voice, the first time I spoke to you: the uncertainty, the doubt. I *need* your doubt – it'll make you listen to me, properly, because you want to find out, don't you? Hardly anyone really listens. Laurie Nattrass certainly doesn't. You'll be objective. The film you'll make won't portray me as a helpless victim or as a killer, because I'm neither one of those things. You'll show people who I really am, who Angus is, how much we both loved Marcella and Nathaniel.'

I stand up, repelled by the determination in her blazing eyes. I have to get out of here before she makes the choice for me. 'Sorry,' I say firmly. 'I'm not the right person.'

'Yes, you are.'

'I'm not. You wouldn't say that if you knew who my father was.' There, I've said it. I can't unsay it. 'Forget it,' I mutter, feeling dangerously close to tears again. *That's why I got upset: Dad, not Laurie*. Nothing to do with Laurie, and so slightly less pathetic. A tragically dead father is a better reason to cry than unrequited love for a complete arsehole. 'I'll go,' I say. 'I should never have come.' I grab my bag, like someone who really intends to leave. I stay where I am.

'It makes no difference to me who your father was,' says Rachel. 'If he was the first on my jury to vote guilty, if he was the judge who gave me two life sentences . . . Though I think it's unlikely Justice Elizabeth Geilow's your dad.' She smiles. 'What's his name?'

'He's dead.' I sit down again. I can't stand up and talk about Dad at the same time. Not that I've ever tried. I've never even talked about it to Mum. How stupid is that? 'He committed suicide three years ago. His name was Melvyn Benson. You probably won't have heard of him.' *Though he'd heard of you*. 'He was Head of Children's Services for—'

'Jaycee Herridge.'

I flinch at the name, though I know it's ridiculous. Jaycee Herridge didn't kill my dad. She was only twenty months old. I feel trapped, as if something that's been gaping open has slammed shut. I shouldn't have said anything. After years of bottling it up, why tell Rachel Hines, of all people?

'Your dad was the disgraced social worker who killed himself?'

I nod.

'I remember hearing people talking about it in prison. I avoided the news and the papers as much as possible, but a lot of the girls couldn't get enough of other people's misery – it was a distraction from their own.'

I swallow hard. The idea of Dad's suffering providing entertainment for the feral incarcerated masses is hard to take. I don't care if I'm prejudiced; if they can enjoy my father's downfall, I can think of them as scum who deserve to be behind bars. That way we're even.

'Fliss? Tell me.'

I have the oddest feeling: that I always knew, deep down, that this would happen. *That Rachel Hines is exactly the person I want to tell.*

Woodenly, I layout the facts. Jaycee Herridge was taken to hospital twenty-one times in the first year of her life, with injuries her parents claimed were accidental – bruises, cuts, swellings, burns. When she was fourteen months old, her mother took her to the doctor's surgery with what turned out to be two broken arms, saying she had climbed out of her pram and fallen on a concrete playground. The GP knew the medical history and didn't believe the story for a second. He alerted Social Services, wishing he'd done so several months earlier instead of allowing himself to be given cups of tea and lied to by Jaycee's parents, who always took great pains to reassure him when he visited them at home, cuddling Jaycee and making a fuss of her in his presence.

The social worker assigned to the case spent the next four months doing everything she could to remove Jaycee from the family home. She had the support of the police and of every health professional who had ever had contact with the family, but the council's legal services department decreed that there wasn't sufficient proof of abuse for Jaycee to be taken into care. This was a catastrophic error on the part of a junior legal executive who should have known that in the family courts, guilt did not have to be proven beyond reasonable doubt. All that was required was for a family court judge to decide that on the balance of probabilities, Jaycee would be safer in local authority care than with her parents, and, given the number and seriousness of her injuries, this would almost certainly have happened if the case had ever made it to court.

As Head of Children's Services, my father should have spotted this mistake, but he didn't. He was overworked and stressed, ground down by the tottering towers of files on his desk, and as soon as he saw the words 'unsafe to initiate care proceedings' and the signature of a legal executive beneath it, he probed no further. He would never have dreamed of trying to take a child from its parents against legal advice, and it wouldn't have occurred to him that a legal executive working in child protection could be so incompetent as to confuse criminal and civil standards of proof.

As a result of his misplaced trust and the legal executive's idiocy, Jaycee was left in the care of her parents, who finally murdered her in August 2005, when she was twenty months old. Her father pleaded guilty to kicking her to death and was sentenced to life in prison. Her mother was never charged with anything because it was impossible to prove she was involved in the violence against her daughter.

My father resigned. Jaycee's GP resigned. The legal executive refused to resign and was eventually fired. No one remembers their names now, and although everyone knows the name Jaycee Herridge, very few people would be able to tell you that her parents' names were Danielle Herridge and Oscar Kelly.

My father never forgave himself. In August 2006, a week before the anniversary of Jaycee's death, he washed down thirty sleeping tablets with a bottle of whisky and never woke up. He must have planned it well in advance. He'd encouraged Mum to spend the weekend at her sister's house, to make sure she didn't find him in time to save him.

I could tell Rachel Hines a lot more. I could tell her I spent the last year of Dad's life lying to him, pretending I didn't blame him for screwing up so horrendously when all the time a voice in my head was screaming *Why didn't you check? Why did you take someone else's word for it when a human life was at stake? What kind of useless cretin are you?* I've always wondered if Mum pretended too, or if she believed what she told him over and over: that it wasn't his fault, and no one could ever claim that it was. How could she believe that?

I drag myself back to the present. I need to finish explaining myself and get the hell out of here. 'What you don't know – because you can't – is that he talked to me about you not long before he killed himself.'

'Your father talked about *me*?'

'Not just you – all three of you. Helen Yardley, Sarah Jaggard . . .'

'All three of us.' Rachel smiles, as if I've said something funny. Then her smile disappears and she looks deadly serious. 'I don't care about Helen Yardley and Sarah Jaggard,' she says. 'What did your dad say about me?'

I feel like a sadist, but I can hardly refuse to answer her question, having got this far. 'We'd gone out for the day – me, him and Mum. One of the many trips Mum arranged to cheer him up after Jaycee died. The fact that they never worked and it was obvious he'd never be cheerful again didn't stop us trying. We were having lunch, me and Mum chatting brightly as if everything was fine. Dad was reading the paper. There was an article about you, your case. I think it must have said something about an appeal – that you were planning to appeal or that you might, I don't know.'

Laurie probably wrote it.

'Dad threw down the paper and said, "If Rachel Hines appeals and wins, there's no hope."'

Her lips twitch slightly. Apart from that, no reaction.

'He was shaking. He'd never mentioned your name before. Mum and I didn't know what to say. There was this horrible, tense atmosphere. We both knew . . .' I stop. I don't know how to say it without sounding awful.

'You knew that if he was thinking about me then he was thinking about dead babies.'

'Yes.'

'And that was a dangerous subject for him to be thinking about.'

'He said, "If they let Rachel Hines out of prison, no parent who murders a child will ever be convicted in this country again. Everyone working in child protection might as well pack up and go home. More children like Jaycee Herridge will die and there'll be nothing anyone can do to stop it." He had this . . . ferocious look in his eyes, as if he'd seen some sort of vision of the future and . . .' *And it made him want out.* I can't bring myself to articulate this. I'm convinced – I've always been convinced – that Dad killed himself because he didn't want to be around if and when Rachel Hines was released.

'He had a point,' she says gently. 'If all the mothers convicted of killing their babies appeal and win, the message is clear: mothers don't and can't murder their children. Which we all know isn't true.'

'He started shouting in front of everybody.' I'm crying again, but this time I don't care. '"Suddenly, they're all innocent – Yardley, Jaggard, Hines! All tried for murder, two of them convicted, but they're all innocent! How can that be?" He was yelling at me and Mum, as if it was our fault. Mum couldn't handle it, she ran out of the restaurant. I said, "Dad, no one's saying Rachel Hines is innocent. You don't know she's going to appeal, and even if she does, you don't know she'll win."'

'He was right.' Rachel stands up, starts to walk in no particular direction. She would hate my kitchen. It's too small for aimless walking. It would make her feel sick. 'My case effectively changed the law. Like your dad, the three judges who heard my appeal didn't see me as an individual. They saw me as number three, after Yardley and Jaggard. Everyone lumped us together – the three crib death killers.' She frowns. 'I don't know why we got to be the famous ones. Lots of women are in prison for killing children, their own and other people's.'

I think of Laurie's article. *Helen Yardley, Lorna Keast, Joanne Bew, Sarah Jaggard, Dorne Llewellyn . . . the list goes on and on.*

'Would I have had my convictions overturned if Helen Yardley hadn't set a precedent? She was the one who first piqued Laurie Nattrass's interest. It was her case that made him start questioning Judith Duffy's professionalism, which was what led to my being granted leave to appeal.' She turns to face me, angry. 'It was nothing to do with me. It was Helen Yardley, Laurie Nattrass and JIPAC. They turned it political. It wasn't about our specific cases any more – Sarah Jaggard's, mine. We weren't individuals, we were a national scandal: the victims of an evil doctor who wanted us locked up for ever. And her motive? Rampant malevolence, because we all know some doctors *are* evil. Oh, we're all suckers for a wicked doctor story, and Laurie Nattrass is a brilliant storyteller. That's why the prosecution rolled over and I was spared a retrial.'

'Because Laurie can't see the trees for the wood.'

'What? What did you say?' She's standing over me, leaning down.

'My boss, Maya – she said you said that about him. She thought you'd got the saying wrong, but you meant it the way you said it, didn't you? You meant to say that Laurie saw you as one of his wrongly accused victims, not as a person in your own right. That's why you want the documentary to be about you only – not Helen Yardley or Sarah Jaggard.'

Rachel kneels down on the sofa beside me. 'Never underestimate the differences between things, Fliss: your flat in a horrible terrace in Kilburn and this house; a beautiful painting and a soulless mass-produced image of an urn; people who are capable of seeing only their own narrow perspective, and people who see the whole picture.' She's pinching the skin on her neck again, turning it red. Her eyes are sharp when she turns to face me. 'I see the whole picture. I think you do too.'

'There's another reason,' I say, my rapid heartbeat alerting me to the inadvisability of bringing this up. *Tough*. Now that I've had the thought, I have to see her reaction. 'There's another reason you don't want to be part of the same programme as Helen Yardley and Sarah Jaggard. You think they're both guilty.'

'You're wrong. I don't think that, not about either of them.' When she speaks again, her voice is thick with emotion. 'You're as wrong about me as I'm right about you, but you're thinking – that's what matters. If I wasn't convinced before, I am now: it has to be you, Fliss. You have to make this documentary. The story needs to be told and it needs to be told now, before . . .' She stops, shakes her head.

'You said your case changed the law,' I say, trying to sound professional. 'What did you mean?'

She snorts dismissively, rubbing the end of her nose. 'My appeal judges concluded, and wrote into their summary remarks so that there would be no ambiguity, that when a case relies solely on disputed medical evidence, that case should not be brought before a criminal court. Which means it's now pretty much impossible to convict a mother who waits till she's alone with her child and then smothers him. There isn't generally much other evidence in cases of smothering. The victim puts up no resistance, being only a baby, and there are no witnesses – you'd have to be pretty stupid to try to smother your baby in front of a witness.'

Or desperate, I think. So desperate you don't care who sees.

'Your father's prediction was spot on. My appeal judgement *has* made it easier for mothers to murder their babies and avoid prosecution. Not only mothers – fathers, childminders, anyone. Your dad was smart to see it coming. I didn't. I might not have appealed if I'd known that was the effect it would have. I'd lost everything already. What did it matter if I was in prison or out?'

'If you're innocent . . .'

'I am.'

'Then you deserve to be free.'

'Will you make the documentary?'

'I don't know if I can.' I hear the panic in my voice and despise myself. Will I be betraying Dad if I do? Betraying something more important if I don't?

'Your father's dead, Fliss. I'm alive.'

I owe her nothing. I don't say it out loud because I shouldn't have to. It should be obvious.

'I'm going back to Angus,' she says quietly. 'I can't hide away here for ever, with no one knowing where I am. I need to start living my life again. Angus loves me, whatever's happened between us in the past.'

'Does he want you back?'

'I think so, and even if he doesn't, he will when I . . .' She leaves the sentence unfinished.

'What?' I ask. 'When you what?'

'When I tell him that I'm pregnant,' she says, looking away.

Daily Telegraph, Saturday 10 October 2009

Significant Lead in Helen Yardley Murder

Police investigating the murder of Helen Yardley, the wrongly convicted mother shot dead at her home in Spilling on Monday, confirmed yesterday that they have a lead. The police artist's image below is of a man West Midlands CID are keen to question in connection with a recent attack on Sarah Jaggard, the Wolverhampton hairdresser acquitted of the murder of six-month-old Beatrice Furniss in July 2005. Mrs Jaggard was threatened with a knife in a busy shopping area of Wolverhampton on Monday 28 September. DS Sam Kombothekra of Culver Valley CID said: 'We believe that the same man who attacked Mrs Jaggard may have shot Mrs Yardley. There is evidence that links the two incidents.' Helen Yardley spent nine years in prison for the murders of her two baby sons before having her convictions quashed on appeal in February 2005. A card with 16 numbers on it, reproduced below, was found in her pocket after her death. A similar card was left in Mrs Jaggard's pocket by her assailant.

DS Kombothekra has asked for anyone who recognises the man pictured below to contact him or a member of his team. He said: 'We can guarantee complete confidentiality, so there is no reason to fear coming forward, though we believe this man is dangerous and should not be approached under any circumstances by members of the public. We must find him as a matter of utmost urgency.' DS Kombothekra has also appealed for information about the 16 numbers on the card: 'They must mean something to somebody. If that someone is you, please contact Culver Valley CID.'

Asked to comment on motive, DS Kombothekra said: 'Both Mrs Yardley and Mrs Jaggard were accused of heinous crimes and found – though only after a terrible miscarriage of justice in Mrs Yardley's case – to be not guilty. We have to consider the possibility that the motive is a desire to punish both women based on the mistaken belief that they are guilty.'

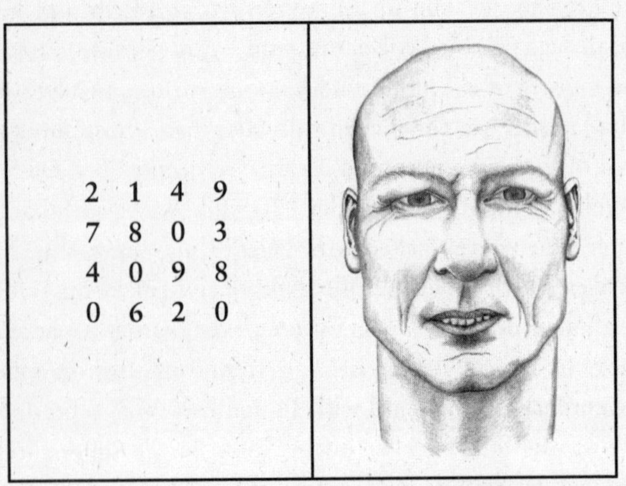

12

10/10/09

'I've no idea whether they were the same numbers or sixteen different numbers.' Tamsin Waddington pulled her chair forward and leaned across the small kitchen table that separated her from DC Colin Sellers. He could smell her hair, or whatever sweet substance she'd sprayed it with. Her whole flat smelled of it. He resisted the urge to grab the long ponytail she'd draped over her right shoulder, to see if it felt as silky as it looked. 'I don't even know that there were sixteen of them. All I know is, there were some numbers on a card, laid out in rows and columns – could have been sixteen, twelve, twenty . . .'

'But you're certain you saw the card on Mr Nattrass's desk on 2 September,' said Sellers. 'That's very precise, and more than a month ago. How can you—?'

'2 September's my boyfriend's birthday. I was hanging around in Laurie's office trying to pluck up the courage to ask him if I could leave early.'

'I thought you said he wasn't your boss.' Sellers stifled a sigh. He hated it when attractive women had boyfriends. He genuinely believed he'd do a better job, given the opportunity. Not knowing the boyfriends in question made no difference to the strength of his conviction. Like anyone with a vocation, Sellers felt frustrated whenever he was prevented from doing what he was put on this earth to do.

'He wasn't my boss as such. I was his researcher.'

'On the crib death film?'

'That's right.' She leaned in even closer, trying to read Sellers' notes. *Nosey cow*. If he stuck out his tongue now he could lick her hair. 'Laurie never seemed to want to go home, and I was embarrassed to admit that I did,' she said. 'Embarrassed to have made plans that didn't involve defeating injustice, plans Laurie wouldn't have given a toss about. I was hovering round his desk like an idiot, and I saw the card next to his BlackBerry. I asked him about it because it was easier than asking what I really wanted to ask.'

'This is important, Miss Waddington, so please be as accurate as you can.' *Can I play with your swishy hair while you suck my nads?* 'What did you say to Mr Nattrass about the card, and what was his response?' For a moment, Sellers imagined he'd asked the wrong question, the X-rated one, but he couldn't have. She didn't look offended, wasn't running from the room.

'I picked it up. He didn't seem to notice. I said, "What's this?" He grunted at me.'

'Grunted?' This was torture. Couldn't she use more neutral words?

'Laurie grunts all the time – when he knows a response is required, but hasn't heard what you've said. It works with a lot of people, but I'm not easily fobbed off. I waved the card in front of his face and asked him again what it was. Typical Laurie, he blinked at me like a mole emerging into the light after a month underground and said, "What *is* that bloody thing? Did you send it to me? What do those numbers mean?" I told him I had no idea. He snatched the card out of my hand, tore it up, threw the pieces in the air, and turned back to his work.'

'You saw him tear it up?'

'Into at least eight pieces, which I picked up and chucked in the bin. Don't know why I bothered – Laurie didn't notice, or thank me, and when I finally got round to asking him if I could leave early he said, "No, you fucking can't." If I'd known the numbers were important, I'd have—' Tamsin broke off, tutted as if annoyed with herself. 'I have a vague memory of the first number being a two, but I wouldn't swear to it. I didn't think anything of it until Fliss turned up here in a state last night and told me about the card she'd been sent and an anonymous stalker who might or might not want to kill her.'

'Did Mr Nattrass say whether the card was sent to him at work or at home?'

'No, but if I had to guess I'd say work. I doubt he'd have bothered to bring it into the office if it had been sent to him at home. He seemed completely uninterested in it – it meant nothing to him.'

'Can you be sure of that?' Sellers asked. 'Anger might be one reason for ripping something to pieces.'

'Anger at having his time wasted, that's all. Honestly – I know Laurie. Which is why I wasn't surprised when Fliss told me he hadn't mentioned getting a similar card himself, when she showed him the one she'd been sent. Laurie doesn't waste words on anything he doesn't consider important.'

Sellers thought it was odd, nevertheless, that Nattrass hadn't mentioned it to Fliss Benson. It would have been the most natural thing in the world for him to say, 'That's strange – someone sent me one of those a few weeks ago.' Why keep quiet about it, unless he was the person who'd sent the sixteen numbers to Benson – a second draft, after he'd torn up the first to put Tamsin off the scent?

What scent, dickhead? On 2 September, Helen Yardley was still alive. Nattrass can't be her killer – he's got an alibi, and looks nothing like the man Sarah Jaggard described.

Everyone had a sodding alibi. Judith Duffy, though she was still refusing to be interviewed, had left a message on Sam Kombothekra's voicemail detailing her whereabouts on Monday. She'd spent the morning with her lawyers, and the afternoon in a restaurant with Rachel Hines. Sellers couldn't begin to get his head round that, but there seemed to be no doubt about it – three waiters had confirmed that the two of them arrived at 1 p.m. and didn't leave until 5.

Duffy's two daughters and their husbands – Imogen and Spencer, Antonia and George – had been in the Maldives. They'd left the country before Sarah Jaggard was attacked and got back on Wednesday, two days after Helen Yardley was shot. Sellers had interviewed the four of them yesterday, and it had put him right off his traditional Friday night curry. He didn't usually let the job get to him, but he'd started to feel increasingly uncomfortable as he listened to them explain, one after another, that they didn't care if they never saw Duffy again. 'She's got no heart,' Imogen said. 'She ruined innocent women's lives to further her own career. You can't sink much lower than that.' Antonia wasn't quite so black and white about it. 'I'll never feel the same about Mum,' she said. 'I'm so angry with her, I can't bring myself to speak to her at the moment. Maybe one day.'

The two sons in law clearly regarded Duffy as an embarrassment. One went as far as to say he'd have thought twice about marrying her daughter if he'd known what would happen. 'My kids keep asking me why other kids at school are laughing at them, saying their granny's in all the papers,' he said angrily. 'They're only eight and six – they don't understand it. What am I supposed to say?'

Sellers hadn't been able to resist asking, though it had no bearing on the investigation, how healthy the relationship between Duffy and her daughters and sons-in-law had been before Laurie Nattrass had brought her lack of professional integrity to the public's attention. 'All right,' Imogen had said doubtfully. Antonia had nodded more enthusiastically. 'We were a normal family before this nightmare started.'

Sellers couldn't stand the thought of his own children one day saying similar things about him – that he had no heart, or they couldn't bring themselves to speak to him. Would Stacey try to make Harrison and Bethany hate him, if he left her?

Suki thought she would – the woman he'd been seeing behind Stacey's back for nearly ten years. She'd told him over and over, and he'd ended up believing her. She talked about Stacey as if she knew her better than Sellers did, even though they'd never met.

Suki didn't want Sellers full-time anyway. She had at one time, but not any more. 'This way you don't have to lose me or your kids,' she often said. Sellers was almost as bored of Suki as he was of Stacey. He'd tell them both where to stick it if in exchange he could have one night with Tamsin Waddington. Even one hour . . .

'Did you hear what I just said?'

'Sorry.'

'I know you're a man, but do you think you could pay attention?'

Sellers risked a grin. 'You'd make a good DCI,' he said.

'There's nothing suspicious about Laurie Nattrass failing to communicate efficiently,' said Tamsin. 'If he'd said to Fliss, "How interesting – I received a similar card myself, also with sixteen numbers on it, only a few weeks ago" – now *that* would have been suspicious. He once said to me, "Where's that coffee I asked for?" three seconds after I'd handed it to him. I pointed at the mug of coffee in his right hand, and he said, "Did you just give me this?" Then he dropped it and I had to make him another one.'

Sellers still wasn't convinced. Nattrass had failed to mention having been sent the sixteen numbers not only to Fliss Benson but also to Waterhouse, during their telephone conversation. He must have known at that point that the card was important, if a detective was asking about it. Waterhouse had asked him if he'd had any unusual emails or letters recently, and Nattrass had dodged the question. He'd described the card Fliss Benson had received and said nothing about being sent one himself. Was that the behaviour of an innocent man?

'I'm worried about Fliss.' Tamsin's haughty tone suggested Sellers had damn well better share her concern. 'I read the paper this morning – why do you think I called the police? I know a card like the ones Fliss and Laurie were sent was found on Helen Yardley's dead body. I know Sarah Jaggard was attacked and whoever did it left a card with sixteen numbers on it in her pocket. It doesn't make sense, though.' Her forehead creased.

'What doesn't?'

'With both Helen Yardley and Sarah Jaggard, the violent part came first, didn't it? He attacked them, then left the cards. Fliss and Laurie both got cards through the post, but they haven't been attacked. So maybe he *isn't* going to hurt them, because if he was, wouldn't he have done it already?'

Which is why Superintendent Barrow won't authorise protection. That and his loathing for the Snowman.

'Fliss isn't in good shape,' said Tamsin. 'I think she's really scared, though she insists she's not, and I'm almost certain there's something she's not telling me, something to do with the card. The numbers. She went off first thing this morning without telling me or Joe where she was going, and I've no idea where she is now. And . . .'

'And?' Sellers prompted.

'She promised a detective she spoke to that she wouldn't work on the film, but she has been. There, I've shopped her,' said Tamsin proudly. 'I'm happy to be a grass if it keeps her safe. She met up with Ray Hines yesterday.'

'Where?'

'At her parents' house, I think.'

'Miss Benson's parents' house?'

'No, Ray Hines'.'

Sellers bit the inside of his lip. This was no good. Waterhouse would be furious.

'You did the right thing telling me.' He smiled. Tamsin smiled back.

All right, love, wipe yourself, your taxi's here. It's four in the morning, love, pay for yourself . . .

Fuck. The voice was back. Recently, Sellers had been finding it hard to banish Gibbs' impression of him from his mind when he was around a woman or women; it was doing nothing for his confidence. He'd heard it last Saturday night, just before he'd made a complete tit of himself. It had honestly been as if Gibbs was there with him, whispering in his ear. He could have sworn he *heard* it. Must have been the drink, since Gibbs was nowhere nearby. Thank God. Absolutely arseholed on a mixture of Timothy Taylor Landlord and Laphroaig, Sellers had tried to pick up a woman he'd seen through the window of a restaurant while walking home from the pub. He'd gone in and propositioned her, oblivious to her companions, a young man and a middle-aged couple. She'd been celebrating her twenty-first birthday with her boyfriend and parents, as she had repeatedly told him, but that hadn't stopped him. He'd continued to insist that she accompany him to a nearby hotel. Eventually the restaurant manager and a waiter had dragged him out on to the street, told him never to come back, and slammed the door in his face. He might have had more luck if he'd propositioned her mother, come to think of it.

'If either Mr Nattrass or Miss Benson contacts you . . .'

'Are you going to look for Fliss?' Tamsin asked. 'If I don't hear back from her soon, I'm really going to panic. Twickenham – that's where you want to start looking.'

'Why there?'

'I think that's where Ray Hines' parents live. And I'm pretty sure Fliss will have gone back there today.'

Sellers wrote 'Ray Hines – parents – Twickenham' in his notebook.

'She's next, isn't she?' said Tamsin.

'Sorry?'

'First Sarah Jaggard's nearly knifed, then Helen Yardley's shot. Ray Hines is number three, isn't she? She's bound to be next.'

* * *

This is the happiest I've ever been, thought Sergeant Charlie Zailer. She'd been in a state of deep joy all morning, but she'd been alone at home, and bliss – as she'd only recently discovered, never having experienced it or anything like it before – pulsed even more strongly through the veins, glowed all the more brightly under the skin, when you were around other people. Which was why she had wanted to throw her arms round Sam Kombothekra's neck and cover him with kisses – platonic ones – when he'd arrived to escort her to Proust's office, and why now, walking beside Sam along the corridor to the CID room, listening to his apologies and proclamations of innocence, she felt her happiness was reaching a peak. Here she was with her good friend, on this brilliant day, talking, breathing air. She didn't care about being taken away from her work, or the manner in which this had been effected. All that mattered to her was the scrap of paper in her pocket.

She hadn't been planning to tell anyone but her sister – it was private, after all – but she was still waiting for Liv to ring her back, and now here she was, strolling along with Sam . . . Well, *she* was strolling. He was marching, glancing back over his shoulder at her every few seconds, scared the Snowman would glaciate him if he took too long to round Charlie up. Who cared? And who cared what Proust wanted? Let him wait, let everything wait apart from the need to reveal that was surging inside her. She'd have preferred to tell Sam's wife, Kate – Kate would have been ideal, better than Liv, even – but Kate wasn't here.

'Simon wrote me a love letter this morning.'

Sam stopped, turned round. 'What?' He'd been too far ahead. It was hard to hear anyone clearly in the corridors in the oldest part of the police station; there was the constant sound of rushing water to contend with, something to do with the pipes. According to Simon, it had sounded exactly the same when he was a kid; the nick had been the local swimming baths in those days. Parts of the building still smelled of chlorine.

'Simon wrote me a love letter,' Charlie said again, grinning. 'I woke up and found it lying next to me in bed.'

Sam frowned. 'Is everything okay? You and Simon haven't . . . broken up? He hasn't . . .?'

Charlie giggled. 'Explain to me how you got that from what I just said. Everything is *fine*, Sam. Everything is perfect. He sent me a *love* letter. A proper one.'

'Oh. Right.' Sam looked perplexed.

'I'm not going to tell you what he wrote.'

'No, of course not.' If ever a man was happy to be let off the hook . . . 'Shall we?' Sam inclined his head in the direction of the Snowman's office. 'Whatever it is, let's get it over with.'

'What are you so nervous about? I'm used to this, Sam. Ever since I left CID, Proust's been in the habit of rubbing lamps and hoping I'll appear.'

'Why didn't he ring you? Why send me to fetch you?'

'I don't know. Does it matter?' Now that Charlie had told Sam about it, Simon's note felt more real. Perhaps she didn't need to tell Liv. Liv would demand to know exactly what it said. She'd pick holes in it, one big hole in particular: the word 'love' wasn't mentioned.

I do. I know I never say it, but I do.

Charlie appreciated the subtlety. She more than appreciated it; she adored it. Simon's note was perfect; those were the best eleven words he could have chosen. Only the crassest of drips would use the word 'love' in a love letter. I'm doing it again, she thought – arguing with Liv in my head.

Liv would ask if Simon had signed the letter, or put kisses at the bottom. No, and no. She'd ask about the paper. Charlie would have to tell her it was a corner of a page torn off the pad of lined yellow A4 she kept by the phone. She didn't care. Simon was a man – he was hardly going to use scented pink paper with a border of flowers. Liv would say, *Would it have killed him to use a whole sheet instead of tearing off a corner?* She'd say, *Big deal. You've been engaged for a year and a half and you still haven't had sex, nor is he any closer to explaining why he won't, but, hey, what does any of that matter now that he's written some words on a scrap of paper?*

Perhaps, after tonight, there would be no need for Simon to explain why he wouldn't. He'd left a message on Charlie's voicemail half an hour ago telling her he'd see her later, to try to get back as early as she could. He had to have written that note for a reason – he'd never done anything like it before. Maybe he'd decided it was time.

Charlie had torn a scrap from the pad herself before leaving for work. She'd written, 'About the honeymoon: whatever you want is fine, even if it's a fortnight at the Beaumont Guest House.' That should make Simon laugh. The Beaumont was a bed and breakfast across the road from his parents' house. You could see it from their lounge window.

'He wants you at a disadvantage,' Sam was saying. 'That's why he's sent me to collect you. You're supposed to wonder if you're in trouble.'

'Sam, relax. I've done nothing wrong.'

'I'm only saying what Simon would say if he were here.'

Charlie laughed. 'Did you just snap at me? You did. You actually snapped. Are you okay?'

Sam's nickname, originally invented by Chris Gibbs, was Stepford, on account of his impeccable courteousness. He'd once admitted to Charlie that the part of his job he hated most was making arrests. She'd asked him why and he'd said, 'Putting handcuffs on someone seems so . . . rude.'

He stopped walking and leaned against the wall, his body sagging as he sighed heavily. 'Do you ever feel as if you're turning into Simon? Too long spent in close proximity . . .'

'I still have no desire to read *Moby-Dick*, let alone reread it twice a year, so I'd have to say no.'

'I interviewed the Brownlees the other day, the couple who adopted Helen Yardley's daughter. Both are alibied up to the eyebrows – I wasn't planning to spend any more time on them.'

'But?' Charlie prompted.

'When I told Grace Brownlee I was a detective, the first words out of her mouth were, "We did nothing wrong." '

'Exactly what I've just said.'

'No. That's the point. You said, "I've *done* nothing wrong." She said, "We *did* nothing wrong." They're basically the same, I know, but I also knew what Simon would have been thinking if he'd been there.'

So did Charlie. ' "We've done nothing wrong" means "I can think of nothing we've done that was wrong". "We *did* nothing wrong" means "That specific thing we did was entirely justified".'

'Exactly,' said Sam. 'I'm glad it's not just me.'

'Even the strongest mind can't withstand the Simon Waterhouse brainwash effect,' Charlie told him.

'I wanted to know what Grace Brownlee felt so defensive about, so I turned up unannounced at her house last night. Didn't take long to trick her into telling me by implying I already knew.'

'And?'

'How much do you know about adoption procedures?'

'You need to ask?' Charlie raised an eyebrow.

'Normally, if there's any chance a child in care might go back to its biological parents, that's the favoured option. While the case is being decided, the kid might go to foster parents. If the final family court decision goes against the birth mother, that's when Social Services start looking for an adoptive family. But some local authorities – and Culver Valley's one of them – have something called concurrent plan adoption that they use in a few select cases. It's massively controversial, which is why a lot of councils won't touch it with a bargepole. Some people say it violates the birth parents' human rights.'

'Let me guess,' said Charlie. 'Paige Yardley was one of those special cases.'

Sam nodded. 'You take a couple that you think would be ideal to parent a particular child, get them approved as *foster* parents, which is quicker and easier than getting them approved to adopt, and you place the child in their care as soon as possible. In theory, there was a chance Paige would go back to her birth family, but in reality everyone knew that wouldn't happen. Once it was official, once Helen and Paul Yardley had been told their daughter was no longer theirs – *then* the Brownlees were approved as adopters, and adopted the child who already lived with them, with whom they'd formed a stronger bond than you'd normally expect in a fostering situation, because, unofficially and off the record, the social workers had given them to understand that they were getting Paige for keeps.'

'Isn't that also a violation of the prospective adoptive parents' human rights?' said Charlie. 'There must be cases where the family court surprises everyone by deciding in favour of the birth mother. Presumably the social workers then have to say to the foster parents, "Oops, sorry, you can't adopt this child after all."'

'Grace Brownlee said they were told repeatedly that there were no guarantees, so in theory they knew things might not go their way – they wouldn't have been able to say they were misled, if it came down to it – but heavy hints were dropped that it *would* go their way, and that Paige would soon be their legal daughter. She was a high-profile baby, the only surviving child of a woman suspected of murder. Social Services were determined to do their very best for her, and they thought the Brownlees would be ideal. Both lawyers – middle class, high-earning, nice big house . . .'

'Nose-rings? Serpent tattoos?' said Charlie. Seeing Sam's puzzled expression, she said, 'I'm kidding. People are so predictable, aren't they? Wouldn't it be fantastic, just once, to meet a respectable solicitor with a serpent tattoo?' She let out a yelp of a laugh. 'Ignore me, I'm in love.'

'The Brownlees were hand-picked,' said Sam. 'They were in the process of jumping through all the hoops would-be adopters have to jump through. One day they were invited to a meeting and told a baby girl was available for them – there were still formalities to be gone through, but that was all they were. But the good news, they were told, was that they didn't have to wait for the legal stuff to be signed off – all they had to do was apply to be foster parents and they could have their future daughter living with them within weeks. Sebastian Brownlee was keen but Grace had her doubts. She's less smug than her husband and more cautious. She hated the nudge-nudge-wink-wink element.'

'So that's what she meant by "We did nothing wrong"?'

Sam nodded. 'Even once it was all done and dusted, court-approved and official, she was paranoid that one day Paige – Hannah, as she is now – might be taken away from them because of the underhand dealings at the beginning. Nothing her husband said to her could convince her it wasn't dodgy.'

'Was that likely? Paige being taken away, I mean.'

'Impossible. Concurrent plan adoption's not illegal. As you say, technically the verdict can still go in favour of the birth parents, and if it does, the prospective adopters have to lump it, which they know from the start.'

'In some ways, it's quite sensible,' said Charlie. 'I mean, from the kid's point of view, it has to be better to be placed with the adoptive parents as soon as possible.'

'It's barbaric,' said Sam vehemently. 'All the time the birth mother thinks she's in with a shot. Helen Yardley must have thought she and Paul stood a good chance of keeping Paige – they knew their sons had died naturally and they believed they'd be treated fairly. Some hope! All along, Social Services and Grace and Sebastian Brownlee – two strangers – knew that Paige was well on her way to her new family. Grace has felt guilty about that ever since, and I don't blame her. It's no way to treat people. It's not right, Charlie.'

'Maybe not, but lots of things aren't right, and a good proportion of those lots of things are stacked up in our in-trays. Why's this got to you?'

'I'd like to pretend my reasons for feeling like crap are noble and altruistic, but they're not,' said Sam. He closed his eyes and shook his head. 'I shouldn't have said anything to Simon. What was I thinking of?'

'You've lost me,' said Charlie.

'There was one thing I didn't understand: how could the social workers be so sure Paige Yardley wouldn't be returned to Helen and Paul? I mean, it was hardly your average care case. I can imagine a local authority knowing all about some unsavoury families' long histories of abusing and neglecting their children, saying they'll never do it again, then getting wrecked and doing more and worse. Those children being taken away from their mothers might seem like a done deal, but Helen Yardley was different. If she wasn't guilty of murder, then she was completely innocent. If her two sons were victims of crib death – which hadn't yet been decided in court, so no one could claim to know – well, then Helen had done nothing wrong, had she? So why risk concurrent plan adoption? That was what I wondered.'

Sam exhaled slowly. 'Shows how naïve I am. So much for innocent until proven guilty. Grace told me the social workers all *knew* Helen had killed her babies, and they had friends at the hospital who *knew* it with as much certainty, who had been there when Helen had taken both boys into hospital, when they'd stopped breathing on several occasions. A social worker even said to Grace that she'd spoken to lots of doctors, one being Judith Duffy, all of whom had told her that Helen Yardley was, and I quote, "the classic Munchausen's by proxy mother".'

'Maybe she was,' said Charlie. 'Maybe she did murder them.'

'That's not fair, Charlie.' Sam started to walk away from her. She was about to follow him when he turned round and came back. 'Her convictions were overturned. There wasn't even enough evidence for a retrial. It should never have gone to court the first time. Is there anything more insane than making a woman stand trial when there's no solid evidence a crime's been committed? Never mind whether Helen Yardley committed it – I'm talking about a high chance that there was no "it" in the first place. I've seen the file that went to the CPS. Do you know how many doctors disagreed with Judith Duffy and said it was entirely possible Morgan and Rowan Yardley died of natural causes?'

'Sam, calm down.'

'Seven! Seven doctors. Finally, after nine years, Helen clears her name, then some bastard murders her, and there I am, supposedly investigating her murder, trying to get some kind of justice for her, for the sake of her family and her memory, and what am I doing? I'm listening to Grace Brownlee tell me about some contact centre care supervisor who claimed to see Helen try to smother Paige right in front of her.'

'Leah Gould,' said Charlie.

Sam stared at her blankly. 'How . . .?'

'I'm reading *Nothing But Love*. Simon wanted me to, but he was too proud to ask. Luckily I can read his mind.'

'I'm supposed to read it too.' Sam looked guilty. 'Proust wasn't too proud to ask.'

'Not your cup of tea?'

'I try to avoid books that are going to make me want to top myself.'

'I think you'd be surprised,' said Charlie. 'It's full of brave, inspiring heroes: the Snowman, if you can believe it; Laurie

Nattrass; Paul, the loyal rock of a husband. And that lawyer, her solicitor – I can't remember his name . . .'

'Ned Vento?'

'That's the one. Interestingly, he had a female colleague, Gillian somebody, who seems to have worked just as hard on Helen's behalf, but so far she hasn't once been described in heroic terms. I get the impression Helen Yardley was a man's woman.'

'Doesn't make her a murderer,' said Sam.

'I didn't say it did. I'm only saying, she seemed to lap up any attention that came her way from valiant male rescuers.' *A classic Munchausen's-by-proxy mother*. Wasn't Munchausen's all about getting attention?

Something else bothered Charlie about *Nothing But Love*: several times in the first third of the book, Helen Yardley had asserted that she hadn't murdered her two babies; rather, they had died of crib death. Unless Charlie had misunderstood, and she didn't think she had, crib death, or SIDS, meant an infant death for which no explanation could be found, so it was odd for Helen Yardley to say that was what her boys had died of, as if it were a firm medical diagnosis. It was as nonsensical as saying, 'My babies died of I don't know what they died of.' Wouldn't a mother who had lost two children to SIDS be more likely to search for a proper explanation, instead of presenting the absence of one as the solution rather than the mystery? Or was Charlie reading sinister undertones into *Nothing But Love* that weren't there?

'What shouldn't you have mentioned to Simon?' she asked Sam.

'Any of this. I was angry about Social Services stitching up the Yardleys and I was letting off steam, but it's got nothing to do with Helen's murder and I should have kept my mouth shut, especially about Leah Gould. Simon waved an *Observer* article in my face in which Gould was quoted as saying she'd made a mistake – hadn't witnessed an attempted smothering, had overreacted, was deeply sorry if she'd contributed to a miscarriage of justice . . .'

'Let me guess,' said Charlie. 'When you told Simon that Grace Brownlee was invoking Leah Gould's eye-witness account as proof of Helen Yardley's guilt, he decided that talking to her couldn't wait any longer.'

'If Proust finds out I covered for him, my life won't be worth living,' said Sam glumly. 'What am I supposed to do? I told Simon no, unequivocally no, and he ignored me. "I want Leah Gould to look me in the eye and tell me what she saw," he said. I should go to Proust . . .'

'But you haven't.' Charlie smiled.

'I ought to. We're supposed to be investigating Helen Yardley's murder, not something that might or might not have happened in a Social Services' contact centre thirteen years ago. Simon's more interested in finding out if Helen Yardley was guilty of murder than he is in finding out who shot her. If Proust gets even a whiff of that, and he will, because he always does . . .'

'Sam, I'm not just sticking up for Simon because he's Simon, but . . . since when do you disregard the life story of a murder victim? Helen Yardley had a pretty dramatic past, in which Leah Gould played a crucial role, by the sound of it. Someone *should* talk to her. So what if it was thirteen years ago? The more you can find out about Helen Yardley the better, surely? About what she did or didn't do.'

'Proust's made it clear what our collective attitude has to be: that she's as innocent and undeserving of what happened to her as any murder victim,' said Sam, red in the face. 'For once, I agree with him, but it's not up to me, is it? It's *never* up to me. Simon flies around like a whirlwind doing whatever the hell he wants and I can't even pretend I've got a hope of controlling him. All I can do is sit back and watch events slip further and further from my grasp.'

'There's something Simon cares about more than he cares whether or not Helen Yardley was a murderer, and more than he cares who shot her dead,' said Charlie, not sure she ought to be sharing this with Sam. 'Proust.'

'*Proust?*'

'He was at the contact centre that day too. Simon's only interested in what Leah Gould saw because he wants to know what the Snowman saw – if he witnessed an attempted child murder and lied about it in his eagerness to protect a woman he'd already decided was innocent. Proust's the one he's going after.' Charlie admitted to herself that she was scared of how far Simon might go. He was too obsessed to be rational. He'd been up most of last night, apoplectic with rage because Proust had tried again to invite them for dinner. He seemed convinced the Snowman was trying to torture him by forcing an invasive friendship on him, one he knew would be anathema to Simon. It had sounded far-fetched to Charlie, but her doubts, when she'd voiced them, had only inspired Simon to flesh out his paranoid fantasy even more: Proust had worked out a new genius way to humiliate him, rob him of his power. How can you fight back when all someone's doing is saying, 'Let's have dinner'?

Easily, Charlie had told him, desperate for sleep – you say, 'Sorry, I'd rather not have dinner with you. I don't like you, I never will, and I don't want to be your friend.'

Sam Kombothekra rubbed the bridge of his nose. 'This gets worse,' he said. 'If Simon's going after the Snowman, I'm going after a new job.'

'Where's Waterhouse?' was Proust's first question. He was arranging envelopes in a tower on his desk.

'He's gone to Wolverhampton to interview Sarah Jaggard again,' said Sam. One he'd prepared earlier, no doubt. Charlie tried not to smile. 'You didn't say you wanted to see Waterhouse, sir. You only mentioned Sergeant Zailer.'

'I don't want to see him. I want to know where he is. The two are different. I take it you're up to speed on our case, Seargent Zailer? You know who Judith Duffy is?' Proust flicked the envelope tower with his finger and thumb. It shifted but didn't fall. 'Formerly a respected child health expert, latterly a pariah, shortly to be struck off the medical register for misconduct – you know the basic facts?'

Charlie nodded.

'Sergeant Kombothekra and I would be grateful if you'd talk to Dr Duffy for us. One pariah to another.'

Charlie felt as if she'd swallowed a metal ball. A faint groan came from Sam. Proust heard it, but went on as if he hadn't. 'Rachel Hines could well be our killer's next target. She's vanished into the ether, and there's a chance Duffy knows where she is. The two of them met for lunch on Monday. I want to know why. Why would a bereaved mother have a nice cosy meal with the corrupt doctor whose fraudulent evidence put her behind bars?'

'I've no idea,' said Charlie. 'I agree, it's odd.'

'Conveniently, Duffy and Mrs Hines are each other's alibi for Helen Yardley's murder,' said Proust. 'Duffy won't talk to us, not willingly, and I was on the point of hauling her in unwillingly, but this strikes me as a better idea.' Proust leaned forward, drumming his fingers on his desk as if he were playing a piano. 'I think you could persuade her to talk to you, Sergeant. Establish a bond. If it works, she'll say more to you than she would to us. You know what it feels like to have your ignominy splashed all over the papers; so does she. You'd know exactly how to approach her, wouldn't you? You're good with people.'

What are you good with?

Pariah, ignominy – they were only words. They could have no power over Charlie unless she allowed them to. She didn't have to think about the events of 2006 if she didn't want to. Recently, she had been choosing not to, more and more.

'You don't have to do it, Charlie. We've no right to ask you to.'

'By "we", he means me,' said Proust. 'The disapproval of Sergeant Kombothekra rains down like an avalanche of tissue-paper, feather-light and easy to shake off.'

'I knew nothing about this,' said Sam, pink-faced. 'It's got nothing to do with me. You can't treat people like this, sir.'

Charlie thought of all the things she'd read about Judith Duffy: she'd cared more about the children of strangers than her own, both of whom had been sub-contracted out to nannies and au pairs so that she could work day and night; she'd tried to fleece her ex-husband when they got divorced, even though she earned a packet herself . . .

Charlie hadn't believed a word of it. She knew what trial-by-media did for a person's reputation, having been through it herself.

'I'll do it,' she said. The Snowman was right: she could persuade Judith Duffy to talk to her if she tried. She didn't know why she wanted to, but she did. She definitely did.

13
Saturday 10 October 2009

My mobile phone buzzes as I emerge from the underground. One message. A lifelong believer in sod's law, I expect it to be Julian Lance, Rachel Hines' solicitor, calling to cancel the meeting I've just travelled halfway across London to get to, but it's not. It's Laurie. I can tell straight away, because at first all I hear is breathing. Not heavy, not threatening – just the sound of him trying to remember which button he pressed, what he wanted to say and to whom. Eventually, his recorded voice says, 'I've got the latest version of my *British Journalism Review* article for you, the one on Duffy. Yeah.' There's a pause then, as if he's waiting for a response. 'Do you want to meet, or something? So I can give it to you?' Another pause. 'Fliss? Can you pick up the phone?' The sound of air being expelled through gritted teeth. 'Okay, then, I'll email it to you.'

Can I *pick up the phone*? No, you numbskull, I can't, not once it's gone to voicemail. How can Laurie Nattrass, recipient of every honour and plaudit the world can bestow upon an investigative journalist, not understand this basic fact of twenty-first-century telecommunications? Does he imagine I'm staring at my mobile disdainfully while his voice blares out of it, wilfully ignoring him?

Is this his way of saying sorry for treating me so shoddily?

It has to be. There's no point debating whether I ought to forgive him; I already have.

I listen to the message eight times before calling him back. To his voicemail prompt, I say, 'I'd love to meet or something so that you can give it to me.' Which might be the perfect casual-but-encouraging teaser, except I ruin it by giggling like a hyena. I panic and end the call, realising too late that if I'd only waited a few seconds, I'd have been given the option of re-recording the message. 'Shit,' I mutter, looking at my watch. I should have been at the Covent Garden Hotel five minutes ago. I pick up my pace, weaving in and out of the convoy of shoppers, glaring at the ones that have enormous bags fanning out from their sides like batwings, ready to smack me in the arm as I hurry past. It's doing me good to be out, busy, surrounded by people. It makes me feel ordinary – too ordinary for anything bad or newsworthy to happen to me.

I expect Julian Lance to be wearing a suit, but the man I see walking towards me as I open the door of the Covent Garden Hotel is wearing jeans, tasselled loafers and a zip-collared sweater over an open-necked striped shirt. He's got short white hair and a square, tanned face. He could be anything from fifty to a well-maintained sixty-five. 'Fliss Benson? I recognised you,' he says, smiling at my questioning look. 'You had your I'm-about-to-speak-to-Ray-Hines'-lawyer face on. Everyone does, the first time.'

'Thanks for seeing me on a Saturday.' We shake hands.

'Ray says you're the one. I'd have met you in the middle of the night, missed Sunday lunch – whatever it took.' Having made clear his commitment to his client, Lance proceeds to inspect me, his eyes taking a quick head-to-toe tour. For once,

I'm not worried about looking a state. I dressed this morning as if for court, as if I was the one on trial.

I allow Julian Lance to steer me towards a table with two free chairs at the back of the room. The third chair is occupied by a woman with dyed red hair with lots of clips in it, and red-framed glasses. She's writing in a ring-bound notebook: big, loopy scrawl. I'm wondering whether I ought to suggest to Julian Lance that he and I sit elsewhere, somewhere more private, when the woman looks up and smiles at me. 'Hello, Fliss,' she says. 'I'm Wendy, Wendy Whitehead.'

'You know who she is?' Lance asks.

I nod, trying not to look flustered. *She's not a killer*, I remind myself.

'Ray said you wanted to talk vaccinations, and Wendy's the expert, so I thought I'd invite her along, give you two meetings for the price of one.'

'That's very helpful, thank you.'

I sit between the two of them, feeling totally out of my depth. Lance asks me what I'd like to drink. My mind is a complete blank; I can't think of any drinks, let alone one I might like. Luckily, he starts listing types of coffee and tea, which jolts my brain into action. I ask for Earl Grey. He goes off to order it, leaving me alone with Wendy Whitehead. 'So, Ray told you I gave Marcella and Nathaniel their first vaccinations?' she says.

'Yes.' *Their only vaccinations.*

She smiles. 'I know what she told you. "Wendy Whitehead killed my children". She wanted to make you listen, that's all. When you're in the public eye in the way Ray was, nobody listens to you. You'd think it'd be the other way round, wouldn't you? Suddenly, you're a household name, you're all over the tabloids and the TV news – you'd think people would be hanging on your every word, eager to hear what you had to say. Instead, they leap to ill-informed conclusions, for and against, and start talking *about* you, telling more and more outlandish stories, whatever they need to say to liven up their boring suburban dinner parties: "I heard she did this, I heard she did that." And your poor little story, your *real* story – that's just a distraction, getting in the way of the fun they're all having. There's too much for it to compete with, so it gets lost.'

I ought to be recording what she's saying. Will she say it all again later, if I ask her nicely? Will she say it to camera? 'Rachel told me—'

'Call her Ray. She hates Rachel.'

'She told me vaccines killed her babies.'

'Vaccines administered by me.' Wendy Whitehead nods.

'Do you agree? Was that what killed Marcella and Nathaniel?'

'In my opinion? Yes. Obviously I didn't think so at the time – I'm not a baby-killer any more than Ray is. If I'd had the slightest idea . . .'

Julian Lance sits down, indicates that she should carry on. I have the sense that the two of them know each other well. They seem comfortable around one another. I'm the one who's uncomfortable.

'Anyway, I'm no longer a practice nurse. Many years have passed since I last injected a baby with neurotoxins. For the past four years I've worked as a researcher for a legal practice. Not Julian's,' she adds, seeing me glance at him. 'I work for a firm that specialises in vaccine damage compensation claims.'

'Marcella Hines was born two weeks prem,' says Julian Lance. 'Babies are supposed to have their first jabs at eight weeks, their second at sixteen . . .'

'It's changed now,' Wendy Whitehead tells him. 'They've accelerated the schedule again, to two, three and four months.' She turns to me and says, 'It used to be three, six and nine months, then two, four and six. The younger a baby is when it's vaccinated, the harder it is to prove it was destined to develop normally, if it has a bad reaction.'

'Biologically, Marcella was only six weeks old when she had her first jabs,' says Lance. 'Ray rang up and asked for advice, and her GP told her to proceed as if Marcella were a normal eight-week-old baby, so Ray did. Immediately after the injections, Marcella took a turn for the worse.'

'Well, not immediately. It was about twenty minutes after. I saw it happen,' Wendy Whitehead takes over the story. 'We always asked parents to wait half an hour after any injection before taking their babies home, so that we could check all was well. Five minutes after she'd left my room, Ray burst back in with Marcella in her arms, insisting something was wrong – Marcella wasn't breathing normally. I wasn't sure what she meant. The baby was breathing, I couldn't see any problems, and I had someone else in with me, another mother and baby. I asked Ray to wait, and when I'd finished with my other patient, I asked her and Marcella to come back in. I was about to examine Marcella again when she had a seizure. Ray and I watched helplessly as her little body bent and twisted . . . I'm sorry.' She presses her hand against her mouth.

'Less than five hours later, Marcella was dead,' says Lance. 'Ray and Angus were told definitively that the DTP-Hib vaccine couldn't have caused her death.'

'All the doctors they spoke to said, "We've no idea why your daughter died, Mr and Mrs Hines, but we know it wasn't the DTP-Hib jab that killed her." "How do you know?" "We just do – because our vaccines are safe, because they don't kill." '

'The timing had to be a coincidence, they were told,' says Lance.

'Rubbish,' Wendy Whitehead says vehemently. 'Even if Marcella hadn't been prem, even if there hadn't been a history in Angus Hines' family of auto-immune problems . . .'

'His mother suffers from Lupus, doesn't she?' I ask. I've got a vague memory of having read that somewhere, perhaps in Laurie's article.

'That's right. And there's a history of crib death in several branches of his family, which strongly suggests a genetic auto-immune disorder. Yes, these vaccines are mostly safe if you take babies with vulnerabilities out of the equation, but some babies *have* vulnerabilities. I wanted to yellow-card Marcella's death . . .'

'That means report it to the MHRA as a possible adverse reaction to a vaccine,' Lance explains. I have no idea what the MHRA is; I make a mental note to look it up later.

'. . . but my colleagues put pressure on me not to. The practice manager hinted I'd be out of a job if I did. I listened to them all, and I shouldn't have. I suppose I wanted to believe them – if they were right, and Marcella dying five hours after having the jab was a coincidence, then it wasn't my fault, was it? It wasn't me that had done it to her. I did as I was told and tried to put it behind me. It sounds feeble and cowardly and it was, but . . . well, if everybody's telling you with great assurance that something's safe, you start to believe them. Over the next few weeks and months I vaccinated babies who reacted normally – screamed a bit but then were fine, and certainly didn't die – and I convinced myself that it wouldn't have done anyone any good if I'd yellow-carded Marcella's death. Ray and Angus would only have blamed themselves, and the last thing anyone wants is negative publicity for inoculations, in case it puts parents off. Herd immunity has to be preserved at all costs – that was what I thought at the time.

'When Ray rang me at work four years later, telling me she'd had another baby and asking my advice about whether to vaccinate him, I opened my mouth to tell her that DTP-Hib was perfectly safe, and I found I couldn't say it. I couldn't make the words come out. I told her it was her decision, that I didn't want to sway her one way or the other. She asked me if a tendency to react badly to vaccines could run in families.'

'Several studies have shown that it does,' Julian Lance leans his head towards me in a slow nod. Is he wondering why I'm not taking notes? Does he disapprove? Something about him makes me feel as if I'm doing something wrong. Come to think of it, I feel that way most of the time – maybe it's nothing to do with Lance.

Several studies have shown. Isn't that what people always say when, basically, they've got no evidence? Isn't it a bit like writing, 'It has been argued that . . .' in an A-level essay, when you're not sure who said what but you want to give the impression of substantial support for the point you're about to make?

'Ray was terrified of something happening to Nathaniel after what had happened to Marcella,' says Wendy. 'She wanted to do what was best for him, but she didn't know what that was. Should she give him the very same jab that she was certain had killed her daughter, even though dozens of professionals had assured her it couldn't have, or should she steer clear of it, and risk Nathaniel dying of diphtheria or tetanus? The chance of her son contracting either disease was extremely small, but she was understandably paranoid and semi-hysterical. I advised her to take plenty of time to make her decision, and speak to as many immunisation experts as she could. Privately, I hoped she'd decide not to give Nathaniel the jab – partly, selfishly, because I knew there was a good chance I'd be the one who'd have to give it to him. The ridiculous thing was, I'd still have said, if asked at that point, that the jabs were entirely safe, that all babies ought to have them at two, four and six months, just as the government advised – I'd have *said* that, but I didn't believe it, not deep down.'

A waiter arrives with a tray: my tea, and a coffee each for Lance and Wendy.

'In the end, Ray and Angus decided to immunise Nathaniel, but later,' Lance takes up the story. 'A doctor friend they trusted had told them that even a week could make a huge difference in terms of the strength of a baby's immune system. They're so much tougher every day, their systems so much better able to cope. That made sense to Ray and Angus, and seemed like a good compromise, so they waited until Nathaniel was eleven weeks old. He wasn't prem, and, although they were a little bit apprehensive, they trusted that he'd be fine. Their doctor friend had convinced them that to let a child go unvaccinated was dangerously irresponsible.'

Wendy Whitehead presses her hand against her mouth again.

'But Nathaniel wasn't fine,' I say.

'Twenty, twenty-five minutes after having the jab, his body convulsed, just like Marcella's,' she says, blinking away tears. 'Then he perked up a bit, and we thought, "Please, God", but he died a week later. Ray and I knew what had killed him, but we couldn't get anyone to back us up. I yellow-carded Nathaniel's death and was made redundant soon afterwards.' She lets out a bitter, throaty laugh. 'Even Angus wouldn't acknowledge that there was a clear cause of death for both his children – though he's big enough now to admit it was guilt that made him side with the doctors – for allowing both babies to have the jab, for the auto-immune problem that was on his side of the family . . .'

'You'll have heard that Angus didn't stand by Ray when she was convicted of murder,' says Lance. It's a question presented as a statement.

I nod.

'The trouble between them started long before she was convicted, or even accused. Angus was angry with her, and with Wendy, for insisting on a truth he wasn't ready to face up to.' Lance takes a sip of his coffee. 'By the time the police turned up at the door, he and Ray were close to splitting up.'

I wait. Politely at first, then, after a few seconds of silence, allowing my incredulity to show. Lance and Wendy are both looking as if that's it, end of story. 'I don't get it,' I say, in case it's a test and they're waiting for me to bring up the very obvious gaping hole in what they've told me. 'If there was a suspected cause of death for both babies, even if it was controversial – why wasn't it mentioned in court? I've looked through the trial transcript and there's nothing.'

'We tried,' says Lance. 'Wendy was ready to testify . . .'

'Ready, willing, eager,' she says, nodding.

'. . . but we were told in no uncertain terms not to refer to a possible adverse reaction to the DTP-Hib vaccine.'

'By whom?' I ask.

'By our four stellar defence witnesses.' Lance smiles. 'Four hugely respected medical experts, all ready to say that there was no evidence of foul play in the case of either baby's death, no medical evidence that couldn't just as easily be attributed to natural causes as to anything more sinister. Quite independently of one another, they each made it abundantly clear to me that if counsel for the defence so much as whispered the word "thiomersal", we'd have a fight on our hands. I couldn't risk it, couldn't let the jury hear our own witnesses calling our story a lie. That wouldn't have helped Ray at all.'

I can hardly believe what I'm hearing. I don't want to believe it; it's too horrendous. 'But . . .' *Ray Hines went to prison for murder. She was locked up for four years.*

'Yes,' says Wendy. 'That was how I felt too.'

'Surely there were other medical experts who'd—'

'I'm afraid not.' Lance frowns. 'I tried, believe me. Most doctors are terrified of speaking out about vaccine damage. Any who do tend to see their careers come crashing down around their ears.'

'If you've got a spare hour or two for Googling, you should read about what happened to Dr Andrew Wakefield and his colleagues,' says Wendy. Again, Lance leans forward and stares pointedly at the table in front of me, where I'm now certain he thinks my notebook ought to be. As if I'm going to forget any of this. I'll probably be able to recite what they're telling me word for word when I'm eighty.

'When Dr Wakefield dared to suggest that a possible link between the MMR vaccine, regressive autism and a particular kind of bowel disorder was worth investigating, a lot of powerful people made it their mission to destroy his credibility and his career. They literally hounded him out of the country,' says Wendy.

This is all very well, but I'm not making a documentary about Dr Andrew Wakefield. 'What's "thiomersal"?' I ask.

'Mercury, essentially,' says Lance. 'One of the most poisonous substances in the world, if you're thinking of injecting it into your bloodstream, and present in the DTP-Hib vaccines given to babies until 2004, when they phased it out.'

Present in the jab given to Marcella in 1998, and the one given to Nathaniel in 2002.

'Of course, they didn't phase it out because it was a highly reactogenic neurotoxin. No, it was completely safe – that was the official story most doctors stuck to. Then why were they phasing it out? They just were – nothing to do with it being dangerous.' Wendy's talking so fast, I'm struggling to keep up. 'Same with whole-cell pertussis – that's the "P" part of the DTP jab. They've phased that out too – the pertussis element is now strands, acellular – much less hazardous. And the polio vaccine, given orally at the same time as DTP-Hib – they now give the dead form instead of the live. But try getting anyone to admit any of these changes have been made because the old vaccines were too reactogenic and you come up against a brick wall.'

'Your tea's going cold,' Lance says to me.

Don't pick up the cup. I beat down my natural impulse to do as I'm told, and say, 'I like cold tea.'

'Why the change of tack, if you don't mind my asking? On the part of Binary Star?'

I don't know what he's talking about. It must be apparent from my expression.

'I spoke to your colleague Laurie Nattrass a few months ago and tried to tell him everything I've just told you, and he didn't want to know.'

'Laurie's working for a different company now. If I'm going to be making a documentary about Ray, I need to know everything.'

'It gladdens my heart to hear you say that,' says Lance. 'I'm sure you'll do an excellent job. Ray's a good judge of character. She was sensible to give Nattrass a wide berth. Man's a coward, one who allies himself with fashionable causes. There's no risk to him in making a documentary about Judith Duffy, the doctor everyone loves to hate. He wants to destroy Duffy more than he wants to help Ray, and he made it clear he wouldn't touch with a bargepole an international health scandal involving governments, drug companies . . .'

'*You* didn't touch it with a bargepole when Ray was on trial,' I say. 'If Laurie's a coward, then so are you.'

For a second or two, as he stares down into his coffee, I think Lance is going to get up and walk out. He doesn't. 'It's slightly different,' he says coolly. 'If I took a risk and failed, that meant Ray getting two life sentences for murder.'

'That happened anyway,' I point out.

'True, but . . .'

'Women like Ray, Helen Yardley and Sarah Jaggard are only a fashionable cause, as you put it, because Laurie brought their predicament to people's attention. Judith Duffy wasn't the doctor everyone loved to hate until Laurie exposed her.'

Lance runs his tongue along the inside of his lower lip. 'I can't argue with that,' he says eventually.

'I read an article Laurie wrote about Ray's case. He says you told Ray to pretend she was post-natally depressed and nearly threw herself off a window ledge, making her seem unstable to the jury.'

'That's wholly untrue.'

I wait for him to elaborate, but he doesn't.

'Did Laurie *say* he was scared of the vaccine issue?' I ask. I can't believe he would be, however many governments and drug companies were involved. Laurie would take on anyone. 'Or did he say he could only make one documentary at a time? You'd need about four hours to do justice to the whole jabs thing as well as tell three women's stories, and the story of how Judith Duffy shafted them. A documentary needs a focal point.'

'Your loyalty is touching, Fliss,' says Lance, 'but I remain convinced that Nattrass is a man who sees only what he wants to see. He had a troupe of doctors lined up to dish the dirt on Duffy. How do you think they'd have reacted if he'd introduced the vaccine issue? They'd have run a mile. Russell Meredew, the GMC's blue-eyed boy . . .' Lance laughs. 'He'd wet his pants at the mere suggestion, and Nattrass knows it.'

'Is Meredew on your radar?' Wendy Whitehead asks me.

'I'm going to be talking to him, yes.'

'Don't believe a word he says. He's probably the most unpopular paediatrician in the country. There's nothing he likes more than testifying against his colleagues at GMC hearings. He's the expert they've asked for an assessment of Duffy.'

'What?' That can't be right. Am I confusing Meredew with another doctor? No, I'm not. 'They both gave evidence at Ray's trial, didn't they? Her for the prosecution, him for the defence?'

'Yup.' Lance sounds resigned.

'But . . . the misconduct allegations against Duffy directly involve Ray's trial. Isn't that a conflict of interests?'

'Just a tad,' says Wendy. 'Funny, isn't it, that that hasn't occurred to the GMC, or to Meredew, who's happy to take their money.'

Russell Meredew – a man I'd trust to carry me across an enemy minefield. That's how he's described in Laurie's article.

'There's something I should probably tell you, if Ray hasn't already,' Lance says. 'She and Judith Duffy have become friends. Unlikely though it sounds, the two of them are a great source of support to one another.'

Friends. Ray Hines and Judith Duffy. I bury my face in my teacup to buy myself some time. 'Just like Ray and Angus are now good friends, if not a bit more than that,' I say eventually.

'Ray's clever enough to know that forgiveness, of oneself and others, is the only happy way forward,' says Lance.

I can't prove it, but I have a sense he knows about the baby. Ray corrected me when I called it that. 'I'm only eight weeks pregnant,' she said. 'It's not a baby yet. A lot of pregnancies miscarry before twelve weeks and if this one does, I don't want to think I've lost another child.'

'Don't judge Ray, Fliss,' says Wendy. 'I'm sure you think that in her shoes, you'd want nothing to do with the husband who'd betrayed you, but you never know – you might surprise yourself.'

I'd have wax effigies of Angus Hines, Judith Duffy and everyone who'd ever said vaccines were a good thing lined up on my mantelpiece, with pins sticking out of them that I'd have made the effort to marinade in cyanide. I decide not to share this with Lance and Wendy.

'Ray doesn't blame Duffy for her guilty verdicts,' says Lance. 'She blames herself, which is fair.'

Did he really say that?

Whose side is anybody on here?

'The window ledge incident you referred to earlier, the one Laurie Nattrass used as an opportunity to lie about me in some article . . .'

'Laurie might have his faults, but he doesn't lie.'

Julian Lance inclines his head and stares at me from beneath his white eyebrows as if I'm the biggest fool who's ever sat across a table from him. 'I didn't tell Ray to change her story. Until we got to court, I'd only ever heard one version: that she'd stayed away from home for nine days because Angus was taking her for granted, expecting her to do everything for Marcella, and all the housework. Then she came back, found his mum in her house, and climbed out onto the window ledge to escape her overbearing mother-in-law. Also, she wanted to smoke, and didn't want Marcella to inhale the fumes.' Lance signals to the waiter to bring him the bill. 'I was worried about how that story would be received by a jury, but there was no way round it – we knew the prosecution were going to bring it up. I nearly had a heart attack when Ray stood in the witness box and started telling an entirely different story about post-natal trances and losses of memory. Not only was it a lie, it was a lie that made her sound exactly like the sort of woman who might murder two babies.'

'How do you know it was a lie?' I ask. 'What if the first version was the lie? It sounds like one.' Why didn't this occur to me when I first read Laurie's article? Would a loving mother really abandon her baby daughter for nine days in order to make a point about equal distribution of housework and childcare?

Julian Lance and Wendy Whitehead exchange a look. 'I know Angus Hines,' says Lance. 'So does Wendy. He would have done his fair share. He *says* he did his fair share, that Ray had nothing to complain about.'

'Then . . .?'

'That wasn't all she lied about,' says Wendy. 'She'd told the police and Julian that she'd phoned an ambulance straight away when she found Marcella not breathing, but in court she said she'd phoned Angus first, then phoned emergency services. Trouble is, there was no record of her call to Angus.'

'She never made it,' Lance underlines the point. I get it. How stupid does he think I am? I'm going to have to read the trial transcript properly. So far I've only skimmed it.

'She lied about Nathaniel, too,' says Wendy. 'The health visitor arrived just after Ray found him and called an ambulance – we're talking *seconds* after, not minutes – and Ray wouldn't let her in, just stared at her blankly through the window. Apart from the health visitor having no reason to lie, there were witnesses: neighbours who heard the poor woman pleading to be let in and asking Ray if she was all right.'

'In court, Ray said she let the health visitor in immediately,' Lance takes over. 'We know that's not true. It was between ten and fifteen minutes before she opened the door.'

I can feel their eyes on me. 'I don't understand,' I say, looking up from my tea.

'Neither do we.' Wendy smiles.

'There's a story here, a story Ray won't tell either of us,' says Lance. 'Part of that story is the reason why she lied so obviously and often in court. She's come close to admitting it once or twice.'

'She's told nobody why,' says Wendy. 'Not Judith Duffy, not me or Julian, not her family. I don't think she's even told Angus, even now. I'd resigned myself to never knowing. We all had.'

'I think she wants to tell you, Fliss,' says Lance. There's no mistaking the seriousness of his tone. 'You're the one she's chosen to hear the truth, the whole truth and nothing but the truth. I hope you're prepared for it. I'm not sure I am.'

It's only when he sees me coming and waves that I realise the man standing outside my flat is waiting for me. My first thought is that he must be police. Two detectives from Culver Valley CID left messages for me while I was speaking to Lance and Wendy: a DS Sam Kombothekra and a DC Colin Sellers. Both demanded I contact them immediately, and DS Kombothekra told me to speak to nobody and do nothing in connection with the documentary: two orders for the price of one. Tamsin also left a message, instructing me to ring her as soon as I could and before I did anything else. I ignored all three of them. I don't want to speak to anyone who's going to try to stop me doing what I need to do.

I slow down as the man walks towards me, combing my mind for a few basic facts about my rights. Can he force me to stop working if I want to work? Can he make me go to the police station with him? Detain me against my will? Laurie would know. *So might you, if you ever read anything that wasn't* heat *magazine* – that's what Tamsin would say. Come to think of it, it's easy to predict what most people are going to say most of the time. That's why I love Laurie. There's plenty wrong with him, but at least he's unpredictable. Not like Maya, who is always going to say, 'What smell? Smoke? Someone must be burning something outside.' Or Raffi: 'I know, I know – a dehumidifier. I'll look into it, Fliss, I promise.'

That's why I mustn't be stopped before I get a chance to speak to Ray Hines again: I don't know what she's going to say and I want to find out. Yes, I'm in danger, but not in the way the police think, from some cards and a photograph. I'm in danger of never being part of anything important, of having my whole bland life go by without anyone noticing or caring. Now I've got a chance to make sure that doesn't happen.

As I get closer, the man's face starts to look familiar. I work out who he is a few seconds before he introduces himself: Angus Hines. I recognise him from pictures in Laurie's files. 'I was wondering how long I was going to have to camp on your doorstep,' he says. He's almost good-looking, but his head could do with being a bit more three-dimensional. He's got a flat, square face that makes me think of a ventriloquist's dummy. When he opens his mouth again, I half expect it to make a clacking sound. 'Ray said you were meeting Julian Lance. How did it go? Was he helpful?' It doesn't occur to him to introduce himself. He clearly thinks I ought to know who he is, how much his opinions matter.

I want to turn and walk away, and not only because of what I know about him already, nothing to do with any ideas I might have entertained about making a wax effigy of him and sticking pins in it. He's talking as if he's in charge of me, brisk and presumptuous.

Seeing that I have no intention of answering him, he says, 'Fliss, I'll be honest. I'm not entirely happy with your . . .

involvement in Ray's life, so I'm going to tell you what I told her: this documentary isn't only about her. It's about me, my family. It really matters to me, and to Ray – the first public account of our lives, to be watched by millions of people all over the country – all over the world, maybe. Laurie Nattrass might be the wrong man to make it, but that doesn't mean you're the right one. It worries me that my wife trusts you when she's spoken to you a grand total of once.'

'I'm not a man, and she's your *ex*-wife.'

'It worries me even more to hear her describe you as "objective". Because you're anything but, aren't you? Ray told me about your father.'

A conciliatory approach might work. Or it might be undermined by virulent secret loathing.

'Do you have someone else in mind to make the film?' I ask.

'No. That's not the point. And none of this is your fault. Ray shouldn't have—'

'It's precisely because of my father that I'll be more objective than anyone else would be,' I tell him.

'How so?'

I don't want to talk about this on the street, but the alternative would be to invite Angus Hines into my flat, and I definitely don't want to do that. 'My father made a careless professional mistake that cost a child her life. It ended up costing him his life too, ruining my mum's, and it didn't exactly enhance mine. If I find myself working on a film that involves child deaths, don't you think I'll do everything I can to get the facts right?'

'No, I don't,' says Hines, apparently not at all worried about upsetting me. 'The trouble with that sort of pop psychology is that you can twist it any way you want. Your father didn't want Ray to appeal – he thought if she got out, baby-murderers everywhere would do their worst and get away with it. But Ray did appeal, and she won. She was vindicated, while he died in disgrace. You're telling me that doesn't make you want to find Ray guilty all over again in your documentary?'

'That's what I'm telling you, yes.'

'Come on, Fliss.' He smiles sadly, as if he cares about me and fears for my sanity. It freaks me out. 'You might think you're objective, but . . .'

'You think you know me better than I know myself?'

What else can I say in my defence? That's what it is: a defence. I'm being attacked in broad daylight outside my home. Just because he's only using words doesn't mean he's not attacking me. Mustering what confidence I have left, I say, 'I don't want to be like my father. When he said what he did about Ray, I hated him. He wanted her to stay in prison because of the effect her release would have on other people – nothing to do with Ray herself.' I'm cold. I want to be inside. I feel as if all my neighbours are listening through their walls, nodding to themselves because they've always thought I looked as if I had something to be ashamed of, and now they know what it is. 'He said nothing about whether he thought she was guilty or innocent – I don't think he knew the first thing about either of her . . . either of your babies' deaths. It was the same mistake he made with Jaycee Herridge – making assumptions and neglecting the details. If I make this documentary, the details are *all* I'm going to care about, whatever they might be, whatever picture they add up to, because I'm *better* than my father. I need to prove to myself that I'm nothing like him, and I don't care if that sounds disloyal!'

'A lot of people think loyalty means suspending your critical faculties and ceasing to think for yourself,' says Angus Hines. He pulls a handkerchief out of his coat pocket and offers it to me.

Am I crying? Yes, it seems I am. *Great*. 'No, thanks,' I say. *I'd rather let my face drip-dry in the wind than take anything from you*.

'You said a few minutes ago that you *found yourself* working on a documentary involving child deaths. Wasn't it your choice?'

'No, not at first. I didn't want anything to do with it. Laurie Nattrass called me into his office on Monday, told me he was resigning and dumped his crib death film on me without asking me what I wanted.'

Angus Hines stuffs his hanky back in his pocket, shaking his head. 'I don't know if you're deluding yourself or deliberately lying to me, but that's not how it happened. It can't be.'

How dare he speak to me like this? 'What? I'm not . . .'

'Your father killed himself in 2006. You started working for Binary Star in early 2007.' He flashes a smug smile at me. 'I work for a newspaper. I'm good at finding things out.'

Anyone would think he was whatever-his-name-is who uncovered the Watergate scandal. I'm not entirely sure what the Watergate scandal was, apart from something shocking involving Richard Nixon, so I'd better not mention it. 'I thought you were only a photographer,' I say, stressing the 'only'. I have nothing against photographers, and I know Hines is something more senior at *London on Sunday*, but at this point I'm willing to say anything that'll make him feel bad.

He pulls out his wallet and hands me a business card. 'Since you're so keen on details, get mine right.' Pictures Desk Editor. Big deal. 'You knew Laurie Nattrass was on the board at Binary Star – you must have known about his connection to Helen Yardley, JIPAC, my wife. You didn't end up working with him by accident, did you?'

I can't deal with this. I push past him and head for my flat, fumbling in my bag for my keys. I let myself in and turn to close the door. Angus Hines is right behind me, so close we're almost touching.

'This conversation's over,' I tell him. How dare he walk into my home uninvited? I try to use the door to propel him out, but he's too heavy. 'Fine,' I say, gesturing for him to go on ahead of me. He smiles again, rewarding me for finally seeing sense.

He heads for the lounge, stopping on the way to look at what I've put up on the walls in the hall. As quietly as I can, I step outside, close the front door and mortice-lock it.

I run towards the main road faster than I've ever run before. I flag down a cab and tell the driver my work address. I need access to a computer, and the one at the office will do just as well as the one at home. It's Saturday, so hopefully no one will be in.

Oh my God, oh my God, ohmyGod. I've just locked the pictures desk editor of a major newspaper in my flat.

In the rear-view mirror, the taxi-driver eyes me hopefully. All I can see of him are his eyes, but that's enough. As a non-driver, I spend a lot of time in cabs, and my instincts are razor-sharp. I'm getting a strong sense that this man has something pressing to tell me about an excellent biography of the Kray twins he's reading. I've already heard all about the bloke who had his smile extended by a knife from several other London cabbies; I don't need to hear it again. As a preventative measure, I pull out my phone and ring Tamsin.

'Fliss?' She sounds as if she'd given up all hope of ever hearing from me again. 'Where are you?'

I'm tempted to say 'Somalia'. 'On my way to the office. Relax. I'm fine.'

'You might be fine now, but the longer you—'

'I need you to do something for me,' I cut her off. 'You're not busy, are you?'

'Depends what you mean by busy. I've just downloaded a test thingie from MI6's website.'

'*What?*'

'I'm going to take it in a minute, under exam conditions. If I pass, I'll be one step closer to getting a job as an operations officer for cases – that's the official job title.'

'You mean a spy?' I can't help laughing, and once I start, I can't stop. *I've got a pictures desk editor locked in my flat and my best friend wants to be a spy.*

'Keep it to yourself, all right? It says on the website that you can't tell anyone.' She makes a dismissive noise. 'Seems a bit unrealistic, doesn't it? They can't mean *anyone* anyone.'

'No. I'm sure they mean you can tell whoever you like as long as they're not wearing an Al-Qaeda T-shirt.'

'Are you crying?'

'I think I'm laughing, but there's not much in it.'

'I'm deadly serious about this, Fliss. I spoke to a detective who said I'd make a good chief inspector, and it started me thinking . . .'

'Why were you talking to a detective?'

Tamsin groans. 'I know it's against your principles, but will you please buy a newspaper and read it? And when you've done that, come here so that I can not let you out of my sight.'

'Tam, I need you to go to mine. Have you still got the set of keys I gave you?'

'Somewhere. Why?'

'Just . . . go to my flat and unlock the door. Let Angus Hines out, lock up again – that's it, then you're done. It won't take you long. I'll pay any expenses – petrol, cab fare, tube fare, whatever – and there's a slap-up meal in it too, at a restaurant of your choice. Just please, say you'll do it.'

'Can we rewind to the "Let Angus Hines out" part? What's Angus Hines doing in your flat?'

'He came in, I didn't want him there, I couldn't get him to leave, so I went out. I had to lock him in or he'd have followed me and I didn't want to speak to him. He's a horrible, self-righteous bully. He gave me the creeps.'

'You *locked* Angus Hines in your flat? Oh, my God! Isn't that . . . false imprisonment or something? Kidnap? Fliss, you can go to jail for incarcerating people against their will. What's wrong with you?'

I press the 'end call' button and switch off my phone. If she wants to let him out, she can go and let him out. If not, they can both stay where they are and have fun disapproving of me.

Maybe I ought to ask my taxi-driver if the Kray twins ever locked a pictures desk editor in their flat, and if so, what happened to them as a result. Except that he's now involved in a phone conversation of his own, which leaves me with no choice but to think.

Yes, I knew Laurie worked at Binary Star when I applied for the job. Yes, I knew about his links to Helen Yardley and

JIPAC. I knew he was trying to get Ray Hines out of prison. No, I didn't for a minute think I'd end up being coerced by him into taking on a film about miscarriages of justice involving crib death mothers. If I had, I'd have run a mile; Dad was dead by the time I started at Binary Star, but Mum wasn't.

She still isn't. It will break her heart if I make a documentary that portrays Ray Hines as innocent. Even if Dad was wrong to say what he said about her that day in the restaurant, that's not how Mum will see it. She'll be devastated.

That used to be enough to make me certain I didn't want to do it.

Then why go and work for Binary Star, alongside Laurie Nattrass?

Could I have been hoping, as early as January 2007, to find myself in the position I'm in now?

If I ring my home number and say all this to Angus Hines, will he finally be satisfied and let me make the documentary? I bury my face in my hands. *Oh, God. What have I done?* I should tell the taxi-driver to turn round and go back to Kilburn, but I can't face it. I don't want to go anywhere near Angus Hines ever again.

The cab pulls up outside Binary Star's offices. I pay and get out. The outer door's unlocked, so somebody must be in. I push through the double glass doors and slam straight into Raffi. 'A Felicity on a Saturday?' he says, hands on hips, mock disbelief all over his face. 'I must be seeing things.'

'Do . . . do you normally work on Saturdays?'

'Yup.' He leans forward and whispers in my ear, 'Sometimes I even work on the Lord's Day of Rest. Don't tell Him.' I wonder if there's something Raffi's scared of, something he's trying to convince himself is nothing. Why else would a person spend the weekend in the office? I decide I'm probably projecting; Raffi looks fine.

'I'm going to be working most weekends from now on,' I tell him, trying to sound busy and professional. He purses his lips at me. *I should think so too, the amount we're about to start paying you*. Is he beaming the words into my brain, or am I being paranoid? Either way, I feel as if I might as well be twirling a pistol in each hand, wearing a T-shirt with 'Stand and deliver' emblazoned across it.

'There's a surprise for you in your office,' says Raffi. 'Come to think of it, there were a couple of surprises for you in Maya's office, last time I looked.' Before I have a chance to ask what he means, he's gone, the doors banging behind him.

Maya's office door is shut, her 'Meeting in Progress' sign hanging from the handle. I can hear her and several other people talking over one another. Workaholic freaks, the lot of them. Don't they know what Saturdays are for? Why aren't they curled up on their sofas in their pyjamas, watching repeats of *A Place In The Sun: Home Or Away*?

Someone with a loud voice says, 'I appreciate that.' I wonder what the 'that' is. Fag smoke? Is this a secret meeting of the Nicotine in the Workplace Appreciation Society? I decide that whatever surprises Maya has for me can wait until later.

In the office that's either mine, Laurie's or nobody's, depending on your point of view, I find what looks like a small silver robot standing in the middle of the floor. It takes a few seconds for me to read the label that's stuck to it and work out what it is: a dehumidifier. My heart sinks to somewhere in the sub-gut region. A week ago I'd have been delighted, but not now. The timing says it all. Raffi knows this is supposed to be my new office, and he knows it doesn't have a condensation problem. Is the dehumidifier his way of letting me know I'll soon be back in my damp old room where I belong?

I lock the door and turn on my computer. Laurie's sent me an email that says, 'Revised article attached', and, beneath that, 'Sent from my BlackBerry Wireless device'. The BlackBerry has contributed more words to the message than Laurie has, and it's never even had sex with me. If I weren't so on edge, I might find this funny.

There is no article attached to the message. Luckily Laurie has sent another email – from his laptop, presumably, once he realised he couldn't append the relevant file to his BlackBerry – this time consisting of no words, only the attachment. I open the article and click on 'print'. Then I root around in my bag for Angus Hines' business card. I send him an email, answering the last question he asked me as honestly and fully as possible, and explain that I ran away because I would have found it too hard to answer face to face. I tell him how painful it is for me to think about my dad, and that I tend to do anything I can to avoid it. I don't apologise for locking him in my flat, or ask if he's still there or has managed to get out.

Apart from the two from Laurie, the only interesting message in my inbox is from Dr Russell Meredew. 'Fliss, hi,' it begins. What kind of greeting is that? Isn't this man an OBE? I check the files: yes, he is. It could be worse, I suppose: *Yo, Fliss, what up?* I read the rest of his email. 'I've spoken to Laurie, who tells me you intend to include interviews with Judith Duffy in the film. He thinks this is a bad idea, as do I. If you want to give me a ring, I'll explain why. I'm not trying to tell you how to do your job – please don't think that – but there's a danger in trying to be even-handed when it's a case of a bird in the hand being worth a pathological liar in the bush, if you get my drift. I think perhaps we should talk on the phone before proceeding with the interview we put in the diary the other day. My willingness to be involved in your project partly depends on what sort of project it turns out to be, as I'm sure you appreciate. Very best, Russell Meredew'.

In other words, don't listen to my enemy's point of view – just take my word for it that she's evil.

I press the 'delete' button, making a gargoyle face at the computer, then ring Judith Duffy's home number again and virtually beg her for a meeting. I tell her I'm neither for nor against her – I simply want to hear whatever she might have to say.

I'm about to grab the new version of Laurie's article and leave the office when I hear voices in the corridor that sound as if they're coming closer.

'... either of them gets in touch, please impress on them how important it is that they contact us.'

'I will.' That's Maya.

'For their own safety, they need to understand that all activity around this documentary film stops until further notice. It won't be for ever.'

'And if you find the Twickenham address Rachel Hines gave you ...'

'I've told you, I haven't got it,' says Maya. 'I gave it to Fliss.'

'... or if you remember it ...'

'I'm unlikely to remember it, since I never knew it. I was probably thinking about something else when I scribbled it down, and I handed it over without looking at it. Bring me a list of all the streets in Twickenham if you want, and I'll see if any of the names ring a bell, but, aside from that . . .'

'All right,' says the louder of the two men, in a strong Yorkshire accent. I recognise his voice from the message he left me: DC Colin Sellers. 'So if we could have a quick look round Fliss Benson's office before we go?'

'Which one?'

'She's got more than one?'

'She's kind of moved into Laurie's old office, but I'm not sure she's finished moving all her stuff yet. And Laurie's not been in to collect his things.'

'We need to see both.'

'Laurie's old office is just along here. Follow me.'

What about a warrant? I want to scream. I leap out of my chair and duck down behind the desk, remembering only when I see its four wooden legs that its bulk doesn't go all the way to the floor. *I knew that. Shit, shit, shit.*

The footsteps are getting closer. I spring up, lunge across the room at the dehumidifier and knock it over. I pick it up, turn it so that the broadest side is facing the office door, and sit with my back pressed against it, pulling my knees up to my chin and putting my arms round my legs, refusing to listen to the voice in my head that's saying, *What's the point? So they won't see you when they look through the glass in the door – so what? In a minute Maya's going to let them in, and they're going to find you, very obviously hiding from them.*

Is there any way I can pretend I'm sitting like this because I'm feeling particularly humid today? I'm sweating buckets; maybe that'll help make the lie convincing.

I hear the quieter of the two male voices say, 'What's that? An electric heater?'

'Never seen one as big as that,' says Sellers.

I tuck my chin into my chest. I had no idea I could do this: make a ball of my body while still sitting up. Maybe I ought to take up yoga. *What are you going to say when they unlock the door, walk in and see you?*

'Sorry, guys, do you want to start with Fliss's old office? It might take me a while to track down one of the spare keys for Laurie's. He was always forgetting his, using the spares, then putting them back in odd places.'

Thank God. My relief lasts about half a second, until it occurs to me that the only good thing about my old room was the view of Laurie's office, across the courtyard. I could lie on the floor beneath the window and not be seen by the police, but then if Maya walks past, she'll see me through the glass in the door. With much panicky swearing through gritted teeth, I shunt the dehumidifier round, so that its widest side now faces the window, and pull it a metre or so across the room. Will the detectives notice it's been moved, or will they assume all four sides are the same?

This is the only place I can sit and not be visible from either vantage point. I assume the tucked-in-ball position again, and wait for what seems like years, listening out for the sound of the police coming back in this direction. *And when I hear them, my plan is to do what, exactly?* Questions flit round my brain: too many moths around a lightbulb, clustering blackly around the source of light, making it dark. Why am I bothering to pretend I might get away with this, and what's the point anyway? Why did Tamsin tell me to read a newspaper? Why do I love Laurie so much when I shouldn't even like him? Why can't I bear the thought of being told by DC Sellers that I can't speak to Ray again until he says I can?

Why are the police looking for her? Do they think she killed Helen Yardley?

Is that the story she wants to tell me?

Footsteps. And DC Sellers' boom-box voice again, faint but getting closer. I scramble across the floor to the window and try to prise it open. It feels as if it's been painted shut. Have I ever seen Laurie with his window open? Did I ever notice anything apart from every detail of the man himself – the hairs on his arms, his ankles in black socks – in all the hours I spent gazing across the courtyard at him? *Silly question.*

I push and shove, leaning my whole weight into the window, muttering, 'Yes, thank you, thank you,' as if it's already given way – a little trick that's sometimes worked for me in other situations. There's a creak, then – glory and hallelujah – it opens. I climb out, and am about to lie down next to the wall when I remember my bag. *Shit.*

I push myself through the window again. Why is it such a tight squeeze? I can't have got fatter since three seconds ago. I'm surprised I haven't lost half my body weight, the amount I'm sweating. Back in the room, I freeze, panic rollercoastering through my veins. The police and Maya are right outside; seconds away. I hear a metallic jangling: a bunch of keys. I grab my bag, and half fall, half wriggle through the window. There's a loud tearing sound as I hit the courtyard's paving stones. Christ, that hurt. I kneel up and detach a swatch of material that used to be part of my shirt from a jagged shard of wood protruding from the window frame.

I hear the key turn in the lock. *No more time.* I push the wood that's come free back into the frame and give the window a shove. It almost shuts. There's no way I can close the catch, not from outside and not with Maya and the two detectives walking into the room, so I do the only thing I can do: lie flat on my side, pressing my sore body against the wall under the window. I scan the rooms on the opposite side of the courtyard. I'm safe – they're all empty.

'It's a dehumidifier, Sarge,' DC Sellers says. So the quieter man's in charge.

'What do you reckon to Maya Jacques?' he asks.

Maya's not with them any more? What the hell's she doing, letting two cops loose in my office unsupervised?

'Good body, good hair, bad face,' says Sellers. Bad personality, I'm tempted to call out, from what I'm trying, euphemistically, to think of as my courtyard retreat. There are weeds sprouting up between the flagstones. One is almost touching my nose. Its leaves are sprinkled with soil and white powder: paint dust from the window. I'm already cold; soon I'll be freezing.

'I think she knows the Twickenham address. She protested a bit too much.'

'Why wouldn't she tell us?'

'Laurie Nattrass has nothing but contempt for the police – he says as much in a broadsheet at least twice a week. Do you think he'd tell us where Ray Hines is staying?'

'Probably not,' says Sellers.

'He wouldn't. He'd protect her – that's how he'd see it, anyway. I think we'd better assume everyone at Binary Star feels the same way. Here, look at this.'

What? What are they looking at?

'New message from Angus Hines.'

No, no, no. I nearly wail out loud. I left my email inbox

up on the screen. This is the part where the police find out I locked a man in my flat. This is the beginning of me going to jail.

'Interesting.'

'Have you opened it, Sarge? Living dangerously, aren't you? Interception of Communications Act, and all that.'

'I must have leaned on the mouse by mistake. "Dear Fliss, here are two lists you might find interesting. One is of all the women, and a few men, against whom Judith Duffy has given evidence at criminal trials. The other is of all the people she's testified against in the family courts. All, on both lists, were accused of physically injuring and in many cases killing a child or children. You might also be interested to know that in another twenty-three cases, Dr Duffy testified in support of a parent or parents and said that, in her opinion, no abuse had taken place."'

'And?'

'That's it. "Best wishes, Angus Hines".'

That's it? No mention of illegal imprisonment in my basement flat? I swallow a sigh. It would be a basement flat, wouldn't it? I hadn't thought of that before. Locking up other human beings is never ideal, but when there's any sort of cellar involved, you know you're dealing with a monster. *Wonderful. Just wonderful.*

'Thirty-two on the criminal list, fifty-seven in the family courts,' says Sellers. I hear a whistle that I think means, 'That's a lot of people'.

'Family court proceedings are confidential. Where's he got these names from?'

A good question, but not the main one in my mind. Why has he emailed me the two lists, with no explanation? Is it his way of saying he wants me to make the documentary? Perhaps by locking him in my flat, I proved to him that I have flair and initiative. *Yeah, right.*

He could have got the names from Judith Duffy. She might well keep a record of everyone she's given evidence against in court. She and Ray are now friends, Ray and Angus are more than friends . . . I press my eyes shut, frustrated. I'm accumulating information, but making no progress. Each new thing I find out is like a thread that leads nowhere.

'Holy crap,' says Sellers.

What? *What?*

'New mail icon just flashed up again. I clicked on it . . .'

'You mean you leaned on the mouse by mistake. And?'

'Look at this photo.'

'Is that . . .?'

'It's Helen Yardley's hand. Those are her wedding and engagement rings.'

'Holding a card with the sixteen numbers on, and . . . what's behind the card? A book?'

I can feel my heartbeat throbbing in my ears and throat. I'm glad they found it, not me. I hope they delete it, so that I don't have to see it.

'*Nothing But Love*,' says Sellers. 'Her own book. Seen the sender's address? hilairious@yahoo.co.uk. He's spelled "hilarious" wrong.'

'Forward it to your own email and close it.'

'Think it's him, Sarge?'

'I do,' the quieter one says. 'That picture was taken in Helen Yardley's living room – see the wallpaper in the background? I think he took it on Monday, before he shot her. Whoever he is, he wants Fliss Benson to know what he did. It's as if he's . . . I don't know, boasting or something.'

I can't decide if I'm relieved or disgusted. The idea that a killer has me on his mind and has contacted me four times makes me want to climb into a boiling hot shower and stay there for a long time. But if he's boasting to me, if I'm his audience, perhaps he's less likely to harm me. I desperately want to believe this.

I hear papers being shuffled. My files.

'Sarge, these are full of stuff about Yardley, Jaggard and Hines. We need to take all this away, and Benson's computer. And Nattrass's, even if we have to break into his house to get it.'

'You read my mind. I'll speak to Proust.'

I assume they're not talking about the dead French novelist.

'We need warrants, soon as possible. I don't see how any judge could knock us back. Helen Yardley's dead, Sarah Jaggard's been attacked, and Ray Hines is missing – presumed at risk until we track her down. The main thing linking the three women is the documentary.'

'Do we know where Benson was on Monday?'

Monday? A chill sweeps through me that has nothing to do with the weather as I realise what they must mean. Helen Yardley was murdered on Monday. It's all I can do to stop myself from leaping up and yelling, 'I was here, in the office. I was here all day.'

'Leave those files as you found them,' says the quiet sergeant. 'I'll tell Maya Jacques to keep the office locked and make sure no one touches anything in here.'

Finally, they go. A few minutes later, I hear the thock-thock of Maya's heels and the sound of the key turning in the door.

That's it. Everyone has finished with my office for the time being – everyone but me. I stay where I am and force myself to count to a hundred before moving. Then I climb back inside and close the window behind me. That's as close as I ever hope to get to a camping holiday, I think to myself as I brush the crumbs of dirt and dust off my clothes.

My hand shaking, I delete the email from 'hilairious' without opening it; the police have taken ownership of it, which is fine by me. I print out Angus Hines' email and put it in my bag, along with Laurie's revised article. Stupidly, forgetting the key sound I heard, I try to open the office door and find I can't. How ironic: I've been locked in. Isn't there something called locked-in syndrome? That's what I'm suffering from, me and Angus Hines. I guess all those irritating people who say 'What goes around comes around' must be right.

I unlock the door, then close and lock it behind me. I take the scenic route out of the office, the one that doesn't involve going anywhere near Maya, and hail another taxi. I give the driver my home address. If I see a strange car camped outside that might belong to the police, I'll tell the cab to drive past, but if I don't, I'd quite like to check my flat's still in one piece – no broken windows or piles of glass on the carpet, no scratch marks on the walls. *No irate Tamsin sitting on the sofa, waiting to deliver a stern lecture.*

Tomorrow I'll have to go back to the office and make copies of everything in those box files before the police take them away. Maya won't be in – Sunday's her manicure and pedicure day. Raffi might be around on the Lord's Day of Rest, as he called it, but the chances of him taking an interest in my activities are slim. If I'm efficient, I should be able to photocopy the lot in five or six hours. The thought makes me feel weak with exhaustion.

And once you've copied it all, where are you going to take it? Where are you going to hide? Tamsin and Joe's flat? Mine? Both are places the police are bound to come back to, if they're as keen to find me as they seem to be.

I think I probably made the decision a while ago, but it's only now that I allow myself to acknowledge it. Marchington House. That's where I'll go. Ray won't mind. I've known her less than a week, but I know she won't mind. There must be spare rooms there, plenty of space for me and the contents of several large box files. Plenty of time for me to plough through all the paperwork Laurie and Tamsin generated, looking for . . . what? Something Laurie missed because he couldn't see the trees for the wood?

I feel utterly drained, but I'm too wired to sleep, or even to stare out of the window. I need to do something productive. I pull Laurie's article out of my bag and start to read it. I stop when I get to a sentence that doesn't sound right:

> Despite never having murdered anybody, Dr Duffy was responsible for ruining the lives of dozens of innocent women whose only crime was to be in the wrong place at the wrong time when a child or children died: Helen Yardley, Sarah Jaggard, Dorne Llewellyn . . . the list goes on and on.

Three names isn't a long list. Why didn't Laurie include more, to prove his point? There *were* more in the original draft, I'm sure of it. I turn to the last page. Laurie has also, wisely – or perhaps because the journal editors gave him no choice – deleted his insinuation that Rhiannon Evans must have murdered her son Benjamin because she's a working-class prostitute and that's the sort of thing they do. It makes sense to cut that out, but why strike names off the list of Judith Duffy's victims – a list that's supposed to go on and on?

I rummage in my bag for the original article, but it's not there. I must have left it at home. I have another idea: Angus Hines' email. I pull it out and start to skim through the names. Two leap out at me: Lorna Keast and Joanne Bew. There's no other way I could know those names. They mean nothing to me. The first time I saw them was in Laurie's article, alongside the names Helen Yardley and Sarah Jaggard. I *did* see them; I'm not imagining it.

In the first draft, Lorna Keast and Joanne Bew were part of that list. So why aren't they now?

From *Nothing But Love* by Helen Yardley with Gaynor Mundy

5 November 1996

I didn't enjoy any of the days of my trial, but the worst was 5 November. That was when I came face to face with Dr Judith Duffy for the first time, when she gave her evidence in chief, which means in response to prosecuting counsel's questions. Unbelievably, I had never met or seen her before, even though she claimed to know so much about me and my family. But I knew what sort of person she was. Ned and Gillian had warned me. She's the sort of woman who is happy to say that a grief-stricken mother committed two murders without even bothering to speak to her or get to know her first. In contrast, Dr Russell Meredew, one of the many heroes of this story and the main expert witness for the defence, had spent days with Paul and me, interviewed us both at length, and painstakingly compiled what he called his 'dossier'. We joked that by the time he'd finished it was as thick as an encyclopaedia! Incidentally, Dr Meredew tried to present the dossier to Justice Wilson in court, and Wilson's shocking response was, 'You don't expect me to read all that, do you?'

I watched Dr Duffy closely as she took the stand and felt real, heart-shaking terror for the first time since the trial had begun. There was something about her that chilled me.

Until that moment, I had assumed I would be going home with Paul at the end of this ridiculous charade. We would get Paige back and live happily ever after. I had no doubts about this because I was innocent. I knew it, Paul knew it, and the jury would know it too. Ned had assured me that once Russell Meredew had explained to them, in his gentle but authoritative way, that it was entirely possible both Morgan and Rowan died of natural causes, there was no way in the world I would be convicted of murder.

But when Judith Duffy's eyes met mine for the first time, I felt as if I'd been punched in the stomach. I saw no compassion whatsoever. Her bearing was haughty and arrogant. She looked exactly like the sort of person who would try to send me to prison for the rest of my life simply because she could, to prove that she was right. I didn't know at the time, but I found out later that Paul had felt exactly the same way about her, and so had Ned and Gillian.

I honestly felt as if I was being tortured as I sat there, helpless, listening to her describe what I must have done to my precious Morgan and Rowan in order to cause the injuries she claimed they'd sustained. I heard her tell the jury, many of whom were in tears, that I had poisoned my children using salt, that I had smothered them repeatedly, with the aim of taking them to the hospital and getting lots of attention for myself. I'd never heard anything so ridiculous in my life. If I'd wanted attention, I thought, I'd have walked down the street in a Minnie Mouse costume, done the cancan naked in my front garden – something funny and harmless. I would *never, never* have murdered my babies.

When I heard Dr Duffy say that Rowan's skull had been fractured, I wanted to scream, 'You're lying! I never hurt my babies! I adored them, I had nothing but love for them!'

I will never forget the way Dr Duffy's examination-in-chief ended. It's painfully etched on my mind for ever. When I checked the trial transcript, it corresponded almost word for word with what I remembered:

Rudgard: Mrs Yardley believes both Morgan and Rowan were victims of crib death, or SIDS. What do you say to that?

Duffy: Leaving aside the fact that it's highly unusual for there to be two instances of SIDS in one household—

Rudgard: Forgive me for interrupting, Doctor – I wish to concentrate on the Yardley family, not other families you've encountered in your professional life. Let's not get into the statistics game. We all know how notoriously unreliable statistics are when applied to a specific case – they're meaningless. Is it possible, in your view, that Morgan and Rowan were both victims of crib death?

Duffy: I'd say that's so unlikely, it borders on impossible. What's overwhelmingly likely is that there was a common underlying cause of both deaths, and that the cause was forensic, not medical.

Rudgard: Then, in your opinion, both Morgan and Rowan Yardley were murdered?

Duffy: My opinion is that both babies died of non-accidental injuries, yes.

I dissolved in tears as Judith Duffy calmly told these lies about me, but, although I was distraught, neither Paul nor I had any idea how much damage had been done by her use of the phrase 'so unlikely, it borders on impossible'. Ned, however, with all his years of trial expertise, knew exactly how dangerous it was for the jury to hear those words. It didn't matter that a few seconds earlier, they'd heard the great Ivor Rudgard QC say that statistics can't be relied upon in cases like mine – that wasn't the part that would stick in their minds. It wasn't as memorable or impressive as Dr Duffy's magic formula for finding guilt where there is none: 'so unlikely, it borders on impossible'.

When Reuben Merrills rose to cross-examine Dr Duffy, Ned flashed one of his brilliant ray-of-hope smiles at me: *Don't worry, Merrills is the best defence barrister in the land – he'll demolish her*. He certainly did his best:

Merrills: Let's be clear: is your contention that it's not possible for more than one baby born to the same two parents and into the same household to die of natural causes?

Duffy: I didn't say—

Merrills: Because I could cite to you several cases of families that have suffered more than one crib death, with no hint of induced injury.

Duffy: Your terminology's confused. Natural causes and crib death aren't synonymous with one another. In a family that contains the haemophilia gene, it's obviously quite probable that more than one member will die a haemophilia-related death – that's natural causes. Crib death is what we call it when no explanation for death can be found.

Merrills: Very well, then, say crib death. Is it possible, in your view, for there to be more than one crib death in one family?

Duffy: Of course it is.

Merrills: To clarify: you're saying that *of course* it's possible for more than one child in the same family to be a victim of SIDS.

Duffy: It's possible, yes.

Merrills: Yet a short while ago, you said the opposite, didn't you?

Duffy: No, I didn't. I said that—

Merrills: You said that for Morgan and Rowan Yardley both to have suffered crib deaths was 'so unlikely, it borders on impossible'.

Duffy: I meant that—

Merrills: You said, and the jury remembers you saying, that for there to have been two SIDS deaths in the Yardley family was 'so unlikely it borders on impossible.'

Duffy: No, I did not say that.

Merrills: Well, Dr Duffy, I'm sure the jury are as baffled as I am, because we all heard you say it. No further questions.

My heart was pounding like the hooves of an excited horse as I listened to this. Thank goodness, I thought. Now the jury will understand what a monstrous liar Judith Duffy is. How could anyone take her opinion seriously now that Reuben Merrills had caught her out in such a blatant lie? But my spirits clouded over when I looked at Paul and Ned and saw that they were both frowning. I found out later that they were seriously worried about the effect of repetition on the jury. Even though Merrills had made short work of proving that Duffy was a flat-out liar, he had twice repeated her original assertion that for Morgan and Rowan both to have died of SIDS was so unlikely it bordered on impossible. Ned told me later that repeating something over and over again is a highly effective way of getting people to believe it. 'The context of the repetition matters less than the repetition itself,' he said. He's right. I was being naïve. Time after time during my trial, the jury heard that phrase: 'so unlikely, it borders on impossible.' I didn't know it on 5 November, but I was going to spend nine years of my life in prison as a result of those six words uttered by Dr Duffy, a woman who had never heard me say so much as a single word.

24 October 2004

On 24 October, a journalist from the *Daily Telegraph* came to interview me in prison. Paul joked that I could barely fit in his visits now that I was a celebrity. That's what the prison staff called me too: 'our resident celebrity'. Everybody at Geddham Hall was wonderfully supportive. They all knew I was innocent, which was a welcome change from Durham, where I was hated and attacked. I knew I had Laurie to thank for people's change of attitude. He'd mounted such a wonderful campaign on my behalf, and even my lovely cautious Ned had been heard to mutter that my appeal next February might just succeed. Laurie had been doing wonders out there in the outside world, and JIPAC was going from strength to strength.

I felt so frustrated, because there was only so much I could do from inside, but Laurie was heroically reassuring, and kept telling me that everyone knew JIPAC was my baby as much as his. I couldn't wait to get out and do more to help women in terrible situations like mine, women the justice system had betrayed and abandoned. There were so many of them and I felt so much love and pity for all of them. I'd heard that Rachel Hines was coming to Geddham soon. Her case was almost identical to mine: an innocent mother wrongly convicted of killing her two children. She'd recently been denied leave to appeal, and my heart broke for her.

One thing I could do in prison was write, and I found I loved it. At first I agreed to keep a diary only because Laurie asked me to, but once I started, I couldn't have managed without it. I told the journalist from the *Telegraph* that one day I hoped to publish a book about my life and everything I'd been through. She nodded, as if this was a perfectly natural thing to want, and only to be expected. I wasn't sure she understood how much it meant to me. She must have had to write all the time for her job, but I hadn't written anything since leaving school. She seemed nice, so I let her have a look at my work in progress. 'I bet my writing style's terrible, isn't it?' I joked.

'This poem's brilliant,' she said. 'Really, really good.' I had to laugh. She might as well have said, 'Yes, Helen, your writing style is terrible.' The poem, the only part of what I'd written that she'd praised, was the only thing in the notebook that wasn't by me! It was a poem I found in an anthology in Geddham's library, and I thought it was beautiful, so I wrote it down at the front of my notebook, to inspire me. It's by a woman called Fiona Sampson, and it's called 'Anchorage':

Those fasting women in their cells
drained a honeycomb brain
of every sugar drop of sense;
they made the skull a silvered shell
where love could live, cuckoo-like –

Would any question what she did
to distance her from how we live,
outside such dedication? – Shedding
the various world, so as to fit
in ways a jealous lover likes?

What flutters still is a bird: blown in
by accident, or wild design
of grace, a taste of something sweet –
The emptied self a room swept white.

I wasn't entirely sure what the poem meant, but I knew that from the moment I first read it, it meant the world to me and became one of my treasured possessions. I almost felt as if it must have been written with me in mind! It was about women in cells, which I was – for the time being at least. I particularly loved the last verse because it seemed to me to be so full of hope. I thought that was what the writer was trying to say: that even when you're locked up and everything's been taken away from you, you still have hope. Hope is the bird that still flutters, 'blown in by accident, or wild design of grace, a taste of something sweet'. And because you've lost everything, in your empty life that is now 'a room swept white', a hope that might otherwise be so tiny and fragile suddenly seems huge and sweet and powerful, because it's the only thing there.

Every night in my cell, I lay in my bed crying for my lost babies and imagining those wings of hope fluttering and flapping in the darkness beside me.

14

10/10/09

'My being struck off is a foregone conclusion,' said Judith Duffy. 'It will happen even if I defend myself, and since I won't . . .'

'Nothing? Not even someone to speak on your behalf?' Charlie made sure to sound curious rather than disapproving. She'd only been talking to Duffy for ten minutes or so, but already it had made her aware of how judgemental she normally was, often entertaining herself while others were speaking by gleefully mocking their clothes, mannerisms, stupidity – all in the privacy of her own mind, of course, and so probably harmless, except she was finding now that she had shamefully little experience of listening to another person in what must (she assumed) be the ideal way – without the secret hope that within seconds her bitchy streak would have something to get its teeth into.

Talking of clothes, Judith Duffy's were a little odd. Individually, each garment was okay, but the ensemble didn't work: a lacy white blouse, a shapeless purple cardy, a grey knee-length skirt that might have been half of a suit, black tights, and flat black shoes with large bows on them that looked as if they would suit a younger woman better. Charlie couldn't work out if Duffy had tried to dress smartly or casually this morning; either way, she hadn't got the look quite right.

Charlie had talked her way into Duffy's house by appealing to what they had in common. It had taken more honesty than she'd thought it would, and she'd ended up almost convincing herself that she and this plain, prim-looking doctor were some kind of outcast soulmates, to the point that to condemn Duffy now for anything would feel like condemning herself, and Charlie was bored of doing that. She'd given it up roughly a year ago.

'Much to my lawyer's consternation, no – no defence at all,' said Duffy. 'And no appeal. I don't want to argue with anyone about anything – not the GMC, not Russell Meredew. Certainly not Laurie Nattrass. That man's appetite for being proved right is insatiable. Anyone who locks horns with him is likely to find themselves still there twenty years later.' She smiled. She and Charlie were sitting on cushionless wicker chairs in her green-tiled, green-walled conservatory. From what Charlie had seen of the house, it was assorted shades of green throughout. The view at the back was of a long, neat, entirely plant-free garden – just lawn and empty beds – and, beyond a low wooden fence, a garden of the same proportions but with shrubs and flowers, leading to a conservatory that looked like an exact replica of Duffy's.

'When I first became unpopular, I used to plead my case to anyone who would listen. It took me more than two years to notice that standing up for myself made me feel worse rather than better.'

'There's something soul-destroying about trying to persuade people you aren't as bad as they think you are,' Charlie agreed. 'My natural inclination has always been to say, "Fuck you all – I'm even worse."' She didn't apologise for her language. If being a pensioner netted you a free bus pass, outcast status surely earned you the right to swear.

'I'm as bad as I am and as good as I am.' Duffy wrapped her cardigan around herself. 'So is everybody else. We all feel pain, we all relieve pain, we all unwittingly cause pain to others. Most of us at some point in our lives deliberately cause pain, of varying degrees.'

'At the risk of sounding like a smart-arse . . . You could fight for your job and your reputation at the GMC hearing and all that would still be true.'

'A GMC verdict doesn't change who I am, and neither does public opinion,' said Duffy. 'Nor does unhappiness, which is why I've given it up.'

'So you no longer care what people think of you?'

Duffy looked up at the glass above her head. 'If I say I don't, it sounds as if I'm dismissive of my fellow human beings, which isn't true at all. But . . . most people are incapable of forming a meaningful opinion about me. They can't see beyond the things I'm famous for having said and done.'

'Isn't that who a person is?' Charlie asked. 'The sum total of everything he or she says and does?'

'You don't really believe that, do you?' Judith Duffy sounded very much the concerned doctor. Charlie half expected her to produce a pad and pen, prescribe a powerful mind-changing drug. *For your own good, dear.*

'To be honest, I'm way too shallow to have given it any thought, so I won't pretend to have an answer.'

'What's the best thing you've ever done?'

'Last year I . . . well, I suppose I sort of saved the lives of three people.'

'I'll ignore the "sort of", which is you being modest,' said Duffy briskly. 'You saved three lives.'

'I should probably qualify that.' Charlie sighed. It wasn't a memory she enjoyed revisiting. 'A colleague and I saved *two* people's lives, though the person who was going to kill them ended up killing—'

'Don't qualify it.' Duffy smiled. 'You saved lives.'

'I suppose so.'

'I have too, dozens of them. I don't know the exact number, but there are plenty of children who wouldn't have lived to see adulthood if I hadn't persuaded a court to take them away from families that would have killed them. What greater gift can you give than the gift of continued life, when someone's threatened with extinction? None. You and I have both given that gift, more than once. Does that make us two of the greatest people who ever lived?'

'God, I hope not.' Charlie laughed. 'If I'm the best the world has to offer, I might have to resort to space tourism.'

'We aren't defined by our achievements any more than we're defined by our mistakes,' said Duffy. 'We're just who we are, and who really knows what that amounts to?'

'You could say that about Helen Yardley. You thought she murdered her children.'

'I still do.'

'But that wasn't *her*, was it, according to your theory? It was the worst thing she did, but it wasn't who she was.'

'No, it wasn't.' Duffy's voice took on a new energy. 'And I wish more people understood that. Mothers who murder their babies aren't evil, they aren't monsters. Mostly, they're trapped in little hells of the mind – hells they can't escape from and can't talk about to anyone. Often they conceal those hells so expertly, they convince the world they're happy and normal, even those closest to them.' She shifted in her chair. 'I don't suppose you've read Helen Yardley's autobiography, *Nothing But Love*?'

'I'm in the middle of it.'

'Have you noticed how many people she writes off as blind and stupid for not taking one look at her and *knowing* she didn't kill her two boys, because she was so distraught and grief-stricken, as surely no baby-killer would be? Because it ought to have been obvious to everybody how much she loved her children?'

Charlie nodded. She hadn't been impressed even the first time the point had been made. *You could have been pretending to be distraught, though, couldn't you?* was the retort that sprang to mind.

'Mothers who smother their babies usually do love them – deeply, as deeply as any mother who'd never dream of harming her child, though I know that's a hard idea to get your head round. Typically, they *are* distraught – quite genuinely. They're heartbroken, their lives are in pieces – exactly the same as an innocent mother who loses a baby to meningitis. Forget the controversial cases – I'm talking about the many women I've met in the course of my work who admit to having felt so desperate that they put a pillow over baby's face, or threw him under a train, or off the balcony. With the very odd exception, these women are devastated by the loss of the child. They want to die afterwards, they can't think of a reason to go on living.'

'But . . .' Was Charlie missing something? 'They caused that loss themselves.'

'Which, if anything, makes it worse.'

'But . . . Why didn't they just not do it, then? Do they think they want the child to die, and only realise too late that they don't?'

Judith Duffy smiled sadly. 'You're attributing a level of rationality to these women that simply isn't there. They do it because they're suffering terribly and don't know what else to do. That behaviour *came out* of them, out of their pain, and they didn't have the inner resources to stop it. When you're mentally ill, it's not always possible to think, "If I do this, then that will happen." Mentally ill isn't the same as mad, incidentally.'

'No,' said Charlie, not wanting to seem unsophisticated. Privately, she was thinking, *Sometimes they're the same. Both can mean going to the shops with no clothes on and shouting when you get there about aliens making off with your vital organs.*

'Mothers who kill their babies deserve our compassion in exactly the same way that mothers whose babies die of natural causes do,' said Duffy. 'I felt like cheering when Justice Elizabeth Geilow questioned, in her summary remarks, whether women like Ray Hines and Helen Yardley belong in the criminal system at all. In my view, they don't. What they're crying out for is empathy and help.'

'Yet you testify against them. You're a crucial part of the successful prosecutions that send them to prison,' said Charlie.

'I didn't testify *against* Ray, or Helen, or any of them,' Duffy corrected. 'As an expert witness in a criminal trial, I'm asked for my opinion about what caused children to die. If I think parent- or carer-inflicted violence is the cause of death, I say so, but I'm not *against* anybody when I say it. By telling the truth as I see it, I'm trying to do the best for everyone. Lies benefit nobody. I'm on every accused woman's side just as I'm on every endangered or murdered child's side.'

'I'm not sure the women would see it that way,' said Charlie tetchily. *Talk about trying to have it both ways*.

'Of course they wouldn't.' Duffy tucked her iron-grey hair behind her ears. 'But I also have to think about the children – defenceless and equally deserving of compassion.'

'You wouldn't say *more* deserving?'

'No. Though if you ask me what I think I'm here for, it's to save and protect children. That's my number one priority. However much compassion I feel for a woman like Helen Yardley, I'm going to make sure she doesn't kill a third child if at all possible.'

'Paige?'

Duffy stood up. 'Why do I feel as if I'm defending myself?'

'I'm sorry, I didn't mean to . . .'

'No, it's not you. Do you want another cup of tea?'

Charlie didn't, but she sensed the doctor needed some space to clear her head, so she nodded. Had she sounded too harsh? Simon would have laughed and said, 'Don't you always?'

While Duffy was pottering about in the kitchen, Charlie looked at the books on the small shelf in the corner of the conservatory. A biography of Daphne Du Maurier, a few Iris Murdochs, nine or ten books by someone called Jill McGown that Charlie hadn't heard of, lots of Russian classics, three vegetarian recipe books, *Forever* . . . No, surely not. Charlie crept across the room to check she wasn't seeing things. She wasn't. Judith Duffy had a copy of *Forever in my Heart* by Jade Goody. Talk about eclectic tastes.

'The Yardleys' inventiveness with names is one of the many

reasons I'm in trouble,' said Duffy, returning with a mug of tea each for her and Charlie. 'I referred to their younger son Rowan as "she" in a report I wrote. I've only known of two other Rowans and both were female, so I assumed Helen's Rowan was too. Laurie Nattrass has made much of that, just as he's made much of my lack of personal involvement with the Yardley family, in contrast to Russell Meredew, who practically moved in with them at one point. I never spoke to Helen or Paul, never interviewed them.'

'Do you regret that?' Charlie asked.

'I regret not having time for the personal touch, but the reality is that . . .' Duffy stopped. 'I'm defending myself again.'

'You can't be. I'm not attacking you.'

The doctor's lips flattened into a line. 'The reality is,' she said less stridently, 'that I was the most sought-after expert witness in the country before Laurie Nattrass declared me the root of all evil, and I didn't have time to get to know every family. I had to leave that to others I hoped were properly trained to give parents like the Yardleys and the Hineses the help they needed. My job as an expert witness wasn't to meet and get to know the family – it was to look at samples under a microscope, look at the slides I was given, and make sense of what I saw. In the case of Rowan Yardley, I was looking at lung tissue and a fractured skull – that was what the paediatric pathologist who performed the post-mortem passed on to me. I wasn't asked to inspect the child's genitalia, hence the mistake about his sex.'

Duffy pushed her hair away from her face. 'I should have known he was a boy. I should have checked, and I deeply regret that I didn't, but . . .' She shrugged. 'Sadly, that doesn't cancel out what I saw through the microscope: clear evidence that in the course of his short life, Rowan Yardley had been subjected to repeated smothering attempts. No amount of sitting in the Yardleys' kitchen and chatting to them would have made the evidence of non-natural airway obstruction disappear. Or the skull fracture.'

Charlie sipped her tea, wondering if there was an analogy to be found in policing terms. If she was walking through the Winstanley estate, and saw a teenager in a hooded top knock an old woman to the ground, verbally abuse her and run off with her bag, unambiguous eye-witness evidence that a crime had been committed . . . Was that how certain Judith Duffy was about Helen Yardley? Were the doctors who testified in Yardley's defence saying the equivalent of, 'He wasn't mugging her, he was rehearsing for his part in a school play about thieves?'

'For what it's worth – and since I never spoke to the woman, you might say it's not worth much – I believe Helen Yardley escaped from her little hell before she died,' Duffy said. 'What she went through gave her a purpose. Her campaigning work on behalf of other women – it was genuine, I think. She believed passionately in their innocence – Sarah Jaggard, Ray Hines, all of them. She suited being a celebrity, the perfect martyr-turned-heroine. It gave her something she needed: attention, recognition. I think she really wanted to do good. That's why she was so effective as a figurehead for JIPAC.'

Charlie heard pride and admiration in the doctor's voice; it made her feel uncomfortable.

'It's always difficult to untangle a person's motivations,' said Duffy, 'but if I had to guess, I'd say Helen's wish to be innocent herself would have fuelled her determination to believe other women were, others like her. The irony is that even if every last one of them were guilty, Helen's support would have been incredibly beneficial to them. By believing in their essential goodness, she probably helped them to forgive themselves for what they'd done.'

'Are you saying . . .?'

'They're all guilty? No. What I'm saying, and what people like Laurie Nattrass seem unwilling to take on board, is that the chances of an unexplained and unexpected child death being murder are far greater now than they used to be, proportionally. Fifty years ago there were 3,000 crib deaths a year in the UK. Gradually, as housing conditions improved, that went down to 1,000 a year. Then with more houses becoming smoke-free, less co-sleeping, and the 'Back to Sleep' campaign – persuading parents it was dangerous to put a baby down to sleep on its front – the SIDS rate came down to 400 a year. But those little hells of the mind . . .' Duffy glanced towards her kitchen, as if her own private hell was somewhere in that direction. 'Presumably there are as many of those now as there ever were, if not more – which means as many adults driven to harm children.'

'So the non-natural deaths are a bigger proportion of the total number,' said Charlie. That made sense.

'I would say so, yes. Though, because I'm not a statistician, I'm not sure whether that's the same thing or slightly different from saying that a reported crib death is more *likely* to be a homicide now than fifty years ago. Statistics might be helpful when you're looking at populations, but they can be horribly distorting if you try to apply them to individual cases. I'm very precise when I talk about these things, which is why it's frustrating when fools misrepresent me.' Duffy sounded more resigned than angry. 'You'll have heard my famous quote: "so unlikely, it borders on impossible"?'

Charlie nodded.

'It's that more than anything else that's going to seal my fate at the GMC,' said Duffy. 'How could I say something so inaccurate and prejudicial about the odds of two siblings being crib deaths, without having firm statistical evidence to back it up? Simple: I didn't say it. I tried to explain what I'd meant, but Helen Yardley's barrister wouldn't let me speak. The exact question put to me was, "Is it possible that Morgan and Rowan were both victims of crib death?" It was *that* question to which I replied with the words I'm now universally hated for, but I wasn't talking about the two-crib-deaths-in-one-household aspect of the situation. On that, I'd have said that for two babies from the same family to be SIDS deaths would be uncommon, but quite possible if there was a medical condition in the family – a genetic predisposition, a history of heart arrhythmias.'

Judith Duffy leaned forward in her chair. 'When I said "so unlikely, it borders on impossible", I meant *given what I'd seen through the microscope* – nothing to do with number of crib deaths per family. I'd studied both boys' files in detail and found what I regarded as incontrovertible evidence of non-natural death in both cases – repeated attempts at smothering, salt poisoning, a bilateral skull fracture . . . Russell Meredew claims a baby can fracture its skull by falling off a sofa; I beg to differ. For Morgan and Rowan Yardley to have sustained the damage I saw and for it not to have been inflicted . . .' She frowned and laughed simultaneously, as if trying to work it out all over again. 'It's as likely as someone with a bone poking out through the skin of their arm not having a broken arm – so unlikely that, yes, it borders on impossible.'

Automatically, Charlie wondered if there was any weird syndrome that might make an arm-bone protrude from the skin without being broken. Acute skin shrinkage? Hole-in-the-flesh disorder?

'Being certain doesn't necessarily make me right, of course,' Duffy added. 'Humility's as important as compassion in my line of work. I made some bad mistakes: I originally said, in the case of Rowan Yardley, that blood results shouldn't be relied upon. Then later, when I found out about Morgan, who also had unbelievably high blood salt, and when I looked at the whole symptom picture, I changed my mind. Taken in isolation, perhaps, high serum sodium could possibly be explained away, but . . . Also, I didn't know, when I said it, quite how high Rowan's blood salt levels were. Another mistake I made was to allow a coroner friend of mine to tell me Marcella Hines' death had to have been natural causes, because he knew Angus Hines and the Hineses were "a lovely family".'

Charlie noticed that Duffy seemed more at ease talking about the things she'd done wrong than about wrongs done to her.

'When Nathaniel Hines turned up on my autopsy table four years later, I panicked. Had I relaxed my usual vigilance and taken Desmond . . . the coroner's word for something when I shouldn't have, and had another baby now been murdered as a result of my giving both Ray Hines and Desmond the benefit of the doubt? It was my worst fear, and I suppose that made me more likely to believe it was exactly what had happened. I went into over-protective, over-cautious mode, and as a result . . .' She tailed off, staring past Charlie into space.

'As a result?' Charlie prompted gently.

'I made a dreadful error in Ray's case. She didn't murder either of her children, but I told the court she did. My defensiveness was partly to blame.' Duffy smiled. 'I used to be very defensive. By the time Nathaniel Hines died, Laurie Nattrass's media onslaught against me had been raging for some time. I was determined not to be cowed by him. To say Nathaniel Hines was a crib death when I had doubts would have felt like a defeat. I suppose I wanted to show the world that mothers can be a very real danger to babies, and it's not just something I invented out of wickedness and because I enjoy ruining people's lives. And I *did* have doubts – I was told on good authority that Ray had suffered from post-natal depression and nearly jumped off a window ledge. What if I'd said natural causes, and the Hineses had had another baby and it had ended up dead too?'

'You and Ray had lunch together on Monday,' said Charlie. Seeing Duffy's surprise, she added, 'That's one of the reasons I'm here. The DI who's SIO on Helen Yardley's murder thinks it's odd that the two of you would spend time together.'

'It's only odd if you look at the world in a limited and limiting way,' said Duffy.

'Yup, that would be our DI.'

'Believe it or not, Ray and I are now good friends. I contacted her when she got out of prison, via her solicitor.'

'Why?' Charlie asked.

'To apologise. To admit that I'd been less than objective in her case. She was the one who suggested meeting. She wanted to tell me the truth about what had killed her babies. She believed it was the DTP-Hib vaccine, in both cases. After listening to her for half an hour, I was inclined to think so too.'

'But . . .'

'Her lawyers didn't bring it up at the trial because all their expert witnesses threatened to deny it, and, with no medical expert to say it was a possible cause of death, they'd have looked stupid. Ironically, if they'd come to me, I'd instantly have thought twice about Marcella and Nathaniel's deaths being murder. At least I hope I would,' Duffy amended. 'I like to think I would have woken up at that point.'

'But Ray's lawyers didn't go to you, because you were the bad guy, giving evidence for the other side.'

Duffy nodded. 'Angus Hines' mother has Lupus. There's a history of crib death in his extended family. That suggests a hereditary auto-immune problem. Plus, a reliable witness saw both Marcella and Nathaniel have a seizure almost straight after they were vaccinated. Vaccine damage – fitting, in particular – would account for all the things I saw: brain swelling, bleeding in the brain . . .'

'That ought to have come out in court. Even if they thought all the doctors would disagree with it.'

'Oh, I'm sure Julian Lance was right about that – that's Ray's lawyer. Everyone admits in theory that a small percentage of babies will react badly to a vaccine and in some cases die – there's even a body called the Vaccine Damage Payment Unit – but when it actually happens, in my experience, everyone closes ranks and says, "It wasn't the vaccine – that's perfectly safe, trialled and tested." '

Duffy smiles suddenly. 'You know, the first time I met Ray after she was released, she thanked me for caring enough about her children not to bow to the pressure I was under – Laurie Nattrass's pressure – and say they died naturally when it wasn't what I believed. That's what she said, even though she ended up going to prison because of my testimony.'

'Do you know where Ray's staying at the moment?' Charlie asked.

'Not the address,' said Duffy. She patted her knees. For a second, Charlie mistook it for an invitation to sit on her lap. Then Duffy said, 'I feel as if I've been talking about myself for an awfully long time. I'd like to hear about you.'

'I've told you about my fall from grace.'

'I'm sorry you had to yell the details through my letterbox,' said Duffy. 'Do you want to talk about it? *Have* you ever talked about it? I don't mean the bare bones of what happened, I mean the emotional impact—'

'No,' Charlie cut her off.

'You should.'

'Even if I don't want to?'

'Especially then.' Duffy looked alarmed, as if a reluctance to discuss past traumas was a symptom of a fatal illness. 'Keeping any kind of emotional damage locked inside you is a big mistake. Pain has to be expressed and really *felt* before it can dissolve.' Duffy half rose from her chair and moved it closer to Charlie's before sitting again. 'It was two years before I could bring myself to talk about Sarah Jaggard's trial,' she said. 'I had to be taken to court in an armoured van and escorted in through a back entrance. I knew then that there was no way she'd be convicted. By 2005, Laurie Nattrass had made me a household name, and not in a good way. My presence as an expert witness for the prosecution was enough to secure an acquittal for Jaggard. People screamed abuse at me in court, the jury stared at me as if they wanted me dead . . .'

A loud ringing sound interrupted her: the doorbell.

'I'll leave it. I'm not expecting anyone. I'd rather talk to you, and listen to you.'

Charlie hesitated. Could she tell this virtual stranger how she'd spent most of the past three years feeling? Should she? 'No, get it,' she said.

Duffy looked disappointed, but she didn't argue. Once she'd gone, Charlie stood up and put on her jacket quickly, before she could change her mind. She grabbed her bag and made her way towards the kitchen. She heard Duffy in the hall, sounding polite but firm, saying, 'No, thanks,' and 'Really, I'm sure. Thank you.'

Charlie stepped out into the hall at exactly the same moment as she heard the shot, saw the gun, and saw Duffy fall backwards, her head cracking on the uncarpeted stairs.

The man in the doorway turned and pointed his gun at Charlie. 'Get on the floor! Don't move!'

'I can't have seen it, can I? She was innocent all along.' Leah Gould raised her voice to make herself heard above the noise in the café. She'd told Simon to meet her here – across the road from her office. Gould hadn't worked for Social Services for seven years. She'd taken maternity leave, then, when her daughter went to school, she'd got a job as a receptionist for a timber company, where she still worked.

'Only you know what you saw,' said Simon.

'But why would she have tried to smother her daughter if she didn't kill her two boys? She wouldn't, would she? Either she's a killer or she's not, and she wouldn't have had her convictions cancelled or whatever if she was guilty.'

'Why do you say that?'

Leah Gould took a bite of her cheese and onion toastie as she considered the question. Simon was starving. Soon as he was alone, he'd get himself something to eat. He hated eating in front of strangers.

'It's like Laurie Nattrass says: the courts'll do anything to avoid saying they made a mistake. They only admit they're wrong when they're forced to, when it's such a bad mistake that they can't deny it.'

'So because Helen Yardley won her appeal, she must have been innocent?'

Leah Gould nodded.

'Before the appeal – what did you think then?'

'Oh, I thought she'd done it. Definitely.'

'How come?'

'Because of what I saw her do.' More chomping on the toastie.

'What you *didn't* see her do, you mean?'

'Yeah. But I thought I did. It was only later I realised I couldn't have.'

Simon's hunger was making him more impatient than he would have been otherwise. 'Do you know anything about any of the three judges that heard Helen's appeal?'

Leah Gould looked at him as if he was crazy. 'Why would I know about any judges?'

'Do you even know their names?'

'Why would I?'

'Yet you trust them more than you trust your own eyes.'

Leah Gould blinked at him. 'What do you mean?'

Simon would have liked to prise the toastie from her fingers and kick it across the room. 'Helen Yardley's convictions were overturned because they were deemed unsafe. It's not the same thing as saying she's innocent. The appeal judges didn't necessarily think she was innocent of murder, though they might have done. One might have done, or two, or all three – they could have had the same opinion or different opinions.' This was useless. 'I'm interested in what *you* believe, based on what you saw.'

'I think she must have been giving her baby a cuddle, like she said.'

Something was missing here. Leah Gould had expressed no regret whatsoever. 'The evidence you gave in court was a big part of the prosecution's case,' said Simon. 'You claimed you saw Helen Yardley try to smother her daughter. You were asked if it could have been a cuddle – a mother in turmoil at being separated from her only surviving child, clinging on to that child – you said no.'

'Because that was what I thought at the time.'

Was guilt an emotion that only intelligent people felt?

'It wasn't just me. There was a policeman there. He saw it too.'

'Giles Proust?'

'I can't remember his name.'

'His name was Giles Proust. He disagreed with you in court. He described what he witnessed that day as an ordinary cuddle.'

Leah Gould shook her head. 'I was looking at him, not at Helen Yardley. He was watching her with Paige. That's when I first knew something was wrong. I saw his eyes change, and he looked at me, like he couldn't do anything and wanted me to stop it. That's when I looked at Helen and the baby and . . . saw what I saw. And I did stop it.'

'You stopped an attempted smothering? By taking Paige Yardley away from her mother?'

Leah Gould's lips thinned in disapproval. 'Are you winding me up? I've told you, I don't think that *now*. I'm telling you what I thought *then*.'

'And you thought, *then*, that DS Proust saw what you saw?'

'Yeah.'

'Then why did he say the opposite in court? Why say he saw only a cuddle?'

'You'd have to ask him.' No curiosity in her expression; not even a flicker of interest.

'I suppose if you could be wrong about what you saw Helen Yardley do, you could equally be wrong about Giles Proust. Maybe you misinterpreted the look he gave you; maybe he was thinking about what he was going to have for his tea that night.'

'No, because he looked petrified. I thought: what kind of policeman can he be if he gets the willies so easily?' She shook her head, her mouth assuming the shape of disapproval once again. 'I mean, he should have stopped it, really. He shouldn't have relied on me.'

'Though now you believe there was no "it" to stop,' Simon reminded her.

'No,' she agreed, looking uncertain for a second. She pushed the last corner of the toastie into her mouth.

'In that case, what would have made Proust look so scared?'

'You'd have to ask him that.' *Chew, chew, chew*.

Simon thanked her and left, couldn't wait to get away. He turned on his mobile. Sam Kombothekra had left a message. Simon rang him back from the car. 'What happened with Leah Gould?' Sam asked.

'She's a bovine waste of space.'

'Nothing useful, then?'

'Not really,' Simon lied. He felt as if a huge weight had been lifted. He'd got exactly what he'd been hoping for. Leah Gould had changed her mind because it was no longer fashionable to believe Helen Yardley was a murderer – simple as that. Simon was certain Gould *had* seen Helen try to smother Paige, and that Proust had seen it too.

Proust must have fallen for Helen's grieving mother act at the first time of exposure, fallen for *her*. He believed she was innocent, and he was always right – that was the one fact he knew about himself, above all others. And he had to *stay* right, even when he witnessed the attempted murder of Helen's third child. His preconceived ideas made it impossible for him to take the action that needed to be taken; he was powerless – as powerless as he'd been making everyone around him feel ever since. With one frantic look, he put the responsibility for saving Paige Yardley's life onto Leah Gould, then resumed the pretence: Helen's innocence, his rightness. He lied at the trial, but told himself he was doing the opposite.

In his heart, he must have known the truth. If he hadn't once visited Helen in prison, as Laurie Nattrass claimed . . .

Deep down, the Snowman had to know how grievously wrong he'd been. Was he afraid of it happening again, in as serious a situation? Was that why he needed everyone to pretend his judgement was flawless?

Knowing all this – knowing the Snowman didn't know he knew – had shifted the balance of power between them in Simon's mind. He no longer felt sullied and threatened by the dinner invitation. Charlie was right: he could easily say he didn't want to have dinner with Proust. Or he could accept, turn up with a bottle of wine and tell Lizzie Proust the truth about the man she'd married.

He had the power now – ammunition. It didn't matter that he couldn't prove it; he knew he could destroy the Snowman any time he wanted to.

'You on your way back, then?' Sam asked, pulling Simon out of his victory trance.

'After I've grabbed a sarnie, yeah.'

'Gibbs spoke to Paul Yardley.'

'Poor sod.'

'Gibbs?'

'Yardley. First he loses three kids, then someone offs his wife, then Gibbs engages him in conversation.'

'He's now admitting he rang Laurie Nattrass before he rang an ambulance. Apparently Nattrass told him to say he rang the ambulance first.'

'Did he, now?' said Simon thoughtfully.

'Not ringing the ambulance straight away looks bad, he said. He told Yardley we'd do everything we could to pin Helen's murder on him. "The filth always frame the husband if they can, and in your case they'll be especially keen to." '

'For fuck's sake!'

'Gibbs thought Yardley was telling the truth,' said Sam. 'Nattrass isn't stupid – he must have known we'd do a telephony check on the Yardleys' line.'

'You think he told Paul Yardley to lie because he wanted us to suspect him? He says to Yardley, "Say this and they won't suspect you", while secretly thinking, "Say this and they *will* suspect you"?'

'I don't know.' Sam sounded worn out. 'What I *do* know is that in the course of their conversation, Yardley told Nattrass about the strange card he'd found on Helen's body, sticking out of her pocket. And wait till you hear this: Sellers spoke to Tamsin Waddington, Fliss Benson's friend, who told him Nattrass had been sent the sixteen numbers too – she saw the card on his desk on 2 September, a month before Helen Yardley was shot. He said he had no idea who'd sent it to him.'

'What?' Simon leaned forward in his car seat, sounding the horn by mistake. He mouthed, 'Sorry,' at two women who turned to glare at him. 'So when Paul Yardley rang Nattrass and told him about the card in his dead wife's pocket . . .?'

'Nattrass should have been straight on the phone to us, scared of being the killer's next victim, yes. Even if he wasn't afraid for himself, when he found out Fliss Benson had been sent a similar card, he should have . . .'

'I spoke to Benson about the card,' said Simon. 'She took it into Nattrass's office and showed it to him, asked him what he thought it meant. He can't have told her about the card Paul Yardley found on Helen's body – Benson didn't mention it to me, and I think she would have. Come to think of it, Nattrass can't have told her about the card *he'd* been sent – she'd have mentioned that too.'

'Would she?' said Sam dejectedly. 'Fliss Benson's agenda in all this is starting to worry me. We can't find her, we can't alibi her for Monday . . .'

'If Benson's a killer, I'm Barack Obama.'

'Sellers and I were in her office this morning. She'd left her email inbox up on the screen. While we were there, someone emailed her a photo of Helen Yardley's hand, holding a card like the others – same numbers, same layout – and a copy of *Nothing But Love*.'

'What?' First a card, then a photograph of a card . . .

'You said Benson was odd,' said Sam. 'Do you think there's a chance she could be sending these things to herself?'

Simon thought about it. 'No.'

'I've just got off the phone with Tamsin Waddington,' Sam told him. 'She's worried Benson's losing her grip on reality – that's how she put it. Benson rang her with a story about having locked Angus Hines in her flat, and could Tamsin go round with the spare key and let him out. When Tamsin got there half an hour later, the flat was empty – no Angus Hines in sight, no broken windows, everything the same as always. Hines couldn't have opened a window and climbed out – Tamsin found them all closed and locked, which could only be done from inside. Benson also apparently claimed she'd been to Rachel Hines' parents' house in Twickenham.'

'Did she lock them in too?'

'Rachel Hines' parents don't live in Twickenham, never have. I've just spoken to them. They live in Winchester.'

'So Laurie Nattrass and Fliss Benson join a police artist's drawing of a skinhead with bad teeth at the top of our "most wanted" list. Are we stepping up our efforts to track them down?'

'*I* am.'

'There's one more thing I need to do, then I'm straight back,' Simon told him.

'A sandwich, right?' Sam sounded suspicious. 'Please tell me you're talking about buying a sandwich.'

'Two more things,' said Simon, and pressed the 'end call' button.

Ten minutes later, he was sitting on a sofa made out of bean-bags at number 16 Bengeo Street, drinking bitty yellow lemonade and watching horse-racing with four-year-old Dillon White. So far his attempts at conversation had been unsuccessful; the boy hadn't uttered a word. It occurred to Simon that one thing he hadn't tried was talking about horses. 'You've seen this race before, then?' he asked. Dillon nodded. His mother had mentioned that it was a recording, Dillon's favourite of a large collection. 'Because his favourite horse always wins,' she'd added, laughing.

'I wonder who's going to win,' Simon said.

'Definite Article.'

'Do you think? He might not.'

'He always does in this one.'

'It might be different this time.'

The boy shook his head. He wasn't interested in Simon and his strange ideas, didn't take his eyes off the screen.

'What do you like about Definite Article, then?' What was it Proust had said? *Try, try and try again, Waterhouse*. 'Why's he your favourite?'

'He's a vegetarian.'

Simon didn't know what answer he'd been expecting, but it wasn't that. 'Are you a vegetarian?'

Dillon White shook his head, eyes still on the screen. 'I'm plain.'

Plain as in unattractive? No, he couldn't mean that. Wouldn't all racehorses have pretty much the same diet? Weren't they all herbivores?

Stella White appeared with a large cardboard box, which she placed at Simon's feet. 'Here's my box of fame,' she said. 'There's quite a bit about JIPAC and Helen in there – hope it helps. Sweet-pea, I've told you, you're not plain – that's the wrong word. You're white. Or pink, if you want to be pedantic about it.'

'He said Definite Article was a vegetarian,' Simon whispered to her over her son's head, feeling like a grass.

Stella rolled her eyes. She sank down to her knees so that she was the same height as Dillon. 'Sweet-pea? What does vegetarian mean? You know what it means, don't you?'

'Black skin.'

'No, it doesn't. Remember, Mummy told you? Vegetarian means you don't eat meat.'

'Ejike's a vegetarian and he's got black skin,' said Dillon tonelessly.

'He's got very dark brown skin, and yes, he's a vegetarian – he doesn't eat meat – but that doesn't mean all brown-skinned people don't eat meat.' Stella looked at Simon. 'If it's not about horses he doesn't listen,' she said, standing up. 'I'll leave you to it, if you don't mind. Give me a shout if you need an interpreter.'

Simon decided to give the boy a break, let him watch his racing in peace for a few minutes. He took a handful of newspaper cuttings from the box Stella had given him and started to look through them. It didn't take him long to piece together her story: she'd been diagnosed with terminal cancer at the age of twenty-eight. Instead of feeling sorry for herself and waiting to die, she'd immediately set about turning herself into a world-class athlete. She'd sought out marathons, treks, triathlons; set herself physical challenge after physical challenge; raised hundreds of thousands of pounds for charities, including JIPAC.

Halfway down the pile, Simon found an article about Stella's relationship with Helen Yardley: how they'd met, how much they relied on one another's friendship. There was a picture of the two of them together: Helen was sitting on the floor at Stella's feet and Stella was leaning in over her shoulder. The headline was 'Two extraordinary women'. Beneath the photograph, a quote from Helen had been isolated and put in a box, separate from the main text: 'Knowing Stella won't be here for ever makes me appreciate her more. I know she'll always be with me, even once she's gone.' There was also a quote from Stella in a box, further down the page: 'I've learned so much about love and courage from Helen. I feel as if my spirit will live on through hers.'

Except that Stella White wasn't the one who died. Helen Yardley was.

'So you like Definite Article because he's got black skin?' Simon asked Dillon.

'I like black skin. I wish I had black skin.'

'What about the man you saw outside Helen's house on Monday, when you were on your way to school? Do you remember?'

'The man with the magic umbrella?' Dillon asked, still watching the horses.

So now it was magic. 'What's an umbrella, Dillon?' If vegetarians were people with brown skin, and white people were plain . . .

'You hold it over your head to keep the rain off you.'

'Did the man with the magic umbrella have black skin?'

'No. Plain.'

'You saw him outside Helen Yardley's house on Monday morning?'

Dillon nodded. 'And beyond. In the lounge.'

Simon leaned forward. 'What does beyond mean?'

'Bigger than infinity,' said Dillon, without hesitation. 'One, two, three, four, five, six, seven, eight, nine, ten, eleven, twelve, thirteen, fourteen, fifteen, sixteen, seventeen, eighteen, nineteen, ninety-nine, a hundred, a thousand, infinity, beyond. To infinity and beyond!' The last part had to be a quote; Dillon sounded as if he was mimicking someone.

'What's infinity?' Simon asked.

'The biggest number in the world.'

'And beyond?'

'The even biggest number of days.'

Days.

'Definite Article's going to win.' Dillon's face lit up. 'Watch.'

Simon did as he was told. When the race was over, Dillon reached for the remote control. 'We can watch it again from the beginning,' he said.

'Dillon? When did Definite Article win the race we've just watched? Did he win it today?'

'No. Beyond.'

'You mean a long time ago?' said Simon. He was sorry Dillon was only four; he'd have liked to buy him a pint. Gently, he took the remote control from the boy's hand. For the first time since Simon had arrived, Dillon looked at him. 'The man you saw outside Helen Yardley's house on Monday morning – it wasn't the first time you'd seen him at Helen's house, was it? You saw him before, a long time ago. Beyond. The first time you saw him it was raining, wasn't it? That was when he had his magic umbrella. Not on Monday.'

Dillon jerked his head up and down: clear agreement.

'You saw him in the lounge. Was anyone else there, in the lounge?'

More affirmative head-jerking.

'Who?'

'Auntie Helen.'

'That's good, Dillon, that's really helpful. You're doing brilliantly. You're doing as well as Definite Article did when he won that race.'

The boy's face lit up, and he beamed. 'I love Definite Article. When I grow up, I'm going to live with him.'

'Was it just Auntie Helen and the man, in the lounge?'

'No.'

'Who else was there?'

'Uncle Paul. The other man. And a lady. And Mummy and me.'

'How many people altogether?'

'All of us.' Dillon nodded solemnly.

Simon looked around the room, hoping to see something that might help him. Then he had an idea. 'One: Auntie Helen,' he said. 'Two: the man with the umbrella . . .'

'Three: the other man,' Dillon took over, speaking quickly. 'He had an umbrella too, but it wasn't magic so he left it outside. Four: Uncle Paul, five: the lady, six: Mummy, seven: me.'

'The other man and the lady – can you tell me anything about them, what they looked like?'

'They were plain.'

'What was magic about the magic umbrella? In what way was it magic?'

'Because it came from outer space and if you opened it you could make a wish and that wish would definitely come true. And when the rain dripped off it onto the carpet, it turned it into a magic carpet and you could use it to fly to space whenever you want and come back whenever you want.'

'Is that what the man told you?'

Dillon nodded.

'This man, did he . . . did he have hair on his head?'

'Vegetarian.'

'Brown hair? Did he have funny teeth?'

Dillon started to nod, then stopped and shook his head.

'You can say no if no's the right answer,' Simon told him.

'I want to watch the race again.'

Simon gave him back the remote control, and went in search of Stella. He found her in a small utility room at the back of the house, ironing and singing under her breath. She looked thin, but not unwell – not like someone with terminal cancer. 'Do you remember taking Dillon round to the Yardleys' house a while back?' he asked her. 'Helen and Paul were there, you and Dillon, two other men and one other woman. It was raining. The two men both had umbrellas.'

'We went round there all the time.' Stella frowned. 'The place was always full of people. Everyone wanted to be around Helen. People flocked to her.'

'All the time?'

'At least twice a week, she'd have us round, usually with other people – her family, friends, other neighbours. Anyone, really. It was more or less open house.'

Simon tried not to look disappointed. He'd assumed that the occasion Dillon had described would stand out in Stella's memory; he should have realised not everyone was as unsociable as he was. Simon had never had seven people in his living room at the same time, not once. The most he'd had was three: him and his parents. The prospect of a neighbour crossing his threshold would unsettle him to the point of sleepless nights, he suspected. He had no problem with meeting people in the pub; that was different. 'Can you remember anyone you ever met at Helen's house telling Dillon his umbrella was magic?'

'No,' said Stella. 'I wouldn't put it past Dillon to have made that up. It sounds like the invention of a four-year-old to me – not something a grown man would say.'

'He didn't make it up,' said Simon impatiently. 'A man said it to him, the same man you saw outside Helen's house on Monday morning, the same man who killed Helen. I need you to put down that iron and start making a list of everyone you can remember meeting at the Yardleys' house – anyone at all, even if you only caught their first name, even the vaguest physical description.'

'In the last . . . how long?' Stella asked.

How many days ago was beyond?

'Ever,' Simon told her.

Charlie didn't know how long she'd been lying face down on Judith Duffy's kitchen floor. It could have been ten minutes, thirty, an hour. When she tried to speculate about time, it seemed to warp, loop back on itself. Duffy's murderer sat cross-legged beside her, holding the gun against her head. She was all right – she kept telling herself that – not injured, not dead. If he was going to shoot her he'd have done it by now. All she had to do was not look at him. That was the only thing he'd said to her: 'Don't look at me. Keep your head down if you want to stay alive.'

He hadn't told her she couldn't speak. Charlie wondered if she ought to risk it.

She heard a series of beeps. He was ringing somebody. She waited for him to start talking.

Nothing. Then the beeps again. 'Fucking answer,' he muttered. A smashing sound told Charlie he'd hurled his phone at the wall. She saw it in her peripheral vision: it had fallen and landed by the skirting board. She heard him start to cry, and the knot in her stomach tightened. If he lost control, that was bad news for her – he was more likely to kill her, deliberately or by accident.

'Stay calm,' she said, as gently as she could. She was on the point of losing control herself. How long would this go on for? How long had it gone on already?

'I shouldn't have done what I did,' he said. A Cockney accent. 'She didn't deserve it.'

'Judith Duffy didn't deserve to be shot?' He could have been talking about Helen Yardley. *Check*. Simon would say check.

'You get too far in and then you can't get out,' he said, sniffing. 'She did her best. So did you.'

Charlie's stomach turned over. When had she done her best? She didn't understand, and she needed to – understanding might save her life.

He murmured an apology. Charlie swallowed a mouthful of bile, thinking this was it, this was when he was going to shoot her.

He didn't. He stood up, walked away. Charlie raised her head and saw him sitting on the stairs next to Judith Duffy's body. Apart from his shaved head, he looked only a little like the police artist's sketch she'd seen in the paper – his face was a different shape. Charlie was sure it was him, though.

'Head down,' he said without feeling. His mind wasn't on Charlie. She had the sense that he didn't care any more what she did. Lowering her head only a fraction, she watched as he pulled a card out of his jeans pocket and placed it on Judith Duffy's face.

The numbers.

Seeing him coming towards her again, she twisted away from him, but all he wanted was his phone. Once he had it, he headed for the front door. Charlie pressed her eyes shut. Being so close to free and safe was hard to bear. If it went wrong now, if he came back . . .

The front door slammed. She looked up and he was gone.

Part III

15

Monday 12 October 2009

'If I'd known Marcella was going to die when she was eight weeks old, I'd never have left her, not for a second,' says Ray. 'I thought I'd have her for the rest of my life, years and years to spend together. Instead, I only had her for eight weeks. Fifty-six days – it sounds even shorter when you say it like that. For nine of those days I wasn't even there. I walked out on my own daughter when she was only two weeks old. For years that made me hate myself. Sorry, should I look at you or at the camera?'

'The camera,' I tell her.

She inspects her fingernails. 'You can always find a reason to hate yourself if you're that way inclined. I thought I was getting better at forgiving myself, but . . . I hated myself yesterday, when I found out what had happened to Judith. I'm not overly fond of myself today.' She tries to smile.

'Did you kill Judith Duffy?' I ask. 'Because if you didn't, then it's not your fault that she's dead.'

'Isn't it? People hated her because of me. Not only me, true, but . . . I contributed, didn't I?'

'No. Tell me about walking out on Marcella.' I sense she's trying to put it off; talking about Judith Duffy is easier.

She sighs. 'I'm scared you'll judge me. Isn't that ridiculous?

It didn't upset me at all when we first met and you told me you thought I'd probably killed my children.'

'Because you knew you hadn't, so my judgement didn't apply to you. But now you're going to tell me about something you did do.'

'I used to have a business: PhysioFit. It was extremely successful. Still is, even though I'm no longer part of it. As well as individual clients, we provided physiotherapy for businesses. Let's use your company as an example – Binary Star. Let's say your boss decides that you all spend too long sitting hunched over your computers. She can see your posture deteriorating, you're all complaining of back pain, the office is a breeding ground for vertebral occlusions. Boss decides to introduce routine physiotherapy provision for all Binary Star employees. First thing she does is invite several companies to tender for the contract.'

'Like PhysioFit?'

'Exactly. Assuming this is years ago, when I was still involved, what would happen is that my colleague Fiona and I would go to Binary Star's offices and give a presentation that would last two or three hours. Fiona would talk about the business side of things, contract terms – all the stuff that I'm not particularly interested in. Then when she'd done her bit, it would be my turn to talk about the physiotherapy itself: what it involves, what conditions it's particularly useful for, how it's not only a last resort for chronic pain but something that can be preventative as well. I'd talk about postural training and cranial osteopathy – that was my specialism – and about the foolishness of believing, as some people do, that a machine can provide physiotherapeutic services as efficiently as a human being. Of course it can't. When I put my hands on someone's neck, I can feel—'

She breaks off, giving me a sheepish smile. 'Sorry. I nearly forgot I wasn't actually tendering for your business.' She turns back to the camera. 'You get the idea, I'm sure.'

'You sound passionate about it,' I tell her. 'I'd employ you.'

'I loved my work. I didn't see why having children meant I had to give it up. When I found out I was pregnant with Marcella, the first thing I did was put her name down for a good local nursery. She was going to start when she was six . . . months. Sorry.'

'It's okay. Take your time.'

Ray makes a tunnel out of her hands, breathes through it. 'That seemed a good compromise to me: six months at home with my baby, then back to the clinic.' She turns to look at me again. 'Lots of women go back to work when their babies are six months old.'

I point to the camera.

'The day after I had Marcella, Fiona came to visit me in the hospital. She brought a box of duck-shaped biscuits with pink icing on them, and some good news from PhysioFit: we'd been asked to give a presentation to the bosses of a Swiss company with offices all over the world, several in the UK. It was a massive contract, one that would enable us to make the leap from national to international, and we really wanted it. We got it, too. They chose us over the competition. Sorry, I'm jumping ahead.'

'No problem. I'm going to edit all this, so don't worry about chronology.'

'I want to see the finished version before it's aired,' Ray says immediately.

'Of course.'

She seems to relax. 'The company's headquarters were in Geneva. That's where Fiona was going, to meet and impress the bosses. "It's such a shame you're on maternity leave," she said. "I've heard you do your spiel a thousand times, and I can recite it word-for-word, but it won't be the same as having you there." She was right. It wouldn't have been the same without me. Of the two of us, I was better with people, and this was such an important presentation for PhysioFit. I couldn't bear the thought of not being there. I couldn't convince myself that my presence might not make the difference between success and failure.'

I think I know what's coming. She went. Obviously she went. But why the lies? Why not tell the story she's telling me to Julian Lance? In court?

'I asked Fiona when the meeting was scheduled for. She told me the date. It was three weeks away. Marcella wouldn't even be a month old when Fiona set off for Switzerland. I . . . this is the part you might not understand. You'll think I should have been straightforward about what I wanted to do, said "Sorry, everyone, I know I've just had a baby, but I simply must jet off on a business trip – toodlepip, see you all soon."'

'Angus would have been unhappy about it?'

Would he have been as unhappy as I was when I worked out how he'd escaped from my flat? I got back to find a note from Tamsin stuck to my fridge: 'No Angus Hines anywhere on the premises, unless you've got a hidden room I don't know about. RING ME!'

I didn't. I couldn't bring myself to contact Angus, either, and ask him how he managed to escape without breaking glass or drilling through a wall. I got my answer this morning when I snuck back home for some things I needed, and bumped into Irina, my cleaner, who is also a PhD student at King's. 'How can you lock your friend in the flat?' she demanded. 'Not nice, Fleece. He was so embarrassed to ring me to say what had happened.'

I ran to the drawer where I keep business cards, spare lightbulbs, takeaway menus and tea towels (there's not much space in my flat, so things have to double up). Irina's card was there – 'The Done and Dusted Cleaning Company' – on top of a neat pile that hadn't been quite so neat last time I'd opened the drawer.

I rang Angus and left a message saying I needed to speak to him as soon as possible. When he called me back, I yelled at him for rummaging in my kitchen drawers and demanded to know why he'd lied to Irina. Why did he tell her I'd forgotten all about him and locked the door behind me by mistake? Why hadn't he smashed a window and climbed out, like anyone normal would have? He said he didn't want to embarrass me by giving my cleaner the impression that I was the sort of person who would lock a man in her flat. 'I don't know what you're so angry about,' he said. 'I was trying to be considerate. I assumed you'd rather not have a broken window.' I told him that wasn't the point, resenting his implication that Irina would have abandoned me in a flash if he hadn't gallantly concealed my true nature from her. The whole conversation made me feel twitchy and paranoid. I tried not to imagine him methodically going through my business cards, putting each one to the back of the pile until he found Irina's.

I haven't told Ray any of this. I don't think Angus has either.

'My plan, at first, was to be straightforward,' she says to the camera. 'It wasn't even a plan – it was simply the obvious thing to do. That night, Marcella and I left hospital and went home. I opened my mouth to tell Angus a dozen times, but the words wouldn't come out. He would have been horrified. Not that he wasn't supportive of my work – he was. He was all in favour of me going back when Marcella was six months old, but going to Switzerland when she was three *weeks* old was completely different. I knew exactly what he'd have said. "Ray, we've just had a child. I've taken a month's unpaid leave because I want to spend time with her. I thought you did too." Then there were all the things he *wouldn't* have said but that I'd have heard anyway: "What's wrong with you? What sort of heartless wife and mother are you that you'd sacrifice precious family time to go on a business trip? Don't you think you ought to get your priorities right?"'

Ray sighed. 'Over and over, I had the argument in my head: "But this is so important, Angus." "And my work, that I'm taking a month off from, that's not important, I suppose?" "No, but if we miss out on this contract, it'll be a disaster." "Let Fiona take care of it – she's perfectly capable of handling it on her own. And it wouldn't be a disaster. PhysioFit's thriving – there'll be other clients. Why does this one matter so much?" "Because it *does*, and I'm determined to go, even though I can't justify it." "And if another equally crucial business opportunity presents itself the week after, and the week after that? You'll be equally determined to go, won't you?"'

'Was he right?' I ask.

She nods. 'I was obsessed with PhysioFit. That's why it was so successful, because every detail mattered to me so much. My drive and passion were so relentless that the company had to do well – it had no other option. Angus doesn't understand what that feels like. He's never had his own business. Yes, he took a month off when Marcella was born, but so what? Were fewer people going to buy the newspaper because Angus's photographs weren't in it? Of course they weren't. I don't know, maybe they were,' she contradicts herself. 'The difference is that for Angus, work's something he does to earn money. He doesn't live and breathe his job the way I did. His passion in life was me. And Marcella and Nathaniel.' She falls silent.

'So you never told him about Switzerland? But you went, didn't you?'

'Yes. I rang Fiona the following day and told her I was going with her, but not to say a word to anyone. She laughed at me, called me a loony. Maybe she was right.'

I think about myself, hiding from the police in order to make sure I can do my work uninterrupted.

'It wasn't only Angus I was frightened of telling. There was also my mum and his mum, both of whom were being super-helpful devoted grannies. If I'd been honest about my plans, I'd have had to have the same argument with them, too. The thought of their concerned faces, the earfuls I'd have got about what I should and shouldn't do – it made me want to curl up under my duvet and never come out. I wanted to enjoy Marcella, not waste time being told how wrong and stupid I was, and having to defend myself. My mum and Angus's mum are both lovely, but they're also rather fond of knowing what's good for everybody they care about. When they join forces, it's a nightmare.'

I try not to notice how lonely this story is making me feel. My mum goes to great lengths to avoid commenting on anything I do, terrified she might offend me. I can ask her what she fancies watching on TV, and she'll jerk like a rabbit that's heard a gunshot and squeak, 'Whatever you want, you decide,' as if I'm a fascist dictator who might chop off her head if she says *Taggart* instead of *Come Dine with Me*.

'As the days went by, I realised I had to make a plan, quickly,' Ray tells the camera. 'Fiona had booked my plane tickets. I'd already lied to everyone about how painful I found breastfeeding. It was a doddle, for me and Marcella, but I pretended it was agony so that I could get her onto formula milk, knowing I was going away. I needed a story to get me out of the house for three days without any hassle. I racked my brains but could think of literally nothing, until one day I realised that was it: nothing was the answer.'

I wait. It's crazy, but I'm tempted to turn to the camera and ask its opinion. *How can nothing be the answer? Do you know what she's talking about?*

'Want to hear my brilliant plan?' says Ray. 'Step one: start acting vacant and dazed. Get everyone speculating about what might be wrong with you. Step two: pack a bag suddenly and, when asked where you're going, keep repeating, "I'm sorry, I have to go. I can't explain it – I just have to go." Step three: go. Go to a hotel near Fiona's flat, because Fiona's flat is obviously the first place Angus will look, so you can't stay there. Stay at the hotel for a few nights, phoning home regularly to reassure everyone you're okay. When they ask you where you are, refuse to tell them. Say you can't come back yet. Step . . . I can't remember what step I'm on.'

'Four.'

'Step four: go to Geneva. Do the presentation with Fiona. Get the contract. Step five: go back to London, this time to a different hotel. Ring home, say you're starting to feel better.

Instead of being monosyllabic, engage with your husband. Ask after Marcella. Say you're missing her, you can't wait to see her again. It's true; you can't. You'd rush back straight away if you could, but it has to be gradual. Everyone would be suspicious if you were suddenly normal again – well, as normal as you ever were, which, come to think of it . . .' She smiles sadly.

'Step six: after a night or two – a gradual recovery – go back home. Say you don't want to talk about why you left or where you've been. All you want is to be with your family and get on with your life. Step seven: when your mother-in-law harangues you mercilessly for what she calls "a proper explanation", climb out of your bedroom window and smoke a fag in mid-air, enjoying the knowledge that you're not scared of anything any more. You've proved to yourself that you're free, and from now on you'll do what you want.' Ray looks at me. 'Selfish, or what? But I *was* selfish when Marcella was born – I don't know if it was the hormones, but I was suddenly much more selfish and self-obsessed than I'd ever been before. It felt like . . . like an *emergency*, like I had to do what *I* wanted, look after me, or I'd be taken over, somehow.'

'If you really felt you needed to go to Switzerland, Angus should have let you go,' I say.

'Step eight: after a policeman's pulled you in through the open window, imagining he's saved your life, and once a shrink has told your mother and your mother-in-law to leave you alone for the sake of your mental health, here's your chance to improve by leaps and bounds. Another day or so and you're happy, full of energy. You got away with it. You've calmed down a bit, the post-natal panic has faded, and now all you want is to have a lovely time with your husband and your beautiful, sweet daughter. Your husband's thrilled – he was so worried about you; he thought he'd lost you. And now here you are: home again, his. Let the celebrations begin.' She looks anything but joyous.

'Wouldn't it have been easier to tell the truth and take the flak?'

Ray shakes her head. 'You'd think so, wouldn't you? But it wasn't. It was easier to do what I did, much easier. It must have been, because I was able to do it, having been *un*able to force myself to tell the truth.' She chews the inside of her lip. 'The way I did it, I avoided responsibility. A zombie who doesn't know what she's doing attracts pity, whereas a successful businesswoman who casts aside her newborn baby to empire-build attracts only condemnation. Angus understands. It's funny, he wouldn't have done then, but he does now.'

'He knows?'

Ray nods.

Interesting. He doesn't know she's staying at Marchington House and he still doesn't know about the pregnancy, but she's told him about her eight-step plan to drive him half-mad with worry. What kind of relationship is theirs, exactly?

'I miss Fiona,' Ray says quietly. 'She's still running PhysioFit. She's got another business partner now. Before my trial I wrote to her and begged her not to say anything about Switzerland to anyone, and she never did. She thought I'd done it, though – thought I was guilty like everyone else did.'

'When did you tell Angus about Switzerland?' I ask.

'Remember the hotel I told you about, where I stayed when I left prison?'

'The one with the urn pictures in every room?'

'When I couldn't stand it there any longer, I went to Angus, to our house in Notting Hill. That was when we sorted everything out. I'd . . . I'd like Angus to be here when I tell you about that,' she says. 'I'd like us to tell it together, because that's when everything came to a head and things finally started to get better between us.'

I try to look pleased for her.

'Don't be cross with him for giving you a hard time, Fliss. He's very protective of me, and he doesn't always treat people fairly.' Ray's tone suggests this is a legitimate lifestyle choice rather than a character defect. 'Neither do I, I suppose. We all do what we have to do, don't we? I lied to my lawyers, lied to Laurie Nattrass, lied in court – was that fair?'

'Why did you? Why did you tell two different lies about those nine days you were away? Why did you lie about how long it took you to let the health visitor in, and about who you phoned first, Angus or the ambulance?'

My phone buzzes. A message. I grab my bag, as sure as I can be that it won't be Laurie. Having ignored twenty calls from me in the past two days, he's unlikely to have decided twenty-one's my lucky number. *Please don't let it be him*.

'I lied in court because—' Ray begins.

'I have to go,' I tell her, staring at my mobile. There on the tiny screen is all the proof I need. I've no idea what to do with it. One press of a button would delete it, but only from my phone. Not from my mind.

'Someone important, by the look of it,' says Ray.

'Laurie Nattrass,' I say neutrally, in the way I might say any old name.

16

12/10/09

They had a profiler.

They also had seven detectives from London's Major Investigation Team 17, none of whom looked as if they'd appreciated being relocated to Spilling. Simon felt uneasy having them around; his only experience of detectives from the Met, last year, had been a wholly negative one.

The profiler – Tina Ramsden BSc MSc PhD and most of the rest of the alphabet after that – was petite, muscular and tanned, with shoulder-length blonde hair. Simon thought she looked like a professional tennis player. She seemed nervous, her smile veering towards the apologetic. Was she about to confess that she hadn't the foggiest? Simon had a few ideas if she didn't.

'I always introduce my profiles by saying there are no easy answers,' she began. 'In this case it needs saying all the more emphatically.' She turned to Proust, who was leaning against the closed door of the packed CID room looking as displaced as a disadvantaged character from the Goldilocks story: *Who's been standing in my spot?* 'I'll apologise in advance, because I'm not sure how much help I can be with the externals that might enable you track this person down. I wouldn't want to commit myself to age group, marital status, ethnicity, social and educational background, occupation . . .'

'Let me commit to some of them on your behalf,' said Proust. 'Baldy's been seen by two eye-witnesses: Sarah Jaggard and our very own Sergeant Zailer. We know he's between thirty and forty-five, white and shaven-headed. We know he has a Cockney accent. There's some disagreement over the shape of his face . . .'

'I discounted the two eye-witness statements,' Ramsden told him. 'A profile's useless if you create it around any givens. You look at the crimes – nothing else.'

'*Could* he be a thirty-nine-year-old white Cockney skinhead?' Proust asked her.

'On age, race, job, qualifications, whether he's single or in a long-term relationship – all the externals, as I said – I wouldn't want to commit,' said Ramsden. 'Character-wise, he could be a loner, or very sociable on the face of it.'

'It isn't particularly helpful to hear that he could be anyone, Dr Ramsden,' said the Snowman. 'We've had more than three hundred names suggested since Baldy's ugly mug desecrated the papers on Saturday, and another hundred or so wild theories about the sixteen numbers, each more preposterous than its predecessor.'

'You want to know what I'm able to tell you about this man? The most striking thing about him is the cards he sends and leaves at the scenes of his crimes. Sixteen numbers, the same ones in the same order in each instance, arranged in four rows of four.' Ramsden turned and pointed to the board behind her. 'If we look at the ones retrieved from the bodies of Helen Yardley and Judith Duffy, and the one Sarah Jaggard found in her pocket after she was attacked, we see that our man likes to be neat and consistent. Wherever the number four occurs, for example, it's written in exactly the same way.

Same with the number seven, same with all the numbers. The distances between the digits are also highly regular – they look as if they've been measured with a ruler to get them exactly the same. The rows-and-columns layout tells us that he values order and organisation. He hates the idea of doing anything in a haphazard way, and he's proud of the workmanship that goes into his cards – that's why the card he uses is thick, high-quality, expensive. Though, unfortunately for you, widely available.'

A few groans from the poor sods who'd spent days establishing precisely how wide that availability was.

'Obsessed with order could mean military,' Chris Gibbs suggested. 'Bearing in mind he's killing with a US army-issue gun.'

'It could mean military,' Ramsden agreed. 'It could also mean jail, boarding school, any institution. Or you could be looking for someone who grew up in a chaotic, unstable family and reacted against it by becoming highly controlled. That's not unusual – the child whose bedroom's unbelievably tidy, but outside his bedroom door, the place is a tip: crockery flying, parents screaming at each other . . . But, as I said, I don't want to talk about the externals because I'm not sure about them. The only thing I want to get specific about is the mindset, at this stage.'

'You say he's highly controlled,' Simon called out from the back of the room. 'Assuming he's got family and friends, won't they have noticed that about him? Sometimes mindset spills over into externals.'

'Aha! Thank you, Detective . . .?'

'Waterhouse.' Simon disliked many things, but high up on the list was having to say his name in front of large groups of people. His only consolation was that no one knew how hard he found it.

'I didn't say he was highly controlled,' said Ramsden, looking pleased with herself. 'I said he might have come from a family that was both practically and emotionally messy.'

'And he might have reacted against it by becoming highly controlled.' Simon knew what he'd heard.

'Yes,' she said, giving him what he took to be some kind of waiting signal with her hand. 'I'd say it's likely that *at some point*, this man was a control freak who ordered his life successfully. But his control's slipping. That's the most interesting thing about him. He's doing everything he can to stay on top of things, he's clinging to the illusion that he's in control, but he isn't. He's losing his grip on the real world, on his own position within it – possibly on his sanity. The same cards that reveal his meticulousness and love of order simultaneously reveal his irrationality and inconsistency. Think about it: he shoots Judith Duffy and Helen Yardley dead and leaves cards on their bodies. He attacks Sarah Jaggard with a knife, not a gun, in broad daylight on a busy street, not in her home, *doesn't* kill her, and places a card in her pocket. He also sends cards to two television producers, whom he neither attacks nor kills, and then, to one of the producers, he goes on to send a photograph of Helen Yardley's hand holding a card as well as a copy of her own book.'

Ramsden surveyed the room to check they were all taking her point. 'He thinks he's got a carefully thought-out plan, but *we* can see that he's all over the place, flailing around without a clue what he's doing, imagining everything's under control when in fact it's accelerating all the time in the direction of uncontrollability. His mental trajectory is like a shopping trolley sliding down a steep slope, picking up speed as it goes, the wheels twisting this way and that – you know what the wheels on shopping trolleys are like, how hard they are to steer.'

A few people laughed. Simon didn't. He wasn't about to take Tina Ramsden's conclusions on trust just because she could demonstrate that she'd been to the supermarket.

'He thinks he's clever coming up with this square of numbers that seems to defy interpretation,' she went on, 'but they could be entirely meaningless. He could be mad, or just plain stupid. Possibly he's got a nihilistic streak: he wants to waste police time by getting you all to chase a meaning he knows isn't there. Or – and I know this isn't very helpful, I know it sounds like I'm saying anything's possible – he might be highly intelligent, and the sequence of numbers could be meaningful, containing a clue either to his purpose or his identity.' Ramsden paused to take a breath. 'But even if that's the case, his choice of card recipients tends to suggest that the part of his brain that knows what it's about is in the process of being swamped by the trolley-rolling-downhill part.'

Simon opened his mouth, but she was in full flow. 'Sarah Jaggard and Helen Yardley – okay, a clear link. Both were tried for child murder. Judith Duffy? Not only does she have nothing in common with Jaggard and Yardley, she's their polar opposite: their opponent in an extremely high-profile controversy. Can't your man decide what side he's on? Laurie Nattrass and Felicity Benson – they're linked to all three women via their work, but otherwise there's no common ground. Nattrass and Benson aren't personally involved in any child death cases.'

'Let me stop you there,' said Proust. 'It transpires that Miss

Benson is personally involved. We found out this morning that her father lost his job over a Social Services cock-up that led to a child death. He committed suicide.'

'Oh.' Ramsden looked a little flustered. 'Well, all right, so Benson's linked to child deaths via her work *and* her personal life. In a way, that proves my point even more. Basically, there's no pattern. These people have nothing in common.'

'Are you serious?' said Simon. 'I can describe the pattern in a sentence: he's sending cards to people connected to the Binary Star documentary and the three cases featured in it: Yardley, Jaggard, Hines.'

'Well, yes, obviously in one sense you're right,' Ramsden conceded. 'Those cases loom large in his mind – I wouldn't deny that. In fact, I'd say he's likely to be someone who's suffered a severe emotional trauma in connection with this issue. He could have lost a child himself, or a sibling, or a grandchild, to crib death perhaps, which might have led to an obsession with people like Helen Yardley and Judith Duffy. But to kill both of them when, as I said, they're polar opposites in terms of what they stand for – there's no sense or rationale to it. And the most worrying thing about the trolley-rolling-downhill type of killer is that he tends to accelerate before he smashes himself to smithereens.'

'Sorry to interrupt, but . . .' Simon waited to see if the Snowman would silence him. He didn't. 'You're talking as if the killer's link to the Binary Star film might be purely thematic – he's a bereaved parent and that's why he's become obsessed with the three cases.'

'I only said he *might* . . .'

'The connection has to be stronger and closer than that,' said Simon. 'I don't know how thoroughly or how recently you were briefed, but Laurie Nattrass sent out an email on Tuesday to everyone connected to the documentary – doctors, nurses, lawyers, police, the women and their families, people at the BBC, JIPAC people. At 3 p.m. on Tuesday, nearly a hundred people got Nattrass's email saying Fliss Benson would be taking over as executive producer on the film. Until that moment, she had no connection whatsoever to these cases. One of the people who received the email must be the card-sender. He or she read Nattrass's message, immediately prepared a card for Benson and went out to post it to her at Binary Star, where she received it on Wednesday morning.'

'Dr Ramsden, all those on the receiving end of Nattrass's email have alibis for one or both of the murders,' said Proust. He might as well have waved his arms in the air and yelled, 'Listen to me, don't listen to him'. 'Without exception. And unless DC Waterhouse thinks Sarah Jaggard and Sergeant Zailer are conspiring to mislead us – which I won't be so naïve as to rule out, for he has a penchant for wrong-headed thinking – then we don't need to bother with "he or she". We know Baldy's a man.'

'Yes,' said Simon, 'and we know he killed Duffy and attacked Jaggard, but we don't know he's the card-sender, and we don't know he's our shooter for Yardley.'

'We're assuming he is, though, right?' said DS Klair Williamson.

'Yes,' said Proust firmly.

'I'm not,' Simon told her. 'Dillon White took one look at the police artist's image and said no, he wasn't the man with—'

'Warning: DC Waterhouse is about to refer to a magic umbrella,' the Snowman snapped.

'There are two people involved in these killings,' Simon presented his theory as if it were fact. He'd worry about maybe being wrong later. 'One's Baldy. The other could be a man or a woman, but let's say "he" to make it easier. That's who's in charge, that's the brain behind the operation: clever, controlling and *in* control. That's who sends the cards, knows what the sixteen numbers mean and is challenging us – letting us know we'll only catch him if we can prove we're as smart as he is.'

'So we've got Baldy and Brainy.' Colin Sellers laughed.

'The Brain could be paying Baldy to do his bidding,' said Simon. 'Or maybe Baldy's loyal to him for some reason, owes him favours. When Baldy said, "You get too far in and then you can't get out," he was talking about the hold the Brain has over him. The Brain, the card-writer and sender, is the person Baldy tried to phone from Judith Duffy's house, after he'd shot Duffy. He wanted instructions about what to do with Charlie, whether to kill her or not.'

'If you're right, then alibis or no alibis, anyone who received Laurie Nattrass's email on Tuesday could be the card-sender,' said Sam Kombothekra. 'Or anyone at Binary Star, anyone either Nattrass or Benson told about Benson taking over as executive producer.'

'I'd expect the Brain to have a firm alibi for Saturday, when Duffy was killed, but not for Monday,' said Simon. 'I think, after Baldy messed up with Sarah Jaggard and got interrupted by a passer-by, the Brain decided he'd take care of Helen Yardley himself. Then, with Duffy, he gave Baldy another chance. Maybe he'd given him a bit more training in the interim.'

'I apologise unreservedly for DC Waterhouse,' said Proust.

Tina Ramsden started to shake her head, and opened her mouth to speak, but the Snowman drowned her out as he warmed to his favourite theme: Simon's worthlessness. 'You have absolutely no reason for thinking two people are involved in these attacks. A four-year-old boy who talks nonsense and the fact that Baldy tried to ring somebody? He could have been phoning his girlfriend to tell her he wanted toad-in-the-hole for his supper. He could have been phoning anyone for any reason. Well, Dr Ramsden? Couldn't he?'

Ramsden nodded. 'When people find themselves in threatening situations, seeking reassurance is a common impulse.'

'What, so he's there in Judith Duffy's hall with a dead body in front of him, holding Charlie at gunpoint, and he suddenly takes a break to ring a mate because he wants the comfort of a familiar voice?' Simon laughed. 'Come on, you're not serious?'

'I'm not convinced there's any loss of control or irrationality involved,' said Chris Gibbs, standing up. 'Whether there's two of them or only one, how do you know everything that's happened so far isn't part of a plan? Just because Helen Yardley and Judith Duffy have both been killed . . .'

'Which strongly suggests the killer doesn't know which side he's on, or maybe he's reached the point where he can only remember names now, and not which side *they're* on,' said Tina Ramsden. Simon approved of her willingness to muck in. She gave as good as she got on the interruption front, and didn't seem to take offence if people disagreed with her.

'It doesn't necessarily suggest that,' Gibbs looked around for support. 'Let's say the killer's Paul Yardley . . .'

'Would that be the same Paul Yardley who has alibis for

Monday and Saturday, no Cockney accent and a full head of hair?' Proust asked. 'Talking of full heads of hair, Gibbs, you appear still to have one. Didn't I tell you to shave it off?'

Simon willed Gibbs to go on with his theory, and he did. 'Let's say Yardley's belief in Helen's innocence wasn't as rock solid as he made out it was – maybe he *did* have his doubts, even if he never expressed them. Most men in his position – let's face it, you wouldn't *know*, would you? Not for sure. All Yardley knows is that his life's been ruined – first he lost his two sons, then his wife was sent to prison, then he lost his daughter to Social Services. Getting out of bed in the morning must have been a struggle for him, but while Helen's still in prison, he's got a purpose, and that's to get her out. Once she's out, there's nothing more to aim for. She's busy with Laurie Nattrass and JIPAC. What's Yardley thinking about, day after day, while he fixes people's roofs?'

'Facias and sofits?' Sellers suggested with a chuckle.

'Make your point, Gibbs,' said the Snowman wearily.

'What if Yardley's the type for brooding? What if he starts thinking someone ought to pay for all the shi— all the suffering he's been through? Whose fault was it? Helen's, perhaps, if she killed his sons. Duffy's? Thanks to her, Yardley lost his wife for nine years.'

'What about Sarah Jaggard?' Simon asked.

'Sarah Jaggard wasn't killed,' said Gibbs. 'She wasn't even hurt. Maybe she was never supposed to be. Maybe she was supposed to mislead us, to broaden the focus out, from Helen Yardley's case to other similar cases.'

'Let me get this straight,' said Proust, smoothing down the lapels of his jacket. 'You're saying Paul Yardley killed his wife and Judith Duffy because he wanted to punish someone for wrecking his life and, of the two of them, he wasn't sure which was to blame?'

Gibbs nodded. 'Possibly, yeah. Or there's another way it could work: not as an either-or, but he blames them both equally: Helen for the loss of his two boys, and Duffy for the loss of Helen and his daughter.'

Simon thought both these possibilities stretched credulity somewhat, but he was pleased Gibbs had put them forward. At least one of his colleagues had an imagination.

Tina Ramsden was smiling. 'You seem to have a whole team full of psychological profilers,' she said to Proust. 'Are you sure you want me to stick around? I have to say, I can't agree about there being two people involved.' She looked at Simon and shrugged apologetically. 'And I'm as certain as I can be about the escalating irrationality. The card-sender as the rational, controlled one doesn't work because the way he distributes the cards isn't regular – sometimes he posts them, with no violence, or emails them in photographic form; other times he leaves them in the pockets of murder victims.'

'The numbers, if we knew what they meant, would lead to us identifying him,' said Simon. 'It's a challenge. He's sending cards to people he sees as his intellectual equals, people he thinks ought to be clever enough to crack his code.' Seeing Sellers open his mouth, Simon raised a hand to stop him. 'Were you about to say that Helen Yardley was a childminder, and Sarah Jaggard's a hairdresser – not great intellects, as the Brain would see it, and yet they got a card each?'

Sellers nodded.

'No. They didn't. Helen Yardley and Sarah Jaggard *did not* get a card each. Judith Duffy *did not* get a card.' Simon listened as the sound of confusion filled the room. 'Yardley,

Jaggard and Duffy weren't the intended recipients of those three cards. Anyway, Duffy was dead by the time she got hers. Those three cards were for us: the police. Our job is to work out what's going on, right? Laurie Nattrass and Fliss Benson's work consists of trying to unearth the truth that lies behind three miscarriages of justice.'

He had everyone's full attention. 'We need to start looking at the two things separately, the violence and the cards. In the first category, two women were murdered and one threatened at knifepoint, all three connected with crib death murder cases. In the other category, five cards were sent, three to the police, however indirectly, and two to documentary-makers – all five to people the Brain thinks might be intelligent enough to make sense of his code. There's nothing irrational about any of it,' Simon addressed Tina Ramsden. 'It makes perfect sense, and it means that Fliss Benson and Laurie Nattrass aren't at risk of attack, any more than we all are.

'The choice of victims for the violent behaviour also makes sense: Helen Yardley and Sarah Jaggard were picked for a reason, though not the most obvious one. The Brain wanted to show us that we'd underestimated him. That's why Judith Duffy was the next victim, not Ray Hines.' Simon was sure he was right about this. 'We forced his hand. On Saturday, Sam here was quoted in every national newspaper as saying that our working assumption was that the killer was a self-appointed punisher, attacking guilty women he thinks have got away with their crimes. But that's *not* his motivation, and later that same day he proved it to us by killing Judith Duffy – I'm using "he" as shorthand for "he or she", remember.'

'Sexist,' a female voice mumbled.

'He may have had no reason to kill Duffy whatsoever,

other than to demonstrate to us that we were wrong about his motivation,' said Simon. 'Just as he's meticulous – writing his number fours and number sevens the same every time – he's also objective, or so he thinks: fair and clear-thinking. He wants us to notice that about him. He's probably someone who associates vigilantism with extreme stupidity – unwashed, tabloid-reading hang-em-and-flog-em proles. He wouldn't like the symbolism of that, because he's clever, and if I had to guess, I'd say he's middle-class. He wants us to realise that any justice doled out by him, or by Baldy on his orders, is exactly that: noble justice, not grubby revenge. By murdering the leaders of the two warring armies – Helen Yardley and Judith Duffy – he's showing us he's fair and impartial.'

Everyone stared. No one wanted to be the first to react. Proust stood with his arms folded, staring up at the ceiling, his neck almost at a ninety-degree angle. Was he meditating?

'Well, if no one else wants to jump in, I will,' said Tina Ramsden, after nearly ten seconds of silence. She held up her notes so that everyone could see them, and tore them in half, then in half again. 'You have no idea how annoying it is to have to do this, after I sat up most of last night cobbling all this together, but I'm no use to you if I'm not honest,' she said. 'I defer to DC Waterhouse's superior analysis.'

'His what?' Proust turned on her.

Ramsden looked at Simon. 'I prefer your profile to mine,' she said.

'So you think his plan was to sweep you up in his arms and give you a good rogering?' said Olivia Zailer enthusiastically. She'd dropped everything and come to Spilling to take care of her sister after her ordeal, having first checked Charlie had no injuries that would necessitate any heavy lifting or staunching of bodily fluids.

'No idea,' said Charlie. 'All I know is, he sent me a love letter – well, a love scrap of paper – and told me to get back as early as I could on Saturday.'

'But then, when he next saw you, he didn't make a move.' Olivia wrinkled her nose in disappointment.

'The next time he saw me was just after I'd had a gun held to my head by Judith Duffy's killer. I was too shaken up even to remember that sex might have been on the cards, and Simon was more interested in interrogating me about the man they're calling Baldy.'

Liv snorted. 'His work-life balance is like a seesaw with a concrete rhinoceros strapped to one end. Still, at least he sent you a sweet letter – that's a big step forward, isn't it?'

Charlie nodded. She and Olivia were sitting at her kitchen table, drinking tea, though Liv had brought a bottle of pink champagne. 'To celebrate you not getting shot,' she'd explained.

The sun was shining as if it couldn't tell the difference between summer and winter; Charlie had had to lower her kitchen blind. Since Simon had sent her those eleven words, the sun had shone almost constantly, even though whenever she caught the local news there were big grey clouds covering the Culver Valley. Charlie trusted her own senses; the TV people had got it wrong.

'I nearly didn't tell you about the love letter,' she said.

'*What?*' Nothing horrified Olivia Zailer more than the thought of not being told something.

'I thought you'd think it was pathetic – not even a proper sheet of paper, the word "love" missing . . .'

'Please! How hard-hearted do you think I am?'

'We're having a bit of a feud over the honeymoon,' Charlie told her. Was she so used to scrapping with Olivia that she had to find something for her sister to attack, so that she could assume her customary defensive position? 'Simon's parents are scared of flying, so he started off saying we had to go somewhere in the UK.'

'Please tell me Simon's parents aren't going with you on your honeymoon.'

'Joking, aren't you? They get palpitations if they go as far as the bottom of the garden. No, they're scared of *Simon* flying. His mum told him she wouldn't sleep or eat for a fortnight if she knew he was going to be "going on those aeroplanes", as she calls it.'

'Stupid mad bint,' said Olivia crossly.

'Trouble is, she means it. Simon knows she *wouldn't* eat or sleep until he was safely back, and knowing he'd return to find a withered death's head where his mother used to be would spoil his fun. Though the difference, it has to be said, would be marginal.' Charlie stopped to check her guilt level: zero. 'I didn't want to spend my honeymoon in the Rawndesley Premier Inn, which is a suggestion my future father-in-law made in all seriousness . . .'

'Unbelievable!'

'. . . so we compromised. Simon agreed to go anywhere that's less than three hours' flight time, and I agreed to lie to his parents and pretend we're going to Torquay – close enough to sound safe, but far enough away that Simon can legitimately tell his mum he can't pop back for Sunday lunch.'

'I assume Kathleen and Michael know cars sometimes crash,' said Liv.

'Ah, but we're going to Torquay by train.' Charlie couldn't help laughing. 'Because people die on motorways. It's so ridiculous – Simon's in his car every day, but because this time he'd be venturing out of his mum's comfort zone . . .'

'People die in train crashes,' Olivia pointed out.

'Please don't tell Kathleen that, or we'll be forced to spend our honeymoon fortnight in her front room.'

'So where are you going?'

'Marbella – flight time just under three hours. Two hours and fifty-five minutes.'

'But . . .' Olivia's eyes narrowed. 'If you're lying to Kathleen and Michael, you could go anywhere: Mauritius, St Lucia . . .'

'I said all that to Simon, and do you know what he said? Go on, have a guess.'

Liv closed her eyes and bunched her hands into fists, muttering, 'Hang on, don't tell me, don't tell me . . .' She looked about six years old. Charlie envied her sister's uncomplicated enjoyment of all life had to offer. 'He'd be too far away if his mum got ill and he suddenly had to fly back? I wouldn't put that sort of ruse past her, you know.'

'Good guess, but the truth is even madder: the less time Simon spends in the air, the less chance there is of him dying in a plane crash and being caught out in a lie by his parents.'

'Which would obviously be the worst thing about dying in a plane crash.' Liv giggled.

'Obviously. Without having referred to any statistics, and completely ignoring the fact that most plane crashes happen on take-off or landing, Simon's decided short-haul flights are less lethal than long-haul.'

'Can't you try to persuade him? I mean, *Marbella*?'

'I've found this amazing villa on the internet. It's—'

'But you'll have to fly to Malaga. The plane'll be full of people with "love" and "hate" tattooed on their knuckles, singing "Oggie, oggie, oggie".' Liv shuddered. 'If it has to be less than three hours, what about the Italian lakes? You'd fly to Milan . . .'

'Is that better?'

'God, yes,' said Liv. 'No tattoos, lots of linen.'

Charlie had forgotten to factor in her sister's colossal snobbishness. 'I thought you'd disapprove of the lying, not the destination,' she said. 'Part of me's tempted to sack it and make the lie true. I do love Torquay, and I don't want there to be anything negative or complicated connected with our honeymoon. In an ideal world, I'd like to be able to tell the truth about it.'

'You can, to everyone but Kathleen and Michael. It's not as if they ever meet or speak to anyone.' Olivia unzipped her bag and pulled out four books with creased spines. 'I brought you these. I hope you're grateful, because they've bent my new Orla Kiely handbag out of shape.' She poked the bag's side with her index finger. 'I wasn't sure how long you'd be off work, but I brought enough . . .'

'I'm going back tomorrow.' Seeing her sister's crestfallen expression, Charlie said quickly, 'I'll have them anyway, though. Thanks. I'll read them in Marbella.'

Olivia adopted her strict schoolmistress expression. 'You're not planning to read a novel until next July?'

'Are they good? Are they ones you've reviewed?' Charlie asked. She picked one up. The cover picture was of a frightened-looking woman running away from a dark unidentifiable blur behind her. Liv tended to bring her novels about women who ended up leaving the useless and frequently psychotic men they'd been wasting their lives on, and going off into the sunset with better men.

'I've got a book I want you to read,' said Charlie. She nodded at the copy of *Nothing But Love* on the table.

'A misery memoir?' Olivia slid it towards her, then made a show of wiping her fingers on her trousers. 'Did you buy it shortly after booking your flight to Malaga?'

'You can't say no,' Charlie told her. 'I've just been nearly killed – you have to be nice to me. I'd be interested to know how you think Helen Yardley comes across – as a genuine miscarriage-of-justice victim or as someone playing a part.'

'Why, do you think she might have killed her kids after all? I thought it turned out that she hadn't.'

Turned out. Liv had trouble distinguishing between real life and fiction. She opened the book at a random point in the middle and held it up close to her face. The optical effect was surreal, as if she was wearing the back cover of *Nothing But Love* as a mask. *Hello, my name's Olivia, and I've come to this party dressed as a misery memoir*.

'There are exclamation marks in it – not inside quotation marks, in the narrative,' she said, horrified. She turned another page. 'Do I really have to—'

Charlie grabbed the book. Her hands trembled, then the shakes spread to the rest of her body. 'Oh, my God. I don't believe this.' She flicked through the pages as quickly as she could. 'Come on, come on,' she muttered under her breath.

'I was reading that,' Liv protested.

The adrenaline pumping through Charlie's body made her fingers too stiff and too wobbly at the same time. She couldn't get them to work properly, and ended up turning too many pages. She flicked back and finally found the page she was looking for. This was it. It had to be.

She stood up, knocking her chair over. Yelling, 'Sorry,' over her shoulder, she grabbed her car keys and ran out of the house. As she slammed the door behind her, it occurred to her that she must look like the frightened running woman on the cover of the novel Liv had brought her, the one whose title she had already forgotten. Her brain only had room for one book's name at the moment.

Nothing But Love. Nothing But Love. Nothing But Love.

17

Monday 12 October 2009

An hour and a half after leaving Marchington House, I'm standing outside the Planetarium, as instructed. I'm not sure if Laurie's late or if he's thought better of meeting me and not bothered to inform me of his change of mind; all I know is he isn't here. After twenty minutes, I start to wonder if he might have intended for us to meet inside. I check the text he sent me, which is full of his usual warmth and intimacy: 'Planetarium 2 p.m. LN.'

I'm about to go and look for him inside when I spot him walking towards me, head down, hands in his pockets. He doesn't look up until he has to. 'Sorry,' he mumbles.

'For being late, or for ignoring my calls?'

'Both.'

He's wearing a pink shirt that looks new. As far as I know, Laurie has never worn pink before. I want to bury my face in his neck and smell his skin, but that's not what I'm here for. 'Where have you been?' I ask him.

'Around and about. Let's walk.' He nods at the road ahead, then sets off.

I follow him. 'Around and about isn't an answer.' I harden my heart, and my voice. 'I rang the JIPAC office this morning – no one there's heard from you for days. I've been to your house more than five times – you're never there. Where are you staying?'

'Where are *you* staying?' he fires back. 'Not at home.'

'You've been to my flat?' *Don't dare to cave in, Felicity. This has to be done*. 'I'm staying with Ray Hines in Twickenham, at her parents' place.'

Laurie snorts dismissively. 'Is that what she told you? Ray's parents live in Winchester.'

I think back over our conversations. I assumed Marchington House belonged to her parents because of the photo in the kitchen, of her two brothers punting down a river. Maybe the house belongs to one of the brothers.

'I'm camped out at Maya's place,' says Laurie.

'Maya?' I'm not the only one lying to the police, then. She neglected to mention that Laurie had moved in with her, when they asked her if she knew where he was.

Maya's keen on pink.

'Is something going on between you?' I ask before I can stop myself.

'Is this what was so urgent that you had to talk to me immediately?' Laurie stops walking and turns on me. 'Look, I don't owe you anything, Fliss. I gave you an opportunity at work because I thought you deserved it. End of story. We had a fuck the other day, but do we have to make a meal of it?'

'Of the sex? No, we don't. There are a couple of things we do have to make a meal of, though. Three things, to be precise – three meals. Think of them as breakfast, lunch and dinner.'

'What things?'

'Let's walk,' I say, setting off in the direction of Regent's Park. I know what this means: I'll never be able to go there again after today. 'Have you been reading the papers?' I ask Laurie. 'Turns out that card someone sent me – remember the one I showed you, with the numbers on it? Whoever killed

Helen Yardley and Judith Duffy put cards exactly like it on their bodies. I've spoken to Tamsin. I know you got one of those cards too. She saw it on your desk long before Helen Yardley was killed.'

'So?'

'Why didn't you mention that, when I showed you the card I'd been sent and asked you what it could mean? Why didn't you say "Someone sent me one of those too"?'

'I don't know,' Laurie says impatiently.

'I do. You knew about the card found on Helen's body, didn't you? You must have done – it's the only thing that makes sense. I don't know how you knew, but you did. My guess is that Paul Yardley told you, and you were scared. You worked out that whoever was sending the cards had moved on to killing. If they'd killed Helen, maybe you'd be next. You and Helen and JIPAC have your loyal supporters, but you've also got enemies. I found several anti-JIPAC websites yesterday, all of which claim you've created a climate of fear for doctors and paediatricians. Most of them are terrified to testify in suspected abuse cases, in case you set out to destroy them the way you did Judith Duffy.'

Laurie says nothing, just walks alongside me, head down. I'm glad I can't see his face.

'You panicked. There was no way you were going to continue with your quest for justice if it meant there might be some actual consequences for you personally, like someone trying to kill you. All that matters to you is you, right? You needed to distance yourself from the crib death murders controversy quickly, so you announced that you were leaving Binary Star, going to Hammerhead. Incidentally, I've been chatting to people at Hammerhead about you. I know when they first made you that offer you couldn't refuse: more than a year ago. Funny how you suddenly decided to accept, the day after Helen Yardley was murdered.'

I stop, so that he can confirm or deny it. He says nothing.

'You emailed everyone telling them I was taking over the film. You chose me because, if you're right and whoever ends up making that film *is* going to be a killer's next target, better that it should be someone disposable like me, someone who's never going to amount to anything anyway.'

I pick up my pace, full of furious energy. Who'd have thought anger would have aerobic benefits?

'Course, you could have gone to the police, couldn't you? Told them about the card you'd been sent, how it was the same as the one found on Helen's body. And when I showed you my card, you could have alerted me to the danger I was in. It's pretty obvious why you did neither. You couldn't risk anyone putting two and two together: your being on a killer's mailing list, and your suddenly dropping the crib death film like a hot brick. People might have concluded you were scared. The great Laurie Nattrass – scared! Imagine if that had leaked out to the press. That was why Tamsin had to go. She was the only person who knew you'd been sent those numbers; she'd seen the card on your desk.'

'Tamsin's redundancy wasn't down to me,' Laurie snaps, making me wonder if this is the first thing he's heard that he disagrees with. 'Raffi said we were overstretched, we had to make some savings . . .'

'And you suggested Tamsin as the sacrifice,' I finish the sentence for him. 'My best friend.'

We're in Regent's Park. I'd probably think it was beautiful

if Laurie and I weren't having the most wretched conversation in the world.

'I had a best friend,' he says tonelessly. 'Her name was Helen Yardley. And I didn't choose you to take over the film because I thought you were disposable and wouldn't amount to anything – that's your paranoia.'

I chose you because I love you. I chose you because the film is important to me, and so are you.

'I thought you'd be easy to control. The film mattered to me, and I thought I could get you to make it the way I wanted it made.'

Oh. Right.

'You've got an inferiority complex.' He makes it sound like a disgusting medical condition, something I should be ashamed of. Surely it's a good thing that some of us are riddled with self-doubt. Don't the people like me balance out the people like Laurie?

'How could you not tell me?' I say. 'When I showed you that card, how could you not say . . .'

'I didn't want to worry you.'

'*You* were worried, enough to—'

'Do we have to analyse everything to death?' he cuts me off. 'You've done what you came to do, staked out the moral high ground.'

I reach into my bag and pull out the second draft of his *British Journalism Review* article. 'I've read this.' I thrust it at him. He doesn't take it. The pages fall to the ground. Neither of us bends to pick them up. 'I thought it was better than the first version. Scrapping those names from the list was a good move.'

Laurie frowns. 'What list?'

'The one that goes on and on.'

'Fuck are you talking about?'

'"Dr Duffy was responsible for ruining the lives of dozens of innocent women whose only crime was to be in the wrong place at the wrong time when a child or children died: Helen Yardley, Lorna Keast, Joanne Bew, Sarah Jaggard, Dorne Llewellyn . . . the list goes on and on." Ring any bells?'

Laurie turns away.

'One problem. In this latest draft' – I bend to retrieve the pages – 'the list doesn't go on and on. In this draft, the list is only three names long: Helen Yardley, Sarah Jaggard, Dorne Llewellyn. I'm no editor, but I think the original version's better. If you want to invoke the dozens of innocent women whose lives were ruined by Duffy, five names works better than three. So what happened? Was it a word-limit thing?'

Laurie is walking away, heading towards the boating lake. 'Why ask if you already know?' The wind brings his words back to me.

I run to catch him up. 'You deleted Lorna Keast and Joanne Bew. Keast was a single mother from Carlisle with a borderline personality. She smothered her son Thomas in 1997, and her son George in 1999. Judith Duffy testified against her, and she was found guilty in 2001. By the time Helen Yardley's convictions were quashed, you'd managed to kick up such a stink about Duffy that the CCRC was forced to act: it started to re-examine similar cases. In March this year – I'm guessing just after you wrote the first draft of your 'Doctor Who Lied' article – Lorna Keast was granted leave to appeal, which had previously been denied. Obviously the honest side of her personality was to the fore that day – she was devastated when her lawyers told her she might be in with a chance of getting out. She'd always protested her innocence up until that point, but when she heard she might soon be freed, she confessed to having smothered both her sons. She said she wanted to stay in prison, wanted to be punished for what she'd done. She wouldn't hear of having the charge changed to infanticide, which was a possibility once she'd confessed, and would have carried a lighter sentence – she wanted to be punished as a murderer.'

'What your Google searches won't have told you is that, as well as being barking mad, Lorna Keast is one of the thickest women ever to drag her knuckles along the surface of this planet,' says Laurie. 'Even if she was innocent, being found guilty and sent to prison might have been enough to convince her she was a murderer and deserved to be behind bars.' He flashes a contemptuous look in my direction. 'Or maybe she preferred the safety of prison life to having to fend for her brainless self on the out.'

'Or maybe she was guilty,' I say.

'So what if she was? Does that make Judith Duffy any less dangerous? Of course I knocked Keast's name off the list – I don't want people reading the article and thinking that if Duffy was right about her then she might have been right about all the others. She *wasn't* right about Helen, Sarah Jaggard, Ray Hines, Dorne Llewellyn . . .' Laurie grabs my arm and swings me round to face him. 'Someone had to stop her, Fliss.'

I shake off his hand. 'What about Joanne Bew?'

'Bew was granted leave to appeal.'

'Whoa, let's rewind a bit. What was she in prison for?'

Laurie's mouth flattens into a thin line.

'Why don't I tell us the story? Joanne Bew murdered her son Brandon . . .'

'Let's fast-forward a bit,' Laurie parodies me. 'There was a retrial and she was acquitted.'

'Then why delete her name from the article? Surely she's your best illustration of the harm irresponsible experts can do: first she's convicted, all because of a doctor's flawed testimony against her, then she's retried and acquitted once that same doctor's been exposed by the wonderful Laurie Nattrass. Come on, she's JIPAC's perfect poster girl, isn't she? No? Why not, Laurie?'

He's staring at the boating lake as if it's the most fascinating expanse of water in the world.

'Joanne Bew, former landlady of what's now the Retreat pub in Bethnal Green, murdered her son Brandon in January 2000,' I say. 'She was blind drunk and at a party when she did it. There was a witness: Carl Chappell, also very drunk. Chappell was on his way to the loo, and he passed the door of the bedroom where Joanne had put six-week-old Brandon down to sleep. He happened to look into the room, and he saw Joanne kneeling on the bed with a cigarette in one hand and her other hand pressed over Brandon's nose and mouth. He saw her hold her hand there for a good five minutes. He saw her press down.'

'As you say, he was smashed. Had form too: GBH, ABH . . .'

'At Joanne's first trial in April 2001, Judith Duffy gave evidence for the prosecution. She said there were clear signs of smothering.'

'Which is the only reason the jury believed Chappell,' says Laurie. 'His eye-witness account tallied with a respected doctor's expert opinion.'

'Lots of other people also testified against Joanne. Friends and acquaintances said she never referred to Brandon by his name – she called him 'The Mistake'. Warren Gruff, Joanne's boyfriend and Brandon's father, said she mistreated the baby from day one – sometimes when he was screaming with hunger, she'd refuse to give him milk and try to feed him chips or chicken nuggets instead.'

'She was a bad mother.' Laurie shrugs and starts to walk. 'Doesn't make her a murderer.'

'True.' I catch him up, keep pace with him. I imagine myself linking my arm through his and nearly laugh. He'd regard that as such an affront; I'd love to see his reaction. I'm tempted to do it, just to prove to myself I have the nerve. 'Bew was already a convicted killer, though, wasn't she?' I say instead. There's no surprise on Laurie's face. He knew I knew, and he thinks that's it, that's my trump card. That's why he's not worried. 'She and Warren Gruff had both served time for the manslaughter of Bew's sister, Zena. They punched and kicked her to death in the kitchen of Gruff's flat after a family row, and each blamed the other. At Bew's first trial in 2001, Zena's death wasn't mentioned – someone must have thought it might prejudice the jury. I can't think why, can you? I mean, just because a woman punches and kicks her sister to death, and is a bad mother – as you say, it doesn't mean she must have murdered her baby. Though, as it happened, and even without the inconvenient Zena anecdote, all twelve jurors *did* believe Joanne Bew was a murderer.'

'You ever watched a criminal trial?' says Laurie scornfully.

'You know I haven't.'

'You should try it some time. Watch the jurors being sworn in. Most of them can't read the oath without stumbling over the words. Some can't read it at all.'

'What about the jury that acquitted Joanne Bew second

time round, in May 2006? How stupid were they? They *were* told that Bew had served time for the manslaughter of her sister. What they didn't know was that she'd previously been convicted of murdering Brandon. They didn't know it was a retrial.'

'That's—'

'Standard. I know.' I walk as close to Laurie's side as I can without touching him. He moves away, widening the gap between us. 'Judith Duffy didn't testify against Bew the second time,' I continue with my story. 'By May 2006, you'd made sure no prosecutor in need of an expert would touch her with a bargepole. I wonder if the jury would have believed Carl Chappell, though, if he'd testified again that he watched Bew smother Brandon?'

'They didn't get a chance to believe or disbelieve him,' says Laurie. 'Chappell updated his statement to the effect that he was so drunk that night, he wouldn't have known his own name, let alone what he did or didn't see.'

'You can tell he's a drinker, can't you?' I'm nearly there, nearly at the end of this protracted worst moment of my life. 'The bulbous nose and the broken veins. He's a prime candidate for one of those makeover shows, don't you think? *10 Years Younger*.'

Laurie stops walking.

I carry on, talking to myself. I don't care if he can hear me or not. 'I can't watch that programme now Nicky Hambleton-Jones doesn't present it any more, can you? It's not the same without her.'

'You've met Chappell?' Laurie's by my side again. 'When?'

'Yesterday. I'd found an article on the internet that suggested he used to be a regular at the Retreat, or the Dog and Partridge as was, so I paid a visit there and asked if anyone knew him. Quite a few people did, and one told me which betting shop he'd be in first thing this morning. That was where I found him. Is that how you found him too, when you needed to track him down and offer him two thousand pounds in exchange for a revised statement, a statement full of lies that would secure a not-guilty verdict for Joanne Bew and another point to you in the battle against Judith Duffy?'

'Look, whatever—'

'Chappell wasn't there when you popped in, so you left a note for him with someone who said they'd pass it on. And they did.'

'You can't prove any of this,' Laurie says. 'You think Carl Chappell keeps notes from years back, just in case the British Library wants to acquire his archive one day?' He laughs, pleased with his own joke. I remember Tamsin telling me a few months ago that the British Library had paid some obscene amount of money for Laurie's papers. I wonder how much they'd pay for a long letter to him from me, detailing exactly what I think of him. Maybe I should get in touch with them and ask.

'Chappell didn't keep the note,' I say, 'but he remembers what happened, and he remembers where you told him to meet you. If only you'd picked Madame Tussauds, or the National Portrait Gallery, or here in Regent's Park, by the boating lake.'

Laurie must think I'm enjoying this. I'm hating every second of it.

'What message did you leave for him, exactly? Was it a bit like the one you sent me?' I pull my phone out of my bag and hold it up in front of his face. 'Was it "Planetarium 2 p.m.,

LN."? "Dear Mr Chappell, Meet me outside the Planetarium – there's two thousand quid in it for you"?'

'You think I gave him the two grand to *lie*? You really think I'd do that – pay a man to pretend he didn't witness a murder when he did?'

'I really think you'd do that,' I tell him. 'I think you did what you had to, to make it look as if Joanne Bew was yet another innocent woman in prison thanks to Judith Duffy.'

'Cheers for the vote of confidence,' says Laurie. 'The truth, if you're interested, is that Carl Chappell witnessed nothing whatsoever the night Brandon died. He was a mate of Warren Gruff's, Brandon's dad. Gruff put him up to lying at Joanne Bew's first trial. He'd made it clear he expected Chappell to lie again at the retrial, which was what Chappell, who can't think for himself, was planning to do. I paid him to tell the truth.'

I try to remember what exactly Carl Chappell told me. *He gave me two big ones to say I hadn't seen nothing*. Have I misjudged Laurie? Have I just done to him what I'm accusing him of doing to Judith Duffy: invented whatever story I needed to in order to condemn him?

'The two grand took care of Chappell's gambling needs, but it did nothing to alleviate his fear of Gruff, who's a thug,' says Laurie. 'You ought to track him down, ask him how much I paid him, out of my own pocket, for a promise not to beat Chappell to death if he gave a new statement.'

'How much?' I ask.

Laurie beckons me to come closer. I take a step towards him. He reaches for my hand, closes his fingers around my phone. I try to hang on to it. I fail.

'What good's that going to do you?' I ask. He can delete

the text he sent me, but not my memory of it. I can tell anyone I want to that Laurie told me to meet him at the Planetarium, just as he told Carl Chappell, and probably Warren Gruff too.

'No good,' he says. 'No good at all.' Running towards the lake like a fast-bowler, he bowls my phone into the water.

18

12/10/09

'Olivia was holding the book up, spread open.' Charlie demonstrated for Proust's benefit. Simon and Sam watched too, though they'd already heard the quicker version of the story. 'I was sitting across the table from her – my eyes must have been on the back cover. I wasn't aware of looking at it – one minute I was daydreaming, the next I was thinking, "Hang on a minute, those look familiar."'

'Every published book has a thirteen-digit ISBN number printed on its back cover and title page,' Simon took over. 'The ISBN for Helen Yardley's *Nothing But Love* is 9780340980620, the last thirteen numbers of our number square. As well as a card, the book was in the photograph emailed to Fliss Benson, to help her make the connection.'

'The first three numbers on the cards – 2, 1 and 4 – we think that's a page number,' Sam told Proust.

'It has to be,' Charlie agreed. 'What else can it mean?' She placed *Nothing But Love* on the desk, open at page 214.

The Snowman jerked his head back, as if someone had put a plate of slugs in front of him. 'It's a poem,' he said.

'Read it,' said Simon. 'And the paragraphs above and below it. Read the whole page.' How much time did they waste, on each case, getting Proust up to speed? His rigidity was the problem: he liked to be told things in a certain way –

formally and in stages, with each logical progression clearly highlighted. No wonder Charlie hadn't wanted to be part of the delivery committee on this one. 'Can't you tell him?' she'd groaned. 'Whenever I try to explain something to him, I feel like I'm auditioning to present *Jackanory*.'

Simon watched the Snowman as he read: a study of forehead compression in slow motion, with the frown lines becoming more and more pronounced. Within seconds, the inspector's face had lost several centimetres in length. '"What flutters still is a bird: blown in/by accident, or wild design/of grace, a taste of something sweet – The emptied self a room swept white." Would someone like to tell me what it means?'

'I'm not sure the meaning matters, from our point of view,' said Charlie. 'On the same page, there's a reference to a journalist from the *Daily Telegraph* who went to Geddham Hall to interview Helen Yardley. We think that's the significant—'

'Track him or her down,' said Proust.

'We already have, sir,' said Sam. 'Geddham Hall keep a record of—'

'You have? Then why not tell me so, Sergeant? What's the point of a perishing update if you fail to update me?'

'The journalist was a Rahila Yunis, sir. She still works for the *Telegraph*. I spoke to her on the phone, read her page 214 of *Nothing But Love*. At first she was very reluctant to comment. When I pressed her, she said Helen Yardley's recollection of their interview at Geddham Hall wasn't correct. Helen did have a favourite poem written in her notebook, or journal, or whatever it was, but Rahila Yunis said it wasn't that "room swept white" poem. She's going to check her old files, but she thinks the poem Helen Yardley copied into her notebook and claimed to be fond of was called "The Microbe".'

'We could only find one poem with that title,' said Charlie. 'It's by Hilaire Belloc.'

'Hilaire spelled h-i-l-a-i-r-e,' said Simon. 'As in hilairious@ yahoo.co.uk.'

'Are you going to make me read another poem?' Proust asked.

'I'll read it to you,' said Charlie.

> '"The Microbe is so very small
> You cannot make him out at all,
> But many sanguine people hope
> To see him through a microscope.
> His jointed tongue that lies beneath
> A hundred curious rows of teeth;
> His seven tufted tails with lots
> Of lovely pink and purple spots,
> On each of which a pattern stands,
> Composed of forty separate bands;
> His eyebrows of a tender green;
> All these have never yet been seen –
> But scientists, who ought to know,
> Assure us that they must be so . . .
> Oh! Let us never, never doubt
> What nobody is sure about!"'

Simon was trying hard not to laugh. Charlie had read the poem as one might to a five-year-old. The Snowman looked startled. 'Give me that,' he said.

Charlie handed him the sheet of paper. As he stared at it, his lips silently formed the words, 'never, never doubt'. Eventually he said, 'I like it.' He sounded surprised.

'So did Helen Yardley, according to Rahila Yunis,' said Sam. 'It's not hard to see why. For "scientists", read "doctors". She must have had Judith Duffy in mind. Duffy can't have been sure Morgan and Rowan were murdered, because they weren't. And yet she never, never doubted.'

'I like it.' Proust nodded and handed the poem back to Charlie. 'It's a proper poem. The other one isn't.'

'I disagree,' said Simon. 'But that's not the point. The point is, why was Rahila Yunis so unwilling to talk at first? Why not say, as soon as Sam had read her the extract, that Helen Yardley had lied? And why *did* Yardley lie, in the book? Why did she pretend that it was "Anchorage" by Fiona Sampson that meant so much to her, and that she'd talked to Rahila Yunis about, when it was Hilaire Belloc's "The Microbe"?'

No reply from Proust. He was mouthing silently again: *never, never doubt*.

'Why aren't we in there?' Colin Sellers had been trying to lip-read what Simon, Sam, Charlie and Proust were saying.

'Because we're out here,' said Chris Gibbs.

'Only Waterhouse'd get away with bringing his girlfriend.'

Gibbs snorted. 'Why, do you want to take all your girlfriends to visit the Snowman? His office isn't big enough to squeeze them all in.'

'How's it going on the name-that-Baldy front?' Sellers asked, not expecting to get away with changing the subject quite so soon.

'Not bad,' said Gibbs. 'Of all the names that have come in so far, only two have come up more than twenty times each.' He stood up. 'I'm off to 131 Valingers Road in Bethnal Green to interview one of them: Warren Gruff, ex-army. I said all along, didn't I? British military.'

'What about the other one?'

'Other one?'

'The other name that's come up more than twenty times,' said Sellers impatiently.

'Oh, that one.' Gibbs grinned. 'Matter of fact, the second one's come up more often than Warren Gruff's – thirty-six mentions, next to Gruff's twenty-three.'

'Then why . . .?'

'Why aren't I going after the second name first? Because it's got no surname or address attached to it. It's just a first name: Billy. Thirty-six people rang in to say they know Baldy as Billy, but don't know anything else about him.'

'Does the sarge know? We need to—'

'Track Billy down?' Gibbs cut Sellers off again. 'I will be doing – at 131 Valingers Road, Bethnal Green.' He laughed at Sellers' confusion. 'Warren Gruff; Billy. You really can't see it? Think along the lines of nicknames. You're supposed to be a detective, for fuck's sake.'

Finally, Sellers made the connection. 'Billy Goat Gruff,' he said.

19

Monday 12 October 2009

'Ray?' The problem with Marchington House is that it's so big, there's no point calling out anybody's name. I'd be better off ringing her on her mobile, except that mine has been thrown into a boating lake, and without it, I don't know her number.

I check the lounge, family room, kitchen, snug, utility room, both studies, the games room, the music room and the den, but there's no sign of her. I head for the stairs. Distributed over the top three floors of the house are fourteen bedrooms and ten bathrooms. I start with Ray's room on the first floor. She's not in there, but Angus's jacket is, the one he was wearing when he accosted me outside my flat. There's also a bulging black canvas bag on the bed with '*London on Sunday*' printed on it in small white letters.

I wrestle with my conscience for about half a second, then unzip the bag. Oh, God, look at all this: pyjamas, toothbrush, electric razor, dental floss, at least four balled-up pairs of socks, boxer shorts . . . Quickly, I pull the zip closed. Words can't express how much I do not want to look at Angus Hines' boxer shorts.

Great. My prisoner has come to stay – the man I yelled at for being decent enough not to smash my window. I'm going to have to see him again and die of shame. This must be how the purveyors of apartheid felt when all that truth and reconciliation stuff started and they had to spend hours telling Nelson Mandela what rubbish human beings they were. I think that's what happened, anyway. I'm considering giving up *heat* magazine and subscribing to something more serious instead, to boost my general knowledge: *The Economist* or *National Geographic*.

I unzip the side pocket of Angus's suitcase, having decided it's bound to be underwear-free: he wouldn't divide his boxer shorts equally between the compartments. I'm surprised to find two DVDs in there, both of Binary Star programmes I produced: *Hate After Death* and *Cutting Myself*. So Angus's investigation of my credentials is ongoing. Actually, *Hate After Death* is the best work I've ever done, so I hope he's watched it. It was a six-parter about families in which a feud between one branch and another had spanned several generations. In some cases, parents on their deathbeds had extracted promises from their children not to let their enmities die with them, to hate on their behalf even after their deaths, to hate their enemies' children, and the children of those children.

Sick. Sick to want to pass on your anger and resentment to others, sick to hang on to those feelings yourself.

I'm not angry with Laurie any more. I don't hate him, or wish him harm. What I wish is that . . . I don't allow myself to think it. There's no point.

As I'm putting the DVDs back in Angus's bag, I hear footsteps. They seem to be coming from the landing above me, but when I go and investigate, I can't find anyone. 'Hello?' I call out. I check all the bedrooms on the second and third floors, but there's no sign of life. I must have imagined it. I decide to go to my room, get into bed and have the protracted pillow-thumping cry I've been looking forward to since Regent's Park.

I open the door and scream when I see a man standing next to my bed. He doesn't seem at all startled. He smiles as if I ought to have known I'd find him there.

'Who are you? What are you doing in my room?' I know who he is: Ray's brother, the dark one from the punting photo in the kitchen. He's wearing a white V-necked cricket jumper and trousers that are more zips than material. I've never understood that: why would you want to shorten and extend your trousers at various points during the day? Who's the target audience: people whose calves only work part-time?

'You've got that the wrong way round,' says Ray's brother, still grinning. 'You're in my room.'

'Ray said this was a guest room.'

'It is. It's my guest room. This is my house.'

'Marchington House belongs to you?' I remember what Laurie said about Ray's parents living in Winchester. 'But . . .'

'You know different?'

'Sorry, I just . . . You're so young. You look about my age.'

'Which is?'

'Thirty-one.'

'In that case I'm younger than you. I'm twenty-nine.'

I feel a fit of tactlessness coming on. 'When did you fit in getting rich enough to buy a house like this? At school, between double Latin and croquet? Or did you make constructive use of a detention?' I'm talking nonsense, still freaked out by having found him in my room. Why was he lying in wait for me? How dare he own Marchington House? Did he open my suitcase? Was he looking at my underwear, while I was looking at Angus Hines'?

'Croquet and Latin?' He laughs. 'Is that what you learned at your school?'

'No, we learned gang warfare and apathy,' I snap. 'I went to an inner city comprehensive.'

'Me too.'

'Really?'

'Really. And I'm not rich, apart from this house. I inherited it last year from my grandfather. I run a window-cleaning business. This isn't where I live – I'm still in my rented flat in Streatham. This place is way too big for me, and the décor's too . . . womanly. My gran was an interior designer.'

'Just you?' I say. 'You inherited this whole house?'

'All six of the grandchildren inherited a property,' he says, looking sheepish. 'My grandfather was very wealthy. Something to do with diamonds.'

'Oh, right,' I say. 'I'm lucky: both my grandads are still alive. One's something to do with an allotment and the other's something to do with sitting in a chair waiting to cark it. Look, Ray said I could stay here, and—'

'You want me to get out of your room? My room? Our room?'

That's it: he's definitely been rooting through my knickers. That was an unambiguous innuendo.

'I'm supposed to kick you out,' he says.

'Kick me *out*?'

'That's right. Don't worry, I'm not going to. I don't see why I should do his lordship's bidding, do you?'

His lordship . . . Angus Hines. I might have known.

Is that why he and Ray aren't here? Too scared to do their own dirty work? Did they watch *Hate After Death*, think it was hopeless and lose all faith in me?

'Do you come from a rich family, if you don't mind my asking?'

I do mind, but I've no right to, after what I asked him. 'No. Poor. Well, ordinary, which effectively means poor.'

'How so?'

'What's the point in having a *bit* of money?' I say crossly.

'You're a strange woman, Fliss Benson. Has anyone ever told you that?'

'No.'

'I hated school, actually,' he says, as if it's the obvious next thing to say. 'My parents could have afforded to send all of us to Eton, no problem. We could have lived the croquet-and-Latin dream, but instead we went to Cottham Chase and had to spend every day fighting to attain the dubious title of cock of the school.'

'Did you succeed?' Eton's a boys' school. Ray couldn't have gone to Eton.

'No. Which was a huge relief. The cock's responsibilities were onerous: you were expected to kick the crap out of literally everybody that crossed your path. I'd have had no free time.'

'Why didn't your parents send you somewhere better if they could afford it?'

'They thought that sending us to the local dump was sure to bring about global equality.' He smiles at me again, as if we're best friends. 'You know the type.'

I haven't a clue what he's talking about. 'Look, about you booting me out . . .'

'I've already told you: I'm not going to.'

'Why don't you evict them instead?' I blurt out. 'I'm not the one causing the trouble. If there were a public vote, like on *Big Brother*, I'm sure I'd get to stay in.'

'Them?' He looks surprised.

'Ray and Angus.'

'You want me to ask Ray to leave?'

'I want you to ask Angus to leave.'

'Is Angus her ex-husband?'

Never trust a man with too many zips on his trousers, that's my motto. 'Don't pretend you don't know the name of your own sister's ex,' I say crossly. 'Though I'm not sure how ex he is any more.'

'My sister?' He laughs. 'Sorry, do you mean Ray Hines?'

I stare at him in disbelief. Who else could I mean?

'Ray isn't my sister. Where did you get that idea? Ray is someone I'm temporarily allowing to stay in an empty house I own.'

This is making no sense. 'There's a photo of you up in the kitchen, punting down a river.'

'The River Cam, yes. With my brother – my nice brother, not the stupid one who uses and discards beautiful women he really ought to treat better.'

What's he talking about? 'I was looking at the photo, and Ray said, "Not much of a family resemblance, is there? Those two got all the good looks." Or words to that effect. But if you're not Ray's brother . . .'

For the first time since we started talking, he looks angry. 'Then who am I?' he says, completing my question. 'If I tell you, you'll hate me on the spot, and it'll be *his* fault, like everything always is.'

Before I have a chance to respond, he's gone. I run after him, shouting 'Wait!' and 'Stop!' and all the other stupid pointless things you shout at people who turn their backs and leave you behind at great speed. I get down the last flight of stairs just in time to hear the front door slam. Through the window, I see him drive away in a car with a cloth roof, probably unzippable, like the bottoms of his trousers.

I storm into the kitchen and pull the punting photograph off the wall to get a better look at it, as if it might be able to tell me what's going on. My fingers touch a flap of paper on the back of the frame, and I turn it over. There's a label on the back; one corner has come loose and curled up. On it, someone has handwritten, 'Hugo and St John take a punt! Cambridge, 1999.' My heart does its best impersonation of a bouncy ball. *Hugo. St John.*

Laurence Hugo St John Fleet Nattrass. His lordship.

I run round the house like a demented person, pulling drawers open, panting loudly. I don't care how long it takes – I'm going to find something, something better than what I've got, something that proves to me what I already know.

I find it in a sideboard in the den. Or rather, I find *them*: photograph albums. On the first page there's a picture of a jowly middle-aged man smoking a pipe. I pull it out and turn it over. 'Fleet, 1973' is all that's written on the back. *Laurie's dad.* Next, I select a photograph of a smiling baby sitting in what looks like the lotus position in front of a chair. I turn it over and read the tiny handwriting: 'St John Hugo Laurence Fleet Nattrass, eight months old, 1971'. This must be the blond brother from the punting photograph, younger than Laurie and older than . . . Zip-man must be Hugo.

Did Fleet Nattrass only know three boys' names apart from his own? Is it a posh family thing, giving all your children the same names in a different order?

Not much of a resemblance, is there? Ray thought I knew she was staying at Laurie's brother's house. She assumed he'd told me.

The person who wants me evicted isn't Angus Hines. It's Laurie.

The house phone rings. I crawl over to the table on my hands and knees and pick it up, hoping it might be Ray.

It's Maya. 'Fliss,' she says. She sounds caught out, as if she wishes I hadn't answered. I don't need to ask her how she knew where to find me. I hear a drawing in of breath.

'Let me save you the trouble,' I say. 'You're afraid you're going to have to let me go. That about right?'

'Close enough,' she says, and hangs up.

I'm sitting cross-legged on the floor in the hall when the front door opens and Ray and Angus walk in. Distractedly, Angus says, 'Hello, Fliss.' He doesn't look as if he's thinking about me locking him in my flat. If he's surprised to find me at his feet, he shows no sign of it. He squeezes Ray's arm and says, 'I'll be down shortly,' then heads for the stairs as if he has something important to attend to.

'Did you tell him you're pregnant?' I ask Ray. His suitcase upstairs can only mean one thing. Not long ago, he didn't even know where she was staying. 'Is he happy about it?'

'Happy's difficult for both of us, but . . . yes, he's pleased.'

'Are you back together, then? Are you moving back to Notting Hill?' Childishly, I want her to say she's moving out because I know I'll have to. I can't stay in Laurie's brother's house. *What did you think, idiot? That someone like you can live in a place like this for ever?* 'Is Angus coming to live here, too?'

Ray's smile vanishes, and I notice how tired she looks. 'No. We're not going to be living together.'

'Why not?'

'Let's get set up for the camera,' she says. 'It's all part of the same story.'

'Did you tell Angus the baby might be Laurie's and not his?' I ask, making no effort to lower my voice. I'm guessing that at some point Ray and Laurie slept together. Why wouldn't he try it on with her? He slept with me in an attempt to persuade me not to interview Judith Duffy for the film; he shacked up with Maya to avoid me and the police, or maybe so that the card-sender wouldn't know where to find him. No doubt bedding Ray was part of his campaign to persuade her to be involved in the film: first he offered his body, then Marchington House as a refuge. He must have been furious when neither did the trick.

From Ray's point of view, why wouldn't she have sex with Laurie? At forty-two she could still have another child. If she has Laurie's baby rather than Angus's, there will be no genetic auto-immune issue to worry about.

She takes my arm and leads me into the den. Closing the door behind us, she says, 'Please don't call it a baby. It isn't one, not yet. And there's no "might" about it. It's Laurie's. Angus had a vasectomy while I was in prison. He wanted to make sure he'd never go through the pain of losing another child.'

'But . . .'

'I told him the truth,' says Ray. 'Don't you think I'm sick of lies by now? Do you really think I'd try to start my new life, and Angus's, based on a lie?'

'So you're going to tell Laurie?'

'Laurie Nattrass is nothing to me, Fliss. Personally, I mean.'

Lucky you.

'I can withhold information from him and it won't be

living a lie, not in the way it would be if I lied to my husband.' She looks caught out. 'Angus and I are getting remarried,' she says.

But you're not going to be living together? 'Will he be able to feel the same about Laurie's baby as he would about his own?' I ask.

'He doesn't know,' says Ray. 'Neither do I. But we don't have the option of "his own". This is all we have, our only chance of being . . . well, I suppose a family, though an unusual one. Are you going to tell Laurie?'

'No.' I'm not going to tell him about Ray's pregnancy, and I'm not going to tell anybody about him bribing Carl Chappell and Warren Gruff. With regard to Laurie, I'm going to do nothing. I don't want to destroy anybody's life – not Laurie's, not Ray's, not Angus's.

'Can I ask you one more favour?' says Ray.

'What?' I haven't granted any so far, unless my memory's letting me down.

'Don't tell Angus you know. It would make it harder for him if he thought anyone else knew.'

What happened to no more lies? I don't say it because it's a ridiculous thing to say, or even think. If no one ever told a lie again, life would quickly become impossible.

Ray nods at the camera. 'Shall we get started?'

'I need to make a phone call first,' I tell her. 'Why don't you sort us out with drinks?'

Once she's gone, I use the antique phone on the table in the corner to ring Tamsin. She doesn't sound pleased to hear from me. 'Just to remind you of the etiquette: you're supposed to drop your friends when you've got a new man, not when you've lost your marbles,' she says. 'In the event of a loss of marbles, you're allowed to spend as much time with your friends as you ever did, as long as you remember to look confused and call them by the names of people who've been dead for years.'

'Please tell me you haven't got a new job yet,' I say.

'Job?' She sounds as if she's forgotten what one is.

'How hard would it be for you and I to set up on our own?'

'As what?'

'As what we are: people who make TV programmes.'

'You mean our own production company? I've no idea.'

'Find out.'

I hear a long, gusty yawn. 'I'm not sure how I'd go about finding out, to be honest.'

'Find a way,' I say, and then I cut her off to show her I mean business. I'm sure that's how MI6 would handle her lazy, uncooperative streak. It'll all work out, I persuade myself. It has to work out.

Now all I have to do is tell Ray and Angus that it's not going to be Binary Star making the film after all.

20

12/10/09

'So we're sure Warren Gruff's Baldy?' Simon asked Sellers.

'I am.' Charlie stared at the grainy photograph on the computer screen. 'That's the man I saw.'

'I am too,' said Sellers. 'Gruff's ex-army, went to Iraq first time round. And look at this.' He leaned across the desk, reaching for an article he'd printed out, and knocked over his can of Diet Coke. 'Fuck,' he muttered as the liquid fizzed over the keyboard.

'I never thought I'd see the day,' said Charlie. 'Colin Sellers on a diet.'

'This was in the *Sun*, June 2006,' said Sellers. 'What diet?'

Simon took the article and started to read. 'Heard of Joanne Bew?' he asked Charlie.

'No. Who is she?'

'She was convicted of murdering her son, Brandon, then retried and acquitted. Gruff was her boyfriend, Brandon's father. He was none too happy about her acquittal. Far as he's concerned, she smothered his son, and he doesn't care if she sues him for saying it. She mistreated Brandon from the day he was born, by the sound of it.' Simon winced and dropped the article on the desk. 'I can do without the depressing details.'

'Are you saying I need to lose weight?' Sellers asked Charlie, covering his gut with a protective hand. 'It's all muscle, this. Used to be, anyway.'

'Sorry. I just assumed, because of the Diet Coke . . .'

'Diet was all the machine had left,' he told her. 'It tastes like shit.'

'His girlfriend killed his kid and got away with it,' said Simon, more to himself than to Sellers and Charlie. 'He's ex-military – maybe he's killed before. Probably has. How easy would it be for the card-sender, the Brain, to get him on side? Easy enough when Sarah Jaggard and Helen Yardley are the targets, women who – like Joanne Bew, as Gruff would see it – murdered kids and got away with it. But what about when the Brain decides Judith Duffy's the next victim? Duffy testified against Joanne Bew at her first trial – it says so in the article. Gruff'd be favourably disposed towards Duffy . . .'

'Which explains what he said to me,' Charlie finished his sentence for him. 'That Duffy didn't deserve to die, that she'd done her best. He meant she did her best to put Joanne Bew behind bars, didn't he?'

'He also said you did your best,' Simon reminded her. 'He meant the collective "you" – the police.'

'So the Brain had some kind of hold over him?' said Charlie. 'If Gruff didn't want to kill Duffy, but did it anyway.'

'Gruff had attacked Sarah Jaggard, provided the gun for the murder of Helen Yardley. What he said to you was spot on: he was in it up to his eyebrows and couldn't back out at that point – the Brain would have made sure . . .' Simon stopped mid-sentence, seeing Sam Kombothekra heading their way.

'Just because I'm drinking Diet Coke and I'm not skinny like you doesn't mean I'm on a diet,' Sellers muttered to Charlie. He tilted his head, inspecting his belly from a different angle.

'I think we've got a solid lead on Ray Hines' whereabouts.' Sam sounded excited. 'Laurie Nattrass has a brother, Hugo, who owns a house in Twickenham. He doesn't live there – he lives in Streatham – which is why it's taken this long to unearth it, but . . . Simon?'

Charlie clicked her fingers in front of his face. 'Wake up. Sam's trying to tell you something.'

Simon turned to Sellers. 'What did you just say? About the Diet Coke. Whatever you said, say it again.'

Sellers gave up trying to pull in his stomach muscles. He sighed. 'Just because I'm drinking Diet Coke and I'm a bit on the heavy side doesn't mean I'm on a diet.'

'That's it.' Simon spun round to face Charlie. He stared at her as if he'd forgotten Sellers and Sam were there. 'That's *it*. A thin person with a diet drink might just like the taste of it, but a fat person with a diet drink . . .'

'Fat?' Sellers sounded outraged.

'So the alibi's bullshit.'

'What alibi?' Sam asked.

'I need to talk to Dillon White again.' Simon's words tumbled out as his thought process speeded up. 'And Rahila Yunis.'

'The journalist who interviewed Helen Yardley in prison?' asked Charlie.

'I need her to tell me why she withheld the most important part of the story about her visit to Geddham Hall. I know why, but I want to hear it from her. Sam, I need photographs: Laurie Nattrass, Angus Hines, Glen Jaggard, Paul Yardley, Sebastian Brownlee.'

Sam nodded. He could have pointed out that, as skipper, he was the one who ought to have been assigning the tasks; he was wise enough not to.

'*Whose* alibi's bullshit?' Charlie asked, knowing the chances of getting an answer at this point were considerably slimmer than Colin Sellers.

'Sellers, you check out the Twickenham address,' said Simon, his eyes darting back and forth as he pieced together the story in his mind. 'If you find Ray Hines there, don't let her out of your sight.'

21

Monday 12 October 2009

'He suspected me from the first time the police came to the house,' Ray says to the camera. I nod, willing her to carry on, to tell me as much as she can before Angus joins us. I'm afraid she won't be quite so open once he's listening. 'He changed towards me, became horribly cold and remote, but at the same time he wouldn't let me out of his sight. He moved into one of the many spare rooms we'd at one point hoped to fill with children . . .' She stops. 'You know we wanted to have lots?'

'No.'

'Angus is one of six. We wanted at least four.' She falls silent.

'He wouldn't let you out of his sight,' I say, prompting her.

'He . . . monitored me. It was as if someone had asked him to spy on my every move and report back. In my most paranoid moments, I wondered if that might be the case. It wasn't, of course. The police would have assumed – did assume, in fact – that Angus and I would stick together. He was watching me closely for his own purposes, no one else's. He was trying to gather evidence of my guilt or innocence.'

'He didn't believe Marcella and Nathaniel reacted badly to the vaccine?'

Ray shakes her head. 'I don't blame him. All the experts tell you vaccines are safe, and he wasn't there when both children had fits. Only Wendy and I saw what happened. For all Angus knew, I was a murderer who'd persuaded Wendy to lie.'

'You were his wife,' I remind her. 'He should have known you wouldn't kill your children.'

'Maybe he would have, if it hadn't been for the zombie-like depression I faked in order to go to Switzerland with Fiona. That made him doubt everything he thought he knew about me. I can't blame him for that – it was my fault. I didn't blame him even then, but—' She breaks off, eyeing the ceiling as if afraid he might burst through it at any moment. *She can't be frightened of him, not if she's planning to marry him again.*

'I quickly became terrified of him,' she says. 'He wouldn't talk to me – that was the scariest thing. I kept asking if he thought I'd killed Marcella and Nathaniel, and he wouldn't answer. All he ever said was, "Only you know what you've done, Ray." He was so blank, so horrendously . . . *calm.* I couldn't believe how composed he was when our lives were falling apart – me charged with murder, maybe going to prison. Looking back, I think he had a breakdown. I'm *sure* it was that. People never tell you it's possible to go mad in a quiet, orderly way, but it is. That's what happened to Angus. He didn't think he'd broken down with grief, he thought he was in full possession of his faculties and responding in the only rational way: I'm accused of murder, so it's his job to watch me and record my behaviour in order to ascertain whether there's any factual basis to the accusation – that's how he'd have put it to himself, I'm sure.'

'When you say "record" . . . You mean he wrote it down?'

'Eventually I got desperate, when he point blank refused to communicate with me. I searched the room he was sleeping in and found all this . . . terrible stuff in one of the drawers: a notebook describing my behaviour, reams and reams of articles he'd downloaded from the internet about the importance of vaccination and the corrupt self-publicists who claim the jabs are dangerous . . .'

'What did he write about you in the notebook?' I ask.

'Oh, nothing interesting. "Breakfast 8 a.m.: one weetabix. Sits on sofa crying, one hour." That sort of thing. I didn't do anything much at that point in my life, apart from cry, answer the police's endless questions and try to talk to Angus. One day, when I couldn't take his staring silence any more, I said to him, "If a jury finds me innocent, will that convince you I'm telling the truth?" He laughed so horribly . . .' She shudders. 'I'll never forget that laugh.'

And yet you're willing to marry him for a second time.

'He said, "You seriously expect me to base my opinion on the views of twelve strangers, most of whom probably aren't educated? Do you think Marcella and Nathaniel meant that little to me?" I completely lost it, then. I screamed at him that he'd never know, in that case, if he wouldn't believe me and wouldn't believe a jury. He very calmly told me I was wrong. One day, he said, he would know. "How?" I asked, but he wouldn't tell me. He walked away. Every time I asked him that question, he turned his back on me.' Ray pinches the top of her nose, then moves her hand as if she's suddenly remembered the camera. 'That's why I lied in court,' she tells it. 'That's why I started being as inconsistent as I could, contradicting myself whenever I could. I didn't know what Angus's plan was, but I knew he had one, and that I had to escape from him and . . . whatever he intended to do to me.'

I nod. I know all about needing to escape from Angus Hines. *Turning round, finding him right behind me in the doorway of my flat . . .*

Where is he? What's he doing upstairs that's taking so long?

'I couldn't bear another day with him,' says Ray. 'He'd become this terrifying . . . *thing*, not my husband at all, not the man I loved. Prison would be nothing compared to the horror of living with *that* any longer – at least in prison no one would try to kill me, and that's what I became increasingly certain Angus would do. That was how insane he seemed.'

'You lied so that the jury would think you were untrustworthy.'

'So that they'd dismiss me as a liar, yes. I knew that once they thought that, a guilty verdict was a done deal. You have to understand, I didn't care where I lived. I'd already lost everything: my husband, my two children. And my home – it was worse than hell. I couldn't breathe there, couldn't sleep, couldn't eat. Prison would be a welcome relief, I thought. And it was. It really was. I wasn't scared all the time, or under surveillance. I was able to spend my time doing the only thing I wanted to do: thinking about Marcella and Nathaniel in peace. Missing them in peace.'

'But you made the world believe you'd murdered them. Didn't that bother you?'

Ray gives me an odd look, as if I've made a freakish suggestion. 'Why would it? I knew the truth. And the only three people whose opinions would have mattered to me were gone. Marcella and Nathaniel were dead, and the Angus I loved . . . I felt as if he'd died with them.'

'So after you found Nathaniel, when you said you let the health visitor in immediately . . .'

'I knew perfectly well that I didn't. I made her wait on the doorstep for at least ten minutes, exactly as she said in court.'

'Why?'

She doesn't answer straight away. When she speaks, it's a whisper, 'Nathaniel was dead. I knew the health visitor would see that as soon as she came in. I knew she'd say it out loud. I didn't want him to be dead. The longer she waited outside, the longer I could pretend.'

'Do you want to take a break?' I ask.

'No. Thanks, but I'll carry on.' She leans into the camera. 'Angus will be down in a minute. I'm hoping that talking about what happened will be the beginning of his recovery. I had therapy in prison, but Angus has never opened up to anyone. He's never been ready before, but he is now. That's why this documentary's so important – not only as a way of telling and explaining . . .' She covers her stomach with her hands.

The baby. That's who Ray wants to talk to – not me, not the viewing public. Her child. The film is her gift to the baby: the family story.

'Angus lied, too,' says Ray. 'When I was found guilty, he told the press that he'd made a decision before the verdict came in: he would believe the jury whatever they said, guilty or innocent. I knew that was a lie, and Angus knew I knew it. He was mocking me from a distance, reminding me of his scorn for the inadequately educated jury and his promise that one day he would find out if I was guilty or not through his own efforts. He knew I'd understand the hidden message behind his official words. For as long as I stayed in prison, though, he couldn't get to me.'

'Did he visit you?'

'I refused to see him. I was so scared of him that when Laurie Nattrass and Helen Yardley first took an interest in me, I wished they'd leave me alone. It took a lot of therapy to persuade me that since I wasn't a murderer, I probably shouldn't be in jail.'

'If you wanted to guarantee you'd go to prison and stay there, why didn't you plead guilty?'

'Because I was innocent.' She sighs. 'As long as I said clearly that I hadn't killed Marcella and Nathaniel, I wasn't letting them down. People had the option of believing me. If I'd said I'd done it, I would have been betraying their memories by pretending there had been a moment when I'd wanted each of them to die. I didn't mind lying about other things, but I couldn't have stood in court and said under oath that I'd wanted my beloved children dead. Besides, a guilty plea would have been counterproductive. It would have netted me a lighter sentence, maybe even a lesser charge – manslaughter instead of murder. I might have been out in five years – less, for all I know – and then I'd have had to face Angus.'

'But when you did get out, after you'd left the urn picture hotel, you went back to him, to Notting Hill. Weren't you still scared of him?'

She nods. 'But I was more frightened of living the rest of my life in terror. Whatever Angus had in store for me, I wanted it over with. When he opened the door to let me in, I honestly thought I might never leave that house alive again.'

'You thought he'd kill you, and you still went to him?'

'I loved him.' She shrugs. 'Or rather, I *had* loved him, and I still loved the person he used to be. And he needed me. He'd gone mad, so mad that he didn't realise how much he needed me, but I knew. I'm the only person in the world who loved Marcella and Nathaniel as much as Angus did – how could he not need me? But, yes, I thought he might kill me. What he'd said to me kept going round in my head: that one day he would find out whether I was guilty or not. How could he find out, if he wouldn't believe me or a jury? The only thing I could think of was that he would let me know I was about to die, that there was no way out. Maybe then I'd finally confess, if there was anything to confess to. Maybe he planned to torture me, or . . .' She shakes her head. 'You think all sorts of terrible things, but I had to find out. I had to know what he was planning to do.'

'And? Did he try to kill you?'

The door opens. 'No, I didn't,' says Angus.

'He didn't,' Ray echoes. 'Which was lucky for me, because if he'd tried, he'd have succeeded.'

No. That's the wrong answer. He did try to kill her. He must have, because . . . Something clicks in my mind: the cards. The sixteen numbers. And the photographs, Helen Yardley's hand . . .

I turn to Angus. 'Sit next to Ray and look at the camera when you're talking, not at me,' I tell him. 'Why did you email me those lists – all the people Judith Duffy testified against in the criminal and family courts?'

He frowns, unhappy with the leap from one subject to another. 'I thought we were talking about what happened when Ray came home?'

'We will, but first I want you to explain why you sent me those lists. To the camera, please.'

He looks at Ray, who nods. I see that she's right: he does need her. 'I thought you'd find it useful to see how many people Judith Duffy had accused of deliberately harming or killing children,' he says.

'Why? Why would that be useful to me?'

Angus stares at the camera.

'You don't want to tell me. You think I ought to be capable of working it out. Well, I'm sorry, but I'm not capable.'

'Isn't it obvious?' he asks.

'No.'

'Tell her, Angus.'

'I assume you know the catchphrase Judith Duffy was famous for: "so unlikely, it borders on impossible"?'

I tell him I do.

'Do you know what she was talking about when she said it?'

'The odds of there being two crib deaths in one family.'

'No, that's a popular misconception.' He looks pleased to be able to contradict me. My heart's thudding so hard, I'm surprised the camera's not shaking. 'That's what people think she meant, but she told Ray otherwise. She wasn't talking about general principles, but about two specific cases – Morgan and Rowan Yardley – and the likelihood that they died naturally, given the physical evidence in both cases.'

'Are you going to tell me why you sent me those lists?' I ask.

'I've got my own likelihood principle, which I'll happily explain to you,' says Angus. 'If Judith Duffy testifies that Ray's a murderer, and Ray denies it, what are the odds of Duffy being right?'

I think about this. 'I've no idea,' I say honestly. 'Assuming Duffy's an unbiased expert, and that Ray might have a strong motivation to say she was innocent even if she wasn't . . .'

'No, leave that out of it,' says Angus impatiently. 'Don't think about motivation, impartiality, expertise – none of those things can be scientifically measured. I'm talking about pure probability. In fact, let's not use Ray and Duffy – let's make it more abstract. A doctor accuses a woman of smothering her baby. The woman says she didn't do it. There are no witnesses. What are the odds of the doctor being right?'

'Fifty-fifty?' I guess.

'Right. So the doctor, in that scenario, might be totally and completely correct in her judgement, or she might be totally, utterly wrong. She can't be a bit right and a bit wrong, can she?'

'No,' I say. 'The woman either did or didn't murder her child.'

'Good.' Angus nods. 'Now, let's up the numbers a bit. A doctor – the same doctor – accuses three women of murdering babies. All three women say they're innocent.'

Ray, Helen Yardley and Sarah Jaggard.

'What are the odds of all three of them being guilty? Still fifty-fifty?'

God, I hated Maths at school. I remember rolling my eyes when we did quadratic equations: *Yeah, like we're really going to need* this *skill in later life*. My teacher, Mrs Gilpin, said, 'Numerical agility will help you in ways you can't possibly imagine, Felicity.' Looks like she was right. 'If, in each case, the probability of the doctor being right is fifty-fifty, then the chance of her being right in all three cases would . . . still be fifty-fifty, wouldn't it?'

'No,' says Angus, as if he can't believe my stupidity. 'There's only a one in eight chance of the doctor being right, or wrong, in all three cases.' Ray and I watch as he pulls a crumpled receipt and a pen out of his jacket pocket and starts to write, leaning on his knee. 'G stands for guilty, I for innocent,' he says, handing me the receipt once he's finished.

I look at what he's written.

Woman 1: G G G G I I I I
Woman 2: G G I I I I G G
Woman 3: G I G I I G I G

'You see?' he says. 'There's a one in eight chance of the doctor being right in all three cases, and a one in eight chance of her being wrong in all three cases. Now, imagine there are a thousand such cases . . .'

'I see what you're getting at,' I say. 'The more cases there are of Judith Duffy saying women are guilty and them protesting their innocence, the more likely she is to be right sometimes and wrong sometimes.' *That's why, in your email, you also made sure to tell me that on twenty-three occasions, Judith Duffy testified in favour of a parent. Sometimes she's for, sometimes she's against – that was your point. Sometimes she's right, sometimes she's wrong*. In other words, Laurie's portrayal of her as a persecutor of innocent mothers is a flat-out lie.

'Precisely.' Angus rewards me with a smile. 'The more wrongly accused innocent women Laurie Nattrass pulls out of his hat, so-called victims of Duffy's alleged desire to ruin lives, the more likely at least some of them are to be guilty. I have no trouble believing in a miscarriage of justice, or that a doctor can get it wrong. But to expect people to believe in an endless string of miscarriage-of-justice victims, in a doctor who gets it wrong every single time . . .'

'And I was supposed to work that out, from those lists you sent me?'

'Hines' Theorem of Probability, I call it: one woman accused of murder by Judith Duffy might be guilty or innocent. A hundred women accused of murder by Judith Duffy must be guilty *and* innocent. *Lots* of them are likely to be guilty, just as lots of them are likely to be innocent.'

'And you wanted to make sure I knew this, because Laurie didn't seem to,' I say quietly. 'He seemed to think *all* the women Duffy accused of child murder had to be innocent. He couldn't see that there must be guilty ones too, hiding among the blameless.'

'He couldn't see the trees for the wood,' says Ray, nodding.

The doorbell rings.

'Do you want me to get it?' she asks.

'No, I'll go. Whoever it is, I'll get rid of them.' I force myself to smile and say, 'Stay put, I'll be back in a second.'

In the hall, I panic and freeze halfway to the door, unable to take the next step. Judith Duffy opened her front door and someone shot her, a man with shaved hair.

The letterbox opens and I see brown eyes, part of a nose. 'Fliss?' I recognise the voice: it's Laurie's zippy-trousered brother. Hugo. Why did he ring the bell? It's his house, for God's sake.

I open the door. 'What do you want?' Without authorisation from my brain, my hand starts performing a winding-up gesture: *come on, get on with it.*

'I wanted to apologise for the way I—'

'Never mind about that,' I say, lowering my voice. 'I need you to do something for me.' I pull him inside and into the room nearest to the door, the music room. I point at the piano stool and he sits down obediently. 'Wait here,' I whisper. 'Just sit, don't do anything apart from sitting. In silence. Turn your mobile off, and pretend you're not here. Don't play the piano, not even one note. Not even "Chopsticks".'

'I can't play "Chopsticks".'

'Really?' I thought everyone could play 'Chopsticks'.

'I can, however, just sit and do nothing apart from sitting. That's a talent of mine that's often been remarked upon by those close to me.'

'Good,' I say. 'Wait here, and don't leave. Promise you won't leave.'

'I promise. Do you mind if I ask—?'

'Yes.'

'But what—?'

'I might need you to drive me somewhere,' I tell him.

'Where's your car?' he asks, also in a whisper.

'Still in the Rolls-Royce showroom, waiting for me to win the lottery or find a rich husband. Now sit quietly until I come back.' I turn to go back to the den.

'Fliss?'

'I've got to go. What?'

'How about me as the rich husband?'

I flinch. 'Don't be stupid. I've had sex with your brother.'

'Would that be a problem for you?'

'I don't know why you're using the conditional tense,' I hiss at him. 'It *is* a problem for me, a huge one.'

'It's a huge problem for me too,' says Hugo Nattrass, beaming like an idiot. 'Do you think that counts as us having quite a lot in common?'

22

12/10/09

Simon passed his phone back to Charlie. 'I don't suppose you're going to tell me who that was or what they said,' she predicted.

'When I'm ready.' He was having one of his workouts, as Charlie liked to call them. Unlike other people's workouts, they didn't involve treadmills or rowing machines; they involved nothing but Simon and his brain. Anyone who tried to join the party was quickly shown how irrelevant they were.

'That's the third secret call you've taken since we set off. Are there going to be more?'

No answer.

'It's a safety issue apart from anything else,' said Charlie tetchily. 'If you weren't so keen to keep me in the dark, you could put your phone on speaker-phone and drive with both hands.'

'Just because you've got a can of Diet Coke and you're fat, doesn't mean you're on a diet,' said Simon, as they turned into Bengeo Street.

'Oh, not this again!' Charlie banged her head on the passenger window.

'You've got an umbrella with you, and it's raining. Doesn't necessarily mean you've got an umbrella with you *because* it's raining.'

'Meaning?'

Simon parked outside Stella White's house. 'Dillon White told Gibbs he saw the man with the umbrella in Helen Yardley's lounge. At first we didn't take it seriously, because it didn't rain on Monday, nor had rain been forecast, and Stella White, our only other witness, saw no umbrella. She also said there was no way her son could have seen the man in the Yardleys' lounge that morning. Subsequently, we find out Dillon saw the man on a previous occasion – in Helen's lounge, where he, Dillon, was too. So were Stella, Helen and Paul Yardley, and another man and woman Dillon couldn't name. That day it *was* raining, and rain from the man's umbrella was dripping on the carpet.' A long pause. Then Simon said, 'Anything you want to ask me?'

'Yes,' said Charlie. 'Will you please tell me what it is you think you know?'

'You don't want to ask me if the Yardleys have a hall?'

'Not especially.'

'Well, you ought to. They *do* have a hall, with a wood-laminate floor. Leading through to the lounge. Why would you take a sopping wet umbrella into a carpeted lounge? Why not leave it in the hall, especially if the hall isn't carpeted?'

'Because you're inconsiderate?' Charlie suggested. 'Busy thinking about other things?'

'What if you're not inconsiderate?' said Simon. 'What if you're thoughtful enough to make up an entertaining story for a little boy, about space travel and magic? And yet you deliberately take your umbrella into the lounge and let it drip on the carpet. Why would you do that?'

'Is the umbrella a crucial prop in the magic story?'

Simon shook his head. He had the nerve to look disappointed

that she hadn't worked it out yet. Had he forgotten it wasn't her case? She wasn't supposed to be in a car with him on the way to Bengeo Street; she was supposed to be getting on with her own work.

'Dillon said the other man who was there, the one who wasn't Paul Yardley or Magic Umbrella man – he had an umbrella too, but it wasn't magic so he left it outside.' Simon took his eyes off the road and looked at Charlie. 'When Stella told Gibbs that last Monday was a sunny, bright day, Dillon said, "It wasn't bright. There wasn't enough sun to make it bright." That's what he'd heard the man say – he was parroting word for word.'

'He didn't mean last Monday,' said Charlie. 'He was talking about the "beyond" day a long time ago, when it was raining and presumably overcast.'

'When *there wasn't enough sun to make it bright*,' Simon emphasised.

'Tell me in the next five seconds, or I'll tell your mother that you're involved in a conspiracy to lie to her about the honeymoon,' Charlie threatened.

'In a way, the man was right about the magic. The umbrella had at least one special power: to create light. That's what it was: a photographer's light umbrella, black on the outside, shiny silver stuff on the inside. It belonged to Angus Hines. He's Pictures Desk Editor at *London on Sunday* now, but he wasn't always. He used to be a photographer, worked for various papers, including one that featured an article about two extraordinary women – Helen Yardley and Stella White.'

'So the other man and woman Dillon mentioned . . .'

'I'm guessing a reporter from the paper and a make-up person,' said Simon.

'How often do we see those things at press conferences, where's there's never *any* natural light, let alone enough?' said Charlie, cross that she hadn't guessed. How many photographers' light umbrellas had illuminated her unhappy face in 2006, when all the papers had wanted pictures of the disgraced detective, and the Chief Constable had told her she had to agree if she wanted to keep her job?

'Angus Hines had no choice but to drip rain on the Yardleys' lounge carpet,' said Simon. 'It was the most photogenic room in the house, and he wanted to take his photos in it. When Stella White gave me a list of everyone she remembered meeting at Helen Yardley's house, of course Hines' name wasn't on it. Stella's been photographed for the papers hundreds of times – the marathon runner determined to defeat cancer. She's not going to remember the names of individual photographers, is she? When I asked her about Dillon seeing the man with the magic umbrella, she didn't make the connection with a light umbrella because I'd already told her it was raining that day – in asking the question, I gave her the reason for the umbrella to be there, so she didn't bother thinking beyond that.'

'But . . . Helen Yardley was part of JIPAC,' said Charlie, frowning. 'She lobbied for Ray Hines' release, didn't she? She must have known who Angus was when he turned up at her house, and if Stella White was there with her . . .'

'Helen behaved as if she didn't know Hines from Adam, greeted him as you would a stranger,' said Simon. 'The first of the three phone calls I've just taken was Sam. He's spoken to Paul Yardley. Yardley remembers the "beyond" day only too well. Angus Hines is one of the bad guys as far as Yardley's concerned – he didn't stand by his wife the way Yardley stood by Helen, the way Glen Jaggard stood by Sarah. When a reporter turned up at the Yardleys' house with Angus Hines in tow to take the photos, Yardley expected his wife to kick up a stink and throw him out.'

'She didn't?' Charlie guessed.

'According to Yardley, Helen didn't want to give Hines the satisfaction of knowing he'd riled her. Yardley could tell she hated having Hines in the house, but she shook his hand and said, "Nice to meet you."' Simon chewed his bottom lip. 'As if she'd never met him before. And he went along with the pretence.'

'Which is why Hines made no impression whatsoever on Stella White,' Charlie reasoned aloud. 'Because Helen treated him as if he were any old press photographer.'

'Exactly.' Simon nodded.

'And then, last Monday, he turned up at her house a second time, and Dillon White caught a glimpse of him and recognised him from the "beyond" day,' Charlie spelled out what she assumed was Simon's hypothesis. 'He stayed all day and ended up shooting Helen dead. Hang on, didn't you tell me Angus Hines had an alibi?'

Simon smiled. 'He does, or rather, he did: a man called Carl Chappell who said he was drinking with Hines at the Retreat pub in Bethnal Green last Monday between 3 and 7 p.m. When Sellers showed us that article from the *Sun* about Warren Gruff, Bethnal Green rang a bell. Gruff lives there, his ex-girlfriend Joanne Bew murdered his son Brandon there . . . but I couldn't think where else I'd come across Bethnal Green recently. Then I remembered: Angus Hines' alibi. Before we set off, I asked Sam to probe a bit further. Didn't take him long to find out that Brandon Bew was murdered in a flat above a pub in Bethnal Green that used to be the Dog and Partridge, that's now called the Retreat . . .'

'Unbelievable,' Charlie muttered.

'. . . and that Carl Chappell testified for the prosecution at Joanne Bew's first trial, claimed he witnessed her smothering Brandon. Sam spoke to Chappell – Angus Hines had given him Chappell's mobile number when he'd offered up Chappell as his alibi. Chappell was drunk enough and stupid enough, when Sam leaned on his story about being with Hines last Monday, to boast about how lucky he was with money, said Angus Hines had paid him a grand in cash for the false alibi. He also said that someone else – a man he'd seen on telly a few times, a man he described as big and fair-haired with a big neck – had paid him two grand not to testify at Joanne's retrial, to say he hadn't seen anything the night Brandon died – he'd been too drunk.'

'Laurie Nattrass?' Charlie wondered out loud. Who else could it be?

'Yeah. Nattrass.' Simon sounded angry. 'Mr Justice-For-All. He must have wanted Joanne Bew to be acquitted second time because he knew it'd look bad for Duffy – yet another innocent woman she'd testified against. And Chappell wasn't the only person Nattrass bribed – he also paid off Warren Gruff, to stop Gruff breaking Chappell's arms and legs when Chappell said he wouldn't testify against Joanne.'

'How the hell do you know that?' Charlie asked.

'Second phone call was Gibbs,' said Simon. 'Gruff's confessed to attacking Jaggard and killing Duffy. He's in custody, and talking – up to a point, at least. I thought the Brain – Angus Hines, that is – I thought he had some kind of hold over Gruff, but from what Gibbs says, it's more a case of misguided loyalty. Gruff thought Hines was the only person who truly understood him – Hines had lost two children, he'd lost one. Hines had been vilified in the press by Nattrass and various other commentators for saying he believed his wife was guilty, but he stuck to his guns. Gruff looks up to him. Which is why he killed Duffy – the woman who did her best to bring his son's killer to justice – even though it was the last thing he wanted to do, because it was part of Hines' great plan. Gruff admired Duffy, but Hines is his hero. He would have done whatever Hines told him – his role was to be the helper. That photograph Sellers showed us of Gruff, on the computer? It was taken by Angus Hines for the *Daily Express*, after Joanne Bew's retrial, when Gruff was briefly newsworthy again. That was how Hines and Gruff met. Hines might have had some genuine sympathy for Gruff, who knows? Either way, he certainly knew how to manipulate him.'

'You said "Hines' great plan",' Charlie talked over him. 'What was it?'

'Gibbs says Gruff won't say, claims he's not clever enough to explain it properly. Says Hines'd never forgive him if he spoke on his behalf. Hines is the one who has to explain – it's his plan.'

Charlie hated the thought that Gruff had admired Duffy but killed her anyway, when he could so easily have come to his senses at that point, listened to his instincts and said no. Why hadn't his hero-worship of Angus Hines ended the instant Hines had asked him to kill someone he didn't think deserved to die?

Charlie hadn't told Simon that Duffy hadn't wanted to answer the door to Gruff, that she, Charlie, had insisted, because she'd been too embarrassed to have the heart-to-heart the doctor seemed to want.

I'll leave it.

No, get it.

Charlie had expected to feel guilty about Duffy's death, but, oddly, she didn't. She could imagine what Duffy herself would have said. *The life you failed to save doesn't make you a bad person, any more than the lives you saved make you a good one.* Something like that, anyway.

'Know why Angus Hines chose Carl Chappell to bribe for an alibi?' Simon asked, glancing out of the car window at Stella White's house. 'Because he knew Nattrass had bribed Chappell.'

'How did he find that out?' Charlie asked.

'Chappell told him himself. Hines tracked Chappell down, told him he'd been researching child-death cases that involved Judith Duffy as an expert witness. He wanted to know why the eye-witness to the murder of Brandon Bew had changed his story. For the price of a bottle of whisky, he got his answer. Chappell was pissed out of his head when he was trying to reconstruct what Hines said to him, but from what Sam managed to piece together, it seems Angus Hines had the idea of using the very same people Nattrass had used, but in the opposite direction – in a direction Nattrass would have hated if he'd known about it. It was one of his little power games – proving he was the one in charge of all the players on the board, not Nattrass. He said to Chappell, "I'm the one paying you now – remember that." I reckon he picked Gruff as his killer-helper for the same reason: Nattrass had controlled Gruff previously, so Hines needed to show that he could control him even more effectively. Up to a point, that is.'

'You keep saying that,' Charlie told him. 'Warren Gruff is talking *up to a point*, Angus Hines was controlling Gruff *up to a point . . .*'

'Yeah,' said Simon defensively. 'Up to the point that as soon as we hint that we're on to them, both Warren Gruff and Carl Chappell give up Angus Hines. Hines is smart: he knew that'd happen, knew he couldn't rely on Gruff and Chappell to keep their mouths shut. He doesn't care. He wants us to know it's him – always has, right from the start. Hence the cards. He wanted to draw our attention to page 214 of *Nothing But Love* because he knew it would lead us to him, assuming we picked up on his clues, which we didn't at first. As I say, he's clever. As a nickname for him, I was spot on with "the Brain". He's got a master plan and he's looking forward to bragging about it – I only wish I knew what the fuck it is, and whether it involves killing Ray. If Sellers doesn't get to Twickenham in time, or if Hines has taken Ray somewhere else . . .'

'Sellers will get there in time,' said Charlie automatically. She had no idea whether he would or not.

Simon shifted in his seat, rubbing the small of his back. 'Hines must have guessed that Gruff and/or Chappell would give up not only him but Laurie Nattrass. I reckon he likes the idea of Nattrass getting done for perverting the course of justice – the irony would appeal to him. Nattrass supported Ray when Hines didn't, he attacked Hines publicly for his failure to support her.'

'It'd be his word against Gruff's and Chappell's, though, wouldn't it?' said Charlie. 'It's a non-starter. Laurie Nattrass'll be just fine – his sort always land on their feet.' There was something niggling at the back of her mind. She was about to give up trying to pin it down when it suddenly came into sharp focus. 'How does page 214 of *Nothing But Love* lead back to Angus Hines?' she asked.

'The third phone call was from Klair Williamson,' said Simon.

'Who?'

'She's one of the detectives on the Yardley–Duffy murders. I asked her to speak to Rahila Yunis, the journalist who interviewed Helen Yardley at Geddham Hall prison and says Yardley lied about the poem.'

'Didn't Sam say Yunis seemed reluctant to talk at first?'

'Right.' Simon nodded. 'Well, now we know why: Yunis was withholding the most important part of the story. Angus Hines was there that day too, at Geddham Hall. He wasn't supposed to be. The rules said no photographers, but Laurie Nattrass and Helen Yardley had briefed Yunis and Hines on how to break those rules, who to talk to at the prison to make it happen. A lot of the guards liked Helen and believed she was innocent, so they bent the rules for her – Hines and his camera were allowed in. The powers-that-be at the *Telegraph* were worried about Hines being the photographer on this particular job, given that he was famous at the time for denouncing his wife as guilty and Helen was equally famous for proclaiming Ray Hines' innocence.'

'Understandable,' said Charlie.

'Yeah. Except, according to Yunis via Klair Williamson, Helen Yardley only agreed to the interview on the condition that there'd be a photographer present. A particular photographer – none other than Angus Hines. Hines was equally enthusiastic. He and Helen Yardley were keen to encounter one another, it seems. When they did, each seemed so focused on the other that they barely noticed Yunis was there, according to her. For nearly half an hour she couldn't get a word in edgeways.'

'What were they talking about?' Charlie asked.

'Ray Hines. Helen accused Hines of disloyalty and tried to convince him of the error of his ways. Hines accused Helen of supporting Ray only as a way of furthering her own cause and underlining her own innocence, using Ray as a symbol for herself, or words to that effect.'

'Interesting,' said Charlie. 'How do the two poems come into it, "The Microbe" and the "room swept white" poem?'

'When Helen presented "The Microbe" as her favourite poem, Hines burst out laughing and accused her of being stupid. "But scientists, who ought to know, / Assure us that they must be so . . . / Oh! Let us never, never doubt / What nobody is sure about!"' Simon recited. 'For Helen, the poem was about Judith Duffy's arrogance in thinking her guilty, but Angus Hines pointed out that it could equally apply to Russell Meredew and the other doctors who testified in Helen's favour. They were as convinced of their monopoly on the truth as Duffy was. The experts on *both* sides told the jury never, never to doubt what nobody was sure about. According to Rahila Yunis, Hines thanked Helen for introducing him to "The Microbe" and told her it was now also his favourite poem, because it validated all the doubts he'd ever had about Ray, Helen, Sarah Jaggard – all the women who cried crib death when accused of murder. Yunis told Klair Williamson that Helen was visibly disturbed when Hines said this, though until that point none of his comments seemed to have bothered her at all. Shortly after he mocked her choice of poem, she put an end to the interview. A couple of hours later, Laurie Nattrass was on the phone to Yunis, saying: "I don't know what Angus Hines said to Helen because she won't tell me, but I've never seen her so angry." All Helen had told Nattrass, apparently, was that Hines had made a fool of her, humiliated her. There was no feature in the *Telegraph* – Nattrass told Yunis to pull it, or she'd very quickly find herself out of a job. She believed he meant it, so she did as she was told. She doesn't like talking about it because Nattrass humiliated *her* – terrorised her into dropping a good story.'

'So Helen lied in her book about the poem that was supposedly so important to her,' said Charlie thoughtfully.

'She didn't only lie,' said Simon. 'She stole. Well, sort of. "Room Swept White" is Rahila Yunis's favourite poem. She told Helen that, before Angus Hines chipped in and pointed out that "The Microbe" didn't mean what Helen thought it meant. Shit.' Stella White had appeared on the doorstep of number 16 and was staring at them, a quizzical expression on her face. 'She must be wondering why we're parked outside and not coming in,' said Simon. 'Have you got the photos?'

'Yep.' Charlie climbed out of the car and stretched. Her knees creaked, as if she hadn't moved for years. She was heading for Stella's house when Simon pulled her back. 'Once we're finished here, you and I are going home,' he said. 'Straight home.'

'Okay. Mind if I ask why?'

'Yes.' He turned away from her, shouted a hello to Stella.

'Is it anything bad?' Charlie called after him.

'Hopefully not that bad,' he said over his shoulder.

And then he was in the house and she couldn't ask him anything else, not without being overheard.

Dillon sat hunched on the sofa, kicking it with his heels. 'I dragged him away from his horse-racing,' said Stella. 'I thought you deserved his full attention for a change.' Her son looked as if he thought otherwise, but he said nothing.

'You look very well,' Simon told Stella. 'Better than when I last saw you.'

'I'm in remission,' she said. 'Just found out today. Can't quite believe it, but there you go.'

'Well done.' Charlie beamed at her. *Straight home*: it could only mean one thing . . .

'Hi, Dillon,' said Simon awkwardly.

'Hello,' the boy replied in a monotone. Charlie wasn't sure which of them was winning on the social skills front.

Simon held out his hand for the photos and she gave them to him. 'I'm going to show you some photographs,' he told Dillon. 'I'd like you to tell me who they are.'

Dillon nodded. One by one, Simon showed him the pictures, starting with Glen Jaggard. 'Don't know,' he said. Sebastian Brownlee also got a 'Don't know.'

'What about this one?' Simon held up a picture of Paul Yardley.

'Uncle Paul.'

'And this one?' Laurie Nattrass.

'I've seen him,' said Dillon, suddenly animated. 'He went to Auntie Helen's house lots of times. Once I was playing outside and he told me to look where I was going and he said a very rude word to me.'

'And this one?'

Dillon's eyes lit up. 'That's him,' he said, smiling up at Simon. 'That's the man with the magic umbrella.'

The photograph was of Angus Hines.

23

Monday 12 October 2009

'When Ray turned up on my doorstep after she'd been released—'

'It was my doorstep too,' she cuts in.

'Our doorstep,' Angus corrects himself. 'When she turned up, I was happy to let her in. While she was in prison, I'd devised the perfect test. Hines' Test of Guilt, I call it.' Ray's eyes are pleading with me: *listen to him, give him a chance. However awful this sounds, don't walk away*.

I remind myself that Hugo is in the next room. That's not as close as it would be in most houses, but it's close enough. If I screamed, he'd hear me. Any time I can't stand this any more, he'll drive me away from here and from Angus, who I'm now certain is a murderer.

Angus Hines: maker of probability tables, arranger of numbers in squares. He sent me the cards. I was supposed to guess what they meant, just as I was supposed to guess his meaning when he sent me the list of people Judith Duffy had testified against in the criminal and family courts. He sent me the two photographs of Helen Yardley's hands. Did he take them just before he shot her?

I had a bad feeling about him from the moment I met him: so bad I locked him up. My instincts must have been screaming at me that he was dangerous. Ray was scared of him too, at one time. Why isn't she still?

'I took Ray up to what had once been our bedroom,' he says. 'The room where years before she'd climbed out of the window and smoked a cigarette sitting on the ledge. I opened the window, grabbed her and dragged her over to it. I pushed her head out, and the top half of her body, and I held her there: half out, half in. She knew I could easily have pushed her out if I'd wanted to. There's no way she'd have survived the fall.'

'You told me you didn't try to kill her,' I say, keeping my voice steady.

'I didn't. As Ray said, if I'd tried I'd have succeeded. What I tried to do was make her believe I'd kill her if she didn't tell me the truth. And I would have done.'

'And then you asked her if she'd killed Marcella and Nathaniel.'

'Hines' Test of Guilt: put a woman who might or might not be guilty of murdering her children in a life-threatening situation. Convince her you'll kill her if she doesn't tell the truth, but that you'll let her live if she does. Whatever the truth is, you'll let her live – tell her that. Then ask her if she committed the murders. Whatever her first answer is, don't accept it. Keep ordering her to tell you the truth, as if you don't believe what she's said. If she changes her answer, do it again. Keep doing it – keep ordering her to tell you the truth, and eventually she'll be so scared and so unable to work out what the right answer is, you'll get the truth out of her. At that point, she'll stop chopping and changing: she'll stick to her story, and that story will be the true version of events. If she continues to chop and change in a way that makes it impossible for you to identify the truth, kill her as you threatened to.'

Don't interrupt him. Don't argue with him.

'Ray passed with flying colours.' Angus smiles at her, as if this is all perfectly normal. Ray keeps her eyes fixed on the camera. 'She didn't chop and change, not at all. She really believed I was going to kill her, yet not once did she say she was guilty. That's what proved to me that I'd been wrong about her.'

'I couldn't have said I'd killed my babies when I hadn't,' says Ray quietly. 'Not for anyone or anything. Not even if Angus was going to kill me if I didn't.'

'Did you tell the police what Angus did to you?'

'No. It'll be difficult for you to understand, but . . . I knew it wasn't Angus who opened the window and . . . It wasn't him. It was his pain and his grief that did it, not the real Angus, the one that existed before the grief. I also . . . You won't understand this either, but I respected him for doubting my innocence. His duty as a father was to do his absolute best for Marcella and Nathaniel, even after they were gone. *Especially* once they were gone. If so many intelligent people thought I'd killed them, how could he not take that seriously? He'd have been letting them down. And . . .'

'What?'

'I understood exactly how he felt about me, because it was how I felt about all the other women: Helen Yardley, Sarah Jaggard . . .'

'I asked you before if you thought Helen was guilty. You said no.'

'I never thought she *was* guilty.' Ray leans forward. 'I thought she *might be* guilty. Same with Sarah Jaggard. There's a big difference. I agree with Angus: the more of these supposed miscarriage-of-justice victims there are, the more guilty ones there must be among them, using innocent women like me as their camouflage.'

Hines' Theorem of Probability. I think of Joanne Bew. Lorna Keast.

'I didn't want anything to do with Helen or Sarah, inside or outside of a TV documentary, because I didn't know if they were murderers,' says Ray.

Yet you know Angus is a murderer, and you're planning to marry him.

'You wanted to find out, didn't you?' I ask him. 'Your Test of Guilt had worked on Ray, so you decided to try it on Helen.'

'Ray had nothing to do with it,' says Angus. 'I discussed my Theorem of Probability with her, but I didn't tell her what I intended to do.'

'You wanted to make someone pay for your pain and suffering, but Ray was innocent, so she couldn't pay. And even if by then you were convinced your children had died from a vaccine, who could you punish for that? Wendy Whitehead? No, she was on Ray's side, *against* the vaccine. It would have been hard to settle on an individual or individuals to blame. Much easier to use your test of guilt to find a baby-killer: Helen Yardley, or Sarah Jaggard. They might be guilty even if Ray wasn't – you could make *them* pay.'

'I delegated Sarah Jaggard to somebody else,' says Angus. 'He made a hash of it – did it in broad daylight in a public place and was interrupted. That's why I did the Test on Helen myself, though I probably would have anyway. Sarah Jaggard killed – or didn't kill – a child that wasn't her own. I was less interested in her.'

'You murdered Helen Yardley,' I say, feeling sick. 'You shot her in the head.'

'I did, yes.' *He said it. He confessed to the camera.*

'And you killed Judith Duffy.'

'Yes. The police seemed determined to mistake me for a pro-Duffy vigilante. I had to set them straight. They needed a lesson in truth and fairness. Impartiality. Unless you're impartial, how can you judge? Duffy made some bad mistakes – she was the first to admit it.'

Next to him, Ray is crying.

'Why didn't you go to the police?' I ask her. 'You must have known as soon as Helen died . . .'

'I had no proof.'

'You knew what he'd done to you.'

'His word against mine.' She wipes her eyes. 'He could have accused me of lying, and . . . I didn't want to hurt him or damage him any more than he's already been damaged. *This* is what I wanted: for him to tell his own story. I knew he couldn't be allowed to carry on, but . . . I wanted it to end in the right way, and I thought I could persuade him.'

'Marriage and a new baby in exchange for a confession and no more killing?' I say. *Laurie Nattrass's baby*.

Ray winces, hearing me put it so starkly.

'Ray's right,' says Angus, taking her hand. She leans into him. *She still loves him*. 'This way's better. I needed to be ready to tell the story.'

Is that what he was doing upstairs, all the time Ray and I were talking? Readying himself?

'Judith Duffy died while you waited for him to be ready,' I tell her.

'I know that, Fliss. How do you think that makes me feel?'

'Judith wouldn't have minded,' Angus says.

I stare at him in utter disbelief. 'Wouldn't have minded being murdered?'

'No. Her children had disowned her, she'd lost her professional credibility – she was about to be struck off, in all probability. She had nothing to live for apart from what she'd always lived for: protecting children, bringing their killers to justice. I think she'd have approved of Hines' Test of Guilt.'

'Fliss, listen,' says Ray. I hear desperation in her voice. 'I know what you're thinking, but everything's going to be okay now. It's finished. Angus's . . . test, it's over. He knows that; he accepts it. I know you think I ought to abandon him and hate him, but I can't, because *this isn't him*.'

'Do you agree with that?' I ask him.

'Yes,' he says without hesitation. 'I didn't used to be like this. I used to be Angus Hines. Now I'm . . . something else, I don't know what.'

A chill runs all the way through me. How terrifying to turn into something you recognise as not yourself – something uncontrollable and horrifying – and yet not be able to define that thing or feel the horror.

'Angus will go to prison, but he won't be alone in the world,' says Ray. 'He'll be punished as he should be for what he's done, but he'll have hope too, and a reason to carry on – a new child to love, me. Even though we won't be together maybe for years, I can write to him, visit him, take our baby . . .'

'What do the sixteen numbers mean?' I ask.

'They mean that Helen Yardley was a liar,' says Angus. 'If she could be a liar, so could Sarah Jaggard. So could any of them. Once Laurie Nattrass worked that out, I hoped he'd be a bit more selective in choosing who to champion. I hoped the same about you, once I heard you were taking over the film. As for the police, they can't say I didn't play fair. Every time I killed, I left a card. All they had to do was use their brains and they'd have worked out that the person most likely to draw those sixteen numbers to their attention was me. I gave them all the information they needed to find me.' He smiles.

He's mad.

But this isn't him. This is his pain and grief, not the real Angus Hines, the one Ray loves and wants to help.

'What's the connection between the numbers and you?' I ask him.

'If you're clever, you'll work it out,' he says.

'It doesn't matter,' Ray whispers. 'All that matters is that it's over, Fliss, and you're going to make a programme that tells the whole truth of what happened. You will do that for us, won't you? For us, and our child, for . . . for the record?'

'Yes. Yes, I will.'

There's one more question I have to ask Angus Hines. I've put it off for as long as I can, because I don't want to hear the answer. 'When you did the Test of Guilt on Helen, what did she say?'

He smiles at me.

'There's no point,' says Ray. 'He won't tell you.'

'Did she confess to murdering her children? Did she insist throughout the ordeal *you* inflicted on her that she was innocent, like Ray?'

'You'd like to know, wouldn't you?'

'Do *you* know?' I ask Ray.

She shakes her head.

'Tell me about Monday 5 October,' I say to Angus, as if it's a different question from the one I've already asked twice. 'Tell me about doing your Test on Helen. Don't pretend you don't want to talk about it. You want me to understand how clever you are.'

'All right, then,' he says easily. 'I'll tell you.'

Just like that?

The doorbell rings. 'No prizes for guessing who,' says Angus. 'Whoever rang the bell before, you told them to go to the police.'

'I didn't, actually.' I hear footsteps, the front door being opened. *No. Not now.*

'Is there someone else in the house?' Ray looks worried.

'It's okay,' I tell her. 'We're going to carry on filming.'

The door of the den inches open and a large sweaty man with messy blond hair appears, with stupid, disobedient Hugo Nattrass behind him. Since when did sitting in silence and doing nothing include letting strangers into the house?

'Wait in the other room,' I snap at them.

'I'm DC Colin Sel—'

'I don't care who you are. Go outside, close the door and wait,' I say quickly, before my resolve has a chance to weaken. 'We're busy here.' Sellers must see something in my eyes that convinces him, because he retreats without another word.

'Thank you,' says Ray, once he's gone.

I move the camera closer to Angus so that his face fills the frame. 'Whenever you're ready,' I tell him.

The Times, Tuesday 29 June 2010

Wrongly Convicted Baby-killer Acquitted

Dorne Llewellyn, 63, from Port Talbot, walked free from Cardiff Crown Court yesterday after being found not guilty at a retrial for the murder in 2000 of nine-month-old Benjamin Evans. The vote for acquittal was unanimous, as was the guilty verdict at Mrs Llewellyn's original trial. In April 2001, in the same courtroom, the prosecution persuaded 12 jurors that Mrs Llewellyn shook Benjamin to death while babysitting for him. She spent nearly nine years in prison.

Mrs Llewellyn was one of many women convicted on expert evidence provided by Dr Judith Duffy, who was murdered in October last year. At the time of her death, Dr Duffy was being investigated for misconduct. She alleged that Benjamin must have been shaken because he had suffered bleeding in the brain, but did not mention that there was also evidence of older bleeds. The second jury to hear the case was persuaded by the five independently appointed medical experts that there was no basis on which to convict Mrs Llewellyn of murder, as she had babysat for Benjamin only once, and there was clear evidence of brain bleeds dating back to before that occasion. Mrs Llewellyn and her friends and family wept on the steps of the court after hearing the 'not guilty' verdict.

JIPAC chairman Laurie Nattrass said on Mrs Llewellyn's behalf: 'The jury demonstrated its utter scorn for this insane and unsubstantiated murder charge by taking a superlative 40 minutes to return a unanimous 'not guilty' verdict. We should celebrate this triumph of justice over its enemies.' Mr Nattrass added: 'Currently the most dangerous of those enemies is the criminally idiotic Tom Astrow.' Professor Astrow, chairman of the Criminal Cases Review Commission, has proposed that in certain cases where possible child abuse is an issue, the jury and all reporters ought to be made to leave the courtroom while the judge examines the complex medical evidence with two experts. Professor Astrow told *The Times* on Monday: 'A layperson jury is simply not able to process the incredibly complex disagreements between experts on the finer points of medical opinion.'

Mr Nattrass disagrees: 'Astrow's proposal is, by any definition, craziness of the worst kind, yet another terrifying by-product of the rash of false accusations sparked off by Judith Duffy and her paranoid cohort of guilt-seeking paediatricians. To exclude jurors based on the assumption that they're too stupid to understand the medical evidence is patently immoral, as well as incorrect. Dr Russell Meredew OBE, author of some of the most brilliant papers ever written on unexpected child deaths, describes Judith Duffy's testimony at Dorne Llewellyn's first trial as "crap". Even a layperson can understand that. Instead of dismissing jurors as stupid and excluding them, why not exclude experts who are biased, devious and arrogant? What kind of judicial system is it where jurors are expected to reach a verdict after being protected from any evidence regarded as too contentious in case it confuses them? As for banning reporters from the courtroom, I can scarcely believe someone in Astrow's position in the twenty-first century would advocate such a move from light towards darkness. JIPAC will put its full weight behind ensuring that Astrow's proposals are seen for the disasters they are and rejected out of hand.' Professor Astrow was unavailable for comment.

A Room Swept White: A Family's Tragedy

By Felicity Benson

This book is dedicated to the memory of my father, Melvyn Benson.

Acknowledgements

Thank you to Ray and Angus Hines for allowing me to tell their story.

Thank you to all the police officers from Culver Valley CID, especially DS Sam Kombothekra, whose generosity and patience have been quite staggering.

Thank you to Julian Lance, Wendy Whitehead, Jackie Fletcher and the JABS contingent, Paul Yardley, Glen and Sarah Jaggard, Ned Vento, Gillian Howard, Dr Russell Meredew, Dr Phil Dennison, Dr Jack Pelham, Rahila Yunis, Gaynor Mundy, Leah Gould, Stella White, Beryl Murie, Fiona Sharp, Antonia Duffy, Grace and Hannah Brownlee.

Thank you to Laurie for giving me the chance.

Thank you to Tamsin and the gang at Better Brother Productions.

Last but not least, thank you, Hugo, for your unwavering support, and for your foresight in predicting that I would one day love you more than I love your house. I do, but only just.

Introduction

On Monday 5 October 2009, Angus Hines got up at 6 a.m. and drove a hired car from his home in London's Notting Hill to Spilling in the Culver Valley. His destination was number 9 Bengeo Street, the home of Helen Yardley. As he drove, he listened to the *Today* programme on BBC Radio 4. Helen's husband Paul had already left for work, so Helen was alone in the house when Angus arrived at 8.20 a.m. It was a bright, sunny winter day, clear skies, not a cloud in sight.

He must have rung the doorbell. Helen must have let him in, though they were not on friendly terms and the last time they had met they had argued. Angus spent the whole day alone with Helen in her house. At some point during the hours they spent together, Angus produced a gun that he'd obtained from an acquaintance, an M9 Beretta 9 millimetre. At five o'clock in the afternoon, he used that gun to shoot Helen dead because, according to him, she had failed a test he'd devised for her – or, rather, not specifically for her, but for all women accused of murdering babies who claim to be innocent of the crime – women like Sarah Jaggard, Dorne Llewellyn, and of course Angus's wife, Ray. It was Angus's own personal connection to a case of this sort that led him to formulate the test that he calls, without any irony, 'Hines' Test of Guilt', though he has twice asked me if I think he ought to change its name to 'Hines' Test of Truth'. Here's how he explained its rules to me:

> 'Put a woman who might or might not be guilty of murdering her children in a life-threatening situation. Convince her you'll kill her if she doesn't tell the truth, but that you'll let her live if she does. Whatever the truth is, you'll let her live – tell her that. Then ask her if she committed the murders. Whatever her first answer is, don't accept it. Keep ordering her to tell you the truth, as if you don't believe what she's said. If she changes her answer, do it again. Keep doing it – keep ordering her to tell you the truth, and eventually she'll be so scared and so unable to work out what the right answer is, you'll get the truth out of her. At that point, she'll stop chopping and changing: she'll stick to her story, and that story will be the true version of events. If she continues to chop and change in a way that makes it impossible for you to identify the truth, kill her as you threatened to.'

The first two times I asked Angus what happened when he subjected Helen Yardley to his Test of Guilt, he wouldn't tell me. He taunted me by saying, 'You'd like to know, wouldn't you?' and seemed to relish his superior knowledge and my frustrated ignorance. Then, suddenly and for no apparent reason, he changed his mind and announced that he was willing to tell me the story of what happened at Helen's house on Monday 5 October. The telling process took nearly three hours from start to finish. I will summarise what Angus told me very briefly, and spare you the more chilling aspects of his account; I wish I could have been spared them myself.

Angus told me that Helen spent very little time – less than half an hour – changing her story from innocence to guilt and back again before finally admitting to having smothered both her sons. That's why he shot her, he said: to punish her, because she was a murderer. But, he told me, before he shot her, he spent several hours listening to her long and comprehensive confession: what she'd done, why she'd done it, and how she felt about it.

This book is the story of the Hines family – Ray, Angus, Marcella and Nathaniel – and of the police investigation into the murders of Helen Yardley and Judith Duffy. Angus Hines' murder of Helen Yardley isn't how the story begins. Insofar as you can pinpoint the origin of any story, I think this one started in 1998, when Angus and Ray Hines had their first baby, Marcella. I've started with this much later incident, Angus's shooting of Helen Yardley in October 2009, not because it's violent and shocking and attention-grabbing – though it is, all those things – but because I want to set it apart from the rest of the book, because I believe Angus's account of it, and therefore my account of it, to be a lie. That's another reason why I have condensed and summarised what Angus told me about what happened between him and Helen that day: I don't want to devote any more space than I must to a story I'm sure isn't true.

By the end of this book, you'll have formed an opinion of Angus, and you'll be able to decide for yourself if he's the sort of man who would ignore the terms and conditions of his own Test of Guilt/Truth, according to which only lying is punishable by death, and shoot Helen Yardley even after she had told him the truth about her guilt. Maybe you'll decide he couldn't risk leaving her alive because she'd seen him and would have gone to the police. My impression, for what it's worth, is that Angus was never afraid of being found out – he freely distributed what he regarded as clear clues to his guilt, as you will see later in the book.

Angus's respect for the law is limited to a handful of detectives: DC Simon Waterhouse and Sergeant Charlotte Zailer chief among them, for reasons that will become clear. In general, however, he has little respect for the police or the legal system, and my theory – though I must stress it is only a theory – is that he doesn't think anybody but him deserves to know the truth about what happened on Monday 5 October 2009 between him and Helen Yardley. I think he feels that, as the sole inventor of the Test of Guilt/Truth, only he is entitled to know its results.

Is that why he shot Helen, so that she wouldn't be able to tell anybody her version of what happened that day? To ensure that he would always be the sole owner of that information? Given his delight in his knowledge, and the power it gives him in the face of others' ignorance, does that mean the story he told me is the opposite of what really happened? Might he get a kick out of misleading me as much as possible, and if so, does that mean his Test in fact proved Helen to be innocent? I believe that's unlikely too, because the fact remains that he shot her dead; Angus's rules clearly state that if you tell the truth, you're allowed to live.

Perhaps Helen didn't waver once but consistently protested her innocence, and perhaps in spite of this Angus didn't believe her – in which case his Test would have been revealed to him as a comprehensive failure. Would that have been enough to make him shoot her? I believe it might. I also believe, given the history between Helen and Angus – a history you will read about – that she might well have refused to say anything at all. Was she determined to resist him, even though he had a gun? Silence from her would have constituted a defeat for him, and she would have known that. Or did she keep 'chopping and changing' her story, to use Angus's terminology? Did she keep saying different things, hoping to stumble on the one that would make him put away the gun and leave? Did he kill her because he simply couldn't ascertain what the truth was?

If Angus didn't discover on that day that his Test was flawed, did he perhaps discover a flaw within himself, an inability to stick to the terms and conditions he'd laid down for himself? Before he was a killer, Angus was a devoted father who lost two children and then his wife when she was wrongly accused of their murders. Did Helen confess to smothering her two babies, and was Angus so overcome by anger and disgust that he couldn't resist pulling the trigger? If that is what happened, he might never tell anybody – he prides himself on being a planner, always in control and thinking ahead. He would never admit to being so swayed by emotion that he went against his own plan.

I am hoping, and Paul Yardley and Hannah Brownlee are hoping, that one day Angus will tell us what really happened at 9 Bengeo Street on Monday 5 October. It's a slow process, but I'm doing my best to chip away at his image of himself as super-rational and in control. I have tried to explain to him that his Test is useless: people do not behave predictably when threatened with imminent execution. Ordered to tell the truth about the most traumatic event in their lives, some might choose the story they wish to believe about themselves – let's say, for the sake of argument, a lie – and stick to it, on the grounds that their lives wouldn't be worth living anyway if they acknowledged the painful truth. Some might tell the truth and stick to it; some might waver, changing back and forth from one version to another. Angus has no way of proving how either a guilty or an innocent person would respond to being tortured. To me this is an undeniable fact, but he insists I'm wrong.

He clams up completely when I point out to him the main flaw of his Test: that it involves judging, condemning and executing other human beings – three things no one should ever do. If what you're about to read proves anything conclusively, it's the necessity for compassion and humility, as well as the undeniable fact that if people could learn to be more forgiving, of themselves and others, there would be less to forgive all round. If attempts to understand and help could replace judgement and condemnation, even when heinous crimes have been committed – *especially* when heinous crimes have been committed – then there would be fewer heinous crimes committed in the future. A popular misconception is the idea that to understand and help a criminal means to let him or her 'get away with it'; this is not the case, as I hope this story will prove. Personally I believe that, irrespective of whatever legal action might or might not be taken, nobody ever 'gets away with' anything: what we do has an effect on us from which we can't escape.

Before handing in the final version of this book to my editor, I went to visit Angus in prison and took the manuscript with me. I made him read this introduction. When I asked him if there was any aspect of it he objected to, he shook his head and handed it back to me. 'Publish it,' he said.

Acknowledgements

I am very grateful to the following people, all of whom helped substantially with the writing of this book: Mark Fletcher, Sarah Shaper, Jackie Fletcher, Mark and Cal Pannone, Guy Martland, Dan, Phoebe and Guy Jones, Jenny, Adele and Norman Geras, Ken and Sue Hind, Anne Grey, Hannah Pescod, Ian Daley, Paula Cuddy, Clova McCallum, Peter Bean, David Allen, Dan Oxtoby (who, without meaning to, inspired a plot twist) and Judith Gribble.

Several medical experts helped me to make sense of many of the controversial issues surrounding crib death: chiefly Dr Mike Green and two other people who would prefer not to be named. All three, and several others, were enormously generous with their time and knowledge, for which I am hugely grateful.

Thank you to Fiona Sampson, author of the brilliant poem 'Anchorage' – which is reprinted in the novel and from which the novel's British title is a quote – and to Carcanet Press for allowing me to use the poem. Thanks also to The Estate of Hilaire Belloc and PFD for allowing me to use 'The Microbe' in this book.

* * *

Sophie Hannah

Thank you to Val McDermid, who invented Reverse L'Oréal Syndrome.

Massive thanks to my inspirational agent Peter Straus, to the wonderful Jenny Hewson, and to my superb publishers Hodder & Stoughton, especially Carolyn Mays, Karen Geary and Francesca Best.

I wouldn't have been able to write this novel if I hadn't read three books: *Unexpected Death in Childhood* edited by Peter Sidebotham and Peter Fleming, *Cherished* by Angela Cannings and Megan Lloyd Davies, and *Stolen Innocence: the Sally Clark Story* by John Batt. The experiences of women such as Sally Clark, Angela Cannings and Trupti Patel were part of the inspiration for *A Room Swept White*, though none of the characters or cases in my novel are based on real people or cases.

Read on for a chilling taste of Sophie Hannah's next psychological thriller

THE OTHER WOMAN'S HOUSE

It's 1.15 a.m. Connie Bowskill should be asleep. Instead, she's logging on to a property website in search of a particular house: 11 Bentley Grove, Cambridge. She knows it's for sale; she's seen the estate agent's board in the front garden. When she clicks on the 'Virtual Tour' button, keen to see the inside of the house and put her mind at rest once and for all, Connie finds herself looking at a scene from a nightmare: on the living room carpet, there's a woman lying face down in a pool of blood. In shock, Connie wakes her husband Kit. But when Kit sits down at the computer to look, he sees no dead body, only a clean beige carpet in a perfectly ordinary room . . .

I'm going to be killed because of a family called the Gilpatricks.

There are four of them: mother, father, son and daughter. *Elise, Donal, Riordan and Tilly*. Kit tells me their first names, as if I'm keen to dispense with the formalities and get to know them better, when all I want is to run screaming from the room. *Riordan's seven,* he says. *Tilly's five*.

Shut up, I want to yell in his face, but I'm too scared to open my mouth. It's as if someone's clamped and locked it; no more words will come out, not ever.

This is it. This is where and how and when and why I'm going to die. At least I understand the why, finally.

Kit's as frightened as I am. More. That's why he's talking, because he knows, as all those who wait in terror know, that when silence and fear combine, they form a compound a thousand times more horrifying than the sum of its parts.

The Gilpatricks, he says, tears streaking his face.

I watch the door in the mirror above the fireplace. It looks smaller and further away than it would if I turned and looked at it directly. The mirror is shaped like a fat gravestone: three straight sides and an arch at the top.

I didn't believe in them. The name sounded made up. Kit laughs, chokes on a sob. All of him is shaking, even his voice. *Gilpatrick's the sort of name you'd make up if you were inventing a person. Mr Gilpatrick. If only I'd believed in him, none of this would have happened. We'd have been safe. If I'd only . . .*

He stops, backs away from the locked door. He hears the same footsteps I hear – rushing, a stampede. They're here.

One week earlier . . .

1

Saturday 17 July 2010

I lie on my back with my eyes closed, waiting for Kit's breathing to change. I fake the deep, slow sleep-breaths I need to hear from him before I can get out of bed – *in and hold, out and hold* – and try to convince myself that it's a harmless deception. Am I the only woman who has ever done this, or does it happen all the time in houses all over the world? If it does, then it must be for different reasons, more common ones than mine: a cheating wife or girlfriend wanting to text a lover undetected, or sneak one last guilty glass of wine on top of the five she's had already. Normal things. Ordinary urgencies.

No woman on earth has ever been in the situation I'm in now.

You're being ridiculous. You're not 'in a situation', apart from the one you've brewed in your imagination. Ingredients: coincidence and paranoia.

Nothing I tell myself works. That's why I need to check, to put my mind at rest. Checking isn't crazy; missing the opportunity to check would be crazy. And once I've looked and found nothing, I'll be able to forget about it and accept that it's all in my head.

Will you?

It shouldn't be too long before I can move. Kit's usually dead to the world within seconds of the light going out. If I count to a hundred . . . but I can't. Can't make myself focus on something that doesn't interest me. If I could, I'd be able to do the reverse: banish 11 Bentley Grove from my mind. Will I ever be able to do that?

While I wait, I practise. What would this bedroom tell me about Kit and me, if I didn't know us? Huge bed, cast-iron fireplace, with identical alcoves on either side of the chimney breast where our two identical wardrobes stand. Kit likes symmetry. One of his reservations, when I proposed buying the biggest bed we could find to replace our ordinary double, was that it might not leave room for our matching bedside cabinets. When I said I'd be happy to lose mine, Kit looked at me as if I was an anarchist agitator plotting to demolish his well-ordered world. 'You can't have a cabinet on one side and not the other,' he said. Both ended up going in the end; having first made me promise not to tell anyone, Kit admitted that, however inconvenient it was to have to lean down and put his book, watch, glasses and mobile phone under the bed, he would find it more irritating to have a bedroom that didn't 'look right'.

'Are you sure you're a genuine, bona fide heterosexual?' I teased him.

He grinned. 'Either I am, or else I'm pretending to be in order to get my Christmas cards written and posted for me every year. I guess you'll never know which is the truth.'

Floor-length cream silk curtains. Kit wanted a Roman blind, which he said would look neater, but I overruled him. Silk curtains are something I've wanted since childhood, one of those 'as soon as I have a home of my own' pledges I made to myself. And curtains in a bedroom have to pool on the floor – that's my look-right rule. I suppose everybody has at least one, and we all think our own are sensible and other people's completely ridiculous.

Above the fireplace, there's a framed tapestry of a red house with a green rectangle around it that's supposed to be the garden. Instead of flowers, the solid colour of the grass is broken up by stitched words: 'Melrose Cottage, Little Holling, Silsford' in orange, and then, in smaller yellow letters beneath, 'Connie and Kit, 13th July 2004'.

'But Melrose isn't red,' I used to protest, before I gave up. 'It's made of white clunch stone. Do you think Mum was picturing it drenched in blood?' Kit and I called our house 'Melrose' for short when we first bought it. Now that we've lived here for years and know it like we know our own faces, we call it 'Mellers'.

What would an impartial observer make of the tapestry? Would they think Kit and I were so stupid that we were in danger of forgetting our own names and when we bought our house? That we'd decided to hang a reminder on the wall? Would they guess that it was a home-made house-warming present from Connie's mother, and that Connie thought it was twee and crass, and had fought hard to have it exiled to the loft?

Kit insisted we put it up, out of loyalty to our home and to Mum. He said our bedroom was the perfect place, so that then guests wouldn't see it. I don't think he notices it any more. I do – every night before I go to sleep and every morning when I wake up. It depresses me for a whole range of reasons.

Someone peering into our bedroom would see none of this – none of the wrangles, none of the compromises. They wouldn't see Kit's missing bedside table, the picture I'd have liked to put above the fireplace if only the hideous red house picture wasn't there.

Which proves that looking at a room in someone else's

house doesn't tell you anything, and there's no point in my doing what I'm about to do, now that I'm sure Kit's sound asleep. I ought to go to sleep too.

As quietly as I can, I fold back my side of the duvet, climb out of bed and tiptoe to the spare room, which we've turned into a home office. It's actually our company headquarters, which is a little absurd given that it's about 11 feet long by 10 feet wide. Like Kit's and my bedroom, it has a cast iron fireplace. We've managed to cram two large desks in here, a chair for each of us, three filing cabinets. When our Certificate of Incorporation arrived from Companies House, Kit bought a frame for it and hung it on the wall opposite the door, so that it's the first thing that catches your eye when you walk into the room. 'It's a legal requirement,' he told me when I complained that it looked uninspiring and bureaucratic. 'Has to be displayed at the company headquarters – that's the rule. Do you want Nulli to start life as an outlaw?'

Nulli Secundus Ltd. It means 'second to none', and was Kit's choice. 'Talk about tempting fate and dooming us to failure,' I said when we were discussing what to call ourselves, imagining how much worse failure would feel with such a conceited name. I suggested 'C & K Bowskill Ltd'. 'Those are *our* names,' Kit said scathingly, as if this fact might have passed me by. 'Have a bit of imagination, for God's sake. Confidence would help, too. Are we launching this company in order to go bankrupt? I don't know about you, but I'm planning to make a success of it.'

What else have you made a success of, Kit? What else that I don't know about?

You're being ridiculous, Connie. Your ridiculousness is second to none.

I press my laptop's touchpad and it springs to life. The Google screen appears. I type 'houses for sale' into the search box, press enter, and wait. The first result that comes up is Roundthehouses.co.uk, which declares itself the UK's leading property website. I click on it, thinking that obviously the Roundthehouses people subscribe to Kit's way of thinking rather than mine: they have no worries about bankruptcy-induced humiliation.

The home page loads: exterior shots of houses for sale beneath a dark red border filled in with lots of tiny pictures of magnifying glasses, each with a disembodied pair of eyes inside it. The eyes look eerie, alien, and make me think of people hiding in the darkness, spying on one another.

Isn't that exactly what you're doing?

I type 'Cambridge' into the location box, and click on the 'For Sale' button. Another screen comes up, offering me more choices. I work my way through them impatiently – search radius: this area only; property type: houses; number of bedrooms: any; price range: any; added to site . . . When would 11 Bentley Grove have been added? I click on 'last 7 days'. The 'For Sale' board I saw in the front garden today – or yesterday, since it's now quarter past one in the morning – wasn't there a week ago.

I click on 'Find properties', tapping my bare feet on the floor, and close my eyes for a second. When I open them, there are houses on the screen: one on Chaucer Road for 4 million pounds, one on Newton Road for 2.3 million. I know both streets – they're near Bentley Grove, off Trumpington Road. I've seen them, on my many trips to Cambridge that nobody knows about.

11 Bentley Grove is the third house on the list. It's on

for 1.2 million pounds. I'm surprised it's so expensive. It's big enough, but nothing spectacular. Obviously that part of Cambridge is regarded as a choice area, though it's always looked fairly ordinary to me, and the traffic on the Trumpington Road is often waiting to move rather than moving. There's a Waitrose nearby, an Indian restaurant, a specialist wine shop, a couple of estate agents. *And lots of enormous expensive mansions.* If the asking price for 11 Bentley Grove is 1.2 million, that means there must be people who can afford to pay that much for a house. Who are they? Sir Cliff Richard springs to mind; I've no idea why. Who else? People who own football clubs, or have oil wells in their back gardens? Certainly not me and Kit, and we're doing about as well, professionally, as we could ever hope to do.

I shake these thoughts from my mind. *You could be asleep now, you lunatic. Instead, you're sitting hunched over a computer in the dark, feeling inferior to Cliff Richard. Get a grip.*

To bring up the full details, I click on the picture of this house I know so well, and yet not at all. I don't believe anyone in the world has spent as much time staring at the outside of 11 Bentley Grove as I have; I know its facade brick by brick. It's strange, almost shocking, to see a photograph of it on my computer, in my house, where it doesn't belong.

Inviting the enemy into your home . . .

There is no enemy, I tell myself firmly. *Be practical, get it over with, and go back to bed.* Kit has started to snore. Good. I've no idea what I'd say if he caught me doing this, how I'd defend my sanity.

The page has loaded. I'm not interested in the big

photograph on the left, the one taken from across the road. It's the inside of the house I need to see. One by one, I click on the little pictures on the right hand side of the screen to enlarge them. First, a kitchen with wooden worktops, a double Belfast sink, blue-painted unit-fronts, a blue-sided wooden-topped island . . .

Kit hates kitchen islands. He thinks they're ugly and pretentious – an affectation imported from America. The avocado bathroom suites of the future, he calls them. He'd got rid of the one in our kitchen within a fortnight of our moving in, and commissioned a local joiner to make us a big round oak table to take its place.

This kitchen I'm looking at can't be Kit's, not with that island in it.

Of course it's not Kit's. Kit's kitchen is downstairs – it also happens to be your kitchen.

I click on a picture of a lounge. I've seen 11 Bentley Grove's lounge before, though only briefly. On one of my visits, I was brave enough – or stupid enough, depending on your point of view – to open the gate, walk up the long path that's bordered by lavender bushes on both sides and divides the square front lawn into two triangles, and peer in through the front window. I was afraid I'd be caught trespassing and couldn't really concentrate. A few seconds later an elderly man with the thickest glasses I've ever seen emerged from the house next door and turned his excessively enlarged eyes in my direction. I hurried back to my car before he could ask me what I was doing, and, afterwards, remembered little about the room I'd seen apart from that it had white walls and a grey L-shaped sofa with some kind of intricate red embroidery on it.

I'm looking at that same sofa now, on my computer screen. It's not so much grey as a sort of cloudy silver. It looks expensive, unique. I can't imagine there's another sofa like it.

Kit loves unique. He avoids mass-produced as far as is possible. All the mugs in our kitchen were made and painted individually by a potter in Spilling.

Every piece of furniture in the lounge at 11 Bentley Grove looks like a one-off: a chair with enormous curved wooden arms like the bottoms of rowing boats; an unusual coffee table with a glass surface, and, beneath the glass, a structure resembling a display cabinet with sixteen compartments, lying on its back. Each compartment contains a small flower with a red circle at its centre and blue petals pointing up towards the glass.

Kit would like all of these things. I swallow, tell myself this proves nothing.

There's a tiled fireplace with a map above it in a frame, a chimney breast, matching alcoves on either side. I didn't notice that when I looked through the window. Maybe I didn't allow myself to notice. A symmetrical room, a Kit sort of room. I feel a little nauseous.

Christ, this is insane. How many living rooms, up and down the country, follow this basic format: fireplace, a chimney breast, alcoves left and right? It's a classic design, replicated all over the world. It appeals to Kit, and to about a trillion other people.

It's not as if you've seen his jacket draped over the banister, his stripy scarf over the back of a chair . . .

Quickly, wanting to be finished with this task I've set myself – aware that it's making me feel worse, not better – I work my way through the other rooms, enlarging their pictures. Hall and stairs, carpeted in beige, chunky dark wood banister. A utility room with sky-blue unit fronts, similar to those in the kitchen. Honey-coloured marble for the house bathroom – clean and ostentatiously expensive.

I click on a picture of what must be the back garden. It's a lot bigger than I'd have imagined, having only seen the house from the front. I scroll down to the text beneath the photographs and see that it's described as being just over an acre. It's the sort of garden I'd love to have: decking for a table and chairs, two-seater garden swing with a canopy, vast lawn, trees at the bottom, lush yellow fields beyond. An idyllic countryside view, ten minutes' walk from the centre of Cambridge. Now I'm starting to understand the 1.2-million-pound price tag. I try not to compare what I'm looking at to Melrose Cottage's garden, which is roughly the size of half a single garage. It's big enough to accommodate a wrought iron table, four chairs, a few plants in terracotta pots, and not a lot else.

That's it. I've looked at all the pictures, seen all there is to see.

And found nothing. Satisfied now?

I yawn and rub my eyes. I'm about to close down the Roundthehouses website and go back to bed when I notice a row of buttons beneath the picture of the back garden: 'Street View', 'Floorplan', 'Virtual Tour'. I don't need a view of Bentley Grove – I've seen more than enough of it in the past six months – but I might as well have a look at number 11's floorplan, since I've got this far. I click on the button, then hit the 'x' to shut down the screen within seconds of it opening. It isn't going to help me to know which room is where; I'd be better off taking the virtual tour. Will it make me feel as if I'm walking around the house myself, looking into every room? That's what I'd like to do.

Then I'd be satisfied.

I hit the button and wait for the tour to load. Another button pops up: 'Play Tour'. I click on it. The kitchen appears first, and I see what I've already seen in the photograph, then a bit more as the camera does a 360-degree turn to reveal the rest of the room. Then another turn, then another. The spinning effect makes me feel dizzy, as if I'm on a roundabout that won't stop. I close my eyes, needing a break. I'm so tired. Travelling to Cambridge and back in a day nearly every Friday is doing me no good; it's not the physical effort that's draining, it's the secrecy. I have to move on, let it go.

I open my eyes and see a mass of red. At first I don't know what I'm looking at, and then . . . *Oh, God. It can't be. Oh, fuck, oh, God.* Blood. A woman lying face down in the middle of the room, and blood, a lake of it, all over the beige carpet. For a second, in my panic, I mistake the blood for my own. I look down at myself. *No blood.* Of course not – it's not my carpet, not my house. It's 11 Bentley Grove. The lounge, spinning. The fireplace, the framed map above it, the door open to the hall . . .

The dead woman, face down in a sea of red. As if all the blood inside her has been squeezed out, every drop of it . . .

I make a noise that might be a scream. I try to call Kit's name, but it doesn't work. Where's the phone? Not on its base. Where's my BlackBerry? Should I ring 999? Panting, I reach out for something, I'm not sure what. I can't take my eyes off the screen. The blood is still slowly turning, the dead woman slowly turning. *She must be dead; it must be her blood. Red around the outside, almost black in the middle. Black-red, thick as tar. Make it stop spinning.*

I stand up, knock my chair over. It falls to the floor with a thud. I back away from my desk, wanting only to escape. *Out, out!* a voice in my head screams. I'm stumbling in the wrong direction, nowhere near the door. *Don't look. Stop looking.* I can't help it. My back hits the wall; something hard presses into my skin. I hear a crash, step on something that crunches. Pain pricks the soles of my feet. I look down and see broken glass. Blood. Mine, this time.

Somehow, I get myself out of the room and close the door. Better; now there's a barrier between it and me. *Kit.* I need Kit. I walk into our bedroom, switch on the light and burst into tears. How dare he be asleep? 'Kit!'

He groans, blinks. 'Light off,' he mumbles, groggy with sleep. 'Fuck's going on? Time is it?'

I stand there crying, my feet bleeding onto the white rug.

'Con?' Kit hauls himself up into a sitting position and rubs his eyes. 'What's wrong? What's happened?'

'She's dead,' I tell him.